THE SECRET AND THE BUTTERFLY

A NOVEL

BY
ROSEMARY LIGHTFOOT NESS-BITNER

The *Secret and the Butterfly* and its companion book *When the Butterflies Come* expose the impotence of our financial institutions' regulatory framework and courts when pitted against a committed wrongdoer. The books were inspired by a matter of civil litigation. All characters, events, and conversations are fictional, the products of the author's imagination, or used fictitiously. Any resemblance to actual characters, living or dead, events past or present, localities, or conversations is entirely coincidental.

A caution and disclaimer

There are opinions expressed in these books which are not those of the author. They are expressions of the fictional characters' beliefs and convictions only. Some or all of these opinions, particularly those of Marty towards married women and their children and David's opinions and actions concerning a wide range of matters some readers may find offensive. They are presented as part of the narrative to illustrate the depths of depravity and sociopathic disorders of the characters. They are in no way intended to convey the feelings or attitudes of the author. The author holds deepest sympathy and highest esteemed regard for the victims of the sociopathic characters. It is the author's hope and intent that, by these illustrations, the reader will gain an appreciation of the presence of the evil forces that lurk in some minds, craftily disguised as normal. If you are squeamish about offensive material, especially cruelty to insects, animals and people, or if you are offended by characters' offensive behaviors and expressions of strong opinions about controversial subjects, you are advised and cautioned to not purchase this book. If you are a child under the age of eighteen, do not purchase this book as it contains erotic adult content.

DEDICATION

To the need for love.

Table of Contents

LOOKING AND LISTENING

Butterfly Poon saw the open barn door and the two people inside. She was determined to get there and rest inside the barn. Much of the kaleidoscope downed and rested behind her in the copse of trees and attached themselves to branches this late afternoon. They were wise and out of approaching danger. Coming toward her were the blue wings of the dreaded barn swallows. Onward she fluttered with about a thousand of the most courageous Monarchs. Her back muscles ached. The sun-glinted blue flashes decimated the vanguard of the kaleido-scope, but Poon and a hundred others made it safely to the brushes and the farm buildings. Poon slipped unnoticed into the barn and attached to the inside frame of the large wooden door. She was safely hidden from swifts and swallows there. And she was in a perfect spot to hear the conversation of the humans below. Humans fascinated Poon. She desperately wanted to become one in her next life. Perhaps one of her eggs would grow to become not a caterpillar like she once was, but a human. She didn't understand such things, but she hoped to learn more about the humans by watching and listening carefully.

Below a woman sat propped upon hay bales with her lower human legs spread out widely, exposing her female anatomy to the man who sat in front of her. The woman's upper human legs braced against the bales behind her and helped the woman hold her head erect. The man stared at the

1

woman and rubbed his front legs' feeler feet slowly back and forth from the woman's anatomical center to her lower legs' knee joints and back again. He was older than she was. The two humans were talking.

Poon heard the woman, Marty, tell the man, David, how her issues with her mother, Susan, gave rise to her exploitations of many men. Marty loved a man named Bob and spoke freely to David about wanting this Bob fellow. Marty had concerns that Bob and Barbara, another woman from the office where the humans worked, had some kind of a secret love for each other. The Barbara woman had a regal look about her and was even more beautiful than the voluptuous Marty. Barbara had a seductive caramel skin tone, which Marty tried to replicate by sunning herself and risking frequent sunburns. Marty envied Barbara's subtle sexuality and worried that Bob considered Barbara more desirable than her. These people were all responsible for the operation of a major financial institution. Whatever a financial institution was, Poon could not fathom.

She observed and listened in amazement as David, seated upon a hay bale closely opposite Marty, knelt down before her splayed anatomy. He kissed both of her upper thighs close to her butterfly tattoo and told her how pleased he was to learn about her seductive conquests. He told her that his chest burst with pride for her evil ways and that he adored everything about her. He confided in her that his company, UGGA, was also the pinnacle of evil achievements and that it also had recently emerged like a regal Monarch butterfly from years in its cocoon. It had devoured innocents as a caterpillar devours milkweed leaves. It had endured insufferable years in chrysalis and was now much like Marty finally open, free, and ready to enjoy its full glory. He told her he intended to adopt the Monarch butterfly for the new corporate logo. That would both recognize her ascendancy to UGGA's exemplary model employee status and also signify his personal approval and immense pride in her debauched behaviors. That would forever idolize her as the corporation's Goddess and standard bearer.

He professed that he and she were kindred souls that had both overcome their need for God and his ridiculous obstacles to human pleasures. They had outgrown the need for the Ten Commandments or Torah's 619 mitzvahs. Working together they would go far for they had both ascended humanity's highest level. They had surpassed any usefulness for God in their quests for pleasure and had triumphed over him. They had swept away his stubborn obstacles to evil. God was now gone from them, a dusty cobweb forever cleansed from the unvisited corners of their minds.

David silently rubbed Marty's legs in a stimulating caress while she talked casually and freely about her relationships and seductions. Poon observed that Marty's tattoos on her uppermost inner thighs formed the wings of a Monarch butterfly, and the Marty woman even referred to her anatomy as the magnificent butterfly. Listening to Marty, Poon could only wish that her next life would be like the woman's. Poon could only expect to copulate one glorious time with flight leader Tang and the others, deep in the wet forests farther south in the jungles of Mexico. She would feel their shafts depositing their semen into her egg sac only one fateful time, but this Marty woman had copulated and felt the joys of intercourse thousands of times, yet she bore no children and continued to live. Marty simply fornicated for the joy of it. She told David she was a nymphomaniac, and how pleased she was to cause the death of the woman who rivaled her. Poon spread her own wings wide in envy of the Marty woman and marveled as she eavesdropped on Marty's vignette, already in progress.

Marty said she proudly embodied the magnificent triumph of evil over goodness. She told David that her Monarch butterfly tattoo on the uppermost reaches of her inner thighs represented the most attractive and best of all butterflies. It represented an irresistible attraction to every man who saw it and melted away any inhibitions he might have about making love with her. When she spread her legs for a man her butterfly tattoo hypnotized him. It signaled him to join her in unimaginable pleasures and welcomed his soul into her evil world of shameless lust. She proudly told David she was the feminine reincarnation of Mephistopheles, Goethe's Satan. Poon listened in amazement as she boasted to David about a man she was having an affair with and her encounter with his upset wife. Marty had already subsumed the woman's husband into her world of lust and sin and through her evil will she cast her archenemies, the man's wife, and young family, into oblivion and death. Marty recanted how she first crushed the spirit of the wife, then shattered the wife's hope of reunion with her husband, and finally annihilated the woman's marriage and induced the woman to destroy herself and her children. She reveled in her role as evil's handmaiden and rejoiced in her triumph. Marty professed inner satisfaction when she inflicted mental cruelty upon women who dared challenge her possession of their husbands.

Poon's antennae quivered as Marty extolled her deeds and explained to David the methods by which she deployed her seductive powers, how she felt transformed into a glorious butterfly when she spread wide her thighs and welcomed her lovers. David seemed to have some sort of dominance over Marty and Poon soon realized that Marty worked for David and David very much encouraged Marty's sexual activities. Poon now listened intently while Marty described to David how one lover's wife confronted her and called her a whore:

"Then she looked into my eyes with this squinty, angry look. 'You're a *whore!*' she said.

"Well, I wasn't about to let her stand there and insult me," Marty said. "As far as I was concerned, this wasn't about me at all. It was about her outrageous behavior interrupting something wonderful and beautiful. I knew by the way she called me a whore that she only used her pathetic, smelly cunt to procreate her two brats. She rarely performed wifely duties. That stopped after the second kid. Carl, the bitch's husband, couldn't stomach the thought of fucking her anymore. I can't imagine what he was thinking when he married that pathetic pile of garbage. I opened my sheer nightgown so she could see my naked body in the moonlight with the flames from the cabin's fireplace silhouetting me and giving a luminous glow to my pussy.

"I gave her a huge, widemouthed smile, as if to acknowledge that her expression looked like she'd just discovered the Easter Bunny, and said to her, 'Why, yes. I am. Did you expect to come up here to meet an ingénue?'

"I continued talking to her in a lowered voice, as if to take her into my confidence. 'But you need to understand, I'm not just some cheap, two-bit whore. I'm a very high-class, expensive whore. I'm also shameless. I'm your worst nightmare, bitch.'

"At that point, she started up the steps. *'Get out of my way,'* she ordered as she tried to brush past me and go in the door.

"I put my hands on her shoulders and gave her a sharp push backward. Then I raised my voice, which startled her. 'You need to understand a few things. You can see, can't you, that I'm the woman, the whore, your husband loves to be with, not you? See my skin? It's soft and lovely. Your husband loves running his hands over my entire body, touching me and caressing me everywhere. I'm the woman who gets massages from a personal masseuse paid for by your husband to keep me feeling good about myself and to keep my skin beautiful. I'm the woman he takes on out-of-town trips to theater shows and fine dining. I'm the one he buys furs and fine dresses for, and I'm the one he buys exotic lingerie and expensive perfumes for. He also pays for my hairdresser, my manicurist, and my pedicurist. When we go to the opera or the theater and when we go to fine restaurants, he always makes sure we have first-class seating. He always makes sure to hold my chair for me and have me seated comfortably. He always holds my car door open for me and always makes sure to get the car and drive it up to the door for me. He just bought a new BMW convertible for me, just so he could prove to me he was worthy to see me more often. Your husband is a wonderful gentleman. He's always good to me. He loves being with me because he loves the thrill of being with a truly wonderful whore. Does that help you better understand how your husband feels about me?'

"'Get out of my way,' she said and tried to step around me.

"'I'm not getting out of your way, dirt pile. You're not going in there. I rented the cabin. You're not welcome here.'

"I stepped in front of her and raised my chin to let her know I'd hit her if she persisted. I looked at her and the clothes she was wearing with scorn and continued talking to her, to enlighten someone who was incredibly stupid. 'Just look at yourself. You wear polyester jackets and torn dungarees. You wear your hair like you're some kind of war orphan. It's no wonder Carl can't stand you!'

"Then I put my hands under my breasts and cupped them, lifting them a little higher. 'Take a good look at my gorgeous breasts. Your husband loves to put his hands on them. He's told me he can't stand looking at your sagging tits. That's true, isn't it? I know it's true. He's told me everything about you.'

"She didn't answer me. She was shocked.

"I could tell she was off balance. I had the initiative and I continued, 'When I'm sitting on Carl's lap, fucking him with my back to him, he loves to hold these breasts in his hands and he loves to squeeze my enticing pink nipples. He makes me squeal with erotic delight when he does that, and sometimes that alone will give me an orgasm. When I sit on Carl's lap, facing him while I'm fucking him, he loves to suck on my beautiful button-hard nipples. He kisses them and plays his tongue over them while he squeezes my luscious, succulent breasts with his hands. I have beauty queen breasts and flawless button nipples. I'm sure you can see that.'

"I seductively wiggled my ass and tugged at my nipples to help her imagine how I moved her husband's penis within me and how his fingers stimulated my buds. That got her fighting mad. She raised her hand to hit me, but I could tell it was a bluff. I was a good three inches taller and much better muscled than she was.

"'You're disgusting. I want my husband. I'm warning you. If you don't stand aside, I'll—'

"I wasn't about to let her take control of the confrontation, so I interrupted her bluff and raised my own hand. 'You'll what? Hit me? Just try it, sweetie. I'll slap you so hard your neck will break.'

"She moved back a half step at that.

"Then I rubbed my hand suggestively over my pussy, stimulating myself by stroking my clitoris with my first two fingers. I taunted her, speaking to her as if I was giving a reality check to an ignoramus.

"'Look at my pussy. This is what you're up against. Take a *real good look* at it! This is the glorious, insatiable pussy your husband begs for. He begs to put his cock into her. You can see I shave the pubic hair off her. You can see how soft and inviting her crown and her outer lips are, can't you? That's because I take exceptional care of her. I rub her with a mixture of baby oil, gardenia and lavender oils, and a few drops of Chanel No. 5 perfume every day. I rub these scents along my inner thighs and outer vaginal walls and on her crown.' I spread my legs and tilted my pelvis upward to show her my Monarch butterfly tattoo with its wings flared open. She could see how my cunt looked in the maiden position when I gave her husband the signal that I was ready to fuck.

"'I'm not going to stand here and look at your cunt, you sick whore! Get out of my way, damn you. You disgust me.' My taunt had provoked her a second time.

"Again she tried stepping around me. That time I pushed her back with one hand, keeping the other on my pussy.

"'Now, I must insist you listen,' I said. 'Whether or not you like what you're about to hear, you're going to learn something.'

"I lowered my voice as if I were once again giving a tutorial to an ignorant child. She stopped as if struck in the head by a brick. She still had a hard time believing I was a serious problem for her at that point, so I continued. 'On her inner walls, I rub baby oil mixed with gardenia and lilac. Your husband loves these scents from my pussy. She drives him insane with lust. She's catnip for your husband. He can't get enough of her. He's crazed when he's away from her. She's not some unshaven wiry mess of pubic hair that irritates him, and she's not some repulsive piss and pus-caked, stench-emitting rat hole that women like you haul around inside dirty, ragged dungarees. She's wonderful! She's loved and adored. And she loves to fuck! She craves your husband's cock. She's insatiably fuck-happy. And, she's such a pampered pussy. In fact, your husband even has a secret name for her. He calls her Gloria. Carl's told me many times that he'd like to give you and your kids up. If I agreed to marry him, if he could be with Gloria all the time, he'd leave you. Your husband loves glorious Gloria! She means everything to him. My cunt owns your husband!'

"That got her attention. When she heard that, she gasped because she knew it was true. She hung her head and her eyes began to tear up.

"'Please, stop. This has gone far enough. I don't want to hear any more of your filth.'

"She spoke in a dignified manner as if she were some sort of upper-class country club pampered poodle. And maybe she was, once upon a time, before I took her husband for my lover.

But she started this and I had no pity for her. So I continued. I wanted to totally destroy this intrusive narrow-minded bitch.

"'I'm not stopping, dirt face. You're the one who drove up here. You wanted to know what's going on. Your dirty little mind wanted to know what was going on with your husband. You wanted to know if he was fucking someone. You wanted to learn something about the other woman. Well, now I'm going to show you.'

"I rubbed my pussy with a circular motion again and smiled at her with a full, joyful smile. I laughed a little belly laugh, taunting her more. I continued explaining the facts of life to her, treating her like the imbecile she was.

"'This wondrous, irresistible pussy loves fucking for the pure joy of fucking. She doesn't fuck just because your husband pays me to fuck him. Can you possibly even understand that? Can you? Can you understand that I love fucking for the sheer pleasure of fucking? Money just naturally follows Gloria. Men want her, and they pay to be with her whenever she can make time for them. They take her wherever she wants to go, and they bid against each other for time with her. That's how badly men want to put their cocks into Gloria. They pay extremely well for her pleasures. Men like your husband throw their money at Gloria because she has this special quality. She creates a bond of love with the men she fucks. Carl pays whatever I ask because he knows Gloria loves fucking so much. He loves knowing Gloria has a great time fucking him, and that's important to him. He always tries to please her, which makes our experience together so wonderful. He always comes back for more. You see, it's like this. Your husband is addicted to my cunt, and we love making love together. We have a perfect arrangement, and there's nothing you can say or do that will change things.'

"She just stared at me, dumbfounded. Now, for full effect, I gave pause to every adjective I used to describe my pussy and its sexual prowess. Speaking slowly, tauntingly, I allowed the full impact of every adjective's meaning to sink into that pea-sized brain of hers.

"'Your husband is among my magnificent pussy's most favorite men to fuck. He also lives for the times he can be inside her. He's madly, hopelessly in love with my wicked, family-wrecking pussy.'

"'I implore you. Stop this. Please, stop.' I could tell from her plea that she was hurting inside. The truth must have made her chest feel like it was being crushed.

"'Your words will never stop what's happened or what will continue to happen. You won't stop your husband from loving me instead of you. Don't you understand anything? You'd have a better chance if you told the moon not to rise or the Colorado River to stop its flow. Your husband's semen will keep flowing into me, sweetheart, not into you.'

"'Jesus Christ, you're unbelievable.' She was dumbfounded. She never expected to hear or see anyone like me.

"'Yes, I am. Now you've hit on something! But you must understand how your husband feels about Gloria. Then and only then will you know what you need to believe.'

"She clenched her teeth and stared at my pussy. Now, albeit reluctantly, I thought she wanted me to go on, so I did.

"'He's told me that there's nothing more wonderful than this beautiful, sensuous pussy in the entire world. He told me he'd rather lose everything he has than lose my tasty, hot, wet, welcoming pussy. We fuck lovingly for hours at a time, sometimes nice and slow and sometimes with strong, sudden bursts of unbridled passion. He likes to enter me from the front but more so from behind, and he loves it when I lie on my back and bring my legs up over the top of me and bend my knees. Then he can hold my legs and caress the undersides of my thighs while he fucks this eager pussy straight down from his standing position above me. Sometimes he holds my legs open while he's fucking me from above, and he even licks my toes.'

"'Please, stop. I don't need to hear any more of your filth.'

"That time she spoke to me as if I were a person she could relate to, kind of woman to woman. But I wasn't about to stop.

"'No, I think we need to keep going. I want you to take a good look at my legs. Really look at them. These are beautiful, sexy legs. I'm sure you can see that. Carl gets really deep inside me when he fucks this glorious, insatiable pussy from above. When Carl fucks her that way, she feels so wonderful and happy knowing she's taken in all of him. When I haven't been with him for a while and I see him coming toward me, my pussy has a warm, moist sensation. She knows she's going to be fucked deeply that way. She's so anxious to receive him. Just my seeing him makes me salivate and gives her a signal that she's about to enjoy several days of wonderful fucking; then she gets very juicy wet and starts throbbing from the anticipation of Carl entering her. He has a wonderful cock, and she loves it when it's inside her. His cock belongs inside my pussy. It's always welcome there. It has a happy home inside me.'

"She turned and started to walk away. 'I told you I don't want to hear any more of this shit, you sicko. That's enough. I'm getting the children from the car and we're going into the cabin to see Carl. He needs us. We will save him from you. You are one sick woman. When I come back, you better get out of our way.'

"'Fine, then I'll give sex lessons to your little girls and explain all the ways I fuck their daddy. Are you sure you want that? And I'm not going anywhere, bitch. I'm spending the night in the cabin with your husband. Maybe we'll stay a few more nights. I'm sure Carl would be up for that!'

"That stopped her. She turned and faced me. She wanted to hit me, I could tell, but she knew she'd get the worst of it.

"'*Just sit down.* You drove up here to see what's going on, so let's make it worth your while. So, you think I'm sick? You and I have a difference of opinion about that. Just sit and listen. You know nothing. Nothing!'

"I sharpened my voice and, amazingly, she sat and glowered at me. She swallowed her saliva and curled her lip. She was boiling mad by that point. I wanted to make her sick inside, so I continued to taunt her until she was ready to throw up.

"'There's so much more I need to tell you about my irresistible pussy and your husband. When he's mounting me from behind, he gives me little love bites on the back of my neck, and he licks me behind my ears. He lays his hands upon my shoulders and gently massages them while he kisses my back. His gentle hands on me and his kisses make my darling pussy's clitoris swell up.'

"'You *don't* say.' She tried to be cynical.

"'Yes, I *do* say. I have this erotic sensation when he loves me with his hands and his kisses that way while his penis is inside me, while he's thrusting into me from behind in the doggie position. I almost go out of my mind with desires. I respond by wiggling my ass back and forth and up and down a little, which makes his prick extremely hard. I tease his penis that way until he's straining in a frenzied state to push deeper inside me. I back my ass hard against his pelvis and this anxiously craving pussy feels him way up deep inside her as we move together in a slow, deliberate rhythm, gliding his hot, throbbing penis over my swollen, juicy clitoris. This marvelous, insatiable, incorrigibly wanton pussy just loves it, absolutely loves it when he shoots his wad into her in that position. His red-hot semen makes my delicious clitoris explode into a wild orgasm. He makes me scream for joy while we both have exploding orgasms.

"'This wondrous pussy has an unquenchable thirst for your husband's penis. I just thought you should hear these things since you seem so interested in my beautiful, delicious, sweet-smelling, joyful, erotic, effusive pheromone-emitting, shameless pussy. I thought you'd like to know just how much joy this precious pussy has while fucking your husband every way imaginable.'

"'Enough! Have you no decency, no shame? Must you go on like a barnyard pig? Don't you realize you're not the only woman who knows how to fuck? Congratulations! You're a nympho! Am I supposed to clap?'

"Her voice hinted that she was becoming less assertive, even a little dejected. She knew she was hearing the truth. A woman knows it when she hears it. By that point, I could see she was beginning to feel slightly nauseous, which was exactly how I wanted her to feel. I hoped if I kept taunting her she'd throw up and leave me alone, so I continued my shameless onslaught.

"'There's more than simple fucking. Your husband also loves to thrust his tongue deep into my pussy. He loves to run his tongue over this beautiful pussy's yearning, welcoming clitoris. He loves kissing the tip of her clitoris. We have spectacular, gushing orgasms when he does that. He loves to savor the juices from my delicious pussy's orgasms. He swallows her juices while he licks her clitoris and makes her gush continuously. This wonderful, worldly, erotic pussy loves to shower her tasty, sweet-smelling juices all over Carl's face, his mouth, and his cheeks while she orgasms from his tongue's caresses of her clitoris.

"'My beautiful, glorious pussy truly cherishes her ongoing love affair with your husband. In fact, Gloria just had a fantastic orgasm right before you drove up. You should have seen Gloria fucking Carl. First, she was on his face. He licked her really good, got her nice and wet. Believe me! Carl was licking this same sensuous pussy that you are now staring at with your mouth open like you've never seen a pussy before. I was having an orgasm from his licking shortly before you drove up! You have great timing!'

"I laughed at her. She started to stand up, but I pushed her back down. She was sitting on the porch steps, and I stood in front of her as she choked back vomit. I almost had her.

"'Your husband kissed this marvelous pussy's clitoris really good just a short while ago. You should have been here to hear me squealing with delight. This pussy was feeling so erotic. She was coming all over Carl's face while he was squeezing these lovely breasts and pinching these beautiful, hard nipples.'

"I cupped my tits again so she could see how excited my nipples were from her husband's pinches. 'Then your husband mounted me and fucked my insatiable pussy so beautifully with his big, hard cock. It was all so wonderful and erotic, so free from inhibition. You should have come here a minute sooner. You could have watched Gloria as she engulfed your husband's penis in her sensuous wonders. Carl just finished shooting a huge semen wad into my marriage-wrecking, sperm-craving pussy a little while ago. See?'

"What I did next positively shocked her. I threw off my nightgown so she could look at me fully naked. Then I tilted my pussy upward, spread my legs apart some, moved closer to her, and canted my pussy toward her face so she could get a close look at my pink inner lips. Slowly, Carl's creamy white, sperm-laden semen oozed from me. I showed her the result of my success. That seared proof of my triumph into her dirty mind. Then I shoved my pussy to within three or four inches of her face, intruding way inside her personal space.

"She pushed me away with a muffled sob. I came right back and stood before her again, right in her face. I wasn't going away."

"'Wouldn't you like to smell my beautiful, victorious pussy? I already explained how I keep her smelling exotic for your husband. With his cum inside me, you can smell that wonderful, erotic aroma of Gloria's and your husband's pheromones blended together. Here, I'll get her closer to you. Take a deep breath. Smell what happened inside her. You can smell the beauty of Carl and I joined in passionate love.'

"She showed great reluctance, but finally took a shallow breath close to my pussy. I think she only did it because she needed to catch her breath, but there was an element of curiosity as well. She was shocked at how I continued taunting her. Then she turned her head away as if to deny I was having Carl, as if her mind refused to believe her husband's semen was oozing from me just three inches from her face. So I continued to humiliate her."

"'Carl fucks Gloria because he craves her. He can't stand your smelly cunt. He hasn't been with you for over a year. Admit it! Carl is addicted to Gloria and will be forever. He will never want you now that he's been with her. Come closer. Go ahead and put your nose into her. She won't hurt you. Inhale her scent and take a really close look at her. She's beautiful. You'll never compete with her. Carl will always want Gloria, never you. He wishes you were dead.'

"I raised my voice to taunt her. She was such a coward. Then I held my pussy open with my hands so she could see her husband's creamy white sperm pool against the pink insides. As I held myself open, I said to her, 'Yes, I'm a whore. I am an unrepentant, unashamed, beautiful, sensuous whore. I am a perfect, unblemished, glorious, iniquitous whore. No one dominates me. You coming here cannot dissuade me from what I'm doing whatsoever. You do not intimidate me one bit. I don't apologize or make excuses for anything I do because I love who I am and what I do. I'm proud of what I can do for a man with my tongue and my beautiful pussy, and I want your husband. I love fucking him, and I'm going to keep on fucking him, and there's nothing you can do to stop me.'

"As she started to get up, she pushed me hard, trying to shove me to the ground. I reeled back a couple steps, regained my balance, and pushed her back down onto the step. I stood over her again.

"'Why must you be so nasty? How can you live with yourself?' she whimpered.

"'Because you tried to get in my way. You must learn respect, and you need to understand you can't interfere.'

"Then she looked up at my face with an expression I'll never forget. She knew I was truthful and determined, and there was nothing she could do to stop me. She knew she'd lost her husband to me. I could see she'd lost her whole reason for living, actually lost her whole purpose in life to me. Her expression must have been similar to the one a victim had when he was sacrificed to the Aztec gods.

"After he plunged the dagger into the man's stomach, the priest reached up above his liver and tore his heart out with his bare hand. It really was a beautiful and awesome moment when you think about it. I felt she was giving me that same pleading death look, as if begging me to spare her and her kids.

"The man sacrificed isn't actually dead yet, but he knows he soon will be. He experiences the trauma of feeling his heart ripped out, and he looks at the priest with eyes of hopeless awe. It's a questioning look, a pleading one. His eyes ask why this had to happen, if there's some faint hope the priest can put his still-beating heart back into him, but of course the priest can't do that. He just smiles at his victim as the man's life expires.

"The priest smiles at the man he sacrificed, engaging the dying man's brain for the last time. Then the dying mind dims and accepts what has happened before fading away into eternity. It had to be a beautiful moment for those priests to witness. It had to give them an incredible rush of power to encounter righteousness being sacrificed to evil.

16

"At that moment, I experienced that same feeling the Aztec priest felt. She stared horrified into my pussy and saw her husband's white life force oozing from me. Then she looked into my eyes. She knew I'd just taken her life from her. I didn't think of myself as being the evil one. I was commanded by my gods, the gods of lust and sensuality, to do what I did to her, just as the Aztec priest was charged by his god to take his victim's heart from him. I was the glorious and triumphant victor over the disgusting, prudish, cloistered mind that directed her possessive heart. I was enthralled with a most wonderful feeling. I had figuratively ripped her heart out. I'll savor that feeling for the rest of my life.

"When she saw her husband's semen burbling inside my pink pussy and sliding out of me right before her face, she held her hand up to cover her mouth and gasped. I took her breath away by doing that, by proving to her the truth of my words. She trembled a little. It shook her that much. Then she and I had this divine, transcendental experience.

"I smiled into her horrified eyes. My mind entered hers, partnered with it, felt and imagined the same things she did. I experienced the crushed feeling she had in her heart. My mind raced alongside hers as it comprehended and visualized how I and my pussy seduced her husband, controlled him, and wrecked her marriage.

"A divinely erotic sensation overcame me at that moment. I decided to make her mind see what I did with her husband inside the cabin. I flexed my buttocks slowly, erotically, and tilted my pelvis upward as I moved closer to her face. Sensuously, I gyrated my hips.

"She visualized how my hot, wet, pulsating pussy undulated in perfect rhythm with her husband's cum-gushing shaft. I saw into her mind. It pictured her husband's penis strokes sliding inside Gloria's slippery, velvety walls. She saw Gloria effortlessly coaxing the life juices from her compliant husband.

I knew she felt the same sensuous rapture that I felt. She saw my gyrations cradle and rock Carl's penis while my legs wrapped around his body and pulled him deeper and deeper into me. She was my victim, captured like a helpless insect within a Venus flytrap, seduced by her own imagination of nirvana, and fated to die with Gloria oozing her husband's semen into her mind. I poisoned her desire to live.

"We shared an amazingly erotic moment. These vivid imaginings were seared into her memory, and she knew she would recall them over and over again in her mind for the rest of her life, for however long she could suffer them until she died.

"I read her mind. It glimpsed peace, acceptance, and surrender. She actually felt a measure of happiness for her husband's erotic bliss, an erotic bliss she never gave him, and she grieved deeply at her own failure. I felt her shocked heart as if I'd torn it from her and held it still beating in my murderous hand. I was victorious. She'd lost and accepted defeat with horrible sorrow. Grief clawed at her stomach.

Her eyes rose from my pelvis and undulating pussy to meet my eyes again. Her pitiful, soulful look begged me to stop, but I was in her mind, tasting an erotic, evil joy. I knew I could force her mind to acknowledge everything it resisted seeing. I wanted her to fully comprehend the joys her husband experienced with me, and I intended to infuse her thoughts with lurid details and drive her insane.

"I called her 'sister.'

"'Come on, sister! We're almost there! Here's what your dirty mind needs to see! Look!'

"I used two fingers to drag her husband's semen from my pussy and sucked it into my mouth, rolling it around on my tongue. Partially opening my mouth, I allowed her to see my tongue basked in his cum. I savored it, immersed her mind in it. I rolled my tongue against the back of my front teeth so she could see her husband's cum in my mouth. Then I burbled his semen onto my lips before licking them slowly, taking his cum back into my mouth. I kissed the tip of my index finger as if it were her husband's cock that had just ejaculated in my mouth. Then I licked my finger, mocking the way I licked the underside of her husband's penis.

"Her imagination and mine united as one. She visualized my lips sucking off the head of Carl's penis, and she saw my tongue lick his balls. She watched me arouse him to an erotic frenzy as I sucked him off. I spared no detail for her imagination. Opening my jaw wide, I extended my semen-drenched tongue, achieving the desired effect. She was a cornered rabbit paralyzed in its death trance by a viper measuring it for a meal.

"She visualized me taking Carl's testicle sacs, one after the other, and putting them fully into my mouth, caressing them and kneading them with my tongue. She imagined Carl's cum responding to my loving mouth. She saw his cock harden as cum left his prostate, rose up his shaft, and pulsed out from his cock into my welcoming mouth and onto my adoring tongue. She saw me roll his cum in my mouth, immerse my tongue in it. She saw her husband adoring me, loving everything about me as I savored his semen before I swallowed it. She visualized his life essence sliding down my welcoming throat. She watched me devour her marriage like a snake devours a rabbit, eliminating every trace of it.

"She even imagined Carl lying under me as I straddled him while he repeatedly thrust his tongue into me and lovingly caressed my clitoris. This erotic moment must have been something like the meeting of minds between the Aztec priest and his sacrificial victim. It was that fleeting moment between the conqueror and the conquered, the living and the dead. I felt an inner nirvana that I wished would last forever. I was glorious in my conquest, proud and unashamed.

"She sought mercy. She looked at me with that same expression a sacrificed man must have had. Her eyes bore into mine with a pleading, hopeless look. They begged me to put Carl's semen back into him, but realizing at the same time that nothing could be put back, that her life would never be the same again. She knew at that moment that her marriage was dying and there was nothing she could do about it.

"I seized the moment. Feeling no mercy, I smiled into her eyes and let a muffled laugh escape me. I felt naughty and empowered by a wonderful otherworldly force, and I was complete as a woman. I had her very life, her universe, entrusted to my mercy. She'd seen Carl's wad of cum oozing from me, her husband's semen on my tongue, but I had no compassion for her. Instead, I laughed at her, mocked her.

"I was as uninhibited as any woman could ever be! I stared deeply into her eyes with the same dispassionate look that an Aztec priest gave to the man whose heart he removed. My imaginary priest and I were one. I stood triumphant, smiling down at my pitiful victim. In my eyes, she saw the same remorseless stare that the dying victim glimpsed from the priest's face. The priest murdered his victim with his knife and hand, while I was murdering mine with the powers of my mind and the hypnotic lure of my cunt.

"I felt her despair in that moment, and the salacious malevolent thought I'd had a moment before recurred. I had her very life in my clutches. I could drive her to such despair that she would actually kill herself. I felt suddenly enthralled with my prospects for ridding this pitiful bitch from my life and the life of my lover. I realized from her pleading look that if I continued to infest her mind with the venom of my unrepentant wantonness and the unshakable reality that I was relentless in my determination to destroy her marriage, she was fragile enough to kill herself. I nurtured that delicious thought. It blossomed into a pernicious, all-consuming driver of my words.

THE SECRET AND THE BUTTERFLY

"I had her mind trapped. I coiled my thoughts around her fragile psyche and squeezed down on her mind like a constrictor snake crushing a hapless rabbit. I wanted her dead. I wanted her children dead. I wanted them out of my life. I instinctively knew this was my perfect chance to accomplish that."

David was amazed at hearing Marty's insight into the wife's mind.

"You actually had the premonition that if you kept taunting her you could get her to kill herself? That's a remarkable ability."

"Yes, David. I've dealt with many wives, and I know how susceptible they are when I attack their marriage, when I go after their husbands. It was my woman's intuition, but also my experience with difficult wives. I only needed to put my mind into hers, take denial away, and replace it with reality. All I needed to do next was play the devil with her mind, push it along this path it feared to go, take away its defenses. Carl's wife was about to go berserk. I had her in deep distress. She was trapped and helpless, and I had complete control of her Carl. He wouldn't come out and save her. I believe, in his heart of hearts, he wanted her dead too."

"And you kept going?"

"You bet I did. When I said I wanted her out of my life, I meant I wanted her dead. Out of my life dead."

"Well, go on, Marty. This is fascinating."

"Gladly. I'm pleased you're enjoying my tale . She didn't want to hear any more of the truth, but there was so much more to tell her. I was determined to crush her spirit, demoralize her, and convince her to end her life. That despicable, smelly, self-righteous bitch had no business trying to interfere with me fucking her husband. He was my lover. Mine! I was angry with her, so much so that if I knew I wouldn't get charged with assault or murder, I'd have had Carl come outside and hold her down while I pissed in her mouth and choked her to death. Then I would have murdered her kids. But I restrained myself. There was a better way.

"My intuition told me I could destroy her if I burnished into her mind the fact that I was on her husband's mind all the time, that there was no room in his thoughts for her or her kids. I simply had to do that. I knew I needed to show her the most evil, wicked essence of myself. She needed to know she could never escape my evil unless she died. I tasked all my mental powers to completely destroy her self-esteem, dismembering it so she'd never recover. After all, the Aztec priests weren't finished with their victims when they took their hearts out. There was another, final act.

"The Aztecs sent the clear message that they were completely in charge, that they totally dominated the people. They were ingenious. They let the people see the victims' heads cut off and tossed down the steps of the temple, followed by the victims' bodies. These heads were permanently displayed upon posts to keep the people in line and obedient. They fed their victims' bodies to the dogs. The Aztecs knew the importance of reinforcing the memory of the sacrifice. They understood the need to impress upon those who would question their powers that they were ever-present, ruthless, and contemptuous of their foes. The Aztecs had zero regard for their enemies. There were no descent burials, only contempt, and disdain.

"I sought to impress upon my victim a permanent reminder, like the Aztecs did. She needed constant reminding that Gloria and I came first, always and forever in her husband's life, and that she and her snotty kids could die of starvation or be eaten by dogs for all Carl and I cared. With that attitude and with malicious intent, I thusly re-entered her mind with a condescending tone. She sat frozen before me, trembling like a rabbit about to be consumed.

"'Sometime soon, you must go to your husband's office and open his lower right-hand drawer. In there you'll see a huge envelope of photos of Carl and me fucking in every position imaginable. He has this excellent camera with a time delay feature. It takes sequence shots of the two of us. Carl takes out the photos and stares at them every single day, sometimes several times a day. He loves me and my craven, sensuous, delicious pussy so much he can't stand being apart from us. We're always on his mind.'

"She put her hands to her ears to block me out, but I continued, only louder.

"'There's one series of shots you really must see. You need to impress them into your mind and remember them for the rest of your life. It's your husband giving all of his love to me. Carl took them after he came into me with a volcanic hot cum spurt deep inside Gloria.'

"'You're demented and sick. I don't know how my husband met you or how you two got involved, but it's time for you to let him alone. It's time to stop this sickness. You have no idea what family life is like. You have no idea all the people you are affecting with your behavior.'

"My inner self-esteem was not about to let this pimple-faced bitch tell me what my boundaries should be. I laughed at her—a low, subtle, knowing laugh—then continued.

"'Well, let's talk some more about my behavior and Carl's involvement with me. What I'm about to tell you is easily verifiable. You can go see for yourself if you so choose. I think you'll see that he very much approves of my behavior. When you look at the photos, you'll understand that your precious Carl encourages my behavior and rewards me for it. You'll understand why I have the furs and the nice car and you don't. You'll see that I do naughty, erotic things with your husband, and he loves it.

"'Carl took the photos when we were here last year, up in the mountains by one of the lakes. It's a time sequence of twelve shots. He had me stand at the edge of the lake. I'm naked, of course, except for my pearl necklace. I love to fuck wearing a pearl necklace. It's very sensuous. I'm sure you'd agree.... But then, I guess you wouldn't know anything about being sensuous, would you?

"'Anyway, Carl waded out into the icy cold water to get this shot. I told him he'd catch pneumonia in that freezing mountain water. I didn't want him getting sick. He responded by saying, "Babe, I'd go anywhere and do anything to get the perfect photos of you. Now, just hold Gloria wide open for the birdie."

"'He captured a perfect photograph my pink inner lips as his thick, white cum oozed out of my iniquitous, fuck-crazed pussy. The camera was angled upward so you can see me smiling proudly and radiantly with my ruby lips peeled back over my perfect teeth with just a hint of my tongue showing as I'm looking skyward, up into the heavens.

"'My eye shadow is perfect, and my eyes look so bright and beautiful. Carl just loves my eyes. They're alive and shiny, not dull and lifeless like yours. He often kisses them and my forehead as if I'm his angelic goddess.

"'Anyway, in this shot, my hips are canted forward noticeably, and my legs are spread slightly apart. I hold Gloria open so the camera can get the full inside view of my lovely, throbbing pussy and Carl's oozing cum wad. The photos show the tip of a mountain above and behind my head. They are erotic, and Carl said the mountaintop reminds him of a giant penis, and my open vagina from that angle gives the appearance that my craven, magnificent pussy has just finished taking in and fucking the entire mountaintop. He calls this series my "fuck the world" photo shoot. His photo sequence shows drops of his semen falling from my heavenly, delicious pussy into the lake. Each photo captures the aboveground scene and its reflection in the still lake. They display your husband's semen drops oozing from my triumphant, wondrous pussy, and their splash rings moving outward from where they meet the edge of the water.

"'The photos in that series show my pussy's shameless wantonness, her beckoning, irresistible, invitation to the cock to enter her, to fuck her again and again, to shoot never-ending streams of cum into her. And they capture the serenity and happiness of my heavenly face with the mountaintop backdrop reflected in the lake. Just as the timed sequence starts, the sun's rays burst forth and shine down upon me, glorifying me and covering me in a warm, angelic halo. I'm being showered in this radiant, shining light. It gives me a heaven-sent, holy goddess sort of look.

"'Carl is mesmerized by that photo sequence. He tells me, when he sees the semen drops coming out of me, he gets incredibly hard. He feels his heart pounding and his erection stiffening, and he knows in his very soul that it's his life's duty to fuck me again and again and put more semen into me. He tells me I should never be without his semen inside me. You really need to go see the photos. It'll help you appreciate what a glorious, shameless, craven, lustful whore I am and how committed I am to my whoring. The photos will also give you a better sense of how irresistible Gloria, my lovely, penis-craving pussy, is to your husband who adores her so much he'd be willing to die for her.'

"'I want to go now. Please, stop.' She started to get up.

"'Oh, no! No! We're coming to the best part. Sit!' She obeyed me and sat back down.

"'There's another set of photos in his desk that Carl took of the two of us up there at our secret lake. He put the camera on a tripod and photographed us making love. They were taken in three different series, showing us in all the different fucking positions. You can see Carl really loving the whole experience, every minute of it. There's one sequence you'd especially like, and I must insist you go see it. It's your husband and me playing around, frolicking with his wedding ring. He's sitting with me on a big rock with his arm around me, kissing my mouth, one hand cupping my left tit. He has your wedding ring placed over my nipple. Then he licks my nipple and takes your ring into his mouth. Then he kisses me some more and your ring is now in my mouth. I'm holding out my tongue to show your ring on it. Then he kisses me again and takes the ring into his mouth again.'

"'Slut!' she screamed and took a swing at me. I stepped back and she missed. Then I finally slapped her. That stopped her from moving. She trembled in fear of me. I shocked her out of her disbelief and continued.

"'The next several photos are of me lying on my back with my legs drawn up over my head so Carl could get his cock deep into me. We call that my bottom's-up position because my insatiably thirsty pussy drinks in all of your husband's semen when we fuck that way. She completely empties him. Obviously, he releases into me with a huge wad of cum.

"'The next several photos you'll like the most. Your husband puts his mouth against my triumphant opening and deposits your wedding ring into my semen-filled, shameless pussy. The photo shows your wedding ring swimming in Carl's semen inside my pussy, like a tiny little lifeboat in a white lake with pink sides.

"'I then hold Gloria wide open with my hands and your wedding ring disappears deep down into my cunt, like it got dropped into a bottomless lake. It's pure symbolism. My lustful, unrepentant, cock-gobbling cunt swallows your marriage in that photo, which of course it also does in real life. Then I squeeze my happy, joyous, playful pussy until she's almost closed and your wedding ring pops back up and reappears, riding atop Carl's burbling, white cum pool. Again, it's symbolism of your reality, that my tasty, , fuck-happy cunt can end your marriage whenever she wants. My sensuous, semen-craving, penis-loving cunt has magical powers that determine whether you're allowed to be married or not. How does that make you feel?'

"She just sat there staring with voided eyes. She was in no condition to speak, so I continued.

"'But we really should refer to Gloria as a pussy instead of a cunt. I only call Gloria a cunt when she feels mean-spirited. Really though, those photos should forever convince you how little your marriage means to your husband. They prove your life means absolutely nothing to him. I'm smiling in these photos because we had so much fun with your wedding ring. Gloria does this open and close sequence several times.

"'Next, I put some of Carl's semen into my mouth along with your wedding ring and I roll your ring on my tongue. I purse my ruby lips as if I'm sucking the tip of Carl's penis, and then my tongue peeks through my lips with your wedding ring around its tip. Finally, I open my mouth to show my sensuous, semen-covered tongue with your wedding ring on it, and I kiss your husband, putting my tongue into his mouth. That's how I give your ring back to him. It's really a neat photo sequence. I do hope you'll look at it and enjoy it as much as we do.'

"I smiled sincerely at her while I described the photo sequence. I was expressing my happy enthusiasm about all the different ways I fucked her husband, but I was, of course, being cynical.

"'Your husband also wanted to do some photos of me pissing on your wedding ring, but I couldn't do that. My pussy doesn't do filthy things, just beautiful things. I just want you to know I'm a high-class whore. I maintain the highest ethical standards. So instead of me pissing on your wedding ring, we did some photos of me with my legs spread out as I'm sitting positioned on three pillows he brought for this erotic photo shoot. There I am, suspended between two rocks and Gloria is spread wide open in the cool mountain air feeling a delightfully soft breeze, just lusting for Carl's tongue to lick her.

"'Carl then puts your wedding ring on the very tip of his tongue as he lies beneath me with his head upon a pillow while he extends his tongue up into my anxiously waiting pussy. He arranged the rocks so well. It's just perfect. I'm completely relaxed and my shameless, whoring pussy is perfectly suspended over your husband's face. There's no straining of his neck muscles or my leg muscles. We're both completely relaxed. We could stay in that position and have Carl lick my tasty, lusting pussy for hours. It was beyond titillating. Carl could lick Gloria forever. It felt that good. My delicious pussy and his anxious mouth are fitted together so divinely, it's almost spiritual. I just love outdoor sex so much! It's more wholesome and joyous than meditation or yoga! If you knew anything about sex, I'm sure you'd agree.

"'Then Carl rubs your wedding ring all along the underside of my luscious clitoris with his talented, lovemaking tongue. You can see the moment in the one photo where my whole body contracts and convulses from a spectacular orgasm. My face looks so serene and heavenly. It's truly a beautiful moment. In the next photo, if you look closely, you can see the glorious, bursting release of my orgasmic fluids as they gush onto Carl's face. My craven, incorrigible pussy is spread widely over Carl's face, displaying how insatiable she is as she engulfs his mouth in all her ravenous ecstasy.

"'Carl's so wonderful and talented with his tongue and the way he uses your wedding ring to bring me to orgasm. When he glides the ring over my clitoral shaft and uses it to tickle the tip, I just lose my mind in the sensation. He makes me scream out in joy. My sweet-smelling, perfumed, tastefully oiled, erotic pussy just gushes and gushes profusely. My clitoris and my loving pussy especially appreciate how thoughtful your husband is to use your wedding ring to titillate them.

"'We're so happy we found a meaningful purpose for your ring. By using it to caress and stimulate my clitoris, Carl told me he can dispel all cares of you and your dirty kids. That act helps him surrender his heart and soul to me, helps him offer up all his love to my ravenous, delicious, insatiable pussy. It's your husband's way of professing his deepest, everlasting, true love for me to both God and nature. Your idea of controlling Carl with that ring is a laughable fantasy that lives only in your mind, not his. We often laugh about you and your kids when we use your wedding ring to stimulate my clitoris. Gloria loves getting stroked with it. When I decide Carl should divorce you, I'll have him give me your ring as my present. We'll use it to stimulate Gloria and memorialize your divorce. It will be my divorce token.'

"I then put my hand on her shoulder to steady her before I resumed. I thought she was going to faint, but she just sat there, stoic. I needed her to hear the rest of what we did at our secret lake. She swallowed hard and just sat there as I continued.

"'The last sequence we made was truly climactic. Off to our left, where the lake spills out over a natural beaver dam, the waters begin a mirthful tumbling stream. I just love fucking Carl to the sweet, cheerful sounds of that little stream. It relaxes me and makes me want to gush out my pussy juices onto his face or his penis. Near the natural dam breast, there are big, green lily pads with bright yellow and white flowers blooming on them.

"'Magically, just as Carl lifted me off my perch on the rocks, and as he was easing my widespread, fuck-loving legs and my pulsating, insatiable pussy onto his swollen, eager penis, a kaleidoscope of little white butterflies appeared. They began fluttering about joyfully, as if they were dancing upon the lily pads and visiting the flowers. We laughed about that. It was as if God sent these delicate little battalions of fluttering wings to watch over us as we made love. It was heavenly. God himself sent the happy little butterflies to lift my spirits soaring upon their tiny fluttering wings to encourage me and cheer me onward as I positioned myself to fuck your husband. I mounted him, facing him, one of his favorite positions for fucking me.

"'He placed his hands upon my breasts, massaging them so lovingly, and his fingers began squeezing my nipples, teasing me into an erotic frenzy as he loves to do, when some of the butterflies began circling about my head. Shortly after they arrived, Carl released an extremely powerful orgasm. I could feel his hot, rushing cum streaming over my clitoris. He always shoots a gigantic wad like that after he's performed cunnilingus with me.

"'This last photo is our best ever. I know you'll be glad you stayed to hear about it. Carl had it blown up to a two-foot-by-three-foot print, which he keeps on his office wall hidden behind his landscape mountain range scene. He often takes the mountain picture down when no one is around and stares at that print. It's a mesmerizing scene. Go to his office some day, see and appreciate it.

"'I tingled all over when that shot was taken. The skin all over my body was warm from my continuing orgasm. Carl does me much better than the other men I fuck. He first brings me to orgasm by gliding your wedding ring along my clitoral shaft with his tongue; then he lets me relax to savor the experience. He never hurries me. He just occasionally taps my clitoris gently with his tongue or rubs his tongue against my clitoris ever so lightly, while my shameless pussy pulsates and streams her fragrant, tasty juices.

"'While I was in this ecstatic state, I was smiling widely because I was having one of the most memorable times of my life. My deliriously happy, pleasure-hungry, unrepentant, lustful, orgasm-pulsing pussy was in her frenzied state of rapture, feeling sensations from our oral sex at the exact moment when Carl ejaculated his huge semen load. It coursed hotly over Gloria's throbbing, swollen clitoris, bathing her, coaxing her to reciprocate and caused my inexhaustible, fuck-happy, penis-adoring pussy to have a fresh, explosive orgasm.

"'Then came the moment caught by the photo, the 'spectacular moment,' Carl calls it. Just as he thrust his penis into me, three things happened simultaneously. My joyful pussy, while still in the throes of my explosive orgasm, released a stream of Carl's semen, and it showered over the shaft of his penis. He was still hard. He's amazing. Then one of those little white butterflies landed upon my hair, right on the little strand of reddish hair I have on the top of my head, close to where my hairline meets my face. Just then, the sun's rays burst out from behind a cloud.

"'The photo caught the butterfly with her wings wide-spread upon my head, and you can see a glint of golden reflection from her white wings. They were like a little angel's imitation of my outspread legs. And the body of the butterfly beneath its wings resembled your husband's body attached to mine by my pussy, naturally joined to his penis. The sun's rays also make the semen on your husband's shaft appear to be a golden cream color, and with the sunshine upon my smiling face, I am angelic and radiant, caught by the camera in a divine moment.

"'The shutter caught the instant when my entire body contracted in ecstasy as I convulsed with orgasmic spasms from my joyous, grateful pussy. I screamed in ecstasy and shouted, "Yes! Yes! Yes!" I smiled with unbridled, shameless fulfillment and happiness. You can see my eyes looking far away up into the heavens. As I stared skyward, I imagined there were a hundred men standing around the lake cheering and clapping their approval of the beautiful fucking they witnessed. They all had rock-hard erections and were salivating and waiting their turn to come and fuck me. And I imagined I was going to be fucking each and every one of them. It's an amazing, unforgettable photo moment because it captures an indescribable feeling. I just love Carl and his magnificent cock so much. You can see how that feeling comes to life in the photos.

"'Carl and I agree—that last photo is our best yet. It represents the triumph of the whore over the wife. It's the embodiment of my glorious conquest over your marriage. It captures the rapture I felt as I savored the victory of my glorious, insatiable, lusting pussy over everything you represent. Over your vile, pathetic life and your sniveling brats' lives, and over your pitiful shambles of a marriage.

"'The butterfly with her wings spread was nature's way of applauding and giving a standing ovation for the sensational fucking your husband gave me. The sunlight on her delicate, heavenly wings represents God's blessed approval and confirmation of the righteousness of your husband's lust for me and my lust for him, consummated in lovemaking. The moment captured in that photo is so profound, my pussy starts throbbing and I become wet just thinking about it. We plan to go back there and fuck like that again and again, but we can only hope to have another day like that glorious day last summer. You simply must go and see that photo. I insist. It's a magnificent piece of art.

"'I'm telling you about the photos so you'll know that, even when your husband is in Plaintown, he's never away from me. He told me he did the wedding ring sequence because his marriage means nothing to him compared to me and my welcoming, understanding pussy. Just so you know, when he looks at the photos in Plaintown, he often calls me and tells me he can't live another minute unless I meet him in a hotel room and fuck him for an hour or two. He pays me a thousand dollars an hour cash for those meetings.'

"By that point, his wife was sitting on the second step with her hands over her ears, just shaking her head and crying. She was appalled, and her chest was heaving in grief. I knew she didn't want to hear anymore, but I persisted. I wanted to leave her with an indelible impression that I could be cruel to her if she tried to push me around. I rubbed my pussy right against her nose, then stepped back a few inches and held my lips wide apart. Her mouth opened in wonder as she fixated on my cunt for the longest time. Her mind was coming under my control.

"I said to her, 'So yes, now you know how things are. I'm not the one who eats bologna lunchmeat and peanut butter and jelly sandwiches and begs for grocery money. I'm the one who is well-fed and cared for, and nothing you can do will change that. Here, inhale deeply and take in the delightful fragrant scents of my iniquitous, semen-filled pussy. Go ahead. Smell her!'

"She did nothing, just sat there continuing her frozen stare, but from the forward stretch of her neck, I knew she was awed and entranced. My cunt was all she could see. I was surprised at how I outdid my own expectations. I was destroying her. I could feel it. Then I moved my hips slightly back and forth in front of her face, brazenly, suggestively. I held my cunt open wide, so she could look up into my pussy's inner lips and fill her vision with her husband's cum in my cum pool. I gave her impressions she would never forget. I meant to harm her ability to think of anything other than my unrepentant, marriage-wrecking cunt.

"The volume of cum pooled inside my cunt mesmerized her. She was like a trapped mouse staring at a predator snake about to eat it alive. She gasped, and her breath quickened. She was enraptured and frozen in shock. In my own cruel way, I was taking revenge upon her for the way I was shunned by some of the girls back in boarding school and the rejection I felt from Mother. Sometimes I find myself disliking all other women, and that was one of those times. Then I took over her mind and her life.

"'You need to understand that this glorious pussy is the goddess your husband worships and venerates. This is the heavenly, angelic, righteous pussy that reflected her godliness from the lake up into the heavens. The holy pussy that is adored and praised by all of nature. Your husband routinely sacrifices you and your children upon the altar of her hot, throbbing, insatiable clitoris every time he fucks her.

"'Your husband routinely enters into her innermost sanctuary, her deepest secret place where he worships her and where she welcomes and awaits union with his penis. He communes with her there in holy intimacy as he heaps everlasting praise upon her with long, coursing, multiple ejections of his hot, sperm-bearing cum.

"'Look closely into her now. Look up into her, into her innermost sanctuary, into her holy of holies. You can tell from his cum pool that he was praising his goddess when you intruded by coming here. You may atone for your sin of intrusion upon her holy acts if you wish, for my pussy can also be a forgiving, loving goddess.'

"That's when I gave her a chance to lick me. I do women sometimes, and I'm always willing to try out a new partner. I doubted she'd go for the invitation, but I thought I'd intimidate her all the more by offering it. She could know with certainty what a ravenous, unrelenting, amoral whore I am. My calculation was that she'd reject my offering, and I wanted her rejection because I really wanted her so revolted she'd kill herself and get out of my life."

"You're deliciously evil, Marty. I love you for that. Just listening to how your mind works makes me desire to fuck you myself, but please go on," David insisted.

Marty laughed. "So I've gone from getting fired to possibly getting fucked! David, you surprise me. You know I'm engaged to Bob now. I'm going to be a changed woman, but I am flattered by your thought. Do you want to talk about having sex?"

"Possibly, after I hear the rest of your story about that pesky wife."

"All right, I'll continue." Marty picked up where she left off.

"'I'm inviting you to rejoice in her glory, to join with your husband in his worship of her and accept her as part of your life, for she is the living goddess before you. So, if you will simply kiss her crown and lick the drippings from her lips and pray your supplications to her, beg her forgiveness for your intrusion upon her pleasures, promise homage, fealty, and honor to her, this one transgression will be forgiven. Your vile deed and thoughts and words will be forgotten as if they never happened. But if you just sit there and fail to kiss me and apologize, my heaven-sent pussy can become an angry goddess.

"'She chooses whether you live or die, whether you eat or starve. She can bless you with her bountiful countenance, or she can place a curse upon you and plunge you into hell. You can see, can't you, that your husband would like you and your brats to die? He wants freedom from you.'

"The bitch refused my offer. She didn't lick me. If she'd chosen to lick me, I'd have embraced her and tried to help her become a passable whore so she could earn a decent living. I'd have even helped her with some introductions. But she just sat there like a passive tree stump, staring into my cunt, fixated on the pooled cum inside me.

"I put my message to her in simpler terms that even she could understand, speaking softly, trying to encourage her. I wasn't threatening, but I didn't yield my superior powers over her and her husband.

"'You need to understand your choice, girl. This luscious, sensuous, glorious, erotic, semen-filled pussy spread wide before you is your goddess, like it or not, kiss her or not. She decides whether or not you get your grocery money, so respect this sacred pussy and honor and worship her! Be grateful to this wanton pussy that she lets you and your brats have anything at all, for she can take your husband and your life away from you anytime she chooses.'

"She just stared her hypnotic stare. I decided to intimidate the demoralized wretch to force her to obey my instructions. I raised my voice to give her my commands.

"'*Look at her!* Look at what's in your face. I'm shoving my spectacular, erotic, unrepentant pussy right against your nose and lips. Put your tongue into her. You need to taste your husband's cum. I know you've never tasted him. He's told me so. He's told me all about you and how wretched you are in the bedroom. So go ahead! I won't charge you for a taste. I won't deduct it from your grocery money.'

"Then I softened my voice, as one woman confiding to another. 'You need to know what your husband's cum tastes like after it's been blended with the precious fluids from my glorious pussy and her rapturous clitoris. You need to become a total woman. You'll never forget the taste, I promise you.

"'Just imagine that you could be a miniature version of yourself. Now you're deep inside my cum pool, holding Gloria in your hands and licking her. Carl's cock is positioned over your head while my cunt squeezes down on it. Huge gobs of white cum spurt out of his semen tube and flood down over your head. You're drowning in cum and cunt juice, and you feel wonderful for the first time in your life. You love it. You scream for more. I squeeze, he comes, and you open your mouth and swallow it. You finally know what it feels like to be happy.

"'You owe it to yourself to know what your husband loves so much about me, this shameless woman you call a whore. I'm standing right here before you, offering you a chance at friendship and understanding. This is all I can offer you. You may taste my pussy. You didn't really expect you could shame me or make me run away from you, did you?'

"The bitch's lips began to quiver, her head and body trembling a little. She was deeply conflicted. She understood everything. She desperately wanted to lick my cunt, but her years of male religious indoctrination restrained her. Her world had spun out of control. I could feel she was about to grab my ass and cup my cunt to her mouth, but she held back. She just couldn't overcome those male taboos. I guessed beforehand that she wouldn't take up my offer.

"I then took some semen and rubbed it on her lips and under her nose as an ultimate insult to her very being. It was my way of replicating disdain for my victim, like the complete defeat the Aztecs showed their victims when they threw their bodies down the temple steps. She was such a timid, mousey coward. She just sat there, her stare fixated on my cunt, whimpering and softly sobbing. She was grief-stricken, devastated, yet in a state of wonderment all at once. Her life was destroyed; her marriage was finished. Her chest heaved. She wanted the same life I had, the life I was offering her, instead of her own miserable life, but she just couldn't take that important first step. She was so conflicted and distraught by the choice I put before her she had difficulty breathing.

"I achieved my desired effect. I gave her the opportunity to cooperate with me, to repent for interfering with me or to accept and honor me and become a whore like me. There was nothing more I could do for her. I let her know her husband, and I went there often, and I let her know her husband carried me and my pussy in his mind each and every day. She knew about the photos. She knew those reminders were available. She could no longer pretend I didn't control her husband. All she had to do was screw up her courage and go look at the photos. She just sat there on the porch softly sobbing outside the cabin door, shaken to her core. Then she spoke in an almost inaudible whisper.

"'Carl. Carl. Please come to us, Carl.' She was pleading for the world to go back in time to one she better understood. I don't think she actually expected her husband to hear her. She was talking to herself.

"Carl ignored her. I don't think he even heard her.

"Tears are a woman's last vestige of hope when another woman has control of her husband, but I wasn't about to show her any mercy. I wasn't about to let Carl listen to her pathetic whimpers and feel guilty about being my lover. I wanted to go inside the cabin and continue fucking her husband.

"It was a decisive moment. I wanted her to just go away and die. I thought I'd made her so dejected that she just might kill herself, and I wanted no chance that she'd feel there was any hope for her marriage. I couldn't let her and her husband see each other. It was time for me to put a final lethal crush to her hopes.

"'Look, you've made your choice, and I have no more patience for you. You and your kids are not welcome here. You are not welcome anywhere in this world. Your husband doesn't want anything to do with you or your kids. You need to do as I tell you now. You'll never be happy in this world. You must go away and die and find peace with the choice you've made. You have something important to do now. You must leave us and go off and die. You must do as I'm telling you. You must think only of my cunt and how badly you want her. You must think how foolish you were not to kiss my cunt and love her. You must punish yourself by dying. You deserve to die. You must kill yourself because you failed to love her. You must think of nothing else until you die. You must go away and die.' I repeated myself to be sure I had her under my hypnotic spell.

"I left her sitting there. I believed my message stayed with her. I went back into the cabin and closed and locked the door behind me. We heard the kids say, 'Mommy, don't cry.'

"We heard her sobbing softly on the front porch. I ignored her and got back into bed with her husband. As he lay there, he said, 'Oh, the kids.'

"I knew at that moment it was imperative to get him to ignore the distraction she was trying to cause, so I used reverse psychology with him.

"I didn't mention their kids. Instead, I told him how upset his bitch wife made me, in order to cleave his sympathies to me for what she'd put me through and to irrevocably cement his love and loyalty to me. I lay on top of him with my naked body pressed against his and kissed him full on the mouth, teasing his tongue with mine, while at the same time I rubbed his forehead, temples, and eyelids softly with my fingers.

"I said to him, 'She just came up here to see what a real woman looked like. She'll be leaving soon. She'll get over it. It's best for us to just ignore her.'

"As I was massaging his face, we heard her car door close. She started the engine and drove away.

"Just so he'd feel no remorse over his choice to continue lying there with me, I whispered softly to him, 'I'm here, my love. I'm here for you. Please help me forget the terrible experience she just put me through. She hurt me terribly. She called me names. I need you to make sweet love with me, baby. Please show me you love me. I need you to help me get her out of my mind. Her behavior was disgusting. I want to fuck you so much. I need you now more than I ever needed you. She's such a vile woman. I felt dirty just looking at her. She doesn't take care of herself. Her appearance was appalling, and she has such a filthy mind. I need you to put her out of my mind. Please hold me and love me. Help me forget her. Make love to me.

"'Here, darling, please kiss my pussy. She loves you and needs you so much, and she needs you to show her you love her. She's very upset by your wife's terrible name-calling. She tried to make my pussy feel guilty about being in love with you. Please put your tongue deep inside Gloria. Let her know how much you love her. Please lick my clitoris. Kiss her softly like only you can do. Make my beautiful clitoris swell up with the joy of your tongue stroking her.'

"I then lifted myself up and straddled his face, lowering my pussy to his lips while I held his face in my hands. His mouth cupped my cunt, and his tongue was soon lovingly caressing my clitoris. He complied with my plea to drive her from my thoughts. I knew in that moment I'd won the decisive contest for his love and his money. I felt euphoric.

"'Yes, my love. Oh yes, that makes me feel wonderful,' I said when he found my clitoris with his tongue.

"I knew my pheromones would overwhelm him, that his serotonin levels and endorphins would surge. He soon forgot he ever knew that bitch. I conquered his mind and body and soul for all time. It was my moment of victory, as when a matador drives his blade into the heart of the bull. I spoke to him in a louder, more authoritative voice, with the tone of praise and encouragement.

"'That's it, my love. I'm the woman who needs you. I'm the woman who loves you. I need you now more than ever. Please be good to me, darling. Fuck me like you've never fucked me before.'

"I had one hand behind me, fondling his testicles and stroking his penis. Turning, I mounted him in the sixty-nine position as soon as I felt his life blood beginning to throb back into his penis. My pheromones stimulated him. We had our intimacy again! I was so thrilled how he responded to me. I felt as if I were fucking him in broad daylight on a mountaintop, with all the splendor of nature around us and an audience of a hundred men watching me, clapping for me and cheering me onward in my victory.

"After he licked me, I turned again, straddling his chest and facing him. I reached behind me and squeezed his testicles and fondled his penis. He was already hard and eager for my touch. I stroked his penis and guided it into me. I was hot and wet inside, and I made him forget everything but me. His hands came up and pressed against my heart. He could feel the rising passions within me and my quickening heartbeat. Then he began massaging my breasts and squeezing my nipples with his fingertips while intensifying his upward thrusts into my pussy. I was so thrilled for him, so thrilled that he stood up for himself by choosing to stay with me instead of leaving with her. I was so incredibly proud of him. I felt an intense, deep, enduring love for him.

"'Oh, yes, yes,' I cried. 'That's it. This is what I need. Fuck me hard, Carl. Fuck me like only you know how. Oh, I love it so much when your cock is deep into me. Fuck me harder, harder. Oh, you are such a wonderful man. I love your cock, Carl. You can make me come like no other man can. Let's fuck all night, baby. This is wonderfully right and good, darling. Oh, that vile, filthy woman! I can't stand the thought of her. Keep fucking me, darling. Your cock makes her go away and it feels so good. Oh, harder, harder. Keep fucking me, my love.'

"At that moment, I felt the greatest thrill of power and union with that man. I had this titillating, naughty feeling, this tremendous surge of victory regarding my controlling power over his wife and his family. It was like the thrill of victory you see from the winning side after a football game, with grown men jumping for joy. He'd proved his love to me, proved that he wanted to be with me, that he loved and desired me so much that he turned away from his wife and kids. I knew by most people's standards I was being positively wicked and sinful, and I didn't care at all."

Perhaps known, perhaps not known, to Marty at that time were the thoughts racing through the mind of Carl's wife as her car slowly ascended the long incline before it crested the top of the mountain pass and began its descent down the winding road to Plaintown. A smoldering hatred and anger in her breast slowly gave way to peaceful acceptance. Her weary eyes closed momentarily and reopened, fighting sleep and exhaustion. Her mind returned again and again to the scene on the cabin porch. The fixated image of Marty's cunt flooded her mind and allowed room for no other thoughts.

It was there, only an inch before her face. Marty held its outer lips wide open to give her a full view of its pink inner lips with Carl's white cum still oozing from deep inside it. What was it about that moment that vexed her so? She couldn't think of anything else. She closed her eyes again and drove onward and upward toward the pass at the top of the mountain. Her mind was playing tricks on her. It imagined she was in a large museum room surrounded by wall and ceiling murals of Marty's throbbing opened cunt. Its butterfly wings were beautiful art, and the pink inner lips mesmerized her. She ran from wall to wall trying to find a way to escape the beckoning cunt, but there was no passage out. Her mind was trapped inside Marty's cunt forever.

Her panic attack stopped as suddenly as it began. In its place, another feeling overcame her. She felt from deep within her breast an irresistible longing. It was the same instantaneous longing she felt when Marty invited her to kiss her cunt, to taste Gloria's juices and pay homage to her salacious pussy. The feeling returned now with overwhelming force, displacing all her previous hurts and anger.

She desperately wanted to return to that moment in time when her face was an inch from the shameless cunt that destroyed her marriage. Momentarily she'd had the urge to lick Marty's cunt, but her years of indoctrination prevailed. She thought it was wrong to do such a thing and she turned away, but now she imagined herself taking Marty's offer. She wished she had clasped Marty's beautiful ass with both her hands as her husband often did and cupped her lips to the lips of the cunt. She imagined softly coursing her tongue over Gloria, the insatiable clitoris, and partaking of the honey juices of Marty's orgasmic fluids mixed with her husband's semen.

The woman felt a great release thinking she could become one of the cunt's many lovers. She imagined Marty taking her into the cabin to join the debauchery. The three of them were there on the bed. Marty's beautiful, shameless cunt was positioned over her face as Marty lowered herself onto her eagerly waiting mouth. Her mouth was engulfed by the opened, welcoming cunt. Her tongue eagerly sought Marty's beautiful little Gloria, and she began to fondle it respectfully and softly with gentle flicks and caresses. The beautiful butterfly wings of Marty's tattooed upper thighs pressed against her cheeks as Marty held her tightly inside her. Marty's cunt and thighs nearly suffocated her, but she reveled in her intimacy with this deliriously delicious evil holiness of unbridled passions. She never knew she had such feelings until Marty unlocked them for her.

Carl was there, but almost as an afterthought. He was kissing Marty's face and fondling her beautiful breasts. The woman's mind escaped reality and felt a euphoric love for Marty, for her delicious, uninhibited cunt and the deeply primal holiness of her evil, carefree lust. It was a feeling of release. She was, in her delirious mind, no longer the captive housewife. No longer was she bonded to drudgery and child-rearing. She was free! Marty showed her freedom from the artificial male hierarchical structures that ruled the world. She was free of all the expectations and burdens heaped upon her by society and her husband. There, sucking Marty's cunt, she found a deep inner release and peace.

The dream state ended as the woman regained her senses. But it was such a beautiful dream! She no longer hated Marty; she loved her! She wanted to go back to Marty and pound on the cabin door to be allowed inside. Suddenly, she wanted desperately to turn the car around and go to Marty, throwing herself upon the mercy of the whore and beg to be allowed to cup her mouth upon the cunt that ruined her marriage and her life. She wanted more than anything she'd ever wanted before, more than she wanted her husband back, to kiss Marty's beautiful, delicious cunt.

The woman was distraught. She realized she'd made her choice. Marty gave her that one brief chance, but she'd rejected the offer to pay homage. She turned away from the goddess of evil and now, belatedly, she realized she loved Marty and all her evil ways because she was finally a free woman. Tears streamed down her face and blurred her vision. She didn't want her children anymore. She didn't want her life anymore. Life without her tongue making love to Marty's clitoris was no life at all. She sobbed as she drove, in deepest despair over her future and the lives of her children. There was a hollow emptiness in her stomach, but she had no thoughts of food. Her heart smoldered in the tormented anguish of a woman who'd lost her husband to another, and then finally realized she'd rejected the love of Marty's cunt, which she now desperately craved.

Her mind would not leave the scene where she discovered the truth about herself. It replayed over and over and relived the anguish and pain. She closed her eyes momentarily, seeking peace, but peace could not challenge the images of Marty, the beautiful, delicious whore. Each time she closed her eyes, she relived the moments where Marty stood naked before her, flaunting her wickedness, proudly proclaiming her revelry in whoring with her husband. Oh, how she wished she had kissed Marty's cunt.

Each time she closed her eyes to escape the memory of what she'd witnessed, her memory of Marty only strengthened. She knew Marty told the truth about the pictures while mocking her, taunting her. She knew she would lose her mind in endless wonderment thinking about the pictures, knowing they existed, knowing her husband cavorted freely with that beautiful, shameless she-devil personified as Marty. Her anguish intensified the further she drove, realizing that only Carl could have Marty now. She was jealous.

The woman hated herself. She intensely wanted to share Marty with Carl, but like a fool, she'd spurned Marty's offer. Oh, how she wished she'd held Marty's lovely ass, squeezed it tightly and pulled her iniquitous, marriage-wrecking cunt hard into her face. Oh, how she longed to cup her face to Marty's welcoming cunt! She knew it now, but too late! She'd realized, belatedly, how she loved Marty and everything the woman stood for! She wanted Marty's cunt more than life itself!

Like a silhouetted statue of Venus, dripping her husband's semen, the image of Marty now laughed mockingly within her mind while Marty's image smeared Carl's semen over its tits, taunting her, reveling in its debauchery. She realized Marty was right; she could never erase those images of Marty from her mind. The beautiful, mentally twisted whore danced in her mind, invited her to play, and beckoned her to freedom. She laughed and shamelessly stood before her while flaunting her sexuality. The gorgeous enchantress was proud of herself!

Marty merely amused herself by destroying her marriage and her budding family, and Carl allowed it to happen! He did nothing to stop the destruction. He loved that whore! He loved what she was doing to their lives. He welcomed it and he encouraged it. And in that moment, she finally understood her husband. He was right to cavort with Marty. Their marriage was a phantom illusion that deserved to be shattered. She saw that now. She loved Marty for showing that to her, and she felt an uplifting of her spirits when she recognized that the true object of her love was no longer Carl, but Marty.

Her mind would never be free of Marty. Her children would never have a happy home again or a real father. That was gone now. Thoughts of Marty and the things she did with her husband, of what she was undoubtedly doing with him even now while she raced down the mountainside to get away from her own thoughts, conjured up demons in her mind.

Marty's laughter rang in her ears. She imagined the naked flesh of Marty, Venetian goddess whore, pressed against Carl's naked flesh, and she winced and whimpered. Carl had Marty, and she would never have her. She'd exiled herself to a life without ever kissing Marty's lovely, welcoming cunt. Oh, what a fool she was! With every breath she took, she remembered the smells that wafted from Marty's proud, evil cunt—the whiffs of Chanel No. 5, gardenia, lavender, sandalwood, and rosemary oils intermingled with Carl's semen.

Every blink of her weary eyes flashed visions of the butterfly brazenly tattooed on Marty's beautiful uppermost thighs. Why had she been shocked at seeing the Monarch tattoo? What sort of woman would do that? What woman advertises her wantonness so openly? What woman flaunts her immorality and carnal lust so boldly? What woman defies shame and embraces evil like this woman who'd captured her husband? It was all clear to her now. Marty was free and alive and full of carnal joy, released from the bondages of confinement imposed by a male-dominated world. But she was not and could never be free. But she could be free still! Marty told her to die. Yes, dying would bring freedom. She could think of Marty's cunt until she died. Marty was beautiful and honest. What she thought was evil was actually truth and goodness. She felt honored to meet Marty now, and she would obey her.

She remembered how those butterfly's wings spread majestically outward when Marty opened wide her beautiful legs to shock and humiliate her. That butterfly was a magnet for Carl. The way its wings spread was like an invitation for a penis to enter and stay within it forever. Carl adored Marty's butterfly and immersed himself in it. That butterfly often held Carl's penis and his tongue in its grasp and controlled him. It controlled his heart and mind and did unimaginable things with Carl. It did things with Carl she herself could not do and would never do. Marty's butterfly was Carl's god now. It was her god too, but she knew she could never attain it, never touch it or kiss it. Fleetingly, the moment was there for her. Marty offered herself, and like the fool she was, she'd rejected Marty and vilified her. Now the moment was gone forever.

And Marty's laughing, smiling mouth held Carl's mouth and tongue to it and in it, and it sucked his penis and swallowed his sperm. And Carl's mouth and Marty's mouth played debauched games with his wedding ring. *Oh, my poor, dear Carl. How tortured your life with me must be.* She blamed herself for everything. Her chest heaved with grief. She wanted to hold her head in her hands and scream. Her mind tortured itself. She'd imprisoned her husband in a chamber, and Marty came into his life to set him free. She held an inner happiness for Carl and his beautiful devil whore. She accepted the reality that they were no doubt fucking again at that very moment, and that she could never join them, never partake of it, not after the things she'd said to Marty.

Carl's wife drove on that night nearly blinded by her tears. There was her inner sadness for what she'd never have commingled with happiness for Marty and her husband. Her mind was by a demon possessed, and her heart ached as if she'd been punched in the chest. She wished her heavy heart would tear away and leave her. She stared at the road being swallowed under the hood of her onrushing car and imagined it was an endless river of semen from many penises flowing into Marty's reveling pussy. Marty's taunting and uninhibited laughter blocked out all other thoughts from her mind. She wished the glorious whore eternal happiness. The road moved speedily under the car and made her dizzy.

She imagined she was swimming, awash in the endless semen stream flowing into the insatiable cunt. She was back in the imaginary museum room, now filled with semen, and swimming from one mural of Marty's cunt to another. A large, soft object arose from the museum floor and swelled up. It rose above the semen pool and presented itself before her face. It was the lovely Gloria. She rubbed against her face, begging to be licked. As she licked the imaginary giant, it grew ever larger and showered her with deliciously fragrant fluids. The fluids warmed and flooded around her, basking her in exotic pheromones. A round opening appeared in the ceiling mural and through it protruded a giant penis. That was Carl's penis! She remembered it. His organ was swollen and pulsing hard. Then it shot a shower of warm juices that drenched her face and flooded over Gloria. It pulsed again and shot a huge stream of thick, white cum onto her head. The bulging clitoris quivered in ecstasy, and the cunt squirted a massive flood of juices.

She imagined wrapping her arms around Gloria and licking her sides. She swam downward to the depths of Marty's muff, submerging herself in the whore's cum pool. Her tongue found Gloria's base and then vibrated against it until the two organs resonated. The inner lip sheaths that shrouded Gloria swelled and gushed, the flood of orgasmic fluids filling her mouth. She drank Gloria's juices and then kissed her lovingly from her base to tip. When she found Gloria's head, she placed her lips upon it and lovingly held it in her kiss. She imagined Marty holding her head with her hands. Then Marty pulled her head close into her sex and held her mouth firmly cupped against her wonderful cunt. She licked Gloria while Marty thrust her pelvis upward, pushing her cunt hard into her mouth. Marty writhed in her orgasmic delight. The woman imagined what her life might have been.

Now the woman's heart beat faster and she felt a deep pressure in her chest. She wished she hadn't defied Marty and had instead accepted her offer. She could have been a love slave to the whore, but like the priest's victim who could not have his heart returned to him, she also could not reverse the fateful choice she'd made. She could not return to the cabin and retract her rejection, but she could at least savor this vicarious union with the cunt she'd foolishly spurned.

She reveled in her mental love fest. Knowing her kids were belted in the back seat, she secretly took one hand off the steering wheel, opened her dungarees, and quietly stimulated herself. She was eager to release. As she masturbated, her juices began to flow. Her fingers and panties were soon wet, something that hadn't happened for years with Carl.

The woman closed her eyes and thanked Marty for freeing her from the living hell that was her prior life with Carl. She now felt relieved of constantly caring for the children, making meals, and begging money from Carl for all their needs. They were undernourished and dressed as paupers. Carl didn't care about them. They were on their own. Marty and Gloria had them consigned to a living hell. She knew she and her children weren't going to make it down the mountain alive, but it didn't matter to her anymore. She didn't know what lay on the other side of life, but she didn't care. She only knew her feelings. She was like a chrysalis straining to free itself of its confinement. She longed to spread her wings like a newly emerged butterfly and leave the life that bound her. When her eyes last stared into Marty's cunt, she loved the wonderment of what was revealed to her. She was attracted to the cum pool but resisted her impulses. However, she knew she could never return to her previous life, or even to life at all. Marty had just told her she must die. Now she only wanted desperately to please Marty so the whore would think well of her after she was gone.

She silently began praying to Gloria and blessed Marty's whole cunt for these brief moments of vicarious happiness. She felt more alive now than she ever had before. Her mind blocked out her children's screams as she took off her mommy tag. Only her imagined closeness to Gloria mattered anymore. She thought of herself as an adolescent girl, brimming with sexuality and singing a tune she remembered from childhood to her friend Gloria. "Oh, you beautiful girl. You great big, beautiful girl. Let me put my arms around you. I could never live without you. Oh, oh, oh you beautiful girl!"

The woman was happier in her imaginary revelry than she'd ever been in her life. She imagined she was hugging Gloria and swallowing giant gulps of cum from the cunt pool, savoring the tastes. Everything was suddenly different, her attitude completely changing. If Carl could have Gloria, so could she! She didn't want to escape from inside the cunt anymore; she wanted to stay inside it and revel there forever. She imagined her body drowning in Marty's cum-filled cunt. Into the pool dove her soul, following her body. It capitulated to Gloria's irresistible allure and was subsumed by the sensuousness of her fluids. The woman's religious learnings and morality were swallowed by Marty's debauchery. She loved where she was. Her mind was free of guilt, her soul lost in her wonderful imaginary world, which she raced to embrace.

The car hurtled swiftly downhill with its human cargo that moonlit night. Marty's ribald, teasing laughter haunted her thoughts as her children's screams reverberated in her ears. The combination of thoughts and voices pushed her over the edge of insanity. She wished to escape from Carl, her own progeny, and the world. She wanted the world Marty invited her to join, not the one that had her trapped. She knew she needed to obey Marty. She needed to die.

The woman sensed a jolt followed by a convulsive shudder. She imagined she was still inside the delicious aromatic cunt, experiencing its latest orgasm. She thought she felt an outpouring of fresh fluids coming from the reservoir of the cunt's juices surging through its walls. She vicariously believed her face was immersed in a fresh glob of cum from Carl's cock. In reality, the car had run over a guard boulder on the edge of the road. It failed to stop the car, to shake the woman into reality. The wetness she was experiencing was the flood of perspiration from her own skin, her sweat pouring over her face and eyes. The warmth that bathed her was the fluids discharging from her own orgasm.

The children's screams went unheard outside the fated car while its driver held its accelerator to the floor. The driver opened her eyes widely too late to realize the onrushing imaginary stream of cum was actually the road and the road was now air. Her last thoughts as the car tumbled end over end for thousands of feet down the mountainside were of Marty's mesmerizing cunt. She fervently prayed it would go on fucking and receiving licks from uninhibited partners for all eternity, liberating them as it had just liberated her. She wanted the cunt to be happy. Just before she succumbed to death, she silently prayed to Gloria, asking her to forgive her foolish rejection.

She said aloud her last words. "Please, Gloria, let me be with you and have you. Allow me into your world." She prayed that someday, in another world, she could enter Marty's holy inner goddess, kiss Gloria, and love her forever.

In those final moments, Marty achieved her goal. That night, as her cunt ingested a powerful spurt of fresh cum from Carl's cock, miles away on a mountain road it swallowed his wife's capacity to reason. Marty's ravenous, multitalented cunt devoured the woman's body, mind, and progeny that night while it simultaneously claimed all her husband's fealty. Like a contented snake digesting its rabbit prey, Marty slept a dreamily sound sleep that night. She knew she'd devoured her amateurish competitor. The next morning, she would claim her rightful prize by fondling Carl's balls, putting them in her mouth and playing her tongue on them, then sucking his cock to full hardness and victoriously straddling her prize. She would place his hands upon her tits. He would squeeze her nipples and breasts while she rocked her cunt forward and back on his cock. She would start his day off fresh with only her on his mind by wildly fucking him before breakfast. In the morning, she would be at the top of her game as the most committed, glorious whore any man ever knew. She slept a beautiful sleep, dreaming of her morning victory celebration. Gloria's lips would shroud and engulf the tip of Carl's cock, and her slippery walls would slide its shaft home.

That next morning, as Carl's hot cum spurted deeply into Marty's unrepentant, iniquitous cunt, miles away some passers-by first noticed the carnage and deaths wrought by her handiwork. Marty French kissed Carl long and playfully after he came that morning. She was rightly confident that only she would ever know the details of the interaction she'd had with his wife the night before. Carl was all hers now for as long as he was useful to her. That was all that mattered.

Marty understood all aspects of her business, her beautifi-cation, makeups and scents, her sexuality and seduction techniques, her muscle control and stamina, her sleep, diet, stimulations and orgasmic regularities, and the psychology of her marks and their female partners. Life for Marty was a quest; her goal was to be the ultimate sex object. She thirsted for conquests of cock and coin. She continually strived to perfect her methods, always seeking to discover methods that worked and discarding themes that fared poorly.

With Carl's hapless, dimwit wife, her tactics succeeded brilliantly. Going forward she used them in her repertoire when matched against other narrow-minded women. Marty was indifferent about the safety of Carl's exhausted, distraught wife who drove away with her children that night. She trained herself to steel her emotions from any empathy for her victims. The lives of these three and all future interlopers were meaningless, inconsequential annoyances to her business. She casually continued her narrative with David.

"I decided from that moment on that, for all my life, I would have my own standards. That meant I would put myself and my needs first above anyone else's. I was feeling unbridled pride and a sense of wonder about myself and my pussy. I wanted to possess Carl, keep him all to myself. Just to make that very point with his wife, I persuaded him to stay with me up at the lake for three days longer than we originally planned. We stayed for six nights instead of three, and we fucked for several precious hours each of those remaining secluded days. I had to let her know that I could take him away from her and keep him away from her as long as I liked whenever I wanted.

"I knew all along I didn't really want him except for his fucking and his sales. After all, David, you know I'm a good company girl and I put the company first. You can count on that. So after his sales fell off and I started going on trips with other men, Carl went crazy. He started sending me flowers and cards, stuff like that. He's settled down some since then, but I know how to drive him insane. He can't get enough of me. His wife never could make him feel the way I can. Fuck her and her pathetic soul. She was a fool for getting in my way. Men always go back to their wives like little boys running to their mommies. If Carl's wife had been smarter, she would have ignored the whole affair and saved herself the aggravation. She must have thought I actually wanted to keep him. Hah!

"Oh, there's one last humorous thing about Carl's wretched wife. She and her kids actually died that night. Carl and I didn't even know about it until we got back to Plaintown. Apparently, she went down the Plaintown side of Mountaintop

Pass. There was one witness who saw it. She was going over a hundred miles per hour into one of those hairpin turns and the car just shot out over the mountainside, rolled end over end down the mountain, and finally crashed and burst into flames. None of them got out of the car. The witness said when she flew by, her little girls had their hands pressed against the back window, and they were screaming, but the witness couldn't hear their screams and of course couldn't do anything to save them."

"Wow, Marty. That's quite an ending to her. Do you feel any guilt or remorse?"

"Oh, no remorse! None at all! I was elated, ecstatic! I felt like a lioness that had just chomped down on the skull of a vile hyena and killed the bitch. I was so proud of myself! That bitch deserved to die. She was the inconsiderate, selfish, uncaring one. She tried to insult me and interfere with my business where she had no business. By killing herself, she just proved how selfish and narrow-minded she was. Her sense of what's right and wrong was ridiculously rigid. Can you imagine a woman like that? She actually tried to make me and her husband feel guilty about what we did.

"I was just surprised at the way she killed herself, that's all. I was sure I'd succeeded in hypnotizing her by using my pussy to put her in a trance. I told her she needed to go away and die. I thought there was a good chance I could drive her to commit suicide, but I thought she would go out as a coward by swallowing a bottle of aspirin and bleeding out. But she amazed me by choosing to go out in flames. It was a hilarious end to a ridiculous life."

"What about her kids? How did you feel knowing she took them over the mountain with her?"

"I was shocked when I heard about the accident. I figured she'd think about our scene at the cabin for weeks or months. After my initial shock, I spent a few days asking myself how I should feel about those kids. After Carl and I came back from the lake, when I was home alone one night sleeping in my own bed, the answer came to me. Just as I was starting to fall asleep, I had an epiphany.

"It wasn't my fault that those kids died! It was the wife's fault. She chose to bring them up to the lake with her, and she chose to drive them back in the car. I had nothing to do with the way she drove that car or the way she decided to kill herself. She was the thoughtless, uncaring person that caused all of this. I had nothing to do with her choices. Her kids were just collateral damage, kind of like what happens in a war when two sides fight and some innocents get hurt. I wasn't driving her car that night. She was. Right then and there, I had peace of mind. I wasn't responsible. I felt relieved and relaxed. Then, just as I was nodding off to sleep, the most wonderful thing happened.

"Miss Iniquity, my soul mate, the one I imagine to be a voluptuous redhead that I'm going to meet in the flesh someday, came to my imagination and embraced me. She's always there for me, and she tells me when I'm making progress. She laid down next to me and began kissing me. Then she spoke to me. 'You've advanced yourself a great deal tonight,' she said. 'By washing your hands of guilt over those little girls, you've reached the pinnacle of immorality. You've claimed your rightful place as a world-class money-making whore. You've managed to place your own needs and feelings above everyone else's and not care about anyone who gets in your way.

"'You can stop thinking about those girls now and look forward. You'll have another forty years here on earth. You have a glorious, golden future before you. You'll fuck and suck hundreds of cocks. The well of your pussy will fill with semen and overflow hundreds of times. Men will worship you and beg you to kiss your cunt. You have your life. That's all that matters. You and I are one and the same now. You are my mirror image. I see myself in you, and I love you. I promise I'll meet you in the flesh one day. I'll place a golden crown upon your head, and I'll anoint your beautiful body with oils. We'll bask together in the sunshine. I'll kiss you everywhere. We'll assume the sixty-nine position and give each other glorious orgasms. Together we'll become immortal. I love you. I'll kiss your sex until you fall asleep, my darling disciple. I am here for you always. You did nothing wrong. Good night, sleep well, my love.'

"I pulled my long goose down pillow close to my body. I imagined it was Miss Iniquity. I wrapped my arms and legs around it and pulled it into my bosom. I fell asleep dreaming I was with her. When I woke the next morning, I was wet and fluid stains from my pussy were on my pillow. I had a whole new outlook on life, and a whole new feeling came over me.

I felt like those Aztec priests must have felt when they threw the severed heads and bodies of their sacrificial victims down the temple steps after their ceremony was completed. I felt an inner release of pent-up joy and vindication for the way I confronted Carl's wife. I felt triumphant, just like those football players when they win that big game. My pussy swelled up and throbbed when I realized Carl would be seeing me more, after he took care of the remains. I knew he'd need me more than ever, but for a different reason. He'd want to be comforted. My frustrations with the wife being in the picture finally lifted from my shoulders, and I anxiously looked forward to rewarding him for his loyalty to me.

"Those deaths had a cathartic effect on me. Now, whenever I'm fucking Carl, or any man for that matter, I think about that woman flying off that mountain, and that fills me with this salacious, titillating joy that is almost indescribable. I visualize her crashing in flames, and I realize the overwhelming powers my sexuality has to be able to cause something like that. I feel like I can control any man in the entire world. I come to my orgasms much more quickly now than I ever did before, and I feel totally released from all inhibitions. I now have no fear of being threatened by another woman in any way whatsoever. I am secure knowing that I can take her man and nothing she does can prevent me from doing whatever I please."

"How did Carl cope with the loss of his wife and kids?"

"He was subdued for a couple weeks, but he soon got over her. Now he's happy to be rid of her, relieved of all the demands she placed on him. He sees me whenever he can and whenever he can afford me. He still worships my pussy, loves fucking me, and he gives us more sales than he had for quite a while. He's working extra hard to make money to see me now, and he's more crazy about me than he ever was, so nothing's really changed. Well, he's more relaxed now. He's finally lost all his guilt about our former adultery and that sort of nonsense. He's a happy widower.

"Before, he'd do this quick glance around the room to see if one of his wife's acquaintances saw us together. Now that silly annoyance has passed, and when we're out to dinner, we're both very relaxed. Our evenings together are much more romantic. He doesn't talk about the kids, and I never mention them. I think he felt some lingering remorse for them, but he's coming around to seeing it as all her fault. He said one time that he couldn't imagine why she'd be so crazy that she'd do such a thing as drive off a mountaintop like that. I just shrugged my shoulders and told him she was an inconsiderate, selfish, vindictive woman, that her behavior that night revealed how evil she was, and then I gave him a warm hug and a kiss. I think that helped him a lot. I've pushed her and the kids out of his mind."

"How do you manage your feelings about a man's children while you are involved with him?"

"That's easy. I actually have absolutely no feelings for them whatsoever. I look at them as pieces in a board game being played between two women. The woman with the kids has an insurmountable handicap when she's up against me. The woman in the man's background and their kids can't concern me. I focus entirely on the man as if his wife and kids don't even exist. I'm thinking only about selling my wares to the top salesman.

"After I've identified which man is the champion salesman and when I've finished my sales presentation, I look to him to see if he approved. Actually, I'm looking to see if he approves of me. I'll lift my eyebrows and give him a smile. If he smiles back, I'll ask him if he liked the presentation. By that time, it's over and the reps are getting up to leave. If he says yes or nods, I then have a brief moment to act upon his interest. Here's the delicate part. I must act like I am suddenly the impetuous school girl who is thrilled beyond words at his approval. I must be spontaneous and believable as I approach him. I pretend to be relieved of some inner tension because he approved of my performance when I'm actually on a mission to hug him and push the crown of my pussy against his leg. I hug him. Perhaps I put my arms around his neck and give him a lingering kiss on his lips. I must have him believe that I am relieved he liked my sales presentation and overcome with joy to have a champion salesman thinking I did a good job. Throughout my little act, I keep my goal foremost in my mind. He needs to come away from that initial encounter knowing without doubt that I've offered my cunt to his cock.

"The state of my mind as I approach the champion is most important. I focus on him alone. I have the urge to fuck him foremost on my mind and I block out all other thoughts. My mental energy communicates intent to him. The way I kiss and hug him must reveal my unmistakable, unashamed intent. He must know I am offering myself with wanton abandon. That intent and offering of my body must come through clearly in that first kiss. A kiss, properly given, can be more intimate than fucking or a blow job. I must perfectly deliver that crucial first kiss. It can't be meek or halting, nor can it be passionate or romantic. The romantic kisses come later. It is a kiss that simultaneously travels the dual paths of spontaneity and purpose. It must leave him wanting more of me, eager to give me sales so he can fuck me.

"If there's any reciprocity from his lips when mine meet his, I will probe inside his mouth with my tongue and tease his tongue with my own. That communicates clearly that I want him to bed me. That first kiss is where I make the implied contract of sales in exchange for sex. I can't care one iota what others in the room think of my advance. They are inferior salesmen and saleswomen, and their opinions of me don't matter. In fact, if they snicker and howl, that makes my shamelessness communicate all the more emphatically that I've surrendered myself to him. I'm depending on him to honor my advance and uphold my honor. I expect him to reciprocate by ignoring the catcalls and giving me sales. After all, we're both professionals.

"If he doesn't push me away at that very first moment when I embrace him in front of other salesmen, I know I'll have him. He realizes he's holding in his arms everything he's ever wanted a woman to be. He knows I'm a beautiful, exciting woman compared to his wife. He has the 'die for' girl in his arms. He wants more of me. He wants to hold my face in his hands, and he wants to fuck me. I can tell all of that if he welcomes my prolonged hug. He understands by the way I push my pussy's crown against his leg that I'm offering him a sexual experience beyond anything he's ever imagined.

"As a champion salesman, he believes he deserves the very best in life, his wife be damned. The telegraphed message in my kiss plays with his mind. He can't forget me or my kiss. Like water drips upon a stone, his thoughts of me wear away his resistance until he becomes crazed with lust. Some men even confided to me that, after my first kiss, they couldn't sleep for several nights. They'd lay in bed next to their wives, unable to get their mind off me. They've even told me they lay there with a huge hard-on. When their wives asked if anything was wrong, they just denied it and rolled over. They told me they couldn't think of sex with their wives anymore. They only wanted me.

"I heard this same story from several men the first time they fucked me. They went on and on about how they couldn't wait to fuck me. It's all in that initial approach and that first kiss. Technique is everything. I've worked very hard to develop my approach to top salesmen. You can't put my experience and what I know into a sales manual and expect just anyone to execute my perfected techniques, David."

"What do you do between the kiss and the time you have the man in bed?" David was always interested in sales technique.

"I wait. I am a woman, and I am expected to wait for his inevitable phone call. Patience is required here. Oftentimes a man must clear his calendar. I time the wait. If it takes a week or two, then I know he's already made a mental calculation. He's thought things through. The delayed call is the best call I can get. He's weighed the risks, and he's willing to chance losing his wife and kids to be with me. In a very real sense, once that phone call happens, I've already won him away from his wife. I have him. He's mine, not hers. The rest is simply going through the motions. I play dating games with him. I meet him for dinner or a sports event, or in some clandestine night spot. It takes me very little time to get my hands on his cock. Usually the same day I get his cock into my hands, I'll also get it into my mouth and pussy. Then the game begins in earnest.

"I approach the game differently than wives. Wives think of holding the family together, as if that holds the key to victory. I think only of loving the man's cock and getting that cock to love my mouth and my pussy. Once his cock loves being inside me, it dominates his behavior. He does what his cock wants him to do, and the cock always wants to be inside me. The wife tries to throw up barriers to that. That's when the game enters its terminal phase, like it did for that wife and kids up at the lake.

"When the wife puts up resistance, my chess moves are to simply fuck her husband as often as I can, anywhere I can, in every position imaginable. I'll meet him on a corner somewhere while his wife thinks he's gone back to the office or out for a trip to the store. I'll fuck him in his parked car and leave my scent on him and his car. That drives the wife totally nuts. I'll meet him in a hotel during business hours, or in the early morning when his wife thinks he's out jogging. I've gone to men's homes and condos to fuck them while their wives were away for a few hours. I get a vicarious thrill from knowing I've been in the wife's bed. I've had that special tickle ever since I fucked my geometry teacher in his wife's bed. After I fuck in a wife's bed, whenever I see her, I look at her knowing I can take her husband from her. I just love the power of that feeling. My philosophy is that the man is my customer and I'll do whatever it takes to please him. The more I show my sincerity, the more sales I can demand. I never work for free.

"My sex-on-request interactions begin as a clandestine game and then blossom into his reason for living. I encourage him and embolden him every step of the way by assuring him that it doesn't matter what anyone thinks of him being with me, especially his wife. It's a process he goes through. He becomes open and shameless about being with me. He stops trying to hide me from her. He becomes a refugee from a harrowing life with his wife and I become his refuge. To stay welcome in my refuge, he needs to give me sales. During this transition, while I'm getting him to depend on a relationship with me, I'm readily available to fuck him whenever and wherever he needs me. I'm always reliably there to reinforce his decision to be with me instead of his wife.

"Eventually, his wife finds us out. That's certain. Most wives use their kids as pawns on a chess board, hoping they'll block me from separating her, the queen, from her husband and taking him away from her. That ploy never stops me. I take her pawns right off the board. I tell him there's always another piano recital or baseball game he can go to, but I'm available at that same time and I really feel the need to have him inside me, fucking me. Trust me on this one: my mouth, and the way I know how to use my lips and tongue, and my cunt with her eager clitoris, always triumph over piano recitals and ball games. Once I've had his penis in my cunt and in my mouth, it's like I hold all the top trump cards in a bridge game. My mouth and pussy partner brilliantly against wives and kids. I book grand slams against them every time.

"I work on the husband's mind as much as his penis. I get him to where he feels he must do his utmost to please me. I want him to feel he can never give me enough sales or presents or money. I say erotic things to him whenever we're together. I tell him what a wonderful cock he has and how great I feel when he fucks me. I tell him how much I love having my mouth on his cock, and how I love sucking him off and tasting his cum in my mouth. I want to always be on his mind. I want him to carry my soul in his heart and blood. I want thoughts of me to pulse his blood into his cock and make it rock-hard. I want him obsessed with me, so crazy with lust that he's anxious to leave his marriage and separate from his wife and kids. I don't actually want marriage with any of these men. I just want them as suitors, like a string line of hooked fish.

"When I burrow into a man's mind, he loses all interest in his wife. In fact, she begins to repulse him. He starts to find faults with her. He dislikes the sound of her voice because it's not soft like mine. He dislikes the way she gesticulates with her hands and arms because she doesn't hold them close to her body like I do and she doesn't move her arms erotically as I do. She can no longer please him in the bedroom. She's just a tarnished familiar boor, like an old food-splattered necktie. She doesn't think to use props like feathers and oils like I do. She doesn't use tricks like alcohol in the mouth to get him hard a second or third time like I do. She doesn't think of mouthing and tonguing his balls to drive him crazy like I do. Her humor is no longer funny, if she even had humor in the first place. He thinks her friends and social demands are ridiculous intrusions into the valuable time he wants to have with me. He becomes miserable with the tedium of home life. Just like I suck all the life out of his cock, I suck all the happiness out of his marriage. I come into the husband's life, I study how to upend his wife, and then I conquer her. I capture her king and it's checkmate. I win. She either puts up with the new circumstances until I tire of her husband, or she gets a divorce, or kills herself.

"So, Marty, is it fair to say you have an unblemished record when it comes to tearing a salesman away from his wife and family?"

"Yes. Unblemished! That's a great way to describe my record." Marty laughed. She had enormous pride in her work. "When I want sales from a man, I do whatever it takes to get him to do our bidding. I take him from the wife until I've sucked him dry of sales. Then I let him go back to his wife because there's no further use for him. The really great salesmen I keep close to me, and I never allow the wife back into the man's heart. The really great salesmen keep going out there, and they keep getting new customers and new sales. The dullards just work their book of clients, and then they are finished. So far, with the keepers, I'm five for five. Four of the wives became alcoholics or bridge players with other women losers, and I just told you about Carl's mouse wife who committed suicide. So yes, I have an unblemished record!"

"Well, Marty, I'm so extremely proud of you and your selfless, unwavering dedication to your work. You've earned your 20 percent raise through your honest hard work. You've also proven you're invaluable in knowing how to deal with pesky, interfering wives. I wish I could have witnessed her flying off the highway into the sky. That must have been hilarious. Anyway, that's how I think about it. Brilliant work, Marty! Good job."

"Thank you, David. Your approval means a lot to me. I deeply appreciate your faith in me. It's easy for me to do a good job in this area because I love my work so much. I just love to fuck. I know I'm a nymphomaniac, known it since I was thirteen. I guess I'm a lot like my mother that way. I know she still has several lovers, but I take my promiscuity much further than she ever did. Mother is happy with the lovers she has. I just love the thrill of taking a man from his marriage, sucking out his sales, and moving on to other men. I enjoy the challenge of seducing a new man. I'm just coming into my prime years as a whore, and I'm hoping I'll be able to fuck hundreds of new salesmen before I retire. It's just who I am.

"There's one other feeling of control I get, since you asked to know all about my feelings, and that's when a group of men take me somewhere for an orgy. As far as I know, my mother, Susan, never did orgies, but I absolutely love them. A lot of salesmen love fucking me in an orgy setting. Mother doesn't know what she's missed.

"When I'm fucking several men and all of them are in the same room, I get the feeling that each one of them wants to be doing to me what the other is doing to me. The guy with his penis in my ass is envious of the guy who has his penis in my vagina, and they are both thinking about the guy with his penis in my mouth. Now, for all the eroticism they are feeling, it's nothing like the feelings of the fourth man whose penis and scrotum I'm stroking with my hand. I can tell he's all excited.

64

He can't wait to enter me somewhere, anywhere. He can't make up his mind where he wants to fuck me. That man is going insane with lust for me. I feel it. When I'm fucking all these men at once, I feel like I have a magical, erotic power over all of them. They'll all do whatever I say. It's as if I own them. They all want to please me. They're all very careful not to hurt me, and they all want to be inside me every way they possibly can. I welcome them to have me in whatever way pleases them. The whole experience is euphoric and loving. It's extremely gratifying for me.

"There's one overriding feeling I get through all of it, and that is that whole group of men are all bonded to me—not to their wives or girlfriends, or their children, but only to me. They feel that special bond with me, and each one of them knows the others feel it as well. It's a special erotic sensation to know several shameless, selfless men simultaneously love me with all their hearts and minds. I love that feeling, David. I'm being totally honest. There is no other feeling like it in the world. When those men and I all know that feeling is there, and all of them are communally fucking me and shooting cum into me, that's when I'm the happiest, most venerated woman in entire world. My mind flies away to another place and time.

"I imagine I'm a pagan temple goddess, and I believe I'm experiencing the same joyous feelings she must have felt when the people worshiped her and Baal. The people paid money to the temple, and the men were required to make love to the temple prostitutes while their wives watched. The prostitutes were holy instruments of the temple. By having orgies with the men, a temple prostitute closely bonded the people to each other and to their temple. The prostitute was honored, loved, and glorified. She held top rank in society.

"When I'm copulating with four or five men, I have the exhilarating feeling that I'm their holy vessel. They love me as their pagan whore and bond with me and with each other forever. It's an incredible experience. It's more powerful than my religion, which regards me as a hopeless sinner. The bonding from an orgy is the strongest faith of all, the faith of communal love.

"I believe the temple prostitutes must have felt they were doing the will of God, as I do. Today many people revile women who think and feel like me, but I can't worry about that. I love who I am. I learned a long time ago that it's pointless to concern myself with how other women feel about me. Like we're talking here, David, I believe what matters is results. I have a lot of good will in the sales community. When a salesman thinks about where to place some assets, he's also thinking about loving me and shooting cum into me. I have a wonderful and dedicated following because I love my work.

"But I always thought you were a practicing Christian, a Catholic. How can you deliberately, consciously choose to violate the commandments against adultery and coveting? Don't you have feelings of remorse or guilt? Aren't you living a contradiction to your own faith?"

"I don't violate the commandment against coveting when I take a married man to my bed or when he joins in one of my orgies. I don't want to replace his wife. Heavens, no! I just want to share the joyous freedom and release of sexual pleasure with him. He can go back to his wife. When a man is with me, when I suck his penis and squeeze his testicles and draw every last drop of his semen into my mouth and swallow it, and then when I kiss him on the mouth and harden him again with alcohol on his penis and then mount him until I come while he joins me for a second release of cum he never knew he had, then I suppose I covet him.

"That's when I want him to know there's no other woman, wife, or girlfriend who will ever hold that special place of wonder in his mind for the rest of his life. I want him to go to bed each night wishing that I was at his side instead of her.

When he dreams of being with a woman, I want it to be me. I want him to love me and hold me in a revered place in his mind until the day he dies, but I do not want to be his wife. I do not want to change places with her, so I am not coveting her possession, which is her marriage license.

"A marriage is simply a business. She may own half a marriage, but she can never own a man's mind or his cock. That man's mind and cock can't be put off limits by any commandment or law. Those who try to define a limit on sexual love are just wrong, and their efforts are as futile as trying to stop the tides or keep the sun from rising. They can't defeat human nature."

"So, you don't think there's such a thing as adultery?"

"Yes, there is such a thing as adultery, and there's a way to deal with it. When Jesus stood beside a woman who made love with a man other than her husband, she was about to be stoned to death as prescribed by the verdict of the Sanhedrin. Jesus spoke up for her and said that the man who is without sin should cast the first stone. No one threw a stone because none were without sin. Similarly, in your religion, there's a lesson in the deaths of Aaron's two oldest sons. The lesson there is that we must simply accept some things. We're not required to understand them, just accept them. People need to accept that it's perfectly natural for a woman to fuck a man who appeals to her.

"If God wanted a world without sinners, he would have made us all perfect and there wouldn't even be such a thing as sin. We wouldn't even need this discussion. But he did make some of us to be sinners because he wanted the world to have good, pure people and hopeless sinners as well. Maybe he did all this for his amusement. Who knows? I freely admit I sin. I love committing adultery with married men, and I get a thrill out of tempting them into an adulterous relationship with me. Who does not sin? I enjoy married men because they appreciate me so much. They're the most grateful lovers, and I love releasing them from their cares.

"Orgies aren't about hurting marriages. They're not like bagging a top salesman, where I need to displace the wife and redirect her money to us. Orgies are about having fun and getting sales and whatever extra gifts the men give me, but none of that is an attack on wives. If a wife takes it that way, then she's the one who is evil. Being narrow-minded and unforgiving or vengeful is against what Jesus was teaching. The ones who would punish for adultery should just forgive and forget instead. They should just be happy that their husbands are away at an orgy with me for the weekend and go play bridge or something. The adultery commandment is a crummy commandment anyway. It's one of God's worst mistakes. He does make mistakes, you know, like when he flooded the entire Earth or when he caused Abraham to sleep with Hagar. Look at all the dissention that caused! God's not perfect either.

"If God didn't want conflict in the world, if he wanted everything to be full of happiness and harmony, he would never have let Sarah wait all those years to have Isaac. But God wants there to be conflicts. That's why we have different religions and different ideas. And God wants there to be sinners too, and he wants all of us to love one another regardless of our ideas, our faults, and our sins.

"So, the way I see things, the wife of a man I'm taking to my bed should love me just as much as her husband loves me. She should be happy for her husband. She should be feeling the same joy he's feeling. You know, the more I think about it, David, I honestly believe before Carl's wife went off the mountaintop she felt some kind of love for me and my cunt. The way she stared at my cum pool and the way her lips quivered, I could tell she wanted to lick me and fall in love with me. I think she just needed more time to see the world as I see it, but she couldn't give herself that time. She was too wrapped up in her nonsensical possessiveness.

"Women in pagan days felt joy for their husbands when the men went to the temple of Baal and fornicated with the temple prostitutes. It was an occasion for happiness, not derision and vengeance. It was glorious and beautiful. Glorious, beautiful sex is a timeless wonder. It transcends and triumphs over all laws and religious doctrines."

"How are you going to be able to give up these feelings when you marry Bob? Or will you continue to have affairs and orgies after you're married to him?"

"Bob's very special, a very special man. He's the only man I've ever felt I could love and care for all the rest of my life, so I have some real mixed feelings about that issue. I don't ever want to hurt him, and once we're married, I will never do anything to hurt him. I'm hopeful that after we are married, he'll get to know me and understand my feelings. Once I'm sure he has no inhibitions and he can love me totally for who I am, and once he understands my deep needs to have that peak intensity of nirvana I get when bonding with other men through orgies, then I believe he'll want to join in that experience. He already understands that I really love making love with him. He can tell I love to fuck. By joining me as I release all my passions during orgies, I believe he'll understand the joy I get from it and he'll love me all the more.

"The only thing that worries me about Bob is his friendship with Barbara. She's so beautiful. Speaking as a woman, she's enchanting and mysterious. I've seen how Bob looks at her and how Barbara looks at him. He never mentions his feelings and she doesn't either, but I see it in their eyes. For the first time ever in my life, I know the feeling a woman has when she feels her relationship is threatened by another woman."

"Ha. I don't think that's something you need to worry about. Barbara is very reserved, very private. In the years I've observed her, many men have tried to get friendly with her, but none have ever succeeded. I think you'll discover she's the least of your worries."

"Thank you for that, David. Are you just trying to make me feel better?"

"Oh no, not at all. You'll find this journey you're about to take has much more important things to trouble your beautiful mind and body than some skinny Indian. Tell me, what about Carl and some of the other lovers you have? Will they still give us sales after you marry Bob? Will you be able to see them and still keep Bob happy?"

"Well, I've given that a lot of thought. Carl is such a wonderful, unselfish lover. He licks me wet, then runs his huge, hard cock along my outer lips until I throb and gush inside. I just go out of my mind crazy when he first penetrates me, when that huge shaft slips into me. I just can't give Carl up. Whenever I think of him and his hard, monster-sized cock, my panties get damp. I can't wait to move my pelvis with his huge cock inside me. I come so easily with him. He stays hard for me while I come like my orgasm will never end. No, I'll never give Carl up. The man adores me, loves me no matter what I do, no matter that I have other lovers. He lives to give me pleasure and make me happy. Every woman should have a man like Carl in their life, even if the man isn't her husband.

"There are a few other men I can't give up either, and I know they'll never give me up, so yes, we'll still get their sales. I'm their only relief from their miserable home lives, and they love me very much. It takes years to develop healthy relationships like the ones I have, and those relationships are a special part of me. They are who I am. My lovers will all understand my situation, and I'm sure they'll all work with me, work around my married-life schedule. I'll just have to manage my logistics and make sure everyone is discreet about their times with me. In a funny way, I have to believe that by having extramarital liaisons, I'll be that much more sensuous with Bob. No man wants a deadpan wife who doesn't know what to do in a bedroom."

"Marty, that's beautiful. Everything about you is beautiful. Thank you for helping me understand you better," David spoke as he thought, *I'm sure I'm right about her. She wants to have her cake and eat it too.*

Poon was exhausted by that point. Her mind was spinning from all that she'd heard. It was essential that she rest before the kaleidoscope fluttered away with the morning sun. As she fell into a deep slumber, she wished she knew more about these human people. What was it like for them when they were little humans? They must lead far more interesting lives than caterpillars. She wished to know what this Bob was like, this man whom Marty seemed obsessed to possess and whom she professed to love. And who, she wondered, was the mysterious Barbara woman whom Marty thought was Bob's true love? She wished the Great Spirit of All Living Things would somehow permit her own spirit to visit with those of the human people so she could understand why their emotional needs compelled them to do the things they did. She wished to know their lives from their beginnings and prayed to the Great Spirit of All Living Things to answer her many questions so she could understand their story.

What was Bob like as a little boy? And what was David like? How did these men come to know each other, and what events transpired to place this Marty woman on these hay bales below, lying in this barn with her genitals boldly and casually exposed for David's inspection while she openly spoke of her insatiable lust for other men and her deeply devoted love of Bob? Did Marty work for David? Who were David's parents, and how did it happen that he was here in this barn with Marty? Who was Barbara, and what made Marty envious, even fearful of her?

Poon could only wonder about the mysterious Barbara, the beautiful, silent woman who knew all the others. Did Barbara also love Bob? Would other tragedies intersect the lives of these humans? Innocent little Poon wished she could fathom what it was like to be one of these humans and what would happen to them. Those events would unfold long after Poon fluttered off to the wilds of Chiapas, Mexico for her rendezvous with Tang and her other breeders.

Before she slept, Poon prayed to the Great Spirit of All Living Things. "Please let my journey be safe and please, somehow, someday, let me become a human woman like the beautiful, voluptuous Marty who knows no limitations to her promiscuity. Let me have a huge male Monarch between my legs just like she does and let me discover what it's like to fuck so many others and so often. Or please bring me back as Barbara so I can discover who she is and why Marty feels threatened by her. Please let my spirit bond with the lives of these fascinating humans. Let me know their lives as they lived them from the beginning." Little Poon fell into a deep slumber. She trusted her prayer would be granted.

STRUBBLER

Arlene received Estella's desperate call a half hour earlier. It was Saturday morning, her only chance to sleep late. A chilling fear stirred her and prompted her to rise, dress, and get out the door. It was mid-May. Robins hopped about in the damp grass, heads cocked for worm sounds. Early leaved trees had the pale green of new life, and newly emerged green crabapples displaced faded pink blossoms. The sky was higher, bluer now. The damp spring rain clouds had spent themselves the night before and dissipated before the early sun. Patches of dew fog lingered in the hollows, but air on the bluff above was dry and fresh, the visibility clear. Billowy puffs of white cumulus lumbered eastward above her. They gradually changed into different imaginary animal shapes for the children below. Some children would soon be flying kites. She envied them and their simple innocence.

It was a glorious, beautiful, blessing-sent day. She'd donned a simple cotton summer dress and wore her white nurse's shoes for walking comfort. She didn't care if she looked mixed up about whether she was socializing or working; she needed to walk briskly, even run a little. Estella could fly into one of her rage states and kill the boy before she got there. She thanked God the woman thought to call her this time.

She hurried along, half fast walking, half jogging. It wouldn't do to walk the sidewalks; that would take too long. She chose to cross half the town diagonally, following the footpaths children made through neighborhood yards and avoiding square corners. She was doing exactly what the teachers admonished the children for doing. *Kids can be smarter than adults, especially when expediency is required.* Besides, the slate sidewalks were slippery traps for a fall. She cut through yards and took Peach Alley, a direct route from Cedar Street up to Coal Street, the same way the kids went.

She wondered as she walked. How was it that, of all the men she could have married, city doctors, even surgeons, she fell in love with Morris Zippen, a territory salesman whose job wholesaled the line towns and the Poconos? He based himself in Milltown, between Rolintown and Rockblack of all places. There was little to do there for a social couple. The menfolk hunted, fished, farmed, or commuted to work at Chipequahapa Steel or Rolintown Zinc. Women quilted, cooked, raised kids, and gossiped. People went down line to Rolintown for hospital care and up line to Blackrock to catch trains down the Shohono Valley to Fortown or Oceanport. Only a night train made a postal stop in Milltown.

Milltown had one doctor. He was old, fond of alcohol, and hard of hearing. Mostly he set broken bones, stuck penicillin needles into the children's buttocks, and prescribed aspirin and bed rest. She'd been there a year now. Doc hadn't delivered a single baby the entire year, although people said he'd done it in the past. Women with child either got a midwife or they birthed unassisted. Most in town didn't trust doctors. That didn't matter for the present situation, though; Doc wouldn't come out for this sort of call, even if he were sober.

She knew why they called her. She was the school nurse and a housewife herself, but above all else, she loved the children, all of them, and the townsfolk noted. For a dollar or a homemade pie, they knew they could count on Arlene to make a house call, take a temperature, give an enema when needed, remove ticks or lice, treat poison ivy or sumac, and test if a child needed glasses or corrective shoes. She was more personable than Doc Rupter. She responded to their calls. She was younger, more up to date on things, much prettier, and cheaper. The Pennsylvania Dutch recognized a bargain.

Estella had called Arlene to her Coal Street row house a month before. That was about the boy too. His name was Bobby. Estella and her sister, Florence, called him "Strubbler." He was a remarkably beautiful boy with button blue eyes and shocks of wild, tousled blond hair that waved and shot out from his head from six different cowlick directions. He appeared wildly uncombed, untamed, with an unmistakable look of awareness about him. Girls and women loved to run their fingers through his hair, as if to touch his wildness. Florence gave him his Strubbler nickname. It was her way of identifying him synonymously with his hair. Arlene figured it must've been some kind of Dutch word, as she'd never heard it before. Childless Florence doted on her nephew. From Florence, Strubbler drew affections; from his mother, wrath.

Arlene reached the northernmost end of Peach Alley. It ended for cars and adults against a steep grassy bank, but kids could scramble up the bank and trot out onto Coal Street. It was a great escape route for their hide-and-seek games or for shaking off pursuing adults. Near the bank, the alley joined a gravel driveway that cut across the backyards of the Coal Street row houses. There were stand-alone ramshackle garages along the south side of the cinder drive and grass yards on the north side. Some empty garbage cans were next to the garages, their lids on the ground attracting wasps and flies. In the middle of the cinder track, three scruffy little girls stopped their play to stare at Arlene. The girls' dresses were patched and dirty and their faces were dirt-smudged. Arlene surmised she'd interrupted them making mud pies.

Each row house ostensibly had its own separate yard, but there were no boundaries or fences between them to pen in the children. The only hint of separate yards was the gardens. Each house had a long, narrow patch of ground turned for growing its vegetables. The plots were bordered and crossed by rotted railroad ties, which facilitated planting and weeding without trampling the plantings.

Children gathered in this secluded little enclave partitioned from the adult world. There they played their makeshift games of tag, hide and seek, capture the flag, baseball, and football. They held their foot races on the cinder track, pretending they were Olympic sprinters. When the children raced on the cinders, the ground crunched under their feet and their footing slipped a bit, just like it did on a competition oval dirt track. From toddlers to teens, local kids all came there to foot race. The cinders helped them all believe they were track stars.

Sometimes the children gathered there to play bean bag tag or blind man's bluff, and in the evenings they squealed with delight as they chased fireflies and captured them in glass jars. Today they gathered for a different reason. The three girls heard the wails and screams. They tried their best to ignore it, but it frightened them for their friend and took the fun out of their pretend pie baking. They stood back and watched Arlene as she hurried up the yard. There was a mentality of "us against them" in the world of these poor children. Arlene was an adult, one of the "them."

Blue and white lilacs bloomed behind the row homes, their rows of fragrant color bordering the carpet of lush green lawn. Midway along the eastern lilac border, a flowering oriental crabapple displayed the brilliant promise of spring. Its pink petals yielded to the bud swell of green apple fruits. There were hedgerows bordering both north and south boundaries of the row yards, and flocks of English sparrows fluttered secretly within the tangled mesh of hedges, safe from maiming cats and ravenous crows.

Would Bobby's life blossom and bear fruit? Could she shield his young life from ignorant adults who purposely caused permanent scars? Were the little mud-pie girls self-appointed child jurors there to watch and listen? She braced her courage for the worst.

Many of these Pennsylvania Dutch spanked their children. Some made an art of it with a switch from a weeping willow or a handcrafted spanking paddle. Their unshakable belief was that a child must be taught obedience, without exception. Parental authority was the Dutch measure of a well-run home; children were to be seen, not heard. A stern look from a parent was enough to tell a child to cease annoying behavior and leave the room while adults conversed. The girls at the edge of the row yards banded close together in their camaraderie of curiosity and fear.

Strubbler's situation was different from the other kids' because everything about Estella and her situation was different. The woman and her sister moved to Milltown in July 1944. Estella was pregnant at the time, though people who remembered seeing her for the first time said she didn't show it then. Little Bobby was born that December. Florence had arrived that same July week. Some said she came a few days earlier than Estella.

Neither woman had family there or in any town nearby. Both fibbed they were from somewhere around Oceanport, and both had husbands. But neither Estella's husband, Nevin, nor Florence's husband, Eddie, had roots in Milltown. The four strangers were just suddenly there, like potted plants set down and left. They didn't know the streets, the history, the people, nothing. The women's speech and mannerisms were overbearing for the casual locals. They didn't appreciate two highbrow German women reminding them how far from their own Germanic roots assimilation had carried them. People were suspicious and maintained their distance.

Both couples bought modest houses by paying cash. Where they got their money was a mystery. Things just didn't click. Neither husband had a job when the two couples first arrived, but both found employment in about a week's time. Nevin was a wretchedly skinny man with a damaged heart from rheumatic fever. He landed business contracts with a local bakery and a downtown grocer and purchased a brand new delivery truck with cash, although he didn't know how to drive. He learned to drive around his neighborhood, grinding the gears of the floor-shift transmission, stalling the engine, and steering the truck wildly as it lurched and careened from curbside to curbside.

Nevin delivered baked goods throughout the town and surrounding countryside. That was his day job. Evenings, he removed the truck's bakery cases and drove his truck seventy miles to Oceanport's fish docks. There he bought fresh fish, gutted and ice-packed them in wooden barrels, then drove back to Milltown.

Nevin's grueling routine hurt in his heart. He arrived in Milltown with his fish during the morning twilight hour, unpacked the fish with near-frozen hands and placed them in the storefront windows at Goodman's Downtown Market. He caught restless sleep on his living room sofa from late mornings until sundown, ignoring the daytime sounds of playing children as best he could.

Eddie also seemed an unlikely husband. He was twenty years older than Florence, a habitual chain-smoker with jet-black hair and stocky build and at least nine inches shorter than his stunning bride. He spoke with an Argentinian-Spanish accent. He opened a pool hall in the seedy part of town, and kept two muscular thugs in his employ.

The sisters were stunning beauties. They had thick, tawny blonde hair that fairly glistened like gold when caught by the sunshine. Their distinctive button blue eyes and pronounced cheekbones hinted of Nordic bloodlines and their mouths had wide, full lips and perfect teeth. They could purse those lips and send a man's imagination soaring. Their skin glowed with health, but despite their beauty people remained wary of their friendship. Local women cautioned their men to avoid them. It was rumored they were fräulein refugees with secret pasts and status, relocated to Milltown by the pro-Nazi Broderbund.

People heard them speak German to each other, but it was not the dialect with its slangs and occasional German instead of English nouns and verbs the locals still used despite generations of Americanization. The immigrant sisters spoke only High German, or Hoch-Deutsch. Their words came rapidly with perfect guttural inflections one only hears in Germany proper. They reverted to perfect German when English failed them, even when talking to locals. They had no experience with the locals' dialect and chose to bypass it altogether, placing themselves at a linguistic impasse in their daily interactions with locals.

There was consensus among the locals that these two were refugees from the Reich, transplanted by Nazi sympathizers who spirited them out of Germany before the Russians crossed the border from Poland. Gossips speculated they were concubines of elite Nazi SS officers, possibly Göring or Hitler himself. Once Bobby was born, the timeline of Estella's arrival in town led to speculation that the boy was conceived sometime before the losses at Stalingrad but before the Russians reached Berlin. He was obviously Germanic with Nordic-like features. Those who suspected his father was a Nazi agreed it was safest to stay silent about their deductions; one never knew whom one could trust. *How did that little boy get his thick wild head of hair?* That was one curiosity amongst the local women that couldn't be silenced.

The town and its environs were an ethnic pocket of pro-German sentiment during the war. Some openly rooted for a

Nazi victory over the allies. They especially wanted the Nazis to crush the impossibly backward Slavic Russians. Many townsfolk and those in the countryside locales of Crow's Run, Otter's Run, Dick's Hollow, Skunk Hollow, Cedar Valley, and Martinson Township spoke only in a colloquial "Dutchy" particular to their own hollow or stretch of modest bungalow homes sited along their particular creek, or "run." Communication with the outside world came mainly from listening to the radio and reading the local newspaper, which was saved up for a few days and passed along to a neighbor. Television was nonexistent in these isolated towns and runs, and telephones were communal party lines that relied on operators to patch people together. Few calls were to the outside. Few people grew up and left, and few wanted to do so. Most locals were cautious of outsiders, couldn't and didn't care to trust or understand them.

Likewise, many outsiders regarded this Appalachian backwater as a mysterious curiosity. It was a beautiful place with low mountains, idyllic scenery, twisting blacktop, and redtop paved roads that meandered about through blended pine and deciduous forests joining this and that town with their hollows and vales. It was a magical storybook sort of place that people from the big cities of the East Coast visited and got lost driving about looking for an address only described to them as the third stone farmhouse from some corner on a dirt road that angled off thataway. Locals tried in their simple ways to discourage city folk from coming to these parts. When a lost driver asked directions, the local farmer often pretended to not understand their questions, or he seemingly understood perfectly where the outsiders wanted to go, and then sent them in the opposite direction.

City folks' government and social service bureaucracies had yet to intrude upon the idyllic line towns in the 1940s. When situations arose, there were better, more personalized sources of guidance in the forms of pastors, priests, rabbis, and caring neighbors. Arlene Hartman recalled that she was so shaken by her first visit to Estella, she'd sought guidance from her spiritual mentor, Rabbi Goldberger, taking her concerns for Bobby to him.

Rabbi Goldberger's wife, a humble, good-natured dumpling of a woman, ushered her into the rabbi's study. The room was the largest in the house, with bookshelves floor to ceiling on all four walls filled with teachings of the great rabbis through the ages. There were books about Torah interpretations, social issues, volumes of histories, life in the home, parenting, humor, and famous quotations. *So many books. So much to know!* She wondered if Rabbi Goldberger had read them all, and she realized, looking at the wizened, bearded face before her, sitting in his favorite chair, that he undoubtedly knew everything between the covers of all of them. She politely settled into his guest chair and unburdened her concerns about Estella's child.

His words resonated in her mind as she walked on the soft grass toward the foot of the long wooden backyard staircase that ascended to the back doors of the row houses.

"You are not responsible for this child's beatings. It can become problematic, even dangerous to meddle in the affairs of these gentiles," responded the venerable rabbi. "Living in these small towns, isolated from the outside world, from socialized civilization, from more advanced cultures, it's hard enough for us to be Jews in this place. Be careful not to offend the boy's mother or her friends. Be patient and always seek reason and compassion for the child. Remember Exodus 22!"

The rabbi raised his index finger to the side of his eye and emphasized the demarcation between man and God. "God hears the fatherless child who cries out to him! God is the one who hears the afflictions of the fatherless! Torah says God upholds them and brings them justice. There is nothing in the

Torah that says it is your duty, Arlene. Only in the Tanakh is justice mentioned for the fatherless."

The rabbi's voice of admonition softened as he placed his hand over hers. "You must listen, Arlene. The scriptures are meant to guide our people. In God's goodwill, it's probably a holy deed to leave the boy some gleanings, give him some of your boundless love and charity, but do not take an active hand in his life. Do not become confrontational with the boy's mother. I can't advise that, no matter how painful it is to watch her beating him. Oy vey! I surely can't advise that. Here in Milltown you must be extremely careful. If you turn the mother in to the police, your efforts will fail. She has powerful friends in their Broderbund, of that I am certain. And she has a way of beguiling men and wrapping them around her finger if she wants, if you know what I mean. Ah! You are a woman, Arlene. Of course you know what I mean." He smiled at Arlene before he continued.

"She and their brotherhood, they could make life miserable for all of us here in our small community. Just be careful," he pleaded, his voice strained. "Always remember they are not like us. At their core of being, they are anti-Semites. They want someone to run the businesses, the banks, and be their doctors, their lawyers, because at their core they are afraid to take the risks of failures in order to succeed. Not all of them, I know, but most of them. But let the Jew take the risks and succeed! Oh yes! Then they will resent the Jew, claim that somehow we stole from them, that they should have the fruit of the Jew's success. They refuse to see labor as a mere factor unit of production cost, that they are replaceable with stronger, faster, and cheaper labor. In their heart of hearts, they are afraid to compete with a Jew. Not all, not all. I know what you think, Arlene!"

He intoned the soft voice of one who confides. "Remember, Arlene, that many, but not all, hate us because they have this underlying fear of us. Remember that. Do nothing to harm our people, our community."

"I won't, Rabbi, I promise," Arlene assured him. She recalled the moment the rabbi rang his little bell. Mrs. Goldberger, the synagogue's blessing of sweetness, smiles, and cookies, dutifully answered her summons and escorted Arlene out the front door. She was Estella's opposite, a gracious, loving, and respectful woman. Arlene's visit seemed like it was yesterday.

As she made her way up the steps to the back porch of Estella's row house, Arlene's memory flashed back to the fall spectacle she saw with her husband. It was the annual Milltown versus Rolintown football game. A rally, complete with a bonfire at Third and Cherry Streets where the high school was located, preceded the game. Students and adult alums whooped and roared themselves into a sort of frenzy. There, high above Shohono's waters, an entire community bonded resolutely to their all-important annual task, to beat Rolintown in football. It was the local German steelworker and coal miner's kids against the lowly Hungarian zinc smelter workers' kids from Rolintown. It was town against town. Two different cultures locked in annual combat. It took on an importance greater than a mere sports rivalry; it bordered on war. Then the parade followed. Arlene and her husband made their way to Cedar Street and watched. The route covered a good half mile west along Cedar Street to the football field.

The procession was led by high-stepping majorettes. They wore spangled white uniforms trimmed in crimson maroon, with tall white stovepipe hats sporting tassels of crimson and white. Their hats were anchored to their heads with crimson chinstraps. Their pleated miniskirts were too immodest to suit Arlene. The majorettes marched, lifting one knee up as high as a knee could be raised while still moving forward. Then they shot their lifted-knee legs forward, reaching their full extent. It was a thrilling athletic move. Boys, young and old, along the march were bedazzled because, in doing this high-stepping maneuver, the girls simultaneously flashed a prolonged view of their crimson underpants. Their outstretched legs exposed pubic hairs and vaginas for the adoring male gawkers. Hot steam rose from the girls' vaginas as their bodies' warmest openings met the crisp, sub-freezing fall air. The menfolk gathered annually for this sexual spectacle; they wouldn't miss it for the world. Arlene remembered how the cheerleaders' steps closely resembled the goose steps of the German army she'd seen in newsreels. The sight of the marching majorettes chilled her.

Then came the drums. A light ratta-tat-tat of the snare drums was followed by a deeper duh-duh-duh-duh of the quad drums. Onward they came, like an army. Ratta-tat-tat, duh-duh-duh-duh, the step beaters cracked the air with their staccato of sharp drumstick taps on frames followed by the repertoire of the drums. The deep booming percussion thuds of the bass drums punctuated the spine-tingling beats from snares and quads. Then the band blasted "Stars and Stripes Forever" followed by "Colonel Bogie," "Onward Christian Soldiers," and the "Marine Corps Hymn" finale, played with blaring trumpets. Ordinary parade-goers became fiercely patriotic pagans, their parade a dress rehearsal for a war between the towns. The crowd cheered with wild enthusiasm. People imagined they were running backs and linemen, stiff-arming and tackling Rolintown!

She recalled the game. Rolintown was assigned the east side, or visitors' bleachers; the Milltownians took the west stands. Beer and hot dog sales soared! The game was a brutal affair. Young boys smashed and collided, fists flew in the pileups on the line of scrimmage; kids got bloodied and hurt. Teeth were left on the field. Some players cried and disgraced themselves before their parents. Catcalls and curses were hurled at opposing players from both sides' spectators. The umpires and referees tried mightily to break up the fights on the playing field, separating the warring factions.

Late in the fourth quarter, Milltown was leading 21 to 17. Milltown's Iroquois needed to stop a Rolintown Mohawk drive. It was third down with two yards for a first down on the Milltown 45-yard line. Johnnie Buberick of the Mohawks carried the ball into the Iroquois line. He surged ahead, first one yard, then almost two. His powerful legs churned forward, ripping up turf as he strained and grunted. He needed to be stopped! Arlie Fronzheiser of the Iroquois linebacker corps answered the screams for "DEFENSE!" Arlie coldcocked Buberick with a jarring right cross to the face. The punch broke Buberick's nose and dropped the boy to the ground unconscious, landing a half yard short of the first down marker. The line judge was from Milltown and knew better than to call a personal foul on Milltown's Fronzheiser. That's when the parents took over the game.

A scream went out from Buberick's father. "You broke my kid's nose, you fucking cocksucker."

Beer bottles flew onto the field at the Iroquois players from the Rolintown stands. The Milltownians responded in kind. Grown men—big, strong-bodied, brawny men from both sides' steel mills and zinc smelters—poured onto the field. The men punched the boys and each other. There was biting, cursing, and more punching. Ears were bitten off and fingers were stomped upon and broken. Remarkably, even women took to the field. Hair was pulled out, blouses ripped. Women spun other women by their arms until they were thrown to the ground, where they were spit upon and kicked by even more women. There was scratching, screaming, and women crying as they hit each other.

The police assigned to the game were inadequate to quell the riot, so they stood on the sidelines and watched the melee. The fire department arrived with two pumper trucks and twenty firemen. They hosed down the crowd with a cold-water soak on that cold fall evening and finally stopped the mayhem. Rolintown's team left the field bloodied, screaming vows of revenge. Next year! Because Rolintown left the field, Milltown's referee recorded a Rolintown forfeit.

Arlene recalled Rabbi Goldberger's words. He understood these people. Many were rooted in European anti-Semitic suspicions with heartfelt affinity to their ancestral German fatherland. Their core traditions were hard work, church, and devotion to family. Beer drinking, guns, blood sports, and fisticuffs added spice to their lives. And lurking below their affable surface demeanor simmered a yearning for revenge.

DIRT

The steps leading up to the back porch of the row house were wooden, steep, and somewhat rickety. There was no handrail. The neighborhood children scrambled up and down these narrow stairs with ease, but adults needed to be mindful of their balance. As Arlene made her way from the yard up the stairs, she recalled her first visit to Estella. It was six months after Nevin died. The woman didn't bemoan his passing much, but she did bemoan her own fate.

Estella presumed Arlene was a fellow gentile, sympathetic to her distress, so she revealed her feelings and prejudices. "A Jew, Gordy Goodman, caused Nevin's death by making him drive five nights a week to the Oceanport docks, gut and pack fresh fish in ice, and get back to Milltown in time to put them in display cases in Gordy's market window. Nevin had a weak heart. The Jew knew that but worked Nevin to death anyway. Hitler was right. Jews are merciless!"

Arlene noticed a copy of *Mein Kampf* on Estella's dining room buffet. It was printed in the original German, an oddity. Not the book itself, for many of the locals had copies of the book—even the local library had six copies of the vile tome—but those copies and all others she'd seen were English versions.

Estella didn't mention her background. She was very protective of her history. Some even thought her name was an oddity. Although she looked Germanic Aryan, she had a name which could easily be Eastern European, possibly Romanian or Hungarian. Florence, also obviously Germanic, had a name that suggested a French homeland. Arlene wondered if the sisters used aliases.

Estella wanted Arlene to correct her misbehaving child. "Please help me. You must, if you can, help me over this! I, my mind, will lose soon!" Estella wailed in tortured English.

"What does he do? What troubles you?" Arlene was sympathetic.

"He digs, digs in dirt. Always he digs. My kitchen spoons he uses. I take his toy shovels and sticks from him, hide them away. Then with his little bare hands, he digs. His clothes never clean he not keeps. Water with dirt he mixes, and holes under back porch he digs. Holes in backyard he digs. I say him to stop, him I shake, him I beat. In corner I sit him, with switch stick I whip him, I slap, I punch arms of him. Still he digs."

"What does he do when you take his shovel and his spoon away? What does he do when you keep him from digging?"

"His head! His head he bangs on wall. Whole house shakes. Bangs hard his head! Cracks plaster from wall he does. I crazy with this! He cracks it with head. Will not stop, not listen. I hit. He cries. He bangs head. I punch. He cries. Bangs head harder he does. Make him stop, you must!" Estella was practically hysterical. Arlene saw the boy was black and blue from beatings. She held Estella close in a warm hug to comfort her.

"First, we must stop beating little Bobby. He doesn't understand why you beat him and it only makes him dig even more. Just love him. Be loving with him. You promise me that, and I will work with him to try to get him to stop. It may take some time, but you will only make it worse if you beat him. Promise you'll stop beating him, and I promise I'll help you. Okay?"

Estella sobbed and nodded. "Okay."

Arlene listened to the mother and learned this cycle of beatings, head banging, and digging had gone on daily for several months. It was a miracle the boy was still alive. She reasoned that deep within the boy's subconscious was an all-consuming desire to continue digging. He shrugged off his mother's interruptions. He even blocked out earlier beatings from his mind and kept digging, not caring about the certain punishments that would follow. After months of this impasse with his mother, Bobby snapped. The toddler no longer regarded his mother as his source of love and affection.

Arlene deduced the boy felt betrayed by his mother. By listening carefully to Bobby and Estella, Arlene pieced together how he came to feel that way. Wasn't he by Estella's side when she cried in the large stuffed chair for months after Nevin died? Hadn't he climbed out of bed and come down the stairs to comfort her? Now she no longer hugged him; she only beat him and tried to prevent him from digging. Shortly before he turned three, Bobby decided to hate his mother. He devised ways to avoid her, resisted her punishments by putting up his little fists. He hit back against her punishing blows and concealed his secret diggings. Bobby viewed his mother with a cold detachment and an underlying resentment. They lived as adversaries now, like two tomcats tossed together in a burlap sack.

In these formative childhood years, Bobby fought the daily fight with his tormenting mother. He boldly struck back at her, resulting in even more severe beatings. Neighbors would hear the wailings and the screams. It was maddening to both mother and child, yet it continued endlessly. It was obvious to anyone who saw them that the child hated his mother. He threw food at her, resulting in more beatings, even public ones. When set in a corner for disobeying, Bobby would scream a baleful, maddening scream and continuously bang his head against the wall before he collapsed on the floor and whimpered until he fell asleep.

Arlene asked Estella how Bobby behaved around other adults. She wanted to isolate his behavior toward his mother by ruling out other possibilities. Estella heaved a deep sigh and shook her head negatively, indicating the hopelessness of her struggle. Her son only hated her.

"One day I bring home two from silk mill where I work, girlfriends, you know. They want see little Strubbler. I told Bobby must be for friends his best behavior. We not have much fun, we women. All piece workers, we make silk stockings for New York and Oceanport rich women to wear. Needle punches from knitting machines our hands, fingers bloody. We hard workers, about us no one cares. A special happy girls' day to have coffee and cake and just talk girls' talk was this day. This happy day Strubbler ruins. Downstairs naked he comes, not napping anymore. In front of the ladies, he pooped on floor and smiled. Ladies thought he'd had mistake, but that it wasn't. Smeared shit all over his body, he did, and through his hair, shit he rubs. Potty-trained I made him over six months. He knew what was it he did. At me with his smelly shit-smeared hands, he runs to rub it onto me. Then I beat worst beating ever had in his life into him. My friends and me, our get-together he ruined."

Arlene left her first encounter with this one-parent household after counseling Estella to just love the boy and let him be.

"Allow him to dig all he wants. He'll tire of it on his own" was her parting advice.

As she knocked on the door to announce her second visit, she could hear Strubbler screaming; then she heard Estella screaming. Clearly her first advice hadn't solved anything. The boy was now over three years old. When Arlene saw him, her jaw dropped. He was covered with welts and bruises all over his head and upper torso. His legs were bruised so badly there were blood blisters on top of blue bruises. His eyes were puffy; he'd obviously been slapped in the face as well.

That time Arlene heeded Isaiah and her heart. She took Estella by the shoulders and looked her right in the eye. "If you hit this child again, I will get the authorities after you. I don't care who you know or who you once knew, or who you think you are, but you are in America now. We don't beat children here. I'll come by here every week from now on, and if I see anything like this again, I swear I'll have you locked up and even get you thrown out of the country, maybe even have you sent to the Russians. Would you like that? Well, I can make that happen to you, and I'll do it to you too. I have a lot more power than you'll ever have. You get no more chances. None!"

Arlene was bluffing, of course, but it worked. Estella agreed to stop beating her son and also agreed to allow Arlene to take Bobby for a couple hours at a time away from home. With this renewed understanding, Arlene left the way she came.

On her way down the long yard, she noticed one of the mud-pie girls standing by a peach sapling near the cinder track. Her two playmates were gone, but she no doubt stayed to learn what she could. Her pale blue dress was mud-stained and her brown saddle shoes were badly scuffed. Arlene guessed she wore hand-me-downs from an older sister, as the kids around there were poorer than most. The tot held a little doll and combed its hair.

Arlene approached the girl. "Hello, how are you?" she asked. "Are you a friend of Bobby's?"

The little girl was shy. She just stood there and looked at Arlene.

"I'm a friend of Bobby's too," said Arlene. "I came to find out why he digs in the dirt. Do you know why he digs in the dirt?"

The girl just stared at Arlene, uncertain whether or not she could trust this adult stranger.

"Well, I believe if we know why Bobby digs in the dirt, we can get his mother to stop beating him. Would you like his mother to stop beating him?"

The girl stood for a long moment. Then she nodded.

Arlene said, "It's all right. You can tell me."

Tears welled up in the little girl's eyes, and then she blurted out, "He keeps digging in the dirt because he wants to find his father down there in the ground. He said they put his father in the ground and he's going to find him and get him out of there."

For the first time, Arlene saw the world the way Bobby saw it, through the eyes and mind of a child. She gave the girl a big hug and thanked her. They were both Bobby's friends now.

Arlene walked home with her thoughts, and the girl ran away to her own house.

NEVIN'S PLACE

Estella reached her first-year anniversary of employment at the silk mill. It was over a year since Nevin died. Florence usually watched Bobby during the day, but the sisters welcomed Arlene's help. Estella punched a time clock and Florence liked to avail herself of some personal time when she could find it. Arlene had considerable freedom of hours, and Estella now trusted her to take Bobby away with her some afternoons. Bobby liked Arlene, and his time with her seemed to calm him some. Estella appreciated the respite from his tantrums and his ongoing fight with her.

Arlene learned Bobby was taken to the Holy Church of Bethany while Nevin's funeral service and burial took place. Arlene called on Big Alma, the Sunday school teacher for children under five years old. Alma was a hefty, no-nonsense brute of a woman. Her hair was cut short in a boy's pixie style, which amplified her massive head and bulging jowls. Her ponderous gut protruded far in front of her. Two elongated pears that ceased being breasts thirty years before hung down to where a waist once was. Standing amongst scattered children's toys, with her fat mush face, gut, and breasts no brassiere could lift, Alma resembled the boss sow in a pigsty. She was a butch of butches.

She wore nylon pants and high-top leather shoes, loosely laced to the last eyelets but not further up to their side hooks. Arlene surmised her higher ankles were fat and puffy, beyond normal obesity. The woman likely suffered from coronary heart disease and high blood pressure. Arlene, as school nurse, cut a slender petite figure, always wore dresses and prided herself on her femininity. Standing side by side, the two women were a study in opposites.

"What was it like the day Nevin was buried?" Arlene inquired.

Alma's reply was guarded. "Why? Nuthin' bad happened, nuthin' bad at all. Bobby wasn't hurt none. I took good care of 'im!"

Arlene pressed for more details. "Yes, I'm sure you did, Alma. No one thinks you did anything wrong. I just want to understand better how a child feels when a loved one dies."

That provoked a response. "Listen! It don't matter how kids feel!" Her voice rose to a low bellow. "You don't need to tink about der feelings. They can't do nuthin' bout der feelings anyways till der older, like round ferteen or so. Till then, they jist need to be taught to mind adults who knows what's best for 'em."

Alma tried a new tactic to draw out this human buffalo a bit further. "Yes, that's true, Alma. I know you are right. I came to see you because everyone says how wise you are about the children." This was not at all true, but Alma felt she was on the hallowed ground of her undisputed authority, so she took the bait.

"Dat's right. I understand 'em. I know what's good for 'em!"

"Well, tell me, then. How do you deal with all the silly little boys and girls? I want to learn from you since I deal with lots of the older kids, but I think all kids must be somewhat the same. For instance, how did you deal with little Bobby Burke the day they buried his father? I understand they left him with you. I bet he was a challenge for you, wasn't he?"

Alma couldn't wait to answer. "Dat one!" she shrieked. "Why, he weren't no trouble at all. The mother, duh Hun bitch from Germany, dropped 'im off here before duh services. He yellt and screamt, carried on like a stupit animal in a trap. I guess he thought he was missin' out on somepin' important, stupit child. I kept 'im inside and had 'im put a puzzle together wid a little girl. I told 'im 'is mama would be back for 'im. Dey had service right here in duh church. I hurd it through dat der thin partition wall." Alma pointed to the partition that separated church from Sunday school. "Dey was going on and on 'bout what a fine man Nevin Burke was, and dey had duh organ blasting away. You'd have thought Jesus Christ himself was in der getting fussed over!"

Then a faraway look came over Alma. "It rained hard dat day. Jesus Christ, it rained so hard you'd think God was gonna drown out duh fires of hell, like he decided to piss on the whole world! Yep indeed."

Arlene was captivated by Alma's retelling. "Did the boy know what was happening?"

"Oh, I don't know fer sure, couldn't say on dat point. Maybe after the service he got wind dat sompin' was happenin'."

"What happened to make you think that?" Arlene was intent now.

"Well, after duh service, they pull duh hearse up here in duh alley by the child's entrance, like dey do. You know duh cars of the relatives and friends line up behind duh hearse here in this here alley before dey takes off for the cemetery. Wouldn't you know it! Duh next thing dat happens, duh mother gets out of duh funeral car, duh one duh undertaker owns, dat big black Cadillac."

Arlene's interest piqued. "She did that? Why?" Her eyes widened.

"Well, she comes inside here to see if dat boy was all right. Of course he was, but she just needed to see for herself. Some parents are jist too attached to der kids. Dat spoils 'em. Anyways, Estella was all bawlin' tears and sobbing and holding the boy. She starts saying dumb stuff to 'im, like, 'We'z gonna be all alone now. Your daddy's goin' away to his final resting place. He's in dat big black car out der. You're gonna have to be a big boy now.'"

"Go on," urged Arlene.

"Well, now she gets the damn kid crying. Den she puts 'im down and goes out and gits into the funeral car behind the hearse. The procession takes off for duh cemetery. Dat kid gets like a wild animal and he pulls himself free of me. I couldn't hold onto 'im. Dat kid's strong as a horse. He runs out duh door just as duh hearse and duh funeral cars is leavin' the alley. Well, I thought that'd be duh end of it, but it weren't. Dat damn kid takes off running in duh rain after duh funeral procession. Mind you, he's screamin' and bawlin' runnin' after doz cars, runnin' really fast for a two-year-old.

"He's screamin', 'Daddy, Daddy! Don't go! Wait, wait! Daddy, Daddy! No, Daddy, no!' That kid must have screamed 'Daddy' fifty or a hundert times. He was sobbin' and snot runt down his face, and he's screamin' duh whole time. What a spectacle! Dat kid was an embarrassment for duh whole church." Alma just shook her head in disgust.

"What did you do?" asked an incredulous Arlene.

"Well, I puts a stop to it right den, dat's what I done," Alma remarked. "Dat little brat ran right out into duh street, into duh traffic, chasing after dat funeral procession. Lordy God Almighty! He could have gotten 'imself run over by a car."

"And you?"

"Why, I runned right after 'im, runned 'im down! I grabbed 'im up in my arms, he's kickin' at me and scratchin' and squirmin' duh whole way, and I runned back to duh nursery with 'im!"

"Then?"

"Den I gave that little son of a bitch bastard duh bestest whippin' of 'is goddamn life. I took 'is pants down right der in front of duh other kids and blistered 'is little backside. I spanked 'im so hard, I made sure he'd never forget dat one, never to ever again try to cross old Alma. Den I locked 'im in duh game closet so his screamin' wouldn't bother duh other kids much. Dat's how you have to deal with dese little brats. Dat's how dey learn to listen!"

"Did you say anything else to him?"

"Well, as a matter of fact, I did. Duh kid wouldn't shut up. He was making 'imself hoarse, so I yanks him back out of duh game closet and gives 'im a really hard shake, and I tells 'im, 'Shut up, you little bastard. Your daddy's gone. He ain't comin' back for you. He's never comin' back. They've gone to put 'im into duh dirt. He's going to stay in duh dirt. He won't be seein' you no more, so stop your goddamn cryin'.'"

"Did he stop crying?" Arlene asked.

"Not at first. I had to spank 'im a couple more times. I knocked some sense into 'im, you know. Every time he cried or screamed, 'Daddy,' I told 'im he was askin' for it and I just hit 'im again. 'Ventually, he cried hisself to sleep in duh game closet over dere." Alma pointed to a small closet in the corner. "Later, 'is mother came and got 'im."

Arlene had followed Alma's narrative closely. "Alma, it just occurred to me. Did anyone tell little Bobby that his father was dead?"

Alma's chin braced, her eyes distant in thought. Then she recovered. "No one needed to tell 'im nothing. He saw the damn hearse, for Christ's sake!"

Diplomatically, Arlene remarked, "Of course! I forgot that."

Alma wasn't finished; she needed to impart Arlene with her diatribe on raising children. "You came 'ere to learn how to deal with kids, so you listen carefully to old Alma. I don't let kids have no feelins. Feelins are like horseshit, soft, mushy, and useless. I'm 'sponsible for dere 'bedience and dere learnin' whiles they 'ere. Dat's 'nuff! When one starts up with feelins, it's the whip for dat little bastard. They all knows I'll use the whip on 'em. Dat way they all obeys. When I whip one, the rest knows dat kid screwed up. Duh rest don't want duh whippin' he's gittin'. They knows I's in charge. They obeys me! You just fergit any book ideas about kids and feelins. Dat's horseshit. Handle 'em my way and it's easier on ya, and duh kids learn more. You member that when you deal with duh older ones. They's no different. Now, whenever dat Burke kid comes 'ere for Sunday school, he minds me. He's learned he must obey me or else I'll whip duh shit outta 'im. Now he just sits quietly and watches duh oder kids. He behaves hisself wid old Alma. He don't dare fuck wid me."

"Doesn't he play games with the others?"

"He will 'ventually, but fer now he jist stares at duh others."

With an understanding gained, Arlene thanked Alma for sharing her know-how, then departed. As she walked away from the church, she told herself she'd just traveled the mind of a monster.

GOOD-BYE

Milltown has a cemetery, called the Segan Treffpunkt, Dutch German for "merciful meeting place." Two and a half centuries earlier, German settlers built a modest settlement upon the fertile game-filled plateau west of the Shohano. The Hackatopas, a fierce warrior band from the great Mohawk Nation, unleashed their fury upon the hapless encroaching settlers. One summer's evening, the Indians burned the settlement to the ground. All the settlers—men, women, and children alike—were massacred and scalped. No life was spared. It's not clear how many Indians died in the attack, as when the horror was discovered, all the bodies were buried in a large common grave, marked by a massive flat stone placed atop the earthen mound. The stone details the settlers' story and chronicles their demise. A metal railing borders the mound and massive elms and leafy maples shade the site, setting a solemn quiet tone for the entire graveyard. The plateau where the massacre occurred rises up from the valley floor midway between Cedar Mountain to the south and Broad Mountain to the north. Few people go there now, but for those who do, they'll likely see rabbits and squirrels scampering about, along with chipmunks and robins. Foxes are sometimes seen, and songbirds practice their melodies there on quiet mornings.

To this peaceful resting place, Arlene took Bobby to remove the scales from his eyes. It so happened there was a burial taking place that day, so they stayed and listened to the graveside service. They heard the preacher say, "Ashes to ashes, dust to dust. Into thy hands we commend his spirit." They watched while the coffin was lowered into the grave and saw the grave diggers shovel dirt onto the coffin.

"This is where dead people go, Bobby," explained Arlene. "There was a person in that coffin box who died. He's now dead." She didn't think the child fully comprehended, but she came prepared for that possibility. From the trunk of her car, she removed a shoebox that contained a little dead sparrow. She opened the box to let Bobby see inside.

"See, the little bird is dead now. He'll never eat again, never fly again, never sing again."

Once she could see that Bobby understood, she took him to his own father's grave. "Now we must bury the little dead bird," she said as she dug a shallow grave next to Bobby's father's. Together, they buried the little bird and covered it with dirt. It was time for the seminal moment.

Arlene patted Bobby on the head. "Look, Bobby, there's someone else who is dead here, buried right next to our little bird. There's a big stone here to mark a grave. There was a hole dug here a short while ago, and a dead person was put into the hole. We call the hole where the dead person is buried a grave, and the big stone on top of the grave is called the headstone. It tells us who is buried here. Let's read what it says on this headstone. It says, 'Nevin Daniel Burke, born June 18th 1914, died March 26th 1947.'

"You see, Bobby, your daddy is dead too. He's gone now, and he's at peace here in the ground, next to the little bird we buried beside him. Your daddy can never come back to be with you again, just like our little bird can never come back to fly again. Once someone's life is gone, they can't come back again. Both your daddy and our little bird are gone. You need to accept this in your own time and understand it. Your daddy loved you very much, and that will always be true. The love he had for you will stay with you forever."

"You mean until I can die too?" Bobby's mind contemplated the benefit of reunion with his father through death. Arlene glimpsed the child's thought.

"Well, not like that. You see, your daddy will go on loving you forever, even long, long after you yourself are dead many years from now, after you've been all grown up and had children of your own and you're an old man. It's what love is, Bobby. It's a feeling someone has about someone else, and that feeling lasts forever. Just like you will always love your daddy, always remember him. You'll never stop thinking about him, and you'll never stop loving him."

As Arlene knelt beside the boy, his eyes began to tear. He nodded ever so slightly as his young mind struggled to fathom concepts that were before unfathomable. Bobby stared at the headstone, fighting to hold back his tears. He looked at the ground where the bird was just buried, then to where the grave diggers were shoveling soil upon the recently interred coffin. He turned once again to stare at his father's headstone, repeating this sequence of looking from the grave diggers to his father's headstone as reality overtook his tender hopes. Young Bobby's mind tried to grasp the concepts of love and death. The child grappled with the realization that he would never see his father again, even while he tried futilely to understand how long never was. His mind struggled to break free of its prison of hopes, which he was reluctant to abandon.

Bobby heaved deep sobs as grief finally broke its shackles. He sat upon his father's grave, trembling. Arlene worried she may have traumatized the child, despite her gentle intentions. Then Bobby fell prostrate upon the ground, pulling at the grass with his tiny hands. "Daddy, Daddy, Daddy! You didn't have to go away. You didn't have to go." Then the child convulsed in sobs. Arlene let him have time to cry. When the sobs stopped, he stood up and faced her. His little face showed resignation, defeat, and a faint measure of acceptance. The tormented frown Arlene had often seen in visits past had melted away to a placid face bearing teary eyes that stared off to a place far away.

The boy imagined an image of his father welcoming him with open arms and fixed this moment to it. It was all Bobby had now. He reached out his tiny arms to Arlene. She gathered him up and held him close.

MARVIN AND SUSAN

When Eloweiss Sustack called, Susan Mallory didn't hesitate. Yes, the Sustack child was difficult to sit. Fussy, brooding, cry-baby, spoiled, and headstrong were all terms that almost, but not quite, described her feelings about the little monster, David. She told Linda, her closest friend, the child was evil inside, but she still agreed to sit that night. Both girls babysat for the yentas of Plaintown's new Skyview District. Couples went out often in these 1920's years. Plaintown was just coming alive from being a sleepy agricultural town, and sitting money paid for housewife freedoms.

Wealth gravitated to the Rockies, and Plaintown garnered the lion's share. Respiratory sanitariums received patients from the east. Sign 'em up, give 'em a room, and let 'em breathe mountain air. They heal or die. Bury the dead, clean the room, and then put in a new Lunger. Consumption was big business.

Legal, accounting and banking services grew from mining, lumbering, and recreation. Count the ore shipments. Count the smelted ore. Pay the royalties. Pay the help. Write the contracts. File lawsuits over claims. Draw up wills for the ones who succeed. Draw up bankruptcy papers for the ones who fail. Incorporate new companies. Liquidate failed ones. Merge them. Spin off subsidiaries. Find a tax break. Go to the club with a client. Take him to Mattie Silks' whorehouse to get him laid. Go to dinner with him and the wives. Get something for the kids. Cattle rustle gave way to hustle bustle.

Retail outlets, recreation and vacation enterprises, hunting outfitters, firearms, and taxidermy businesses sprang up. Elk, deer, antelope, moose, cougar, grizzly bear, black bear, wolf, coyote, geese, duck, and ptarmigan were all waiting to be killed. Trout streams teemed with cuts, bows, and natives. Muddy, rutted dirt country roads yielded to paved streets and, gasp, civilization.

A proliferation of railroad companies took place here. Doubled and tripled engines pulled trains up the slopes, over the tops, and then braked hard going down. Inbound trains from Chicago and Saint Louis moved goods through the new Metro Station to Plaintown's vast rail yards. Outbound assembled long trains moved outpoured resources eastward. Ribbons of steel railroad tracks knifed through the mountains attacking Mother Nature, making her heel to the will of man.

Ribbons of track wound their way through the steep mountain passes, carrying the trains, moving their cargos of rebar steel and finished goods from the east to the new buildings sprouting up in the mountain towns across the west. They carried the backbones for the mines' tunnel frames, shafts, and head frames, and they carried oil country pipe and drilling rigs. Plaintown was awake, alive, vibrant and bustling. She became known as the magnificent "Shining City of the Plains," a proud moniker for a proud can-do city.

The mushrooming new wealth drew the enterprising young Marvin Sustack to Plaintown from nineteenth-century Chicago. He quickly succeeded with his investment advisory company. Many regarded him as brilliant. He understood markets, money and banking, financial analysis, and was an early reader of Charles Dow's column for a specialized business newspaper named *The Wall Street Journal*. Marvin had a wife and son.

Barely two hours passed since the Sustacks left the house. Young baby David slept in his crib. They returned earlier than expected. Wife, Eloweiss, complained of a headache and retired to her bedroom, leaving Marvin to settle monies with the sitter. Eloweiss never emerged from the bedroom suite after she retired. Alone in the living room with Susan, Marvin asked the usual checklist questions.

"How was David? Did he eat his dinner? Any trouble getting him bedded down? How long have you been here? How much do we owe you?"

"He was fine. Yes, he ate. No trouble getting him to bed. He's sleeping soundly. Two hours, so one dollar. Thank you, Mr. Sustack."

Susan sat on the sofa, skirt slightly above a leg crossed at the knee. Her back bowed, her chest protruded, and her firm young breast mounds pressed hard against her blouse. Marvin's and Susan's eyes met. Something beyond routine checklist questions and answers happened. Facial expressions relaxed, each face yearning for the other's. Passions flared. Simultaneous urges heated their bloods and raised neck hairs. Two knew simultaneously. Nature opened a path. They wanted and needed to fuck. Neither knew this intersection of lives had lifelong ramifications for all four in the household, and for persons yet unknown and unborn. How could they? Fucking was on their minds.

Susan harbored concealed resentment toward Eloweiss. Mrs. Sustack was twenty years her senior, but the woman looked and acted like late fifties or early sixties, not late thirties. Eloweiss often called Susan to cater the Sustacks' parties. The young girl tolerated her work but disliked her matron. Her earnings were endurance pay. Mrs. Sustack commandeered her when she was twelve for all sorts of duties. Susan's mother brokered her services; she had no say in the matter. For six years, she tolerated Mrs. Sustack's insults. She was called schlep, clean-up girl, garbage girl, and mop-up girl. That grated and irritated Susan, but it was Eloweiss's tone that she resented most. Often Susan heard Eloweiss's shrill voice call staccato variants of angry rants in front of house guests.

"That's not what I want, you stupid girl!"

"I told you before. Serve the champagne first! Can't you do anything right?"

"If you spill one more morsel from a serving tray, you will not be paid, and I'll tell your parents how impossible you are!"

Eloweiss relished using these cruel threat tactics. She loved the power she held over the young girl. Susan's Irish family was terribly poor; her father made very little and her mother depended upon the children to bring money into the household. The poor girl could not defend herself, nor leave Eloweiss's employ.

But trapped animals, human or otherwise, are dangerous to the trapper. Marvin noticed how Eloweiss abused the girl. He empathized with Susan's dilemma and respected her perseverance. His sympathies cheered the underdog while his heart turned cold to Eloweiss. A flammable situation awaited a match strike.

Susan thought of Eloweiss as an impossible wealthy pig. The woman was fat and slovenly, with a face kindly described as ugly. It had oversized, wide, sloppy lips and a bugle-sized nose. The nose and lips drowned out the narrow-set gray eyes, deeply recessed behind bulging eyebrows. The woman's puffy face was comic-book-like, as if a mound of cheeky dough and drooping jowls had some outrageous features haphazardly stuck onto it. Likely she compensated for her looks with callousness toward her help.

Eloweiss didn't care a wit about her appearance. Cosmetic surgery was a new, dangerous experiment, so she gave up and surrendered to chocolates and pastries. Now she flaunted that body, even bragged to her friends about it.

"Marvin likes a soft landing when he comes home at night," she boasted to her friends, many of whom had already bedded Marvin or hoped to do so. All knew her boasts were hollow; Marvin liked women's bodies tight and lively.

Eloweiss accentuated her monstrous presence with grandmother-styled boots and accessorized with oversized, garish handbags. Her dresses were large-sized floral prints, sometimes resembling flour sacks with paint splattered upon them. And she wore brightly colored patent leather belts, in reds, bright blues, and greens. Her earrings were equally as garish as her dresses and handbags, and she adorned her presence with teased wasp hive-styled hairdos.

Linda joked to Susan, "Some hapless wasp might someday mistake her hair pile for home. Then everyone could see if the hair is real or fake!"

Susan thought a rhinoceros with paint thrown on it would look more attractive than Eloweiss, but she always held her tongue. She coped with Eloweiss much like an abused dog cowers from its master, careful to maintain distance, always deferring and avoiding confrontation.

Notably, Marvin never once criticized Susan in public or in private, even when Eloweiss excoriated him to "Do something about that stupid girl!" Little did she expect the girl, who was far removed from stupid, could ever turn the tables on her and "do something" about her. Susan was primed to strike an emotional dagger into Eloweiss's heart and then twist it, leave it in to ache and ache and then twist it more. She was about to enjoy visiting endless sorrows upon Eloweiss. She would taunt her former mistress and savor the distress she inflicted. No matter how often Eloweiss begged her, Susan would never relent, never give quarter, not even in death. The die was cast for these two women, Marvin's women.

When she was prepubescent, Susan never gave Marvin a passing thought, except that she felt some sympathy for a man who was saddled with such an impossible partner. Susan changed from a girl to a woman the past three years. Her puberty began when she was thirteen. The awkward years from thirteen through sixteen were tumultuous for her.

She allowed her innermost urges to override her mother's cautions. With two different boys her own age, she'd experimented with sex. Frank was big-boned, pimple-faced, and clumsy. He'd penetrated her hymen and then acted like a terrified child about it. Her distressed gasps from the pain and blood were more than he could cope with. His only concern was how quickly he could get away from her and get the scary blood wiped off his prick. After their experiment, he shied away from Susan at school, avoiding her stare as if she were dirty. Larry was an upgrade from Frank. He was a tall, skinny boy, played forward on the high school basketball team, and already had a girlfriend, with others eager to take her place. Susan felt a surge of sexual power when she bedded him. His parents owned a mortuary; she professed a profound interest in seeing a cadaver and Larry obliged. There, after working hours in the embalming room, she made her advance.

"I'm actually much more interested in your live body than these dead ones." She smiled as she kissed him full on the mouth. She'd read about the French kiss and decided Frank would be an all-or-nothing experiment. Her tongue was well inside his mouth as her hands deftly opened his zipper. Frank offered no resistance. They found their way to a viewing room sofa, and Susan, for the first time, had sex she thoroughly enjoyed. Too quickly, Frank finished, pulled out of her, and shot his semen all over her stomach. He stood, washed up, and urged her to hurry and clean up before somebody caught them. Good, maybe not the best, but for the next two years, she and Frank watched for their opportunities and fornicated when and where they could.

At age sixteen, Susan noticed that boys and men noticed her. She was beautifully formed with her enchanted Irish lassie's face of high cheekbones, bright blue eyes, and inviting, shapely lips. She'd crossed the intersection that separated her from coquettish schoolgirls who were easy to impress, easy to bed, and eager to please. Now she transited into the full bloom of womanhood. She knew she could choose from among many men, but like all women, she also knew that as she grew past twenty-one or twenty-two, her physical appeals would peak and decline. She began sizing men up as potential mates who could support her and her children yet to come. She contemplated life with this or that man in it, not just for a few years ahead but for a lifetime pairing. What was the glory of a large family if you couldn't provide for them?

Susan's mother and father avoided acknowledgment of their own poverty while at the same time urging her to marry a nice Catholic boy and have lots of kids. Education for a girl past high school was beyond their comprehension. All any girl needed to learn, by their way of thinking, could be learned from her mother. Therein lay the rub. Susan saw how the wealthy lived. The scales that fell from her eyes still covered her mother's and father's eyes. Her parents were devout regular Mass-goers. Her mother's life was penurious. Mrs. Mallory mothered six children and found respite and refuge in her church. The woman was the proverbial church mouse, one of the many who attended often but paid little. That lifestyle didn't resonate with Susan. Silks, furs, and jewels had more appeal to her than the cross. She viewed sinning abstractly.

She memorized each of the Ten Commandments when she was ten. She understood and agreed that killing and stealing were strictly forbidden, but now the others seemed a bit of a muddle. How could there only be one God when the pope himself called Jesus Lord? How could she be expected to honor her parents when she became ever more convinced they were clueless about the potentials that life held, and only harped advice that would certainly lead her into a life of drudgery? Lying? Sometimes she simply had to lie, if only to avoid trampling upon someone's feelings. As for coveting, how could she be expected to not desire what others had? Wasn't that just the human drive that made the world go around? Coveting another's man! Well, was it justified for a man to be harnessed by an oppressive woman rather than be free to enjoy happiness and love? Wasn't that a theft of the man's happiness? Weren't misery and oppression sins enough, though not enumerated by the church?

She pondered the weight of these moral questions and ultimately rationalized the credo by which she chose to live her life. As long as she didn't hurt anyone, and as long as things were manageable, she considered herself a willing participant in matters otherwise immoral by the doctrines of her teachings.

Marvin first piqued her interest shortly after puberty, during her first year as the Sustacks' babysitter. As a girl of thirteen, she saw a handsome, educated, dashing, well-socialized man sixteen years her senior, possessed of drive and status far beyond the imagination or aspirations of her own father. Whenever he looked at her, spoke with her, patted her on her head, she inwardly fumed at her lack of maturity and wished he'd notice her, at least on a level above Pal, the Sustacks' family dog. By fifteen and sixteen, when she helped cater the garden parties, she noticed how frequently other women flirted with Marvin, how they rubbed against him, trailed their hands over his arm, his back, and even his buttocks. She'd heard that Jews touched more than gentiles, but these touches seemed like overt sexual invitations by women seeking at least a dalliance with him. Whenever Susan saw another woman touching him, she felt an inexplicable tinge of jealousy. She blocked the tinge from her conscious, knowing she needed to mind her place and duties.

Mrs. Sustack had a keen eye for potential rivals. Often enough, Susan saw Eloweiss frown, squint, or nervously bite her lower lip when another woman brushed against Marvin.

The normally repulsive face, when squinting, assumed the look of a snarling dog about to bite. On one occasion, when Susan was impressed into the service of Mrs. Sustack, there was a party to celebrate Marvin's success at becoming the investment advisor to the largest trust company in Plaintown. The fees earned from the position would assure his firm's future for beyond his lifetime. He stood to make millions and would be influential in the financial affairs and decisions of Plaintown's most elite families.

Already wealthy and successful, Marvin first moved there to escape a troubled law firm in the throes of breakup. As competing factions vied for whom would receive the rights to the firm's well-known telephone number in the expansive Chicago Jewish community, Marvin decided he'd have none of it. Instead, he harkened to the lure of the west and the promise of Plaintown. From a modest office and door-to-door solicitations, he rose to community prominence. In Plaintown, attitudes were wide open. There was opportunity everywhere. People wanted to do business there, wanted to grow their assets. The political class had not yet infested the business world with progressive socialism and nonsensical regulations. People there were proud to work to get ahead. The Plaintown culture of the early twentieth century had no room or patience for people who thought they were entitled to a free ride.

This was the party where Mrs. Sustack unwittingly revealed her vulnerability. A perky, attractive newcomer to these affairs, Goldie Blinkly was a jeweler's wife who had inherited a sizeable fortune. She approached the covey of women where Eloweiss was holding court. As Goldie breezed by her, Susan detected the faintest hint of cigarette smoke. It was a dank, stale, stomach-turning, putrid odor that made heads turn away and gasp deeply for fresher air. It hung in Goldie's clothes. Susan held a tray of hors d' oeuvres and stood near the periphery of the women's circle. When Mrs. Blinkly extended her white-gloved hand to Eloweiss, Susan noticed their interaction.

"You must be Eloweiss Sustack, the wife of that hand-some Marvin," interrupted Goldie with her soft, seductive, unhurried voice. The woman was dressed to the nines, with a midriff that accentuated her breasts upward, overlain with a low-cut formal gown that plunged the viewer's eyes downward from her pearl necklace to a resting place an inch above her navel. The gown had a slit opening along the left leg, revealing everything from ankle to the middle of her thigh, and it wrapped tightly across her firmly toned buttocks. She could've easily been taken for a competitive working girl. She walked with an accentuated sideways thrust of her hips, as if she were a lively worm on a hook wriggling its wares to entice any hungry trout that happened to be near her waters. Susan surmised this woman came dressed for Marvin and gave no thought to the impression she'd leave upon the other women, who dressed for each other.

Blunting the obnoxious intruder before she could roundly introduce herself, Eloweiss retorted, "That's right, dear." She then raised her voice in an exclamatory lilt. It was her resounding slam down, a hammer's ringing noise intended for this impertinent, intrusive nail of a woman. "And I'm the one he sleeps with, sweetie!" The jaws of several ladies dropped as their eyes quickly darted from Eloweiss's to search each other's. Eyebrows lifted ever so slightly and heads turned to the side in secret contempt for the boastful hostess.

If she was anything, Susan was astute. Eloweiss's retort, the unspoken repartee, the unguarded eyes of the other women revealed the truth. Susan's suspicions were confirmed—Marvin slept around. Did he sleep with all of them? She'd heard many Jews were adulterous, even overheard some of them wishing they could put the pesky seventh commandment to a vote!

Susan brushed aside her compunctions about being jealous of these wretched pretenders to Marvin's favors. Why not her? Was she not far younger and far more beautiful than any of these women? Was she not unconstrained by marriage to another man as these women were? Was it not true that many Jewish men sought the beds of gentile girls? And why was that? Maybe the gentile girls were less demanding of gifts and more giving of passions? She couldn't be sure about that, but she thought perhaps she could learn more in time. Or was the act of sex with a gentile some sort of tribal drive to symbolically vanquish a conquered people? Or was it vice versa on her part, the way she coveted Eloweiss's husband?

What was that Abraham and Hagar business all about, really? Maybe Abe's ninety-nine-year-old Sarah was just like these yentas gathered here today. They came to show off their diamonds and silks, boast their positions and standings, and brag about their sons becoming doctors or lawyers. Or they came to brag about their daughters marrying a successful professional or businessman. Maybe old Abe just grew exhausted listening to it all and decided what he needed most was a great fuck! Maybe that's what Marvin needed too! The more she thought about it, the better Susan liked her chances. None of these neurotic nags could hold a candle to her beauty or her sexual endurance. Didn't she exhaust Frank after just one or two ejaculations? And he was sixteen years younger than Marvin, as was she!

On that fateful evening, after the checklist questions, Marvin, ever so slightly and with subtle indifference, opened the possibility of a direct communication with Susan. "The night air has a bit of a chill, I've noticed. Would you prefer that I drive you home?" Marvin's proffer of kind concern for her comfort was casual enough, yet Susan brushed aside his vague opaqueness. The distance home and the cooler air were inconsequential. They both knew that.

"Why, Marvin, I was just sitting here thinking the same thing and hoping you'd want to be with me. Yes, I'd love to go for a drive with you." As she spoke, she brushed her golden hair away from the side of her face, revealing her ear. She opened her legs a bit and put her hand on the sofa behind her. The effect was to thrust her breasts up and forward as she arose, as if serving up her mountains for sacrifice.

Riding in Marvin's new Cadillac, Susan felt the luxury of the crushed velvet piled seats under her legs. She rubbed her fingers softly over the burled walnut dash. There was the new car smell of fresh interior fabrics, carpet and wood, and there was another smell. There it was! The faintest hint of stale cigarette smoke was barely discernable, but it was the exact same smell Goldie carried on her clothes. Neither Marvin nor Eloweiss smoked, so it likely came from her. The pieces all fit together neatly for Susan. Marvin had consorted with Mrs. Blinkly and Eloweiss had issues because of it. Maybe Eloweiss also noticed the cigarette smell? Maybe having her husband boinking someone in her immediate social circle was too much for her to tolerate? For whatever reason, Susan reasoned she was about to become Goldie's replacement. She was becoming more and more stimulated by the car, rubbing her hands over the fabric, imagining she'd soon be rubbing them over Marvin's cock. He noticed her hands.

"Are you in a hurry to get home?" he queried.

Susan responded as if on cue. "No. No hurry at all! My parents are away, actually. They're in Evergreen visiting my father's sister. They're not expected home until tomorrow evening."

Marvin knew the gratuitous information was Susan's signal, encouraging him to advance. He pleased her hopeful expectations. "Well then, since there's no hurry, I wonder if you'd like to take a look at a small property I own. I'd like to know what you think of it."

Susan's juices began flowing in contemplation as Marvin drove her to an empty house about a mile from her parents' home and two miles from his. It was a beautiful stone, three-bedroom bungalow in the Rondel Hills area. It was unoccupied! As Marvin unlocked the door, Susan knew she was leaving one world and entering another. The home was well-appointed with leather sofas and chairs. Beautiful oil paintings of country scenes decorated the subtlety colored walls. There was a spacious fireplace with a massive mantle for those cold nights on the high plains. She could see herself there on a quiet snowy evening, straddled atop Marvin in front of the crackling fire. She made a silent promise to herself that she'd have many such evenings with him.

There were two bedrooms without beds, only walls of bookcases filled with books. Her lover-to-be was very well read. There were books about the Jewish religion, the Christian religion, even the Buddhist and Islamic religions, many books about history, and biographies of famous people, presidents, world leaders, kings, dictators, and odd things of interest to few people, such as habits of different animals, astronomy, geology, map books, and books about revolutions, births of nations, world conquests, fictions, classic literature, and political intrigues. And there were books about psychology, anatomy, and studies of sexual practices amongst different tribal peoples, and animal behaviors.

Susan was in awe of Marvin and all he knew. She thirsted to open all those books herself and read every one of them. She loved learning new things. She so greatly wanted to be accepted by this man and to have him open his world to her. Even the smell of the book rooms excited her, the idea that so many brilliant people had committed their thoughts to written word. She'd made many trips to public libraries, but here was a private world-class library, brimming with knowledge and arranged by subject matter. It was all dreamily intoxicating.

One room contained a massive rolltop desk stuffed with papers. She noticed it held an inkwell. The pigeonholes within contained envelopes of bills and records, she presumed. It was plain this was Marvin's home away from home. He came here for solitude and quiet study.

Lastly, he showed her the master bedroom suite. The room was cavernous, giving off a beckoning summons to relax, to be uncaring. It was the grand feature of the dwelling. The bed was king-sized with an extra-firm mattress and appointed with six overstuffed down pillows. It was all decorated with soft, sound-absorbing maroon drapes. It adjoined a bathroom, complete with an oversized claw-footed bathtub, with a privacy curtain and massive showerhead. There was also a bidet. She'd never seen one.

"What's that?" she giggled, gesturing toward her never-before-seen curiosity. "A toilet for little children?"

"Actually, it's called a bidet," Marvin explained. "Originally they were used by European royals to bathe their sexual organs. It helps maintain a person's cleanliness and minimizes the chances of diseases of any sort. Many of the royals use it before and after sexual intercourse. It's very stimulating and refreshing. Would you care to try it?"

Susan knew all masks of pretense were now removed. With delight she made full use of the bidet. As the water shot up to her vulva, she felt the sensation of preparation. Her mind raced and wondered about the unknowns that lie ahead. When she finished, she trembled with excitement and anticipation.

How would she be this first time with him? Would he find her girlish and inexperienced? Could she please him? Would he be gentle with her? Was he a different person in lovemaking than the mild gentleman she knew? Would she try too hard? Would she make him self-conscious? Finally, she took a deep breath and decided she would just live each second of the experience, be her natural self, and love this man as if there never was nor ever would be another. After all, he was older and experienced; if he wanted to fuck a certain way, he'd surely show her what pleased him. She immersed herself in a thick, red terrycloth robe, conveniently hung on a bathroom wall. Then she opened the door to the bedroom. Her mind was set upon being the best lover Marvin ever knew. He was standing there waiting for her in a white terrycloth robe.

"I've often wondered what being with you would be like," she teased, putting her arms around his neck. Marvin would not be anything like Frank. He smelled of musk-scented cologne. He was cleanly shaven and his face was smooth as silk. There would be no facial abrasions, just warm skin against her soft cheeks. He was a thoughtful man. There was no perfunctory kissing, no tearing away of shirts, no awkward positioning of tangled limbs. There wasn't hurried penetration, savage jabbing, and guilt-tarnished retreats. Unlike sex with Frank, there would be no haste to reassemble discarded garments or wash off hurriedly to reappear as if nothing happened.

Marvin took his time. The seasoned lover was deliberate, thorough, and expert in the craft of lovemaking. Susan never imagined such pleasures existed, let alone that she'd be chosen to receive them. There first came the French kissing, tongues deep in each other's mouths. Their robes opened as their bodies came together. His caresses covered her while she stood. He touched her softly everywhere as he kissed her face and neck. Slowly, he would bed her, she thought. She was partly right. As they lay on the bed, she expected him to mount her as Frank would. That would have to wait.

He rubbed her nipples with his fingertips. She didn't know where he got it or how he concealed it from her, but he'd dipped his fingertips in warm baby oil. He played with her nipples for what seemed an eternity, arousing her passion, and had her wishing he'd begin intercourse.

Marvin understood the mitzvah to kiss your wife before intercourse in the most robust sense, and he obeyed it for his soon-to-become mistress as well. Susan lifted her hips as he bid her to do as he positioned one of the large pillows beneath her pelvis. She was at first apprehensive but quickly concealed it, determined to do as he pleased. She'd heard of oral sex but thought it was something only very strange people engaged in. She never gave the practice any thought beyond that. No one had ever performed cunnilingus with her before that evening. Marvin kissed her stomach and upper thighs. He was ever so gentle, and it felt so titillating. He loved what he was doing, she could sense that. She felt he was falling in love with her, and he was.

Then, Marvin began kissing her outer lips and moistening them with his tongue. As Susan's clitoris awoke, his tongue glided over it smoothly, softly tickling it with a darting motion at its base. Then he stroked it upward, all the while keeping her moist. The educated tongue next explored both sides of her joyful organ, first one side, then the other. His pursed lips found her tiny head, held it softly, squeezed it ever so gently while his tongue again caressed its shaft from bottom to top. Just when she thought she was going to lose her mind in a bout of sensual madness, he began to rub her clitoris with the underside of his tongue. That unleashed a sensation of irresistible passions and desires. She wanted him inside her. She wanted to explode from uncontrolled desires. Her vulva swelled as her clitoris stiffened.

She cried a muttered, "Yes, Marvin. Yes, darling. Don't stop. Oh, Marvin, my love. Yes. Yes. Yes." Then the volcano of her desires burst through its containment and she exploded in a wild, gushing orgasm. Marvin's tongue continued to titillate her throbbing clitoris as the gushing continued. She writhed in a frenzy of desire; it was all deliriously erotic. She desperately craved to have his penis inside her. She'd never experienced an orgasm before and never imagined any woman having these feelings. She was in a different world with this man, and she never wanted to leave it. Whatever costs she must bear to be with him, she would.

He finally entered her, sliding his shaft in so smoothly. Already lubricated, it was a frictionless entry, unlike the jabbing irritations from Frank. Marvin expertly rubbed his shaft against her still-throbbing clitoris, and she pulsated with delirious enthusiastic joy as her pelvis moved with him. She cradled his shaft as they rocked rhythmically, feeling each other's sensations. They fucked slowly at first, then faster and faster, until Marvin ejected his hot burst of seminal fluids. She simultaneously came a second time. Marvin remained inside her until he was spent and limp.

They were exhausted and sweaty as their bodily scents intermingled. A long time passed. Neither said a word. His thoughts were that he was now responsible for her, that he needed to meld their lives together in a way that would benefit and not harm her, if she'd want that. Susan's thoughts were about Marvin, the man himself and how gentle he was. He was the one who was always giving, like he must be in his business.

There occurs a rare moment in many persons' lives where they suddenly glimpse their future and perceive how they might live the rest of their lives. She was transfixed into a euphoric state of near meditation and could see herself with Marvin, making him the center of her world until death would part them. Her purpose for living seemed revealed, her path made clear.

Marvin was truly a great man and a genius, but he was a man with needs unfilled until now. Susan believed if she could fulfill his need for female companionship, that she could help him stay great and perhaps help him become even greater. He had an aching void that Eloweiss, Goldie, and none of the cackling yentas could ever fulfill because they did not love him. She knew that only she loved him.

Marvin held her close, kissed her cheek tenderly, and touched her face lightly with his fingertips, letting his hand feather over her closed eyelids and softly rub her nose and forehead. He told her he couldn't help himself. He told her that first night he'd fallen in love with her.

Over the weeks and months that followed, they made love often, experimenting with each other and making their sexuality a kind of adventurous, uninhibited team sport. They also reached some lifelong understandings. Susan would become Marvin's mistress. Jews would see them together and come to call her Marvin's shiksa. She would steel herself against the whispers and the jeers made behind her back and block out concerns over what others thought of her. There would be a social stigma to be known as Marvin's woman. The stigma would envelop her like a gossamer coat that warded away and repelled those who knew her before she took up with him, including her parents and especially her mother.

"What are you thinking, taking up with this older Jewish man? This is not how we raised you. What will your brothers and sisters think? You're our oldest. You need to set a good example for them. And our friends and the priests at church, Susan, what about them? How long do you think you can hide something like this? What possesses you to shame us this way?" Susan's mother confronted her about her affair with Marvin. Mrs. Mallory was horrified at the thought that her daughter's honor was soiled, the family's image tarnished. She was applying Catholic guilt. Susan expected a follow-up caution from her father about fire and brimstone, sins, and the path to hell, but it never came. The household was dominated by his wife, but he loved his daughter dearly. He knew Susan was a bright, strong-willed young woman now, and he wanted to avoid a confrontation that might drive her away from him. He wisely stayed silent and listened to the tiff between mother and daughter.

"Mother, first of all, I'm not 'taking up with him.' I love him and he loves me. Second, I'm not trying to hide it. Our love is nothing to be ashamed of, so I don't care what your friends or the priests think. I'm not possessed any more than you are, Mother. Like you, I want a man who loves me. That's what's important here. I've found that in Marvin, and I'm not going to let you shame me for being in love. I'll still go to church. I don't plan to become a Jewess, and Marvin and I don't plan to marry. He already has a wife."

"Listen to yourself! He already has a wife! Oh, the shame of this. I won't be able to hold my head up. I will pray and light candles for you until you come to your senses. Your soul will suffer for all eternity for this."

"You've been a wonderful mother to me. This is not something you've taught me to do, so you need not feel ashamed. I am a woman now. This is my choice. Save your candles. Don't waste your money, Mother. People who have a problem with this will just have to get over it. Mrs. Sustack doesn't love her husband. She loves her lifestyle and her sweets. She's not going to miss much. She's just a pig who needs a feed trough and a bed to sleep in. She'll just have to learn to accept me in her husband's life, that's all. Marvin and I are going to have a life with each other, Mother. The world will just have to make room for us. I don't wish to discuss it any further."

And that ended the discussion. Mrs. Mallory looked to her husband to take her side, but her hope for support was only met by his languid stare as he just sat there and shrugged. There was nothing to do, not for him anyway. He puffed on his pipe and stared through his smoke haze out a nearby window. His mind escaped from the two women even if his body could not.

Susan's parents' ambitions for her were dashed. She would not be their doting, docile church mouse. Neither would they have a clutch of four to six grandchildren by her for them to fawn over. Nor would they be able to hold their heads high when she sat with them in church. Susan only came with them for Christmas, Easter, and the Saint Cecilia masses anymore. Her absence from the family pew caused her mother conflict. Susan was a source of bruising to her mother's pride when she wasn't present for services and a deeper, more painful shame when she took her rightful place next to her mother during special religious holidays.

Marvin provided for Susan and bought her a home of her own. It was larger and better appointed than her parents' abode and thus another source of shame for them. She put their feelings out of her mind and moved on with her guilt-free life. Marvin paid for her education at State University. She graduated with a bachelor's degree in business administration and joined Marvin full time in the business. He introduced her to business associates and clients as his office administrator, and he delegated to her the responsibility for managing the administrative functions of the firm. As best his clients and business contacts could ascertain, Marvin and Susan were equals, and on most matters requiring corporate decisions, they evolved a policy where both had to agree on a course of action. Deciding to take on or terminate a client was largely Marvin's decision, although on ambivalent choices he sought Susan's opinion.

Working out their roles required Marvin and Susan to reach a solemn understanding. They would become office husband and wife in a common bond that transcended traditional conventions and mores. This secular arrangement eliminated Susan's Catholic requirement to be married to a Catholic man in a Catholic church by a Catholic priest. No priest could sanction a union such as theirs. Increasingly, Susan saw her church as being hopelessly behind the times. Marvin had his own reasons for their secular arrangement.

In order for Marvin to marry Catholic, Marvin would need to divorce Eloweiss. Was it possible? Yes. Would it be harmful to the business and his father's heart? Definitely! He'd also have to get his marriage to Eloweiss annulled, even though he and Eloweiss weren't Catholics, just to mollify a pope in Rome for whom he had little regard. Eloweiss would not consent to that, and he could never deny his son. Also, Marvin would be an impossible Catholic. He thought the religion was far too dour, too judgmental and unforgiving. Joining it would neuter him and require him to become too rigid. He loved his religion, his friends, and his community of fellow Jews. Could he give up everything and everyone he held close to his heart so Susan could please her mother, who knew nothing about anything worldly? Impossible and ridiculous! Could he turn back the lessons and nuances of the Torah and reject the insights of Cabalism? That could never be. Impossible!

Marvin pulled fanciful thoughts of marriage to Susan up like weeds by their roots, discarded them forever, and accepted himself for whom he was, a good man who sought to harm no one and was comfortable in his own skin. Sometimes the world's structured institutions fit a person like outgrown clothes. Marvin decided the firm would be their institution and they'd make their life around that. He did not ask Susan to become a Jewess, or to marry him into his religion. That would be far too complicated, hurtful to his and Eloweiss's families, and likely deleterious to the business. It would cause Susan irreparable animus with her family. He loved her with his whole heart, but he recognized he could not have her completely without destroying her relationship with her parents, knowing they would shun her if the couple married as Jews. The whole notion of marrying Susan would cause immeasurable pain for far too many people. Was his bone-hard little head causing him to think boneheaded thoughts? He laughed at himself for even giving the marriage matter a passing thought.

Marvin next wrestled with the morality of involving himself with this gentile woman outside of marriage. What was morality anyway? Was it not to do no harm, to live and to love, to liberate a mind from its constraints, to liberate this beautiful caged bird and let her soar to her full potential? The office marriage seemed Marvin's best and wisest venue choice to be forever with this gentile woman, this partner he adored and deeply loved.

CUCKOO EGG ARRANGEMENTS

Educated Susan went to work with Marvin in his business. She learned to know his mind and anticipate his wants. She would always be deferential to him, his clients, and even his obnoxious son, David, whom Marvin hoped would one day join him in the business. Susan noted that Marvin was not possessive of her. He never acted as if he had any right to confine her. Among Marvin's greatest strengths was his understanding of human needs.

Marvin respected the natural urge women had to procreate and have progeny. He affirmed to Susan that, if she wished to marry and have children with another man, it would be her business. He would never speak of their relationship to her husband, nor should she to his wife. Marvin and Susan would have love, power, and wealth together. He would be most generous with her, even giving her a full half of the business profits. He would keep his assets, to later give to his son, Jewish charities, and, after World War Two, to the State of Israel once it was chartered by the United Nations and allowed to take its place among nations.

Susan embraced her role and learned the business well, especially the administrative and all regulatory aspects of investment advisors. She managed the office staff with a quiet authority; she expected competence and treated the employees fairly. They were paid about 15 percent more than they could realize elsewhere. They all knew there was a personal relationship between Susan and Marvin, but they dared not question it or pass judgment. Employees knew the firm made money and lots of it. They also understood they were well compensated and replaceable.

As Marvin's mistress, Susan always endeavored to please him. She learned the Kama Sutra and became expertly skilled at fellatio. She kept a silent promise to herself that for all Marvin's life he would never feel the urge or the need to seek a woman's favors elsewhere.

The Sustack firm had street credence. Working at Sustack Associates carried an air of prestige. The place hummed and the office tempo was upbeat. People wanted to know what Marvin was buying and selling, but the employees kept mum. Divulging secrets was punishable by dismissal. The firm had a reputation for secrecy, the staff for being tight-lipped. Corporations feared the firm's power. It successfully engineered proxy wars to gain control of several Plaintown-based mining companies and one large banking institution. Inefficiencies at these firms were eliminated, managements replaced, and their enterprises sold for sizeable profits. Corporate heads were wary of Sustack Associates prowling around. A Sustack analyst visit or attendance at an annual corporate shareholder meeting was a signal to double-check their bylaws and anti-takeover provisions. Marvin could be very pleasant luncheon company, but many a CEO knew he could also eat their lunch and put them out on the street.

No two people can think alike or agree about all things, and Marvin and Susan were no exception. Susan's political persuasions favored the Wilson Democrats, believing the government's involvement in social betterment was important to the advancement of human progress. Marvin's opinion of Wilson was in sharp contrast to hers, regarding Wilson as a nitwit, a buffoon, a demigod, and a pathetic puppet of the New

York banking establishment. Marvin believed Wilson involved America in The Great World War for reasons having nothing to do with "Making the World Safe for Democracy," Wilson's slogan to justify his decision, but had everything to do with keeping bank loans to England and France on "performing" status, instead of "non-performing."

Unchecked banking powers are inherently predatory to a free people, Marvin averred. Allowing Wilson to establish the Federal Reserve Bank, which was a private banking company made up of wealthy shareowners, was a disaster for America, he explained to Susan. The new bank, under the Federal Reserve Act, could simply print debt obligation notes called money, or currency, owed by the U.S. Government, and then use those notes to buy the government's bonds. This arrangement destroyed the very foundation of the United States, which was founded upon the principle that only the people of the country could have control of the country's money, and that the nation's money would always be backed by gold and silver.

This new arrangement would do away with the American people having real money, backed by valuable gold and silver. Money would become pieces of government debt chit paper, no longer having any real value. Thus, Wilson flipped the tables on a free people, and Marvin hated the man for that.

From Wilson onward, the government no longer worked for the benefit of the people. The people worked for the benefit of the government as little debt slaves to a government that could now commandeer resources by merely printing paper currency to steal labor and material from the people who had to work for phony government debt chits disguised as money.

The vilest, damning, despicable part of the new Wilson arrangement was the coupling of the Federal Reserve Act with the introduction of the Federal Income Tax. Marvin explained to Susan that this tax gave the new Federal Reserve Bank a way into tax revenues that streamed into the federal government to pay down or pay off the government debt it acquired when it exchanged its printed paper for government bonds. There was a rub to this arrangement, a really sweet, orgasmic clitoris rub for the shareholders of the Federal Reserve Bank! The interest on the money they made by issuing paper to the government out of thin air could and would be used for the Federal Reserve Bank's private shareholders to buy up all the gold of the United States. It was an ingenious scheme to suck away the nation's wealth and to steal America's gold from its rightful owners, the people.

The whole arrangement was a nifty way for the nation's richest families, along with some rich European families who were also shareholders in this monster, to steal all of America's gold. They were like leeches with their suckers rooted into the nation's tax revenue flow. Marvin's opinion was that they should all be found out and thoroughly audited, that the Federal Reserve arrangement with their country should be changed to a system that had no central bank, but instead many privately owned small banks. Money should be once again backed by gold and silver, and the U.S. Constitutional provisions regarding money and the U.S. Treasury should be strictly followed forever.

Constitutional peoples' money was a brilliant original concept that served the nation well for one hundred and thirty-one years and should never have been changed. Wilson was, in Marvin's mind, a president who made a terrible error that resulted in burdening the nation with growing debts that would never be repaid, and those debts would grow so large that the interest service costs would eventually impair the nation's ability to fund its budget. The only time Susan ever saw Marvin become upset was when the name Woodrow Wilson was mentioned.

The new Federal Reserve Bank would also destroy private capital formation within the nation. By the Bank's policies, which were to smooth out business cycles by fiddling with natural market interest rates and by printing money, the Bank was certain to cause misallocations of the nation's private capital pool by directing flows into stabilizing enterprises that should be allowed to fail. Also, established failing enterprises likely had corrupt politicians as friends who would pass laws and persuade the government to loan these failing businesses cheap, low-interest money to keep the unsustainable sustained. The whole concept of this privately owned central bank was a formula for ruin of the nation, according to Marvin. He railed that so few people understood the disaster that was the Federal Reserve and that politicians were too meek to voice a challenge to this corrupt scam and enemy of a free people.

He forecast that government solvency would erode and disappear because of this new Bank, and that it would slowly, imperceptibly erode the value of the public's money. He said money would be slyly changed from gold- and silver-backed, by degrees, to non-backed worthless fiat paper that other nations would come to distrust in trade.

Susan's defense of Wilson's social engineering was that people at the bottom rungs of society needed government to give them a ladder to climb upward, to facilitate social mobility. Marvin's retort was that such notions were misguided. Government agencies, he opined, merely sought to obtain bigger budgets for themselves, stealing from the wealth generated by the sweat and enterprise of the people and their businesses, like big hogs crowding out little hogs at a trough. These big hogs, or government agencies, cared not one wit for the people they were supposedly helping, only in getting fatter themselves. According to Marvin, most government employees were overpaid parasites, and the mere fact of their government employment was in itself a ruse. His view was that government employment was welfare in and of itself. He believed private employers would not hire such worthless idiots and paper pushers.

Marvin told Susan that in the lifetimes of her grandchildren, the Federal Reserve Bank would totally destroy the United States like termites totally destroy a home. The Fed's grand beginnings would devolve the nation into socialism or possibly a worse tyranny. In this process, it would unjustly enrich its own shareholders. After all, he explained to her, monopolies exist to enrich their owners, and a monopoly on money is the greatest of all.

In the world to come, according to Marvin, society itself would become totally corrupt, dishonest, and immoral because of this wretched bank, for a nation without honest money is doomed to become a nation of dishonest, immoral people. His theory was that people intuitively knew their money is dishonest; therefore, the people themselves would behave in a way to give less-than-honest goods and services for dishonest money. They would structure deals with not just the interests of the two parties contracting in mind, but the debasing of money over time by their Federal Reserve Bank would cause parties to try to arrange payment terms in a manner which disadvantages one party for the benefit of the other. This would cause mutual long-term goodwill amongst businessmen to erode, and it was detrimental to the overall economy as well as each individual enterprise. This immorality in business bred a certain cynicism in society as a whole and caused increases in crime and poverty for those who were not amongst the most privileged insiders. Marvin predicted America would become a whorehouse.

He blamed the plight of the Russian people not on the communist Bolsheviks, but on the U.S. Federal Reserve Bank, which financed the communist revolution behind the scenes. The wealth of the czars was stolen and the production and resources of Russia looted, not by the communists who got a share, but by the Bank, which took the lion's share. The Russian people had a stable silver-backed ruble for five hundred years before the bankers and the Bolsheviks. Then, over the next four years, the new paper ruble was devalued to one new ruble for a million old ones.

In Germany, National Socialism was on the rise. Marvin blamed that on the Bank also, for imposing impossible reparations upon the German people. He foresaw an intractable situation festering in Germany, which could lead to yet another war, and the Bank would be to blame for the catastrophic losses of life and property to come. But the Bank cared not about the consequences of its actions; it only cared about getting paid. Marvin explained that stealing wealth from the people was what central banks did.

Only private charity could help those in need. Why? Because they, the people involved in the charities, the doers, cared enough about the needy to put in their own money and their own time to help them. Government workers weren't putting in their own money or their own time. They were taking their salaries from the tax trough and gobbling up precious resource dollars that should have stayed in the private sector, put to better use to fund a company so the company could employ people and enable them to feed their families. The government hog didn't care about the people. He got a salary, that's all he cared about. That and figuring out how to become a bigger hog!

Nikolai Lenin had it pegged, said Marvin, when he boldly stated that people who were social liberals were merely useful idiots. They clung to the naïve belief that taxing wealth from those who worked, then taking a cut for the government and giving the surviving portion to those who will not work would somehow grow the world's wealth, when such policies actually destroyed wealth and assured a dependent social class. If you gave money to someone who didn't work, all you were doing was rewarding him for not working. That didn't create wealth; it created dependency and crime. Marvin noted that no trust fund liberals in his client base actually gave their own wealth to charity, but they unwaveringly voted policies to make sure that those who did work would be raped by socialism's progressive taxes and unlikely to reach the same wealth plateau they had already inherited. Liberals were do-nothings befriending other do-nothings.

Susan pondered Marvin's predictions that the Federal Reserve's currency was a cuckoo's egg that would destroy its nation's nest of honest gold- and silver-backed money, and ultimately the entire world. While Marvin's ideas sounded a little futuristic when she first heard them in the 1920s, by the Great Depression years of the 1930s, with the Roosevelt Democrats madly debasing the currency, abandoning America's gold peg, and confiscating gold, Susan was convinced he was uncannily accurate. She began to quietly accumulate gold and silver coins from the coin dealers on Plaintown's South Street. Each month she set aside 10 percent of her earnings, as Marvin suggested, and each year when the firm divided profits, she took half of her share, and with those portions, she accumulated gold and silver coins. She secreted the coins away in private hiding places, as Marvin advised her, and never placed any of them in the custody of any bank. After Roosevelt confiscated private gold holdings in the 1934 gold revaluation, it was clear to her that the government would steal private gold if it were left in a bank.

With Marvin's blessings and guidance, Susan also steadily, imperceptibly, and without compunctions of guilt or remorse, shoved aside his loyalty to his wife and, to a lesser extent, his son. The thought crossed her mind that her cuckoo bird arrangement with Marvin was similar to the Federal Reserve's arrangement with America. She quietly, methodically shunted off a half portion of Marvin's wealth for herself instead of watching all of it go to David and Marvin's Jewish interests. Like the Fed, Susan liked her deal. Over the years, she amassed a fortune in gold and became one of the wealthiest people in the West.

JOSEPH AND MARTY

By age twenty-five, Susan yearned to have a child, a progeny she could raise and into whom she could impart her love, knowledge, and guidance, even if some considered her moral compass unsuited for motherhood. She married a man whom she'd met at her church, introduced to her by her parents in their forlorn hopes of saving her from perdition. Like her, Joseph Maloney was from good Irish-Catholic stock. He was tall and handsome, with a happy face quick to lift into a broad smile, bright blue-green eyes, and a shock of orange-red hair. Joseph was a year younger than Susan, and he already had a girlfriend.

Her name was Bonny. She was a plain-faced, wholesome girl of twenty-two, a homebody type his parents adored. She giggled a lot whenever they were together, hung on every word he said, and talked often about having a family with lots of kids. Bonny loved kids. She taught the little ones in the church daycare, played their games with them, picked up after them, wiped their snotty noses, tied their shoes, and rocked some of them to sleep for their naps. Outside of children, the church, her friends, and Joseph, Bonny had few interests. News of the world beyond her cocoon seldom reached her.

Bonny noticed when Joseph began talking with Susan after church. At first she brushed it off because Susan rarely attended church, but now Susan was coming almost every Sunday, and always after church she could be seen talking with

Joseph. Susan even took his arm and pressed herself close against him. The two of them laughed together, talking longer than Bonny felt they should have considering Joseph was her boyfriend. The matter came to a boil when Bonny watched Joseph walking Susan to her car. He held her door open for her and it seemed they talked for an interminable time before he came back to the church to give Bonny a ride home.

A piqued Bonny attempted to open a ticklish subject while dissing her apparent rival. "What is it about men and that Susan Mallory? She must put a sort of spell on you fellas, huh? I even see you kind of puppy scampering after her."

"She's just a friend. She's kind of fun to talk to." Joseph tried to escape the subject, but Bonny wouldn't have any of it.

"That rubbing her tits on you stuff looked like something more than just two friends talking. I'm not blind, you know. I can tell when a woman is after a man."

"Well, what of it, anyway. She just likes to be that way, I guess. It's her nature, that's all."

"Joseph, she just likes to be that way with you. I don't see her putting moves on any other men. I'm warning you as your long-time friend, as someone who cares about you. You watch out for her. She's after you for a reason. There's something about her I just don't like. She's got money by working very closely with some Jewish man who runs an investment company downtown. Where I come from, girls don't make that kind of money unless they do something extra for it. She's no good for you, Joseph. You should put your trust in a woman who really loves you."

"And that would be you, I suppose?"

"Yes, as a matter of fact, that *would* be me. You know I love you, Joseph. You're not going to be seeing her, are you?"

Joseph ignored Bonny's pleading question, and that told her all any woman needed to know. They drove to her place in silence. He dropped her off after giving her a peck on her cheek.

The next Friday evening, when Marvin was in Schull with his wife, Susan invited Joseph back to her place in Skyview after the two of them saw a movie. She went to her bar and made two martinis. As Joseph sipped his drink, Susan unzipped the back of her dress and let it fall to the floor. Her black silk stockings, black panties, and black brassier were suddenly standing there in front of Joseph. This woman was nothing like Bonny. Joseph wanted more of Susan, all of her.

While he was still sipping the martini, Susan unfastened his belt and unbuttoned his trousers. She slowly rubbed his organ to attention and then began fellatio. Joseph had never had oral sex before; he was mesmerized. In the course of the evening, Susan had him enter her vagina from behind, canine-style. Joseph had a long, full, hard member. She backed herself against him and squeezed his testicles until he came deep inside her. Joseph's inhibitions about this mysterious woman gave way to an insatiable lust to become completely lost in her. Susan had Joseph in her clutches, as Bonny tried to warn him, but his thoughts of Bonny were slipping further and further away.

Susan methodically erased Bonny from Joseph's mind, having sized Bonny up as a naïve child. Taking Joseph was like taking candy from a baby. Susan knew exactly what she needed to do to destroy the relationship between Joseph and Bonny. She gauged his feelings for Bonny were being further decimated each time he shot off his semen into her and every time he groaned and pleaded to see her again. Susan's strategy was to fuck Joseph often, and soon he was spending evenings at her place. She fucked him before they went to sleep and in the mornings she made him breakfast and gave him a blow job before she went to the office. Joseph had no time for Bonny and no reason to think about her. In short order, Bonny's hopes for a life with Joseph were obliterated.

Bonny, you simple fool, thought Susan. *I need a husband to have my child. I picked the man I wanted. I picked your man. You foolish girl, you wasted four years of your simple life on him and received no proposal, no engagement ring. I took him from you in one night. One night! I can't wait to see your simple, sad face and your parents' negative head shakes when I walk into church with Joseph on my arm.*

I know the three of you and many others have talked about me behind my back. You whisper and call me Marvin's whore. You think I'm not good enough for the rest of you. Well, I just took the best man amongst you, the best marriage prospect any of you had to offer. Now he's mine!

So, go ahead. Imagine that I seduced him, because I did! Whisper about what you think I'm doing to him, because I am! Imagine that I'm fucking him every moment he's away from the rest of you, every which way it's possible for a man and a woman to fuck, because we are! In fact, Joseph is getting fucked in ways the rest of you have never even thought possible.

And all you men in the church, I know you'd secretly like to be Joseph, if just for one night. And all you women, I know all of you are worried that I'll take your man next. I know all you hypocrites. I know how you think and I know how limited you are. I am not like any of you. I'm not the sweet little mommy's girl I once was. I don't believe for one minute that I'm going to hell for what I'm doing. I'm not buying into guilt anymore.

I'm fucking two different men now. In fact, I often fuck in the morning, in the afternoon, and in the evening with two different men the same day. And do you prudes want to know how I feel about that? I feel great! I am not one bit ashamed of who I am or what I'm doing to Joseph and Bonny, or what I do to make my living, so you all can just live with it!

Susan smiled roundly at all of them as she sat down in a pew that seated just her and Joseph.

His family always thought he'd marry a nice homebody girl like Bonny, but after a few evenings with Susan, Joseph began to fancy having a prosperous woman of independent means as a mate. He told himself that there was nothing personal going on in her relationship with Marvin. He accepted her partial truth that Marvin was a kind benefactor who'd known her since she was a little girl. Marvin had no daughter, but an errant son whom Susan babysat when she was younger, and Marvin was open and encouraging about giving her opportunities.

Susan told Joseph she was Marvin's female protégé. Perhaps he wanted to be duped, or perhaps sex with Susan was so wonderful he couldn't imagine her performing like that with another man. Men sometimes delude themselves into believing they are the mountain's king and the world's champion stud.

After three months, Joseph and Susan married in the church. It was a small ceremony and both sets of parents came, both mothers crying from agony more than joy. Susan sent Bonny an invitation to drive home the message to the hapless girl that she'd now been completely vanquished, and that all the godly goodness that she represented was being rejected by her former boyfriend. Bonny did not attend the wedding, staying home and crying for Joseph as much as for herself.

Joseph was a government auditor for the state. He had a dull sort of personality, accustomed to doing routine chores, following the directions promulgated by his superiors, and willing to travel. His assignments took him out of town with some frequency, usually for a week or two, and sometimes for three weeks at a time. He went to the far-flung corners of Colorado, to Grand Junction, Durango, Fort Morgan, Lamar, Pueblo, Aspen, Cripple Creek, Creed, Alamosa, and Colorado Springs. He traveled by train when he could, as there was no interstate highway system in those years and the Eisenhower Tunnel wasn't even imagined yet. Trips to the Western Slope had to go by train through the Moffat Tunnel or brave auto transit over treacherous Loveland Pass.

The western passes had no guardrails. There was constant danger from large logging and freight trucks on the high mountain roads. Many drivers were from either coast, and they underestimated the steep lengthy declines in Colorado's mountains. Trucks' brakes failed because drivers ignored warnings to use lower gears, and large semi-tractor trailers frequently jackknifed, sweeping oncoming cars cleanly off the road. Often enough, the victims' cars shot off the highway and plunged down into the ravines and creeks below.

The scenic beauty of the vistas and canyons caused still more drivers to lose their focus and have accidents. Deer, elk, and moose on the roads caused inexperienced drivers to often swerve to their deaths. Experienced drivers ran rigs with big steel bumpers fashioned from oil country pipe. They simply ran over wayward animals and kept on driving. This was Joseph's working life. He was home for a week or two, then away for a week or two or even three. He lived in hotel stops far away from Susan's bed at home.

Intercourse with Joseph became more like a bland duty for Susan, the thrills of conquest no longer there for her. Neither husband nor wife dwelt long on foreplay. Being with Joseph was so unlike her liaison with Marvin. She loved sex enough to tolerate Joseph's savage, rapacious thrusts, but when he was schlonging her in her maiden position, she imagined she was back in the mortuary with Frank. Then, after Joseph spent himself, she'd coddle him and compliment his ejaculation with her soothing, "Way to go, baby" assurances, all the while wishing she were cradling Marvin instead.

Frequently she copulated with both men multiple times on the same day. She never denied either man's desires, although intimacy occurred three to four times more often with Marvin than it did with Joseph. Joseph just wasn't home that much. Susan and neither man took precautions. Before Joseph, she kept Marvin in rhythm with her menstrual cycle and avoided pregnancy. Now that she was married, she wanted nothing to do with precautions while with either man. The sire of the child born of this sexual threesome would be unpredictable. Susan wanted it that way, her main objective in marriage being parenthood, but she secretly hoped her child would be Marvin's.

Many fathers live their entire married lives raising and supporting another man's child. About one woman in three saddles her spouse with the burdens of her dalliance with other lovers. Some harness their marital plow horse as a spiteful sort of thing, as payback for her mate's own infidelities. Others simply lose all passions for their husbands, but need a good breadwinner for her household while her natural passions take her to the beds of other men, and sometimes other women.

Susan was neither of these types. She was independent in every sense. With her professional credentials and profit-sharing agreement with Marvin, she had no need for Joseph in her life from a financial or intellectual standpoint. His usefulness to her was the legitimacy he provided her unborn child. After six months of trying to conceive with Joseph and Marvin, fortune smiled on Susan. She became pregnant and later gave birth to a beautiful, healthy baby girl.

Joseph and Susan named their baby Marty Maloney. Susan adored the child, as did Joseph initially, but he became suspicious of Marty's paternity. He couldn't help but wonder how a buxom, blue-eyed Irish-American woman and a green-eyed, red-haired Irish-American man could possibly create a dark-haired, brown-eyed daughter. Marty also had a tiny protrusion jutting outward from the base of the little finger of her right hand. It was a tiny genetic defect; Mother Nature tried to create a sixth finger for Marty, but gave up. The nub's growth stopped after it formed a quarter-inch in Susan's womb.

Marvin once had the identical defect on his own right hand, but had it surgically removed just a few weeks before he took Susan to his rental home for that first time. Plastic surgeons did a remarkable job removing any trace of the growth on Marvin's hand. Genetic deformities were less rare in

Ashkenazi Jews than other genetic pools, likely the result of tribal inbreeding that took place beginning in the eleventh century. That tribe was a latecomer to Judaism. The people did not have the direct blood lineage of Abraham. They were Kazarian Jews, forced into their religious choice by Ottoman rulers of their ancestral lands between the Caspian Sea and the Caucuses. They were a band of thieving highway robbers and gypsies who adopted a new way of life. The bloodline was greatly diluted by generations of intermarriage with Ashkenazi and Sephardic bloodlines, as well as additions to the blood pool through assimilated gentile converts. Marvin carried a faint trace of the Kazarian bloodline, which he passed to David, although David had no physical defects, only mental ones. Now little Marty, through Marvin, carried the bloodline as well. By the way he held his hand, Marvin kept his defect concealed until he had it removed. As far as he knew, Eloweiss and David were the only ones in Plaintown who'd ever seen it.

Susan admonished Joseph for his unanchored musings. "Well, genetics certainly is a strange new science. Who knows? Why, there are thousands of brown-eyed Irish lassies, don't you know?" As a matter of fact, Joseph didn't know. He never personally saw a brown-eyed Irish, but he was afraid to challenge her assertion.

Then she reasoned with him even further, as a way of reassuring him. "Who knows, if we trace our genealogy back far enough, we probably all have a bit of Negro within us. Maybe there's a tiny bit of that in her somehow from thousands of years back. Then too, every once in a while, a pair of white swans will produce a black swan offspring. Please, let's not give this any more thought. I assure you, she is our baby. We are her parents, and we must love her with all our hearts." What Susan told Joseph was, at least, half true.

Joseph felt trapped, outmaneuvered. Was he saddled with raising another man's daughter? He told himself it wasn't true, that the child was his, but in his heart of hearts the suspicions persisted. He suspected he'd been cuckolded by Marvin, but what could he do? Susan refused to confess to an affair.

Susan maintained a steel-willed resolve to exclude Joseph from any discussions about Marvin or the business. She made it clear to Joseph by what she said and what she refused to disclose to him that she and Marvin had some sort of inseparable bond. It was an almost holy pact. They seemed happily unholy in their investment firm, their private cash machine.

Joseph long felt that he was somehow secondary in her life to Marvin and Susan's business. He held his thoughts while Marvin and Susan went out of town to conventions together. He tried to understand when she told him they often needed to work late hours to prepare for a client, to make a regulatory filing, to make an overseas call to some company they'd invested in, to do this or to do that. But he wondered what was really going on.

Was it all just so they had time to fuck? His mind raced with anxiety. He remembered Bonny's warning to him. "She's not like us." Those words echoed and reechoed. That had to be it! His wife had been making love with Marvin for years. He was just a convenience for Susan! He was Plaintown's biggest fool.

Then Joseph's rationalizations came. Sustack's was a very successful firm. They had to be working down there, just like she said. Maybe it was true. The child could be a black swan event. Something special must have happened. Maybe it was God's way of testing him; after all, didn't the Virgin Mary have a child by a holy spirit? Didn't Joseph also doubt the Virgin Mary at first? Susan was, after all, a good Catholic girl from a good family, just like Mary, the mother of Jesus, was a good woman. Yes, it must all be true. Susan was a good girl, a wonderful woman, and a blessing to him. He felt ashamed for his doubts.

Joseph and Susan went to the same Sunday school together when they were little kids. Joseph reassured himself that Susan learned the same things he learned. He told himself she wouldn't lie to him; she didn't know how. After all, she'd told him she loved him, that he was the man she'd been waiting for all her life. She'd said her life would be incomplete without him. He'd believed all of it then, and now they were in life together with a child. Nothing had changed; he told himself he was just acting like an ungrateful fool. He hoped God would forgive his suspicions. He'd pray the rosary. He believed if he prayed enough, he'd be forgiven his sin of doubting his wonderful wife. Yes, he would accept all of it. Everything she told him had to be true. He was her husband; he'd learn to accept what he couldn't fully understand. It was, after all, the miracle of faith.

Joseph decided he'd accept her late hours, her priority of Marvin first, him second. And whether little Marty was his or Marvin's, he would accept Susan's promises that Marty was his child. He would love little Marty, would raise her in a household filled with love. His suspicions were swallowed up and contained within his rationalizations.

In a perverse sort of way, Joseph began to love Susan even more deeply than he had before. He worshiped her, palpitated and salivated at the thought of making love with her. A kind of obsessive madness possessed him. When he suspected she could be making love with Marvin, he shoved those thoughts from his mind and he wanted her all the more. He tried mightily to please her, but somehow he always felt inadequate.

Joseph's income didn't help matters. He worked hard and diligently to earn paltry government bonuses, but his income never reached a fraction of hers. In the bedroom, she grew more and more distant from him. Their pillow talk was increasingly superficial. Pretense of romance was replaced by bland, inconsequential commentary about the day's happenings and reports from the sitters about what little Marty did.

While Joseph stoked his flames of deep passions for Susan and pined for their hot romantic nights gone by, she became clinical about her lovemaking. She was a woman only doing her wifely duty now, no longer the writhing siren of passionate desire he'd known before. He often felt she might as well be a prostitute who just laid there with spread legs until he finished. No longer did she lick his balls or suck his cock. Never again did she straddle his face and lower her delicious cunt onto his mouth. His back rubs and French kisses were ancient history. He wondered if marriage became too dull for her.

Years passed and little Marty turned four. Susan began taking her along to the office on occasions. She had some staff girl who could watch her, and it avoided the annoyance of getting a sitter, she declared to Joseph. It seemed plausible enough, so Joseph didn't object. Who wouldn't want their child to spend time being close to her mother? Little Marty might even learn something about how the investment business worked. Joseph rationalized, what could possibly be wrong with that?

Then one day at a company party at the Sustacks' residence, in the same garden where Susan used to cater parties, the scales fell from Joseph's eyes. There, in front of him and Susan, all the firm's employees, and Eloweiss Sustack, little Marty climbed up on Marvin's lap without being summoned, like she'd done it hundreds of times before. Marty gave Marvin a huge, uninhibited child's hug around his neck and kissed him lovingly on his cheek. She called him Uncle Marvin. Marvin smiled, Susan smiled, but Joseph was mortified. Everything was suddenly obvious to him.

What he'd refused to see before he could no longer pretend not to see. Marty wasn't his child, but Marvin's little girl.

She'd known the comforting warmth of his lap many times before this. Susan's motherly smile at true father united with daughter confirmed the bitter truth for all to see. Marvin's son, David, seemed happy with little Marty. David was in his late twenties by that time, enjoying his learning years and not too anxious to begin working. He was shy around girls as he'd always been, but he liked playing with little Marty. The two of them acted as if they were big brother and little sister, laughing and bouncing a beach ball between them.

Up his neck and outward from the back of his brain, a hot flash of blood coursed through Joseph and flushed into his face. He resembled a chameleon changing its colors from white to red. Susan noticed the unspoken tell Joseph revealed. She knew for certain that he would no longer pretend away the truth.

Even Eloweiss noticed the innocent affections of Marty toward Marvin, and her heart sank. Marvin was lost to her in a hurtful way. A woman can feel a terrible pain when she realizes her man sired a child with another woman. Eloweiss held her tongue though and never spoke to anyone of her revelation. Joseph noticed Eloweiss's reaction and it served to confirm his own.

Susan knew her masquerade could no longer continue. It was time for her to become calloused with Joseph. She had the child she wanted, and she had the man she wanted in Marvin. She had the money and power she craved, and she no longer saw a need for Joseph. Susan waited for the inevitable confrontation. That night, when Marty was asleep in her room, Joseph could hold back no longer. "She's Marvin's child, isn't she? Admit it."

"I don't know what you're talking about. Don't be silly." Susan sought to deflect Joseph's hostility until she was ready to unload her own hostility. She wanted him to leave their home and never return.

"I saw the way she kissed him. I saw the way you beamed your motherly countenance upon that father-daughter scene. I'm no fool! What do you take me for? That's some nice, cozy whorehouse you work in with your Marvin, isn't it?" There was a long moment of silence, but Joseph would not be put off. "Isn't it!" He was shouting. "Goddamn you, you whore bitch. Answer me!"

For the integrity of the business, for her reputational narrative, she could not admit to anything. "Stop it! Just stop it! I've told you before. Marty is yours, ours."

"You're lying! Lying! Tell me the truth or else!"

Tempers flared. Joseph raised his hand to slap her, but the angered Irish mother would have none of it. She advanced face to face with this man who was no longer a compliant cuckold husband. Now the stupid man represented a threat to her, her child, her way of life, and to Marvin and their firm.

"Or else you'll do what?" she screamed in his face. This was no longer the little girl Joseph knew in Sunday school. This woman was brazen, ruthless, and heartless. Her face was vacant. There was no love there, not even the pretensions of love he'd glimpsed before. This face wanted him to disappear. This woman had already separated from him in her mind; all that remained for her were the formalities. Susan knew she'd pushed Joseph into retreat. He was too much the gentleman to slap her, too much the coward to stand toe to toe with her. She unsheathed her claws, dug them into his soul, and punctured his confidence and masculinity. Never before had she belittled him, but now she would sink her fangs into his jugular and kill his self-respect.

"I've told you before, Mr. Maloney," she snapped with a bite in her words. "And this is the last time I'll tell you! Ever!" She was screaming in his face. "Marty is your child! Now you listen to me, Mr. Maloney, and you hear me well. If Marvin were her real father, that would be a better thing for her! He's a much better *man* than you! He's more of a *man* than you'll ever be! You just mind your own business in this family, mister. Marty and I don't need you." She snarled the words in the most derogatory way. "Let me warn you. If you try to do anything about your ridiculous suspicions, Marvin and I will find a way to get you fired. You'll never find another job in Colorado again. We have friends, and we have power. You? Hah! You are a nobody, a nothing!"

She was screaming. She could see her tactics were working. Joseph blanched, taking a step backward as she thrust her face into his once again. He saw her as a wild, ruthless demon, intent on his destruction. Never in his wildest imagination had he ever believed her capable of this sort of behavior. She continued, showing him no mercy.

"Now, you listen to me, you stupid son of a bitch. If you want a divorce over this, you'll get one, but I'll destroy you in the process. I'll make a record about how you mistreat us, how you molest our child, how perverted you are. You'll never marry again! I'll never give you an annulment either, so you'll never be able to crawl back to your sappy little Bonny. If you won't leave, your only other choice is to stay married to me and to love that child who's asleep in that bedroom. You never let her hear what you said here tonight. You work. You go out of town and you do your stupid audits, and you stay out of town and away from us as much as you can for as long as you can. You forget about ever having sex with me again. I don't want you ever touching me! You find that somewhere else. Find yourself some roadhouse whores. That's your business, I don't care. From now on, you and I sleep in separate bedrooms when you are here.

"And furthermore, since you're so suspicious about Marvin, maybe I'll make your suspicions come true. Do you hear me? Maybe I *will* start fucking Marvin. What if I do? What do you think you're going to do about it? Do you think you could get me fired? Do you think you're going to hit me? Or hit him? Do you want to spend a couple years in jail, big boy? Huh? Why don't you just go someplace and fall off a cliff and die! I hope you do die, and soon. I hope the rats come and eat you. I have no use for you. I'm sick of you. Do you think I like fucking you? You're disgusting. You have nothing to offer me. You are a nobody."

Her berating tactics worked. She watched as Joseph sat down and placed his head in his hands. She knew he couldn't stand up to her barrage of heartless cruelty. She watched him stare into empty space, to somewhere far beyond his unimaginable predicament, shocked at her words. She could tell that he realized now, too late, that he never knew her at all. She silently laughed at him, knowing that he wished he had stayed with his simple, innocent Bonny. But, she knew she'd trapped him. She knew his need for her love coursed through his veins and that she could treat him however she pleased.

It was with this inexplicable ache for her love deep within his heart that cleaved Joseph to Susan, no matter how she mistreated him. It was an attraction to her evilness, her ruthlessness, her abuse of him and his very life that he could not explain or begin to fathom. She was like a black widow eating the guts out of her mate, but he still loved her even as she destroyed him. There was no going back to Bonny. After making love with Susan, he couldn't imagine being apart from her, no matter how painful it was for him to know she preferred another man.

Joseph lived in a world of purposeless, mindless drudgery. He buckled to Susan's will and stayed away for extra weeks on his audit trips. He found some roadhouse whores and took up drinking and whoring with women he pretended were Susan to ease the pain in his heart. Ultimately, after a night of heavy drinking, he gave Susan the ultimate gift. He decided he loved her enough to die for her, hoping that someday she'd understand what love really was and that she'd repent from her evil ways.

He had a long drive home from Aspen and two weeks until his next road trip, but he didn't want to go back to Plaintown. The thought of seeing Susan again churned his stomach. She hated him now. He wasn't man enough to confront her. Their house was no longer a place he could call home. He couldn't tell his parents the situation; they were so disappointed in the marriage, as they never approved of Susan. Bonny deserved a man better than him. He couldn't go back to her after the mess he'd made of his life. Even she would probably laugh at him. She told him something like this could happen. Why hadn't he listened? Why did he turn his life over to this whore?

He was despondent. He hated his job. All he had to look forward to was thirty more years of tedium. He drove faster and faster. Then he turned his headlights off and looked up at the twinkling stars above. Maybe there was happiness somewhere in the universe. He wanted to end things this way. Ultimately, he'd prove he made a decision to do something on his own terms.

His car was found a week after he drove it off Independence Pass outside Aspen. While taking his death plunge, Joseph thought of what life might have been like with Bonny. But he knew himself, knew Bonny wasn't what he wanted. In his final seconds, he saw Susan realizing her ultimate joy, outwardly playing her role as the grieving widow but inwardly relieved by his tragedy. She was free from the marital chains that bound her to him, free to commit unfettered and uninhibited to Marvin. As his automobile crashed and tumbled end over end down the thousand-foot drop, he hated himself for being the willing dupe, for being the person he was, and for still loving her even as he committed suicide. He wished the good times and the sex with Susan had never ended. He never got her out of his mind or his blood, obsessed with her until the end.

His final thought was of Marty. A lot goes through a mind in the final seconds before death. Marty would wonder why her daddy went off the road. Would Susan ever tell her the truth? She likely wouldn't hear that, at least not until she was much older. Would Marty hear about how the coyotes and ravens savaged and mutilated his corpse? Probable she would hear that. Susan would like thinking about that and would enjoy sharing her depraved relief with her daughter, most likely Marvin as well. It would make his death so final.

Would Marty hear about the bulldozers needed to pull the wreck up from the bottom of the slope below? As his head was bludgeoned and crushed from colliding with the steel roof of the crumbling car, his final thought was of the child he had come to love, even though she wasn't his. He believed Marty would find comfort and consolation with Susan and Marvin.

CHOOSE TO GO FORWARD

Five weeks had elapsed since Joseph left for his Western Slope trip, three weeks since anyone had heard from him. Little Marty was accustomed to her daddy being away, but the child noticed this absence was prolonged. Would Daddy bring her a toy this time? Candy? Perhaps he'd bring her some Enstrom's toffee from Grand Junction?

"Why is it taking Daddy so long, Mommy?"

Even Susan couldn't say for certain why this trip was so elongated, so she made something up. "Daddy's on an unexpected assignment and will tell you all about it when he returns."

A five-year-old's imagination could cope with that explanation. Perhaps Daddy went to Aspen to get her some skis! Maybe he went to Mountaintop Lake to buy them a cabin! Then she dreamed she and Daddy could go hiking together, look at the elk and the deer, and go boating and fish for tasty Kokanee salmon. That had to be it. She relished the idea of taking a friend along on a mountain trip with her dad, but it was not to happen. Marty's dreams of time with her daddy were swept away when the local sheriff came calling. She was at home with her mother when he sat them down and told them of the tragedy. Marty went to her room and cried on her bed while Mother talked with the sheriff.

The news of Joseph's demise shocked Susan. It was all so sudden, although not entirely unexpected. There were no skid marks; the car just shot off the road into the open air and careened down a thousand feet of steep mountainside, where it came to rest against some boulders at timberline. Suicide? That was a definite possibility, the Gilpin County sheriff told her.

"Now, Mrs. Maloney, we jist don't know what happened here. The animals molested his dead body some befores we's even able to git to it, so's we jist can't say fer sure. Now, some folks, day jist comes up here and they don't git nuf oxygin in der brains, ya know wut I means? Well, den dey git takin wid da beauty of dees montins, and they jist stops payin' tentin to drivin'. Dat's probly wut happened here. It happens to lots of flatlanders up here."

The old sheriff tried to be reassuring and matter of fact about it, but beneath that cowboy hat he knew it was likely a suicide. No skid marks, highest point on the pass, huge drop-off. No animals ranged up there. No, this guy wanted to check himself out of Hotel Life. Maybe this dame who looked like a fox in heat had something to do with it. There was no note. No one at Hotel Jerome, where he stayed, could say when they'd seen him last.

She was down in Plaintown. No phone calls to the wife. That was strange. *Poor bastard*, thought the sheriff. *He's working his ass off out here while she's probably back in the city fucking some other guy. He probably loved her and she was just eating his guts out.* The old sheriff had seen it all. He knew people and could spot what they were all about pretty quickly. Give him a half hour with somebody, let him watch their face when they talked, see how they cried about a death, what they said about the stiff. He spotted this bitch's true feelings from a mile away. She never gave a shit about this poor devil, and there was nothing he could do about it.

Back in Plaintown, knowing her spouse ended his life so tragically, stirred some emotions Susan didn't think she had—not so much for Joseph, but for Marty. Poor Marty! Now her baby girl was fatherless. How could she shield her daughter from the big wide world without Joseph's help?

Damn you, Joseph. You were a coward to the end.

There she was, poor innocent Susan! She was widowed. Would people think about why it happened? Would they annoy her with consolations she didn't want? Would they, God forbid, try to find her another husband, which she definitely didn't want? How could she console Marty in a genuine sort of way while secretly bursting for joy at her own newly unfettered freedom? What could she do about Marty?'

No strong male figure was going to raise her little girl. Her parents were getting older and couldn't reliably watch Marty while she was downtown working. How could she ensure her child was well-raised and well-schooled without his involvement? She was not about to give up her career; she made tremendous money, wielded enormous power. Surely when Marty was older and had all life's advantages, she would understand.

Momentary grief, anger at her now deceased husband, quandaries about others' perceptions, and her motherly duties were quickly decided. Marty would go to boarding school. Her daughter would be raised correctly, instructed in manners and etiquette, and the child would be out of her way. Marty could come home for a month during summers and two weeks at Christmas. With Susan's new freedom, the firm could grow larger and richer. And, if she played her cards well, she foresaw the possibility that she could get Marvin's ownership sometime in the future.

The Sustack firm occupied a high floor in the prestigious King Building, midway on the Main Street financial district. The firm was figuratively and literally where the action was. Marvin and Susan occupied adjoining corner office suites, both expansive with commanding views of the automobiles and foot traffic bustling below. The suites were joined by a private door between them, not a feature that could be seen from the long narrow hallway that joined the publicly accessible elevator doors at the other end. Each suite had its own door opening to the hallway, but the door between the suites was behind the wall at the end and was invisible to the public. The office staff was not allowed in Marvin's office unless summoned or to deliver his morning mail and papers. He kept his hallway door locked for privacy.

Susan also locked her hallway door from time to time, leaving instructions with her staff that she didn't want to be disturbed until a given hour later in the day. Her office had been modified at considerable cost to include a private bathroom and a bidet. The plumbing for the general restrooms was at the other end of the hall, and the plumbers had to disturb the floor below to accommodate the unusual demands of the Sustack firm. Marvin used the facilities at the other end of the hall, which had the men's room on the right side, the women's on the left. He, being the only man in the firm, never considered his bathroom privacy an issue.

Marvin's office had a huge, semi-circular walnut desk. He sat behind it in a massive, high-backed black leather throne chair. Around the desk were lesser, shorter black leather audience chairs. All chairs in the office swiveled on their bases and were on steel rollers. It was an exceptionally comfortable office.

There were two other pieces besides a credenza behind the throne chair, a huge, overstuffed black leather sofa, which Marvin used for naps when he needed rest and a mysterious seven-foot long black leather bench. It was only two feet wide and sat just up off the floor at about footstool height. Most who saw it thought it was a sort of footstool, or possibly Marvin sat on the floor and read papers on it; but then, what was his credenza for? Whenever he was asked about it, Marvin gave a softball response. "Oh, that. It's just a piece I saw and liked, so I picked it up." The lie was in the leather; the piece matched the chairs. Marvin had it custom-made, but nobody ever pursued the matter further.

The funeral was a week past. Susan's mother and Marty were boarded on a train and sent to Maryland to enroll Marty in the Wexler Baxter School for Girls. Susan sent her widow's dresses back to consignment where she'd purchased them. Her outer mantels of marriage and motherhood now shed, Susan sought the taste of her new freedom. The very afternoon she put Joseph in the ground, she sat on the floor next to Marvin, who lay naked on his low bench. The two of them gave their "do not disturb" message to the secretary at the front receptionist desk. All calls were to be held. They were "in conference" and not to be disturbed under any circumstances.

Susan performed perfect fellatio, and she loved sucking Marvin's cock. As she stroked and held his lower shaft with her left hand, she suckled the head and upper shaft with her velvety lips. Simultaneously, she tickled the sensitive underside of his scrotum with the fourth and fifth fingers of her right hand, all the while kneading his testicles ever so softly with her right thumb and first three fingers.

After a brief while, Marvin surrendered what no man could possibly retain under Susan's unrelenting seduction. He moaned softly, holding her head gently in his hands as his semen erupted in a hot, volcanic gush into her mouth. She continued working her mouth, stroking the shaft with her wet, juicy lips while sucking up Marvin's semen. She squeezed his testicles more firmly, causing semen to continue rising from deep within his scrotum. She swallowed all his ejaculation and relaxed her grip from his testicles as his shaft began to soften, but she was not yet finished. Her sexuality was fully aroused.

She coaxed Marvin into a shared state of delirious ecstasy, swishing a small swig of vodka in her mouth before taking his shaft into her mouth, basking it in the alcohol. The shaft responded to the cool, evaporative sensation, stiffening immediately. Her vagina was throbbing to receive him, so she mounted her custom-made low bench, straddling it with her knees upon the floor on either side. It was the perfect height, the perfect width for the deepest penetration of her vagina. She'd specified its dimensions to the carpenter, and he'd succeeded perfectly. She could use this position to rock her pelvis and rub her pulsating clitoris against Marvin's rock-hard cock. They usually maintained this coupling for anywhere from ten to twenty minutes.

Susan loved the thrill of their in-office lovemaking. She relished the naughtiness of hiding their fornication breaks from their suspicious staff, and she was empowered with the knowledge that she was stealing Marvin's affections from his wife and other would-be lovers. As she joyfully rode his cock that afternoon, Susan felt freedom from her troubled marriage and from the responsibility of raising Marty. She felt omnipotent.

Her subordinates were at the other end of the hall, minding the store. Marvin often said the stock and bond assets, once chosen, pretty much managed themselves whether they were watched or not. Clients might've been appalled if they knew the goings-on at Sustack's, but of course they didn't know. Besides, Marvin and Susan convinced themselves that sexual stimulation invigorated their minds; thus, they were copulating to help their clients' assets grow. Susan wondered—nay, rejoiced—that she possessed an unquenchable, sinful lust that drove her to be ever more daring and uninhibited. After a short while, Marvin broached an unspoken but persistent thought. "What will we do if my wife ever comes to the office and demands to see me?"

Susan had long anticipated that trepidation. She immediately quelled it.

"We'll do nothing," she said. "Our doors are locked. She has no key. I'll simply tell the front receptionist to tell Mrs. Sustack to wait in the reception room until I'm finished fucking her husband!"

Marvin chuckled. He loved it when Susan took control. "But what if she comes storming down here, knocking on the door? She can be pretty persistent."

"Then I'll call Mrs. Rodriguez and have her call security and have your wife removed from the building."

"Would that work?" Marvin wondered.

"Of course it would work." Susan smiled. "A wife has to know her place. I know how she thinks. She would never jeopardize you or me or the firm. You are her meal ticket." She kissed Marvin full on the mouth, a deep French kiss. "Relax. Don't be silly. You could, if you'd like, take me home with you one night and fuck me right in front of Eloweiss, right in her bedroom, right in her own bed. She couldn't and wouldn't do a thing about it."

"You're crazy!" Marvin's reaction surprised Susan. She thought he'd salivate at the idea.

Susan took his shaft into her hand and stroked it softly. Then, as it stiffened, she plunged it deep into her vagina once again. Both their organs were pulsating, titillated by the naughty thought of fucking in front of Eloweiss, driving her to near insanity with their bald lewdness.

"Oh, my love, I am not crazy. I am a woman in love with you. I'd love to flaunt my pussy right in her ugly face. I'd like to fuck you in front of her until she screams and begs us to stop. Someday, when you've had enough of her, you'll be ready to do just that, my love. You tell me when you've had enough of her abuse. You tell me and I'll go with you. Together, we'll laugh in her face. We'll fuck right in front of her until she goes insane."

Susan couldn't know the effect her words. She had no comprehension that the Torah's admonition to first do no harm were resonating in his consciousness in opposition to her words as he visualized cavorting and copulating with Susan in front of Eloweiss. She couldn't appreciate how much wickedness and hurtfulness repulsed him. She only sensed his mind slipping away to another realm that she could not enter. She wisely stopped urging him to fuck her in front of his wife. Her instincts correctly guided her to redouble her passions and stay focused in the moment. She felt Marvin's moral dilemma fade and disappear into serenity as her sheath undulated expertly, squeezing its captured shaft from scrotum base to penis tip, drawing his spurting nectar into her cradle of creation. When she felt his hot, shooting fluids coursing into her, she knew she and Marvin enjoyed a special intimacy which would forever bind them both. Her orgasmic juices gushed, titillated by her own vicarious thoughts of becoming Mrs. Sustack and displacing Eloweiss. She looked into Marvin's eyes. He seemed to read her mind and his body stiffened involuntarily as his face betrayed a slight grimace.

Susan, expert at reading expressions, realized she'd inadvertently overstepped some boundary she didn't understand was there. She'd broken a taboo of some sort, but she wasn't sure what it was. They'd laughed about Eloweiss before. She was repulsive to Marvin, a foul-mouthed sexless dominatrix with a miserable personality, repugnant appearance, and a ghastly malodorous, unwashed bodily scent.

My God, she'd often wondered, *why on earth does Marvin stay married to her? How can he sleep in the same bed with that human sow?*

Still, mistakes were easily made in love and war. Whole armies got slaughtered or captured because of the simplest miscues, the most innocent miscalculations. Susan thought it best to not pursue the subject of taunting Eloweiss any further at that time. She calculated that, with the passage of time, she'd triangulate her nemesis. She'd work to understand the invisible armor that shielded Eloweiss, chip it away, and destroy her. Marvin would be hers, all hers!

For the moment, she thought it best to change the subject. Fondling his testicles, she lightly kissed his face, reverting to her role as the ever-compliant mistress. She would ask Marvin's opinion on some subject. He liked her curiosity, liked sharing his thoughts with her. It was a comfortable place for them.

"Tell me, Marvin," she cooed. "I'm uncertain about the best way to think about charity. I give some to my church and to different causes, but I don't put much thought into it. Mostly, I just send money out of habit, to be done with it. Do you put a lot of thought into it, or are you like me, just give something and be done with it?"

Marvin answered her inquiry as if he didn't know she'd recognized his grimace. She'd wisely changed the subject, avoided direct confrontation about his wife, but it was too late. She'd revealed her ultimate intent. She wondered if Marvin would take certain measures to redirect her focus, and noted that he ignored her lewd proposal as if he had not heard it. Marvin passed over her bedroom idea and directly responded to her inquiry about charitable giving. "Charity is a matter of individual choice, always. Many religious organizations expect their members to give 10 percent of their income if it doesn't cause hardship."

"But what is your personal view? Tell me. I'd really like to know. Sometimes I see rabbis leaving your office and they seem unhappy. Why would they be unhappy? Isn't there anything you can tell me?" She massaged his testicles, as if focused on squeezing his true thoughts from him. Marvin yielded.

"The sincerest gift to charity is the one given anonymously, which, in your confidence to never repeat, I do. With respect to the rabbis, they are just that way. You can never give them enough. When they go away with less than they ask, I know I

ROSEMARY LIGHTFOOT NESS-BITNER

have a good relationship with them. That just means they'll be back. These men are my friends, my closest friends. You see, they are wise and learned beyond the rest of us. They give their lives to understand people and morality. They can look into situations that seem impossible to resolve and they resolve them. They are great company, and I enjoy their conversations always. When they come up with a project they need help with, I listen carefully. I find out what they need. Then I give them part of their request. Then they come back. They cry and complain that no one will open a purse for this or that.

"Then I ask again what they still need. I can then tell how much others have put in. If they are still short, I give some more. And then they get an anonymous gift that is maybe about what I just gave. By then, they should be almost at their goal. If no one else is giving, maybe something's wrong with their idea, and I want to know that. They are really terrible at business, the worst of everyone. But they are great with humanity, very loving men for all humanity. They're just terrible with business. If they can't raise money, maybe I'll then get involved to help analyze their project, de-risk it, make it more appealing, or I'll help them see what it needs if it's supposed to make money. I enjoy them. I love them, as good people and good friends. They are a kind of pleasant diversion from ordinary business."

"So, that's the best charity, the 'silent helper' sort?"

"No, I didn't say the best. The most amusing would be a better way to put it. The best charity is a business investment, a cold-blooded business investment where you expect to make a profit. That's what actually employs people. That employment enables families to thrive and have self-respect and dignity. There are many liberal progressives who believe it's the government's calling to take from the wealthy and the wage earner and have all sorts of social programs to help people rise up from poverty. Unfortunately, a lot of rabbis buy into this

THE SECRET AND THE BUTTERFLY

thinking. I guess that's because they gloss over economics in rabbinical school. Too many rabbis urge their congregants to vote democrat because they wrongly believe the government social programs are the best way to order society. I guess that's another reason they leave my office unhappy. I couldn't disagree with them more."

"But why do you disagree?"

"Because the Torah says I must disagree. It's the true lesson of the Exodus story."

"Please tell me. I want to know," implored Susan.

Marvin loved her most when she asked questions like an inquisitive schoolgirl. He sensed his shaft stiffening once more. Soon she'd again guide it into her insatiable cunt. Perhaps she thought he'd overlook her earlier transgression. He'd think about that later. Now he only wanted to be in the moment with her, the two of them sharing their thoughts and their love.

"The Exodus is not just about getting out of Egypt, or about getting freedom from slavery. Most rabbis think that's all there is to the story, but it has a more subtle, deeper meaning. For background, when the tribe left the Sea of Reeds, they crabbed and complained every step of the way. God gave them manna and water, so they'd make it and not starve or die of thirst. The gist of the story is that they wandered for forty years, without any vision of how precious their freedom was. They needed constant reassurance. They just couldn't see that somehow, no matter how tough the circumstances, God always comes through. You just have to believe that.

"Then, there's the time when the tribe is at Mount Sinai. Moses gets the Ten Commandments and comes down the mountain. Now, while he was up on the mountaintop, the people down below built a golden calf and were worshiping it, cavorting about, generally going crazy over this thing. There was a faction in the tribe that wanted to throw Moses over, get a new leader, worship this calf, and go back to Egypt. Now, part of this is that Jews always disagree about something or other. We are impossible!

"But the key to the Torah story is this: The ones who wanted to go back to Egypt wanted to go back because the pharaoh would take care of them. Imagine that! They wanted cradle-to-grave care! It's too hard to be free. Can't you see it? They were willing to become slaves again because the pharaoh would take care of them! So they were willing to worship an idol—in other words, sell their souls—if the authority that tells them to worship the idol also promises to take care of them. See it yet?

"How are modern people any different? People want to vote for the established parties and their controlling bankers because the government promises to take care of them. They are willing to be slaves to a debt-based currency system, worshiping paper money as if it were a god. Paper money is just a modern version of the golden calf, and the paper money system lends itself to all sorts of debauchery. People are willing to pay taxes, or a modern-day levy, which is their slavery tribute to the government slave owner, from their wages, just like the pharaoh system in ancient Egypt. You see, God would have none of this. He killed those people. God has no patience for idiots. He had the true and faithful Israelites put their swords to them and brother killed brother. God wanted the people to get it right, meaning no idols, and by extension no fiat money, no paper currency, no currency created by brokers' credits on stock margin accounts, none of it. God said they were turning away from 'the way,' meaning God's way, meaning freedom. He did not want his people to return to slavery, so I take it as a mitzvah to never vote for any party that wants big government.

"So, when a rabbi tells people to vote for big government, and they do tell them that, those rabbis do not understand the real lesson of the Exodus story in the Torah. The real lesson is that there is only one God. And the next big lesson is that there is no going back to slavery. You die if you go back to slavery. Now, think about this. If you have all these social programs, you have to follow logically that you will engineer a weak, dependent, immoral, decadent, slothful society. You will grow a rotten tree with dead limbs that never get pruned. The slightest breeze will topple it. It will collapse, either from an external opponent or from internal unrest. It's analogous to a debt-laden society with unsustainable social programs. It carries too much dead weight, and it will collapse inward upon itself. Surely and for sure! It's obvious from the Torah.

"Voting big government is a formula for destruction and disaster. When big government becomes your god, and you worship paper money as your golden calf, you are screwed. Just like God destroyed those wrong-thinking Israelites, he will surely destroy a country run by wrong-headed big government. Whenever I hear a rabbi talking up big government, I feel like I need to give him a head slap, or a 'Shemah! Listen up! What you are doing is against your religion and you are being galactically stupid.'"

"But the rabbis are your community leaders. How can you say they are stupid?"

"The leadership of today is no different from the leader-ship at Sinai the first time Moses went up the mountain. Those leaders couldn't see the big picture. They wanted immediate creature comfort. They wanted big government and were willing to return to the pharaoh to get their cradle-to-grave care. The social forces that drove those leaders to create the golden calf idol are the same forces that drive today's rabbis to champion big government socialism over freedom. Those are the forces that say to accept dishonest money as your idol, to be immoral and decadent because it's okay. The government will take care of you and smooth over the consequences of your immorality. Today you have free abortions, welfare, rehabilitation and assistance programs of all sort, all brought to you by big government and dishonest money. Today we live under a pharaoh in the form of the big political parties and the Federal Reserve."

"Life is good though. What's so terrible about big government and dishonest money? Can't the government and the Federal Reserve manage the economy and keep things going indefinitely?" Susan threw Marvin a challenge. She saw nothing of consequence from the current structure.

"The problem with the status quo is it is not sustainable. It creates favoritism. People and companies curry favor from government, government creates winners and losers, and wealth gets distorted. Some get extremely rich, others get progressively poorer. This seeds revolution, anarchy, or terrorism. Some societal, political, or external terrorist threat arises. They see discontent. They have money, real money of gold and silver. They pay the disaffected in the pharaoh society to cause radical change, and society changes radically as a result. You get a dictator or a communist politburo, or total anarchy with individual fiefdoms. You lose the America the Founding Fathers structured with the Constitution and precious, honest money. You replace gradual, manageable change with chaotic, disruptive change that capsizes the boat called America."

"So, you're convinced that honest money is the key to perpetuating the nation's future. You are, aren't you? There's no other way?" Susan thought Marvin's great mind could conceive of other ways for society to transact and save.

"There's absolute certainty about it. There is no way for the nation to have a sustainable future without honest weights and measures. Amazingly, the Founding Fathers of the United States got it right when it came to money, prescribing and codifying only gold and silver. Also, when you think it through, the second most important cabinet secretary, after Secretary of State, is Secretary of Treasury. That highlights the importance the founding fathers attributed to honest money. By my reasoning, every president, including Lincoln and the South's Jefferson Davis, who both took people away from honest money, did the great concept of the United States a horrible disservice. From Woodrow Wilson's presidency to the present, all presidents have been traitors against the core principal of honest money upon which the nation was founded. Lincoln and his southern opponent Jeff Davis used greenback and confederate paper money to essentially destroy an entire generation in a terrible, deadly waste that should have been negotiated to a settlement.

"The legions of dead men in the Civil War are testimony to the fact that very few in government actually understand the sanctity of honest money. The Lincoln Memorial is a national monument to a man who hoodwinked millions into believing they didn't need honest money to fight the war. It was an unnecessary war. Slavery would have died a natural death because the industrial age was already replacing it. Hundreds of thousands of lives and families could have been saved through compromise and honest money. The Civil War was a naked power grab by the forces of national unity, which is a necessary step on the march to communism. If the American people understood honest money, they'd audit the Federal Reserve, put it out of business, and go back to honest money as prescribed by God in the Torah and the Founding Fathers in the Constitution. They'd destroy the modern-day rendition of the golden calf, just like God and Moses did. They'd pull the Federal Reserve and the present-day banking system of fiat paper money up by its roots and start over from scratch, back to the way the founders prescribed money.

"Look, Susan, this is important to grasp. It's not a right in the Bill of Rights, not an afterthought. It's a core constitutional principal. It's in Article One, in two places. The Constitution talks about coining money, not printing it. It also prohibits any state from using anything other than gold or silver as money.

Those old guys got it right, Susan. They were smart. They thought this through correctly. Honest money equals a country under God, or for those who are atheists, replace God with goodness. Dishonest money equals no country at all. Without honest money, the end is chaos."

Marvin's brilliance was Susan's primary attraction. Every day with him, she learned things and gained in wisdom in ways that were never possible before. She considered herself fortunate to be with him to her exclusion of all others, including her parents, her daughter, and her former husband.

Some people were just created different than others. Some had no sense of moral duty to family, regardless of how warm and loving the family they came from, regardless of how their siblings were bound to family. A person could have all that warmth surrounding them when growing up, yet still turn out to be amoral, cold, and detached from a moral compass. It's not that they were denied something in the home and hearth department of life, or that they were loved less than another child. They could have even been far more lavished in love because the parents saw that there was no love coming from within the child.

Susan was one such person. All her energy of love and heartfelt goodness was lavished upon Marvin. She craved his acceptance and approval and love, and she was enthralled with her good fortune of being his lover. She continued to gush and pulsate, moaning as her pulsing, cum-thirsty cunt stroked his resurgent shaft with the rising and falling undulations of her pelvis. She didn't want their relationship to ever end.

FOCUS AND DEVELOP

Marvin needed to address Susan's impossible illusion and unbounded ambition before their arrangement became unworkable. She could not become his wife; that was out of the question. Marriage to Eloweiss gave him acceptance and respectability in the Jewish community. Maintaining a shiksa was perfectly acceptable. Many men found monogamy intolerable and needed relief and diversions. As the ancient Romans would say, "De Gustibus non est Desputandum," or "the preferences of an individual are not to be disputed." The present arrangement was workable, but to divorce Eloweiss and marry his shiksa would cost the firm a good measure of business. Clients would castigate him as disloyal to the tribe, and they'd voice their disapproval with their feet; their money would walk, and new business would dry up. It was impossible for him to fulfill Susan's fondest wishes, despite his deep love for her. How could he tell this woman whom he loved more than anyone, even more than his wife and son, that her goal of marriage to him was unattainable?

Marvin, ever the consummate businessman, first sought to define the problem. He needed to keep his shiksa well lubricated, happy in her fucking and her work, while at the same time not having her become cemented solely to him, too one-dimensional, too sticky, so to speak. How could he channel her quest for greater wealth and power without incensing her, without causing a scandal, and without losing her? As much as he loved her, he was wise enough to see that if he married her he'd lose his business and they'd both have nothing. She was excellent at managing people, establishing procedures, and delegating authority for all the office functions. He not only loved her, he also depended on her.

As vice president and corporate secretary for the firm and its subsidiaries, Susan was outstanding. Everything ran smoothly, deadlines were always met, reports were filed accurately, and regulators were pleased with the firm's procedures and its policies regarding handling of client assets. She managed the firm so well she had ample time to satisfy his personal needs. Since Susan affiliated with Sustack Associates, Marvin's life had become a kind of nirvana. It would be business foolish to disturb her office empire and personally foolish to cool her ardor for him. What she excelled at, he reasoned, should be continued, but it was apparent that what she already had was not enough for her.

She shied away from direct money management, from the investment decisions. She had little education in economics, investment theory, money and banking, or technical analysis, so she allowed Marvin to nurture his first love, his true obsession of managing money. He correctly assessed the odds of her leaving the firm were miniscule. His quandary needed to resolve itself in a way that gave her the challenge of obtaining greater money and power, without detracting from her amorous devotion to him, and in a manner which also enhanced him. After some weeks of cogitation, Marvin broached a suggestion most delicate to Susan.

"Would you be interested in doing a little marketing to bring in additional assets to the firm?" He had a mischievous twinkle in his eye, and a slightly devilish smile.

She, a trifle apprehensive about leaving her secure domains of office whip and mistress, answered cautiously, "I can tell when you've been thinking. What is in that mind of yours?"

"I was thinking of John Hilbert and the railroad pension plan. Remember them?"

"Of course, they interviewed here. Did they decide to take their account to Chicago or New York? Have you heard anything?" Susan asked.

"I had a lawyer friend make a discreet inquiry. They're still undecided. They're going to want a second meeting and a detailed presentation."

"Should I get some materials together? What would you like us to show them?"

"Not them, just John. And I thought you could do the presentation solo, if you'd like."

"Me? I don't get into investment strategy and portfolios. I'd be terrible." Susan was taken aback.

"Au contraire, my love. You wouldn't have to get into anything. My thought is that you'd allow John to get into you." Marvin looked at her with a sly upward turn of his lips.

"You mean…?" A long silence followed her puzzlement while she absorbed the implications of Marvin's suggestion. She finally spoke to ask confirmation of what she previously presumed was inconceivable "You want me to fuck him to get the business? That's what you're suggesting, isn't it? You want me to fuck him!" Her jaw dropped as she raised her eyebrows. It suddenly occurred to her that Marvin didn't consider her to be a virtuous woman. He'd caught her completely unawares.

Susan realized their relationship was about to change. It was similar to that moment when she was a girl growing weary of obeying her mother without question. She'd grown tired of giving away her dolls, her dresses, her best things to her younger sisters so her mother could scrimp on expenses. Mother had always said it was because they had to be penurious, but suddenly there was that one day when a different reality awakened in her young mind. It wasn't as Mother said it was at all. They didn't have to be penurious because God wanted it that way. No! They needed to be penurious because it was mother's decision to forgo birth control and have so many children; there was really no other reason!

From that moment on, the relationship she had with her mother changed, but she concealed from her mother that she regarded her differently. Mother wasn't some sort of divine, infallible, all-knowing wise person she idolized as before. Mother was just a regular person like herself, but a bit more stupid. Here it came again, a realization she hadn't considered before.

Marvin was not her perfect, infallible prince. He was, by broaching this idea, unlikely to ever marry her, unless Eloweiss died. Even then, her feminine intuition told her that marriage was off the table, that it never was on the table.

Marvin was her office mate, her fantasy love, but he'd never commit to anything more. No, he saw her as a whore, although she was the only whore he had and the only woman he loved. Nevertheless, he saw her as his whore. Like Mother, Marvin wasn't perfect either. Just as she arrived at a new feeling about Mother, she would come to a new feeling about Marvin. She believed that now as his voice interrupted her thoughts.

"Just hold your thought for a minute." Marvin couched his answer as if the idea originated from Susan. "We're looking at a $40 million account, with a 1 percent management fee and a half percent for expenses. We'd make $600,000 per year. I saw his eyes during your part of the presentation. They were fixated on your legs. He was practically salivating. He's the key guy on their selection committee. Forget the other two. They're rubber stamps. Let's say you call him, tell him there are some additional items you forgot to put into the presentation. You'd like to pick him up and take him out for a drink so you can show them to him."

This was a bitter pill for Susan to swallow. She saw Marvin's plan as a diminishment of their relationship and a degrading of her esteem, but she was in business to make money and she understood she was not an inexpensive mistress. The firm's costs kept rising relentlessly, and performance growth alone shouldn't be depended upon to always provide new revenue. A firm needed new business to grow. She knew she'd come to understand and accept her expanded role in time, and the bitterness she tasted today would be made sweeter by receiving more of what she loved above everything—money and power.

"Then, Marvin, tell me what do I do?" Susan asked him frankly, speaking through her hurt as if it weren't there.

"Then you take him to my rental house. You fix him a cocktail. He'll take care of the rest."

She was skeptical of the whole idea and wondered if Marvin was preparing to get rid of her and end their relationship.

"And why should I want to do this?" She wore a quizzical look, as if she might agree to Marvin's scheme but was unsure of what was in it for her.

He saw his opening and took it.

"You'd be doing it for yourself, for both of us, my love," he continued with a hint of urging. "If you bring in the account, you can have half the fee, right off the top. We'll split the fees fifty-fifty. That's $300,000 per year each."

"And what if he wants me all the time? What happens to us?" She was hoping Marvin would say John couldn't have her after she got the account.

"He won't. He's married with two kids. That's a collar we could use to yank him back at any time. Maybe you'd need to see him once a quarter. After we get our quarterly fee, you could call him and give him a bonus for keeping the account here. Look, if I perform well, he won't be able to take the account away very easily. Once we have it, we should be able to keep it for at least three years before he could stir up some reason to take it elsewhere. Other firms give kickbacks of hunting and fishing trips, and that's no competition for you. We should keep the account for at least three years, which is $600,000 each if I double the money. And if I double the money twice, we'd be making $1.2 million per year, each and every year." Marvin was enthused. She could see excitement in his eyes.

"What about us, Marvin? What about our love?" Susan asked again, in a voice that intoned she was potentially accepting the idea. And she was, but the lingering shock of her new role made her understandably cautious. She was about to become the firm's whore, not just Marvin's, and he was going to pimp for her. No doubt it was probably one of the best deals any whore ever had, but the realization of Marvin seeing her as one, using her as one, weighed heavily upon her. She deeply loved him, and the thought that he was willing to share her hurt her heart. His reply shocked her even more than the proposition.

"Oh, absolutely it will affect us! I'll love you that much more for doing this. I'll wait anxiously to hear you tell me of your conquest. We'll play John like a fiddle. We'll keep him thirsty for you just enough to keep the account, and we'll soon make over a million per year each on just this one account. Let's just look at it as our business, and you'll be giving a large account exceptional service."

Susan saw Marvin in an entirely new light. Perhaps she was hearing the truth. Maybe he needed her to become a whore, and maybe somehow that would cause him to love her even more than he already did. Maybe he was perverted in a way she never suspected. After all, he craved having oral sex with her, and that was unusual for most men. Sometimes he'd spend a solid half hour kissing her pussy. She'd often have to beg him to stop because he enjoyed driving her to near insanity. He had everything to do with making her into a raving sex maniac. Maybe she didn't really understand him after all. She felt she had to assume he was telling her the truth.

She began to think about John. He was handsome enough and appeared to be a virile man. He had excellent manners and showed her every courtesy when he came to the office for the presentations. She thought he was about five or six years older than Marvin. He was a railroader, a working-with-his-hands kind of man. The broad shoulders he carried were the first thing about him she'd noticed. She remembered thinking he must have laid track in the mountains. She imagined him mounting her during that very first instant of greeting, before she retreated into her professional demeanor. Surely he hadn't noticed her reaction to him.

She had a difficult time visualizing him in a union office signing papers and making phone calls. He was an outdoorsy, rugged man's man, uncomfortable and a tad awkward when out of his natural element. She began to imagine herself in her new role and slowly began to warm to it. Maybe she could learn to enjoy her expanded duties as the large account exceptional service provider. She was practically being ordered to experiment with another man! How could any harm come of that? She called John and arranged to pick him up for his additional presentation details that Friday afternoon.

Marvin and Eloweiss would go to synagogue together that same Friday afternoon at sundown to celebrate Shabbat together, just as they had always done through their entire marriage. For Eloweiss, who was very religious, this was the most special time of the week. It was a magical spiritual experience that Marvin dutifully shared with her. From the time of the lighting of the Shabbat candles and the immersion of the light of God, through the *Shema Israel*, the rabbi taking the Torah from the arc and then dancing the Torah through the congregation while the music and the chanting voices sang their joyous praises, Eloweiss felt serene and one with her husband and her God. Then came the words she loved hearing, the words in the Mezuzah on their doorpost, the words that kissed Eloweiss's and Marvin's mouths each day as they went and came into their home:

'You shall love the Lord your God with all your mind, with all your strength, with all your being. Set these words which I command you this day upon your heart. Teach them faithfully to your children. Speak of them in your home and on your way, when you lie down and when you rise up. Bind them as a sign upon your hand, let them be a symbol before your eyes. Inscribe them on the doorposts of your house and on your gates. Be mindful of my mitzvoth and do them, so shall you consecrate yourselves to your God. I, the Lord, am your God who led you out of Egypt to be your God. I, the Lord, am your God.'

Marvin can have his shiksa. That's his business. Eloweiss accepted that no one was a perfect human being, and one should not question the ways Adonai, their God, fated things. She strengthened herself with this acceptance, just as Aaron, the brother of Moses, needed to strengthen himself when God, as mighty Yahweh, took his first two sons. No one could ever know why God did what he did that day, consuming Aaron's sons with a flame as he did. Many speculated they made an improper offering, while others speculated that they disobeyed and went into the Holy of Holies where they were forbidden to go. But a Rabbi she'd studied with when she was a little girl explained it differently, and that was the explanation that gave her strength to accept Marvin's shiksa in their lives.

The Rabbi explained that it was God's will to kill the sons as a lesson to Aaron and to all Jews, that there were things that happen to good people in their lives that were so incomprehensible, so horrible, that we screamed out for an answer, "Why?" But there was no answer to the why. The answer was in the fact that the act happened, that God wills things to happen, good things and bad things too. The lesson to take away from all of it was to accept things as God made them for you to live with. And you must love God with all your heart, mind, and soul, regardless of whatever things happen in your life, just as Aaron did after losing his first two sons. Aaron continued to love God and so would she, Marvin's shiksa notwithstanding.

How many times had Marvin come home later than he used to before he took Susan into the business? She tried to count them at first, then stopped. How many times had he come home to her with the smell of that gentile's filth on him? Sometimes he didn't shower before bed and took that whore's smells on his genitals into bed with her, as if he couldn't be apart from his whore, as if she were more to him than Eloweiss, his wife, was.

Maybe Marvin didn't know she could smell the whore on him. Maybe he was so often into his whore that he didn't know what it was like to not be immersed in her smells anymore. It was a madness Eloweiss lived with. Maybe there was a simpler explanation. At least she could hope there was. Perhaps Marvin worked so hard he just forgot to shower properly and the smell was from days before. She learned to lie to herself to give herself peace.

When services began, a woman from the congregation went up onto the dais and lit the Shabbat candles. Eloweiss watched in tingling anticipation as the woman opened her arms and her whole being to the light of Shabbat and waved the light toward her, motioning it to cover her head, heart, and soul. Eloweiss felt great comfort in the lighting of Shabbat candles. Ordinarily, at that moment, she only thought about welcoming God's holiness into her life, but that night, for some strange reason only a woman's intuition can understand, she also thought of Susan and silently prayed that God's holiness would find its way into her heart and mind as well. She wished the shiksa health and happiness. If she made Marvin happy, there had to be some goodness within her, Eloweiss rationalized.

As the congregants began their prayers with the lighting of candles and the welcoming of God's light, in another part of town Susan was fumbling for the key that opened the door to Marvin's rental. It was pitch black inside. Susan let herself and John Hilbert enter the darkness. She put her arms about his neck and kissed him before she turned on the light.

The rabbi said there were reasons for terrible things that we could not know. Eloweiss must accept, and she did. Marvin was there with her, at services. As the Torah passed by them, she touched it with her prayer book and then kissed her prayer book. Marvin touched his tallit to it and then kissed his tallit. This affirmation of the Torah lifted her heavy heart. She beamed with glory and pride at that moment each Shabbat. Her heart lifted up in joy to God. She, Marvin, and God were all one for that moment and forever. He would go with her again to temple on Saturday as they always did whenever there was a Bar Mitzvah. They would be one with God and their friends, all members of the same congregation, all congregations and all members of the tribe. They were one people with their God. No shiksa could ever have that, could ever share those times of joy with her, and that was enough. God deemed it to be as it was. She suffered a terrible, aching hurt, but she accepted.

As Eloweiss sealed her love of God's word by touching her prayer book to the Torah and then kissing her prayer book, Susan sealed her own destiny as corporate prostitute. She had John in the bedroom, where she deftly undid his belt and unzipped his trousers, then took his penis in her hand and kissed it. She licked it and suckled it briefly to give John a preview of his evening to remember. Susan also was to forever remember the evening, for it was to be a time of definition of who she was, and who she was not. She knew Marvin's heart, that there was this religious barrier she couldn't cross as a person, but she also knew that the love she and Marvin had for one another crossed that barrier. She took great solace in that knowledge as she went to the bar to prepare cocktails for herself and John.

On the other side of town, services were coming to an end. Marvin and Eloweiss joined their voices with the other congregants as they began chanting the Kaddish. For Marvin and Eloweiss, the Kaddish was a somber, reflective moment, praying for the souls of those they so loved and shared life with, their parents, friends, relatives, and all Jews who had ever lived and for all to have everlasting peace. The prayer was for this married couple a deep reaffirmation of who they were and what their values were, as well as a communal remembrance that they would be always loyal to one another.

That same evening, Susan would recall her late husband, Joseph, with scorn and relief to be free of him. She anticipated John's shaft plunging into her while he took her doggie-style. John was very strong. His shaft was a large, full-sized organ that she anxiously anticipated receiving to its fullest extent. She would wriggle and squirm upon it and relish the sensations it provided her, all the while mentally mocking her dearly departed Joseph and even mocking that foolish girl Bonny for being unable to save Joseph from her lusts and desires. Susan felt deliciously wicked and uninhibited as she mixed the drinks.

Before the services broke for the Oneg sweet treats on that Shabbat, Susan was shaking a cold Tanqueray martini for John Hilbert at Marvin's rental home that never rented. Her fantasy of becoming Marvin's wife faded from her priority of ambitions. She reflected with a tinge of remorse for where her life had arrived, the disdain of her parents.

When they looked at her or talked to her, it was always with a painful reaching to her past, to the little girl she once was. Her husband was dead and gone, and she'd sent her daughter away to a school eighteen hundred miles from

Plaintown. What remained in her life was her bondage to Marvin. She was like a beautiful butterfly trapped in a web she'd helped him spin around her. Her parents could see it, feel it. They looked beyond her money, her corporate power, and wondered why this all happened, unable to comprehend how family could mean so little to her.

America was a great mixing place, the melting pot into which many migrated. If Susan's ancestors had never left Ireland, or if they'd stayed in Boston, perhaps she would have never met her Marvin. But they didn't stay—they came West, to Plaintown, and there they "mixed." What did it all mean to have a mixture of cultures, anyway? For each it must somehow be different. Some may live side by side, an Irish family next to a family from Algeria, or France, or a family of Jews whose ancestral roots were in Russia or Prussia, or possibly one could live side by side with a family from Mexico. But one could, in America, be all mixed together this way and yet never interbreed with their neighborhood's other families.

The real mixing came for Susan's and Marvin's families when two people, as individuals, saw something in the other person that they sought to incorporate into themselves. It was a recognition effect. In Marvin's and Susan's mixing, it was sexual attraction, but in many people's it could be a sudden sharing of a laugh or a tear, or a fear or a joy. But likely it was a deeply human thing, perhaps greed, anger, or any other sort of human emotional driver. For Susan, it happened when she no longer saw her mother as the wisest woman to follow. When she saw the Sustacks' way of life, and that Marvin wanted her sexually.

She saw Marvin and wanted to bed him, and vice versa. Once mixed, each person changed from what they were or would have been if left in isolation from the other. In the mishmash, lives were altered, some were enhanced, others less so, and it was up to each affected by the mixing to determine for oneself whether it was all beneficial or detrimental. Some made lemonade of the lemons handed to them, others wallowed in remorse. Regardless, mixing was the essential nature of human life, and life did move forward.

As Marvin and Eloweiss went into the synagogue's recreation hall to partake of sweets and coffee with their closest friends, Susan was at Marvin's rental removing John's tie and unbuttoning his shirt. One martini seemed about right to help him relax. She wore a black silk dress that plunged open in front, inviting a man's mind to vicariously grope her breasts. It featured a raised waistline and flared trim at the bottom in a dazzling revelation of ravenous feminine beauty.

She chose black attire often since Joseph died, as if she could assuage her guilty feelings of being rid of him, but her selections were the opposite style from modest sorrow. Many a man looking at Susan in her black dress would naturally be curious about what she would look like if he could lift it over her head. That sort of exercise wouldn't be necessary that evening. As she led John into the bedroom, she sat him on the bed, stood before him, and let the dress fall to the floor. Her under panties were black silk, a compliment to her dress. She unsnapped her black silk stockings, teddy and unhooked her brazier.

I stole Joseph from Bonny and used him. I seduced Marvin and stole his heart from Eloweiss. I sent my daughter away so I could have more money and more power, and, yes, greater freedom to satisfy my lust. I have to accept myself for what I am, a woman without morals. I am what I was meant to become and I cannot explain it even to myself. As depraved and as shameless as I must be to excel at my new role of office whore, I must see it as the logical progression of who I have become. I must make the most of it and not be timid or cautious. I must love my expanded role. I must find myself loving this man and the others to come, and I must relish my duties to please them. Above all else, tonight I must give John Hilbert the greatest fucking he's ever had in his life.

As Eloweiss took her first bite from a delicious blintz, Susan removed John's trousers, retrieved his penis, and tantalizingly suckled it. While Eloweiss took her first sip of coffee, Susan removed her panties and brazier. John Hilbert would soon experience the most memorable evening of his life. Susan guided his shaft into its new home away from home. She enjoyed her new conquest and lost all inhibitions about sharing her cunt with the firm's clients. She warmed to her expanded role, thoroughly enjoying herself and wanting to service additional top clients. Eloweiss and Susan both had very pleasurable evenings.

A week later, Marvin called John to congratulate him for his wise decision to move the pension plan to Sustack Associates. He assured John that the account would be handled with the utmost in professional management and discreet account services. It was always good business to reassure the client after the sale. For Marvin, it was a perfect outcome, and a problem solved. Susan's new role did not cause Marvin any jealousy; in fact, it drew the two of them even closer to one another, if that were even possible.

In her new capacity, Susan would go on to service two additional large accounts, and she and Marvin evenly split over $6 million each year until Marvin died some twenty years later. They did indeed talk of Susan's bedroom exploits. They were astounded by how desperately their largest clients needed her intimacy and, to Susan's everlasting relief, Marvin did not mislead her. Together, they replicated their clients' most perverse fetishes and laughed about their clients' closest bedroom secrets. Their debaucheries transcended all normal morality. It seemed their sexual bond grew even stronger. Marvin stayed harder longer, while Susan had more frequent orgasms and gushed longer and more readily than before. They made love twice as frequently, often taking entire afternoons away from the office. They traveled out of town together for conferences and intimate playtime. Marvin's management and Susan's cunt were perfectly matched, and the cash register that was Sustack Associates rang loudly and often. The pair remained inseparably intertwined in their deeply shared love for each other and their business.

The world news was disturbing in those years at Sustack's. A small angry man named Hitler was stoking flames of hatred in Germany. There was a civil war raging in Spain, and a murderous dictator named Mussolini was rampaging through Ethiopia. The Japanese invaded Manchuria as the Japanese emperor appeared to be sidelined, reduced to mere puppet status. Their government was controlled by a brilliant military general named Tojo. It appeared all of China and Southeast Asia would succumb to the bloodthirsty Japanese army.

Reports reaching Marvin were unsettling. Jews were being persecuted in Hitler's Germany, and the little angry man seemed interested in territorial conquest. Having solved his problem of focusing Susan on her enhanced career path, Marvin now needed to turn more of his attentions and problem-solving skills upon positioning Sustack's to best benefit from the erupting worldwide turmoil, and to develop the business abilities of his son, David.

DAVID

"Oh, how I hate him! God forgive me for hating, but I do hate him so much. It's so bad, Marvin. Please forgive me, but I spend most of my waking hours thinking how much I hate him. I should not be a mother. I pray to Adonai, Marvin. I pray for him to take back this terrible mistake, to somehow take him back. I wish he'd never been born."

Eloweiss was sobbing softly, sitting in one of the large wing-backed blue velvet chairs in the Sustack living room. Their home was a small, three-bedroom ranch-style in the Rondell Hill neighborhood, built in the early 1920's. Diffused light filtered into the living room through the multicolored block glass that formed a structural wall that framed a bay picture window, where the curtains were discretely drawn closed. The multicolored light rays played upon Marvin's head as he leaned in toward Eloweiss from his matching companion chair. With each passing month, it was becoming more difficult to help his tormented wife find peace. Her hysterical sessions, as Marvin thought of them, used to occur once every two of three months, but now they happened weekly and lasted much longer, going from after the dinner hour into the late evening.

Eloweiss's occasional trembling was recently diagnosed as Parkinson's. She was terminally ill and less and less able to manage their child. Her doctor's prognosis was that she would likely live with the disease for another twenty to thirty years and that she could possibly outlive Marvin, but she would become progressively worse. His son's caregiver would be in need of care as well. Marvin was oft distraught by his domestic trap and tried not to dwell on it. Divorcing her was out of the question, especially now that she was ill. He couldn't stand being anywhere close to her outside of temple, or her "impossible project," as she referred to their son. But he needed, for her sanity's sake, to once again listen and sympathize with her.

"Perhaps we could take him back to see Rabbi Wasserman?" he suggested half-heartedly. He knew she'd reject the idea, but it would give her an opportunity to speak more freely.

"No!" She was emphatic. "The man doesn't understand David at all. Every time we see him he says to be patient and loving, and David will grow out of it. David needs more than a rabbi. He won't tell a rabbi anything. He just stands there with his hands in his pockets and stares down at the floor. He won't even make eye contact with the rabbi, Marvin. He needs something much more. He needs to be constantly supervised. If you don't find someplace to institutionalize him, so help me God, I'm afraid I'll kill him!" Her blubbering jowls shook as she dabbed her tearing eyes with her handkerchief.

"Now, let's not say crazy things. Get a hold of yourself. You must not go on like this. It worsens your condition. I promise I'll look into it and try to come up with something. Just give me a little time. I'll work out a solution."

"That's what you always say!" she screamed at him, distraught and sobbing uncontrollably. "That's what you've said ever since he was two years old! That's what you said when he rubbed dreck all over himself! That's what you said when he used to stand there smiling at me while he pissed on the carpets. You said then he'd grow out of it! Well, now he goes to the bathroom and pisses on the floor, never in the toilet. He's ten years old, Marvin! Listen to me. I am your wife, Marvin! *Shema!*"

Her voice rose in a hoarse, choking shout. "What boy is like him, Marvin? Huh? What boy pulls the wings off flies? What boy pulls legs off grasshoppers, lights butterflies' wings on fire? The magnifying glass you gave him, remember? Well, he's using it, Marvin! He uses it to focus the rays of the sun onto ants! Marvin, your son is spending his afternoon hours burning ants! Who does that?" She was nearly hysterical. There was silence for a few minutes before she resumed.

Her voice grew soft, resigned to exasperation, almost a whisper. "He plays with matches, Marvin. Where he gets them, I don't know. If he burns our house down, how's that going to look for your business? How's that going to make people feel about having their money with you and your shiksa whore? Think about it, Marvin. Think about it! And there's more," she continued with a stronger voice. "He kicks at dogs and cats. He spits on the other children. Parents tell me things almost every day. They don't want their children anywhere near him. He punches them. He took a kitchen knife, Marvin. I can't watch him every minute. He tried to stab little Kenny! He's thrown rocks at windows, and just today, he broke one of Mrs. Nelson's bedroom windows. Of course he denied it, but she said she saw him playing around her house just before it happened.

"You need to worry about him, Marvin. Lately he and Hirsch have been seen playing in the narrow strip between our garage and the Keegans'. Well, he and Hirsch have been back there, taking their pants down and playing with each other's little weasels, and that's not the worst of it. There's more. Mrs. Trout, the gentile woman from down the street, with the little blonde girl who wears pigtails, well, she came here yesterday and just pounded on our front door!"

"What did she want?" Marvin was feeling besieged. He was now sipping on a gin and tonic he'd fixed himself.

"She claims her daughter, little Betty Trout, was playing behind the garage with David and Hirsh. She said the boys pushed her to the ground and punched her." Eloweiss's eyes were watering as if she knew there was trouble for her son for all his life to come. She didn't want to talk about it, yet she must. Things had to be said. She reached out to her husband. Marvin knew from that gesture that she was deeply troubled.

"Well, now. It might not be true. You know kids make stuff up all the time." Marvin voiced his paternalistic skepticism, hoping to shield his son.

"No, Marvin. No! It's true, all right. David did something much worse than punch that little girl." She was bawling like a wounded cow. She couldn't get a hold of herself.

Marvin became frightened of the unknown. "What? Tell me! Stop holding back."

Eloweiss halted her bawling enough to get the words out in her low whisper. "Marvin, David bit that little girl. He bit her hard, with his teeth."

Marvin's jaw dropped. Violence never solved anything. It was against everything he held descent and good. "Did he draw any blood?" he asked, hoping not to hear the worst.

"Oh, yes, he sure did." Eloweiss held her head in her hand and nodded slowly.

"Well, where did he bite her? Was it on her finger?" Marvin was still a bit dismissive of the significance of this revelation, as if fingers were gratuitous extra parts that God just stuck on people for no good reason. This was the bait Eloweiss was just itching to hit, like a bass fish slamming into a frog on the surface.

"Oh! No, Marvin, not on her finger!" She was shouting loudly, as if he were five blocks down the street and her voice needed to carry her message the distance. "David bit little Betty Trout on her leg. And not just anywhere on her leg! He bit her right up close, right next to her pussy! He tried to bite off the little girl's pussy! Your son is a monster. I can't cope with him anymore. David is a sick human being. It's got nothing to do with how we are raising him. He's just a nasty, evil, disgusting little creep. I am so sorry he is our son, and I do mean it when I say I wish he were dead. May God forgive me, but I wish he had never happened. God should find a way to take him back. Marvin, God made a mistake here. David should have never been born."

"Look, hopefully it's just a physical condition of some kind. Maybe it's the mastoids he has in his ears." Marvin tried to be hopeful, wishing the hope would become contagious. "The doctor said he might get pain in his ears. Maybe he tries to do things to take his mind off the pain? The doctor said—"

Eloweiss became enraged, cutting Marvin off in mid-sentence. She hated when her supposedly intelligent husband reasoned things as if he were a retarded simpleton. She went into her she-bear roar and shout mode. "Marvin, I don't give a fucking shit what that fucking quack doctor said!"

Marvin quaked in terror at her outburst. Most men shrunk into mice when a woman erupted suddenly. Marvin, for all his stature and leadership in the community, was no exception.

Eloweiss continued. "Marvin, pain in his ears does not make him piss on floors or try to hurt or kill everything that lives. He was laughing when he was playing with Hirsh's prick. There was no pain. Do you really believe mastoids make a boy try to take a bite out of a little girl's pussy? Do you? Show me in a medical book! You can't show me anywhere where little boys who have mastoids want to take bites out of little girls' pussies! Mrs. Trout brought the little girl to me. I saw the bite mark, and I saw the blood running down her leg. The poor little girl was traumatized. His ears must not hurt that badly. It's all a big phony act he puts over on us. He does that screaming, holding-his-ears routine whenever he can't have his way or whenever he wants attention. Take him to another doctor, a specialist in ears, whatever! Just do something before I lose my mind and kill him! I mean it, Marvin. I am done with our little monster. Done and done!"

Marvin was in full retreat. "All right, tomorrow I'll make some calls. I'll find the best ear man here or in Chicago, and we'll see if it's the ears."

"And if it's not the ears? We're not doing this 'let Eloweiss handle it' shit anymore, Marvin. I'm telling you. I'm done with him!"

She was shouting herself hoarse. Finally, she slumped back into her chair, completely exhausted. She was the picture of a woman to be pitied. For all his dislike of her, his contempt for her grotesque body, and despite his passions for Susan and his priorities that had placed her and their son far below his business, he felt a genuine pity for Eloweiss. Many of her travails were foisted upon her by him and their parents, and in a deeply human way he understood her and loved her as he could love no other.

It was at Marvin's insistence that they lived there, on Plaintown's East Side, so they and little David could better assimilate with the gentile Christians. Marvin wanted his son to grow up away from the cloistered community that hugged itself to the Shalom Conservative Synagogue on the West Side.

Now a doubt flickered across his mind. What if he'd made a mistake? What happened behind the garage? What made David so violent? And why was that little girl's vagina exposed? Were the boys demonstrating how hard it was for them to assimilate with the gentiles? He couldn't ask David or Hirsh. He didn't think that would produce the truth, as they'd likely just stay silent. He resolved to deal with what was manageable for the time being. He'd take David to an ear specialist, and he'd look into a boarding school for boys. Securities, clients, women, he could manage. He resigned himself to the fact that he did not understand how to manage his son.

Unbeknownst to Marvin and Eloweiss, David was just around the corner, listening in the hall. The boy had excellent hearing and was taking in the entire discussion from the time he first heard his mother say she hated him and wished he'd never been born. As he listened, he had a hard time holding back his urge to burst out laughing at them. He thought life was one great joke, and the world's creatures were there for his pleasure to maim and torture.

GROOMING DAVID

From the moment of David's birth, Marvin dreamed of having his son follow in his footsteps. At the infant's bris, after the circumcision was completed by the mohel, Marvin kissed David's forehead and held him aloft for the world to see.

"Meet David, my son, descended from kings, my successor to come and a glorious man to become, who will become a king in his own right."

By his sixth birthday, David's behaviors set Marvin wondering. The boy was fiercely independent and headstrong, even defiant toward his parents. His open defiance of Eloweiss's authority caused her unending cycles of consternation, exasperation, and resignation, and David's antics were taking a toll on her health. Perhaps these were the traits of a king, Marvin rationalized, always willing to imagine the best possible outcome for his protégé. Then again, David's behaviors could not be trusted to self-cultivation.

Historically, there were many examples of despotic kings. Most were eminently successful as they extracted tributes from those they vanquished and terrorized their subjects. Marvin could see that David would have made a great Caesar or Genghis Khan, but the world he would grow into would be a democratic society, a capitalist system framing a corporate America. Perhaps his son's development should be channeled into public service and politics? Marvin seriously pondered the issue, for David's natural proclivity was to be a dictatorial tyrant who brutalizes his subjects. When Marvin looked into David's eyes, he hoped he'd see some spark of joy, some childish happiness. Instead, deep into those dull gray pools, all Marvin saw was a vacant anger, a cold, vacuous, inhuman distance from him and everyone else. Marvin was vexed.

The political world beckoned David. Although the boy was too young to understand how his own tendencies telegraphed the venue into which his development might best be channeled, Marvin clearly recognized the perfect match. But allowing David his natural pursuit would deny Marvin his own cherished goal of having his son working with him in the business. He wanted to groom David and share with him all he'd learned over the years. He yearned to leave a legacy firm that would survive him and continue indefinitely. Marvin, the great problem solver, correctly focused on the problem first, as was his scientific approach to these challenges.

There needed to be a way, a venue, that accommodated David's ruthless, domineering personality and facilitated Marvin's dreams of nepotism. Marvin set upon a long-term plan for David, recognizing one key to being a successful nepotist was to start work on one's protégé as early as possible.

Socializing David to a passable level was a critical first objective. Pissing on floors, torturing insects, biting people, screaming inconsolably, and flaunting homosexual tendencies would not likely serve his son well in the investment advisory business.

Each client has a unique and confidential relationship with their advisor. Sometimes this could be a contact, relationship sort of person, but in most cases the client would insist upon a direct communication with their portfolio manager. No matter how expert and exhausting the analysis, how sound the advice, or how gratifying the results, it was inevitable that there would be periods of underperformance. Most clients, assuming their advisor was a civilized, well-meaning sort of person, would weather rough seas with the advisor, even through elongated storms, for the inevitable sunny days that follow. However, if the client ever discerned their advisor was some sort of misanthropic sociopath, the client would likely move their money elsewhere.

Client's greed and fear were ultimately determining factors for many of them. Some could had the most unbalanced nutcase managing their money, and as long as results were good, they'd ignore the personality of their manager. Others would move money at the slightest hint of a darkening sky, regardless of the integrity of the manager or the soundness of the investment strategy. Many—in fact, likely the majority of advisory clients—did not understand their own emotions in the least. Many would document that they could tolerate considerable risks and valuation fluctuations because, in the abstract when they were documenting these issues, they truly believed they could. This was natural enough because of greed.

All investors knew that, to get superior results, they must accept risks of losses; thus, they signed aboard with bravado. They were entirely different personas when their accounts declined, even if the accounts rose beforehand. They then became fearful and antagonistic, or snarky. Counseling patience and explaining the long-term rewards likely to come from a chosen strategy would avail to naught when emotions displace reason. Should the client have any inkling that their advisor was somehow an alteration of the fair-haired smiling face they first trusted, there would be no quarter brooked. Assets liquidated and fled. There was a "take no prisoners" attitude as they left, even though the advisor designed a portfolio exactly according to their instructions. For many it was impossible to have a decline or loss without affixing the blame on someone other than themselves.

David's behaviors had to be corrected, unlearned, masked, or somehow made unapparent to clients, or he would never be suitable in a client-advisory relationship. Marvin had nightmares where he saw David punching clients in their noses, spitting at them, throwing their papers at them, or even kicking them. In one dream, David tore the dress off an older female client with a large trust and threw hot coffee on her underpants, then kicked her posterior. Clearly, his dreams were trying to tell him something. He needed to be able to sleep peacefully before he could turn David loose on clients.

Marvin did not have the time, patience, skill sets, or personal inclination to invest a personal effort and precious time in his "civilizing David" project, as he referred to it. Thus, during the years when a son most wants to look up to a father, when the son seeks to have a bond, to have the big guy show him the ways of the world, when the boy in his heart of hearts hopes his father will come to him and talk with him about the things he's doing wrong, Marvin just watched David from a distance.

Maybe it was just the vestiges of the old Hassidic cultures, where the fathers didn't think sons were worthy of being spoken to until they were full-grown men. David couldn't know that, if that's what it was. All David knew for sure was Marvin was too busy for him, yet he often heard with his excellent hearing his mother muttering under her breath about Marvin having time for "that whore." David had to ask Hirsh to tell him what a whore was. When Hirsh told him, David decided his father had no time or love for him or his mother. David began hating all women, even little girls. Betty Trout was the first to reap his anger, but she would not be the last.

There would be boarding schools, camps, doctors, sessions with rabbis, and more doctors for David, but not much time with his father. Marvin's interests were drawn to financial statements, economics, markets, asset accumulation, and his unquenchable passion for Susan. In Marvin's fantasized naivety, David would go into some abstracted project box at the age of six and come out the other end as a finished, polished adult, ready to work shoulder to shoulder with Dad at age twenty-one.

Initially, Marvin sent David to live during the week with a trusted rabbi in Plaintown's immigrant neighborhood. The boy was enrolled in a Yeshiva for Talmud and Torah Studies School, where he received a rigorous instruction in Orthodox Judaism in the mornings and basic school studies in the afternoons. At the rabbi's insistence, David was also given a dog, a male collie. The rabbi's hope was that the boy would receive some measure of unconditional love from the dog that he seemed unable to feel from his parents. All the initial reports from the rabbi and the school were encouraging. The consensus of his teachers was that David was doing well. He did average work and was rated in the middle of his class.

In actuality, David was learning to conceal. He glimpsed that others learned the 619 mitzvahs because they intended to follow them, and these others would naturally assume that he, like them, would do the same. Nothing was further from the truth. David understood early on that if he could get someone to give him something of value presently, in exchange for his promise to return his end of the bargain later, most people would assume, to their detriment, that he would uphold his part of the bargain. David's intent was to apply the mitzvahs in reverse.

While home from school on vacation, David and his friend Hirsch set upon their neighborhood. They went knocking on doors telling the housewives they were taking orders for Boy Scout cookies. They wore no Boy Scout uniforms. They weren't Boy Scouts. The Boy Scouts didn't even bake cookies, but that did not deter these intrepid souls. Taking their cue from P.T. Barnum's quote, "There's a sucker born every minute!" the boys raised over a hundred dollars. They dutifully took down the housewives' names, how many and what kind of cookies they wanted, and promised they'd have their cookies delivered in about two or three weeks.

After about a month's time, Eloweiss and Hirsch's mother began receiving calls from neighborhood housewives asking when the Boy Scouts were going to deliver their cookies. The boys couldn't give the money back. They'd spent it on candy, cookies for themselves, movies, soda pop, and arcade games. They also burned their order lists, so there was no way to trace to whom and for how much refunds were due. The boys claimed they only raised ten dollars, but they had no credibility with their parents or the miffed housewives. David blamed Hirsch for the idea, and Hirsch blamed David. The parents never could sort out who was telling the truth, but they made restitution to the housewives. For the remainder of his vacation, David was confined to the backyard. Often enough, Eloweiss could hear him crying softly while he sat on the ground hugging his dog. That was Eloweiss's first inkling that, in addition to his general dislike for the human species, David also didn't like David.

Incorrigible, David's next outbound deportment was to a youth mountain camp near Rocky Mountain National Park. His dislike for the great outdoors was palpable. He thought the mountains were stupid; the animals were boring; the trees, flowers, and grasses were a major annoyance. He refused to get out of bed for breakfast call, and then he bit another boy's ear, causing it to bleed and sending David to confinement in the recreation hall for two days. That suited him perfectly because he hated hiking about outdoors and looking at all the glories of nature. He told his fellow campers that nature made him want to throw up. His final camp escapade was to get himself purposely lost on a simple daytime nature walk. One of the counselors drove David back to Plaintown, back to Eloweiss.

Marvin's goal to socialize his son received its final coffin nail while David was attending a Hebrew outdoor camp for troubled boys in Arizona. His antics generally paralleled his behavior at the Rocky Mountain camp, only it wasn't practical for a counselor to drive him home to Plaintown from a ranch near the Mexican border. To go home, David needed to dramatically escalate his defiance.

A simple confidence-building exercise the camp employed was to have the boys walk on a rudimentary foot bridge across a six-foot-deep gully. The bridge had rope handrails and wooden planks set upon a taut rope floor, and it swayed slightly as the boys walked across. Last in his group to cross, David deliberately swung hard back and forth on one of the rope handrails. He succeeded in making the bridge swing with abnormally high amplitude, straining the floor ropes at the top of the swing. Then, screaming as if in a panic, he flung himself off the bridge just as it reached the top of its arc of travel. David succeeded in breaking his arm in this self-destructive stunt. He was sent back to Plaintown, back to Eloweiss.

David spent the rest of his adolescence with the West Side rabbi and received schooling at the Torah school Paul was a religious studies classmate of David's. He was a superior student and he took a disliking to David; but he gained David's confidence in order to play a trick on him. He pretended to listen to David relate his horror at what his mother did to his father with her pussy. He assured David that pussies were something to be enjoyed and he promised to set David up with a very understanding girl named Connie. At the appointed time when her parents were away Paul took David to the farm where Connie lived. She was a winsome lass with a compelling anatomy and a willing smile.

"Hello David. Paul told me all about you. He was right. You are very handsome. You don't need to be shy with me. Let's go to the tack room in the barn. Follow me."

"Paul said you'd like to make love with me because I'm a virgin. Is that really true?"

"Sure it's true, David. I want to be your first!" She smiled a suggestive smile that held out the promise of a naughty treat for David.

David and Connie walked hand in hand to the tack room. It was a lovely spring day. The smell of sweet freshly mowed grass was in the air. *Paul's a good friend to fix me up with a girl who wants to do it. I'm afraid of girls, but if one of them is willing to have sex with me I feel I'd disappoint Paul if I didn't to give it a try.*

"Here we are at the tack room. I want this to be perfect for you David. Just stand here while I tie this blindfold over your eyes." Connie produced a large piece of cloth and tied it tightly over David's eyes. "Now, I want you to stand here while I get undressed."

David did as he was told while Connie went into the tool shed. After a moment she called to him from inside the shed. "David. I'm naked in here. I want you to keep your blindfold on and take your clothes off so I can see you naked." Again, David did as he was told. "Now, David, I want you to walk forward very slowly. I will guide your steps until you are standing right in front of me. That's it, David. Keep walking forward. Now hold your arms out in front of you. You're soon going to touch me. That's good. That's very good." Again, David did as he was told.

Suddenly, a pair of arms grabbed David and pushed him forward. He fell headfirst into the pigsty at Connie's farm. As he struggled to sit upright Connie, several other girls and a dozen of his classmates were leaning over the rails of the sty and laughing at him. "Pig, hog boy, oink, oink, sue e. pig boy, fatso, hog face, you stink. Phew," were called out as David was made the butt of their cruel joke. David took off his blindfold and saw his situation for what it was. Paul had befriended him in order to make a fool of him.

David didn't cry nor did he laugh at himself. He just sat there without speaking, but he inwardly seethed with rage and hatred. All the feelings of loneliness he had as a child rushed back to him with more force than ever. Eventually the other young teens stopped their name calling and their laughing, but David didn't move. He didn't look up at them. He never said a word. Something profoundly transformative took place in David's personality that day. He crossed over the threshold that separated his prankish tricks and sadistic behaviors towards insects into the behavior of a determined vengeful sociopath. As he sat there up to his waist in pig waste he promised himself that he would never again allow himself to trust anyone; and that he would, in time get revenge on all the pranksters. He would tear pages from their books when they weren't guarded, shower his piss on their clothes in their lockers when they were in gymnasium, slash their bicycle tires, steal their bicycles and sell them, and pour glue in their snow boots. And, he vowed that he would never forget the lesson of that day. He would always be a loner out to get everybody else. No evil that he could inflict upon another human being would be off limits. He convinced himself that he could never trust anyone, not his parents, or his classmates, or any woman. He liked the budding feeling of hatred toward his fellow man that grew from the revenge seed within him and he promised himself that he would nurture it and perfect it and grow to love it. He resolved to commit himself to the hatred of all other humans. Demeaning others, mocking and belittling their lives and pursuits, destroying their businesses and families and in all possible ways bringing harm to them would henceforth be his source of satisfaction.

Book learning never held much interest for David outside of his religious studies and he struggled with his academics through his public high school years He simply couldn't see how he could use any of the secular subjects to help him take advantage of others. Therefore he saw no value in learning the subject matter. He put in enough effort to get passable grades but nothing better. He and Hirsch were in most of their classes together. They continued their bad influence on each other, devising ways to cheat on exams and bribing other students to do their homework papers for them. One ninth grade civics teacher, Mrs. Harney, took a particular disliking to David.

"David. Since you seem to be so interested in talking to Hirsch while I'm talking about the Constitution and the Bill of Rights, I suppose you know all these things already. So, please stand up here next to me in front of the class and you and I will show the class how much you know about the subject matter."

David grudgingly walked to the front of the class and stood with his hands in his pockets.

"Now then, David, recite for the class, since you know so much, each of the ten rights in the Bill of Rights." Mrs. Harney stood with hands akimbo, holding a ruler in the hand that rested on her left hip.

"I don't know them." David smirked.

"Hold out your hand, David." David did as instructed. Then, what David never imagined would happen, happened. Mrs. Harney slammed her ruler down hard on his right hand causing David to cry out I pain. "Now, David. Please tell us What Article One of the Constitution is about." Again, David replied that he didn't know. Mrs. Harney again instructed him to hold out his hand, this time his left, and again she slammed his hand with her ruler causing him to scream in pain. "Now, David. Stand still while I place upon your head this dunce cap." Mrs. Harney took a two foot tall cone shaped headpiece from her classroom closet and placed it upon David's head. It was the sort of class embarrassment that a teacher might mete out to an elementary school student, but Mrs. Harney did it to David. Many in the class laughed at him while Mrs. Harney ordered him to sit in the corner in front of the class, facing the class.

Mrs. Harney's attempt to focus David on his school work had unintended consequences. It drove David deeper into his sociopathic outlook on others, particularly women and people in authority. Inwardly, David seethed in raging hatred for Mrs. Harney. He plotted revenge to destroy his teacher. After an interlude where Mrs. Harney believed David was making progress with his studies, some bizarre things happened. One day, when she noticed a foul smell coming from her teacher's desk, she opened her drawers to discover that someone had deposited urine in each drawer. Her papers were ruined. The desk needed to be removed and sanitized. A week passed. She walked out on her front porch on her way to school to discover that someone had thrown a bucket of red paint all over her door, porch, and the exterior walls of her house.

About a week later, as she walked to the school building she noticed a crowd of youngsters standing about the flagpole, looking up. Horror of horrors! There was a cat hung dead by its neck from the flagpole where the American flag should have been. And, gasp! It was Boo Boo, her beloved calico cat! Who would do such a dastardly deed? Who could possibly be so cruel as to harm a defenseless adorable animal? How vile! How despicable! She was horrified into a state of shock. She fell to her hands and knees weeping inconsolably and blubbering incoherently for her loving cat, imagining her animal's terrible final struggles. Shock overcame her constitution and she vomited on the sidewalk in front of the flagpole. David watched the scene from a distance. His faint smile and far away gaze revealed his inner glow of satisfaction. She suspected these foul deeds were David's work, even caused him to be investigated by the school's principal, but he denied any knowledge of them and nothing was ever proven. David had slipped deeper into his sociopathic pathology. With these deeds he crossed another barrier into an even lower level of base conduct. He would willfully use filth, property destruction and the heinous murder of other mammals to demean and destroy his enemies. David's sociopathic behavior was sinking lower, plunging toward its bottom boundary. He embraced depravity and mastered the advantages of patience, stealth and secrecy.

And, his tactics worked. Hatred expressed in depraved deeds got results for David. Mrs. Harney requested and received a transfer to another school in the district, and from then on all teachers handled David with kid gloves. He always earned passing grades on his papers and tests whether he knew the materials or not.

Later, David attended the prestigious Plaintown University, where he took up the study of public administration in defiance of his father's exhortations to learn accounting, finance, economics, money and banking, and investments. He did poorly but just enough to earn a bachelor's degree in six years. Book learning never held much interest for him. By now Marvin was near exasperation with his son. He'd learned nothing about investing or any of the disciplines related to investing in six years at an expensive private college for which Marvin footed the tuition bills and the costs of David's room and board. It was time to take control of David.

"We're going to be making some serious changes in your life style. I've paid for your college and now you've been out of school for over a year. You say you have no interest in investing, but you seek no employment elsewhere and you choose to continue living at my expense. So, I'm going to give you a choice. If you wish to have me continue supporting you, you will do the following. You will come to this office each day at 9AM sharp and you will go to the office I provide for you and you will sit in that office all day and you will study investment subjects. I will give you the books I want you to read and you will read them. I will ask you about them and we will discuss them. If you do not wish to do this then your monies from me will stop and I care not what happens to you.

You may move to another country for all I care. I will have nothing to do with you. You will not inherit and you will no longer be welcome in my home except to see your mother if you ever choose to see her. If you choose to come to the office you will not interfere with the members of the office staff. You will at all times respect my privacy, Mrs. Maloney's privacy, and the privacy of all the employees.

"Second, you will marry a woman and live under the same roof with her. I understand that you are a homosexual, but that is not acceptable in the image of many investors and it is not acceptable in my firm. I have arranged with a good family in Chicago for a woman who will marry you. She is, from what I am told, a lesbian woman who has no interest in having sex with you or any other man. Her family wishes that she leave their household and make a life for herself. She is a generally quiet, docile and plain featured woman who will make no manly demands upon you. She will frequently be away from you to spend time with her girl friends, but she has agreed that she will keep house for you and she will cook for you. That is all I know about her except she likes to read and is somewhat religious; she also likes to ride horses and travel occasionally. You will share the same bed with her for appearances sake, and I will get you a super large California King sized bed so you each have your own space in the one bedroom apartment where I pay your rent. When you advance enough in the company I will give you enough money to buy a house so you and she can have separate bedrooms if you so choose. Remember always, I am your father and you are my son. I make the rules here and you will follow them or you will be dismissed and cut off from me. You either accept my terms now, David, or you leave me and we will not speak again." David accepted his father's terms, but inwardly he felt humiliated and he chafed at his new controls. He resented sharing his bed with a woman but out of necessity he acquiesced.

During David's investment learning years, war broke out in Europe. European Jewry was about to be eradicated by Hitler. Because of his reputation for shrewdness in market economics, Marvin was summoned by the War Department to develop gasoline and other vital materials' rationing plans to ensure the military could build up its readiness for America's inevitable entry into World War II. Marvin designed the most efficient use of resources he could, which helped put America on a wartime footing and positioned the military with sufficient supplies to engage in offensive battles and win them. The time Marvin and David had available for each other diminished in large measure due to their mutual dislike and in lesser measure due to the convenient exigencies of war.

With his high-level contacts in the Roosevelt administration, Marvin gained access to the diplomatic contacts that reached into Germany through Switzerland. He understood the plight of the Jews trying to escape the Holocaust. He used his capital and borrowed all he could to finance those Jews who could pay, in diamonds, for their escape from Hitler's clutches. He, with diplomatic help, ferreted out those few Nazis who would take bribes to look the other way when questionable papers were presented to them. Marvin did business on the basis of the American value of diamonds on the wholesale market.

At first, his returns were quite good. He fronted the bribe money and sold the diamonds advanced from the Jew before he made it possible for the Jew's escape to Switzerland. Marvin's initial return in the early months was 5 percent per month, which is excellent for any venture, but as the Holocaust gained momentum, as the gates out of Germany were closing, his returns rose to an outstanding 100 percent per month. The price for a Jew to save his or her life rose exponentially. Alas, few could pay Marvin's price. Most Jews perished.

Marvin would later explain to David that it was essential for every Jew, everywhere in the world, even in America, to have several pairs of shoes with hollow heels in which to hide diamonds in case one needed to bribe one's way out of a country that closed its gates. He swore often to David that the most important thing he could teach him as a father was that all societies had a dangerous undercurrent of anti-Semitism coursing through them. What seemed democratic and stable one day could turn anti-Semitic the next. Usually, it happened when the economy was stressed, and it took a noble people to forgo blaming Jews for their own excesses that brought them to hard times in the first place. Lack of education in the populace naturally bred anti-Semitism, so he encouraged David to always seek to advance his education as well.

Marvin told David that anti-Semitism would surly arise in America because of the Federal Reserve Bank and the deficit spending engendered by Keynesian economics. There would come a time that the massive build of debt caused by such a monetary system would inevitably lead to a collapse and a prolonged depression in the United States. The people would not be capable of understanding the cause of this hell when it was finally unleashed upon them. It was inconceivable to Marvin that Americans would be able to affix blame where it properly belonged, upon Woodrow Wilson, the Federal Reserve banking system, and all the government administrations and banking institutions that operated within this unconstitutional system. America was in dire peril because the nation hadn't allowed natural forces to cleanse unserviceable debt from the nation's banks or the government. Even worse, the government's policy was to ensnare other nations into the same debt-based system through cross-border agreements for dollar reserve currency status and currency swap lines between

allied central banks. This convoluted mishmash of intercon-
nected agreements insured a worldwide domino-like collapse
where banks and nations would all someday, nearly simultaneously, fail.

There were never enough bribable channels available to
accommodate the volumes of people trying to escape Germany.
Those taking bribes were occasionally caught and summarily
shot, and their personal and family wealth confiscated by
Hitler. By war's end, Marvin counted himself as one of the ten
wealthiest Jews in Plaintown. His wealth from the diamond
chain operation increased twenty-thousand-fold from what he
had prior to his involvement with the government, and that did
not include over three thousand gem-quality diamonds, which
he retained in a secret place that only he knew about.

From the late 1930s into the 1950s, both Eloweiss and
Susan were seen sporting a sizeable array of diamond
accessories with their wardrobes. Eloweiss went for the huge
rocks worn on the fingers and oversized diamond earrings,
while Susan opted for a gorgeous diamond necklace choker and
another necklace that sported a huge fifty-carat pearl-shaped
diamond on a silver chain. She suspended the rock between her
breasts about one-third of the way down her cleavage channel.

When Susan wore the gem in her executive presentations
to clients, it sent a subtle message that exceptional account
service was available, but expensive. The tactic worked, three
large accounts doubling their assets under management. Oddly,
two of her newest large accounts rewarded her for her services
from union and corporate funds beyond what their agreements
required. John sent her a mink coat, and another key money
placer sent her a lynx coat. Both men justified the expense to
their boards by stating that it would be unacceptable for their
exceptional service representative to be cold during Plaintown's
chilly evenings.

Susan wore her stunning diamond when she fucked her clients, who were filled with more lust for her than ever before. No man wanted to be outdone by any other, each seeking to be her favored lover. The price to fuck Susan skyrocketed, and management fees were increased from 1 percent to 2 percent. Every client paid the increased freight and none defected. Fucking Susan was seen as a prestigious honor by these men, and she and Marvin were soon splitting $20 million each and every year.

In those days, there were few regulatory oversights for such practices. Brokers gave sailboats and hunting trips to bankers, villas to top executives who placed investment banking business, and lavish trips for those further down the food chain. Susan often fulfilled her initial dream of making love with Marvin in front of the massive fireplace in the rental. Now she lay victorious upon furs given to her by men she held in secret contempt while Marvin had intercourse with her.

Many winter evenings she laid there naked while the flames from the fireplace flicked glowing orange mixed with black shadows across her irresistible body. Marvin loved this scene and loved her more in her new role as a greedy, calculating, ravenous whore. While he often licked her clitoris by these crackling flames, he finally felt he had the perfect relationship with the woman he'd shaped to reach her fullest potential. He was so proud of her and so deeply in love with her now, he could never have any life without her. Together they reveled in her triumphs, symbolized by her delicious cunt spread widely open upon the fur gifts offered up by her conquests.

By the late 1950s, there was a significant change in the investment landscape. The markets had finally shrugged off the disastrous losses of the depression years. The second World War and the Korean War ended. The public's confidence was improving and, most intriguing to Marvin, there was a burgeoning new source of investing funds and an increasingly accepted way of capturing those funds. The mutual fund industry, before that time, was a kind of investment backwater area for small-saver types who invested pittances each month. Now, the industry found itself ideally positioned to benefit from changes taking place in the insurance industry. A number of upstart insurance companies were marketing "Buy Term Insurance, Invest the Difference" programs. The upstarts were lowering insurance premium costs compared with the premium costs associated with traditional whole life policies, which included an investment and cash value component. Business was about to boom in this budding venue, and Marvin could see it clearly.

Many insurance sales organizations were realizing juicy commissions by cannibalizing whole life policies' assets and placing those cash values in investments, but those looking to enter the market needed to overcome a small obstacle. To make investment transactions, these insurance salesmen needed to be securities licensed.

Marvin pounced, quickly incorporating a mutual fund organization comprising a fund, a broker-dealer to sell its shares, and an investment advisor to manage the fund, thus providing a fee-based income stream from an investment product. He solicited many small- and midsized insurance companies and offered to sponsor their sales representatives for securities' licenses, provided that, when an insurance competitor's whole life policy was cannibalized, the insurance proceeds would be invested in his new fund. It was a very attractive commission proposition for the participating insurance companies and an easy sale for their freshly licensed representatives.

Marvin's advisory firm did spectacularly well managing wealthy individuals, pension plans, and bank trust department assets. The Sustack Associates advisory firm could have managed the new mutual fund, but by starting a second advisory firm, Marvin's goal of having a place for David beside him in the investment business could be realized.

The new organization Marvin created would be ideally suited for David. The clients of a mutual fund, or shareholders, rarely or never met their portfolio manager. Most didn't even know the manager's name. David could manage other peoples' monies and they'd never have to know anything about him! He still exhibited little more than a passing interest in investments, or any of the disciplines associated with investing, but that didn't matter; Marvin would show David some rudimentary tools for deciding when to get into or out of markets. In the ten to twenty years of life he had remaining, Marvin believed he could teach David enough so his son could survive and make a successful living after Marvin's death. David was already in his mid-thirties and had accomplished absolutely nothing with his life except obtaining two collegiate degrees in public administration, which Marvin considered completely useless.

Marvin rented additional office space and shared staff with his son and the new fund complex. He gave numerous sales talks to the newly licensed sales representatives of the fund's broker-dealer charged with distributing its shares. Monies for management began to flow into the new venture. Until shortly before his death, Marvin controlled the fund's advisory company with voting-class X shares, while David was given non-voting-class Z shares. Marvin paid David a living wage and spent countless hours drilling him on basic investment principals. These sessions were often frustrating for Marvin and often resented by David, who wanted to do things his way but didn't understand the different market cycles, interest rate cycles, the way institutions configured their assets and liabilities, and a whole host of other details pertinent to being a successful investor. Still, Marvin doggedly pushed onward.

Susan was in her early forties, still able to keep the Sustack Associates firm running like a smoothly functioning Swiss watch and still maintaining her allure to the firm's largest clients, who relished her exceptional services. She kept her face and body looking ten years younger than she was, and her cunt was more prized by large clients than ever.

David harbored resentment toward Susan dating back to his childhood. He saw how her involvement with his father was a continuing source of torment for his mother—not that he had warm feelings toward Eloweiss. He merely disliked her less than he disliked Susan. David enjoyed taunting Susan and challenging her office authority, frequently giving instructions to her staff that contradicted her own.

David also took a disliking to Mrs. Rodriguez, the Hispanic woman who was the main receptionist for the firm. She had been there fifteen years before David's father gave him his office. Mrs. Rodriguez did not like her legs to show and preferred to wear pants to work. There was never an issue about whether women wore pants or dresses or skirts to work before David's tenure, but he insisted on making it an issue.

One day David told Mrs. Rodriguez to wear dresses to work from the next day onward, and to never wear pants to the office again or he'd have her fired. For Mrs. Rodriguez, this was a very serious matter. She had terrible scars on her legs from being in a fire when she was a little girl, and she didn't want the embarrassment of revealing her injuries, nor did she want people talking about it or asking her how it happened. The poor woman was distraught. Naturally, she went to Susan.

"David told me he would fire me if I ever wore pants to the office again, Ms. Susan."

"He'll do nothing of the sort. You report to me. I'm your supervisor, not him. Just wear your pants and forget what he says. I'll have a talk with him." Susan was confident and reassuring.

David was out of the office, hiding from confrontation with Susan, or his father. His deportment was very much the same as when he was a boy. His modus operandi was to cause a stir—punch a girl, bite a girl, steal money under a pretense—and then run off and hide from the consequences. Susan didn't see him that day and David escaped a confrontation, as planned. The following day, he came in earlier than usual and before Susan arrived, again as planned. He walked off the elevator straight into the reception area and stood in front of Mrs. Rodriguez.

"Stand up!" David ordered. She did as commanded. "I see you are wearing pants. I told you to wear dresses from today on, didn't I?"

"But Ms. Susan said—" Mrs. Rodriguez began, but David cut her off.

"It doesn't matter what Ms. Susan said. You are fired for disobeying my direct order. Pack up your desk and leave immediately."

David was expecting Mrs. Rodriguez to be gone before Susan arrived. He miscalculated.

Susan knew her antagonist and his methods. She'd endeavored to arrive an hour earlier than her usual time that day, just in case David tried to make trouble with Mrs. Rodriguez. When she came off the elevator, there stood the receptionist, bawling her eyes out. Susan knew the poor woman supported three children and a husband who was wheelchair-bound from two splintered legs he'd sustained while in the Army. The woman was a top-notch talent and ran the front office to Susan's exact specifications. There was a professional love between the two women, a "we'll get it done right and on time the first time" kind of respect. Susan was infuriated. She'd always regarded David as a disgusting imp and constantly reminded herself to never let her Irish temper to turn its fury upon him. Still, this was more than she could bear.

"What are you doing?" She was only six inches from David's face.

"I've just fired Mrs. Rodriguez. She's leaving as soon as she gets her desk cleaned out."

"Sit down, Mrs. Rodriguez. You're not going anywhere. You're not fired."

"I said she's fired. I'm an officer of this company—"

Susan whirled from comforting Mrs. Rodriguez to again put her face in David's, only that time she closed to two inches. She put her hands on David's shoulders and pushed him backward, catching him totally off guard. She pushed him as she screamed in his face: "Don't you ever fuck with my staff again, you little dipshit, or I'll kick your fucking balls off and there's nothing your daddy will do about it. Get it straight and keep it straight."

Susan kept shoving David toward a small trash can behind the adjacent receptionist's desk, and then she did the unthinkable—she lifted her knee and jammed it hard into David's testicles. It must have been the Irish temper thing she'd always controlled before, but she had a great fondness for Mrs. Rodriguez after working with her for many years. The groin pain bent David forward.

Susan wasn't finished. She grabbed his head and lifted him back to the upright position, exacerbating his groin pain, and then shoved him backward until he fell onto the trash can. It was too small for him and he broke it, ripping his trousers in the process. Susan stood over him with a fist in his face as David cried from his injuries.

"Don't you ever disturb my office personnel again, you got that?"

Susan stood over David demanding an answer, but he just lay there whimpering. She still wasn't finished. She put her foot on David's face and probably would have kicked him, but she gave him another chance.

"I asked you if you got that. I want your answer."

David finally realized Susan was about to kick his face in and she didn't care about any consequences from his father. He'd never been cowered like that and he was suddenly terrified of Susan. His former babysitter still had the upper hand.

"I get it," he said meekly. His confidence that Marvin would take his side against Susan was never there; he'd been bluffing all along. In his heart, he knew Susan's cunt controlled his father and there was nothing he could do about it.

"Good! Now let's all make sure you get it. Stand up and apologize to Mrs. Rodriguez."

David looked up at Susan with an expression of resentment, but she wasn't about to be trifled with. When her ire was raised, she had more strength than he did and a raging determination. She grabbed David's ears and began lifting him. If he didn't scramble to his feet, she'd have torn his ears off.

"I said you are going to apologize to Mrs. Rodriguez. You are going to apologize sincerely and with respect for her, or I will smash your smug little face into this desk and break your goddamn nose. I'm not joking, David. I'll enjoy smashing your face. Apologize!" Susan had her hand on the back of David's head and was ready to slam it into the reception desk.

David mustered up the sincerest demeanor he'd ever exhibited in his life. "Mrs. Rodriguez, I apologize for the problems I've caused you. Please accept my apology."

Mrs. Rodriguez was still crying and trembling from the scene she'd just witnessed. Two other women from the staff also saw what happened. They were all glowing inside, happy Susan put an end to the petty nonsense.

"I accept your apology, Mr. Sustack," said Mrs. Rodriguez.

Never in her life had a white man apologized to her. Except for Marvin and Susan, she had never felt equally treated or respected by white people. Tears ran down her cheeks as she looked at Susan, her expression one of complete gratitude. She wanted to stand up and hug the other woman but thought better of it. After all, Susan was her boss.

The office staff had sensed the tensions between David and Susan for some time. Now that it was out in the open, they were especially cautious and alert to not give David cause to make trouble for them. Morale sagged for years afterward and staff turnover increased. Susan's administrative camp and David's marketing camp grudgingly coexisted for the next fifteen years. Marvin was the glue that bonded the competing factions together.

The thought occurred to him that Susan might actually kill David if she had the chance. It never occurred to Marvin that David could murder. He knew his son could be cruel and sadistic, but Marvin was confident that the rabbis had some good effect on him and likely David's childhood behaviors were a thing of the past.

In his desire to keep Susan in the firm and to buy her tolerance of David, but not kill or injure him, Marvin gave her a codicil to his will that provided that as long as she was an officer of Sustack Associates, upon his death, she would inherit all the stock of the company. He also passed a corporate resolution that provided the new fund company would pay her company a handsome monthly fee; specifically, she would receive a salary equal to half the fund's expense allowance fee as long as she lived. Thus, even though his advisory clients would likely leave after his death, his life-long mistress would receive cash from his son's fund for the remainder of her life. Susan was already rich, so she didn't need the money, but she also felt Marvin's desire to have her continue to babysit David; therefore, she agreed to this lifetime arrangement.

As the years passed, Marvin became progressively weaker. He suffered from leukemia. It began with a general fatigue—he needed frequent naps to maintain his strength—but gradually, other symptoms appeared. His weight began to drop, which was something he initially welcomed because he had grown somewhat of a stomach. But Marvin's weight loss continued and the stomach protrusion increased. His libido failed and he experienced nosebleeds. His blood tests confirmed the disease, and in the '60s and '70s, there was little hope for a cure.

The office staff talked in whispers about any news of Marvin's health. Susan was stoic about the end times of her lover. She was strong enough to keep the firm operating as if nothing were different from before his affliction, but in the afternoons, after the staff had gone home, she would sometimes go into his empty office, sit in one of the audience chairs, and look at his empty throne chair, as if the brilliant man were still sitting there, explaining what would happen next in the markets. She missed him so. She carried a terrible ache inside her, and she cried quietly to herself as she tried to imagine life without Marvin. But she couldn't project those thoughts into the future.

About five years before, when he was still in his handsome prime, with the glow of life in his face, she insisted that he go to the Big Steer Hotel Portrait Shop and have an oil portrait made. Marvin scoffed at the idea at first—he was a modest man when his own aggrandizement was suggested—but he did eventually sit for the portrait sessions. He knew it was something Susan wanted for the firm after he was gone. Now she had the portrait, the version of him that would always be in her mind. He was Marvin, the majestic lion, the leader, the wise one, and he was such a handsome man. Now he was dying. The doctors said he could not return to the office. He would go home to die in his own bed, attended by his wife and son.

It was a sad and bitter time for Susan, for she knew in her heart's deepest corners that he loved her like he could never love any other woman. She'd learned to accept the religious boundary that bonded him with Eloweiss and separated him from her. But she believed there was a human element of kindred souls that plumbed a depth of love that bonded two people. That love didn't need God to join them within a religion; this was a bond that resided in their thoughts and cares for each other. Marvin and Susan were bonded across all barriers. She ached to be with him now. He needed her. She knew he was thinking of her in his dying hours, and she cried for him. She cried that he couldn't hold her hand at the very end.

Then it was Marvin's time. The time she wished would never come, came.

She originally planned to hang the portrait in the reception area, so that when clients arrived they'd be reminded of the great man who founded the firm. But with Marvin's death, it was likely most of the advisory clients would drift away and go elsewhere. Few of David's mutual fund shareholders would ever bother to come to the office. David didn't love his father. Susan knew he'd hated Marvin from childhood on, and that he harbored jealousy toward Marvin, slighting his father's accomplishments and taking personal credit for building the firm. David dishonored Marvin at every opportunity. Susan was the only person on earth who genuinely loved Marvin for the human being he was. She kept his portrait and hung it in her office on the wall directly across from her desk.

Marvin was always there with her. Every time she would look up at him, she'd remember him and the glorious times they had together, how they laughed and loved and held each other close until the wee hours of the mornings. And how each time they parted they would promise to wish each other a kiss good night. He was a handsome lion of a man with his waved silver hair and stunning profile. He looked like a victorious general or a statesman's statesman. And he was so good-hearted and kind, so ready to listen, so easy to talk to, so easy to understand when he explained things.

"Sleep well, my handsome prince. I am with you now and always. I know what love is now. I feel you in my heart and I will adore you forever. No woman ever felt a greater love." Susan pursed her lips and blew a silent kiss to the picture. Her heart wept.

While on his deathbed, Marvin executed his final will, which gave David all of Marvin's controlling class X shares of the mutual fund's investment advisor. This transfer was actually illegal since it required a majority of fund shareholder votes, but that was rectified by the lawyers at a later time.

Marvin bonded David to his wishes from the grave. The will contained the proviso that David was to receive control shares only on the basis of his solemn written pledge to Marvin, to be kept in a safe at the orthodox temple, that upon David's death, the shares of the fund's broker-dealer and advisor would be given, or the proceeds of their sale would be given, to the new State of Israel.

Marvin's will was copied, as he instructed, and given to two Plaintown rabbis, and filed with the Plaintown Probate Court. Marvin was a committed Zionist. He deeply regretted he couldn't rescue more Jews from Hitler's evil, and he hoped by this bequest that he could help ensure that never again would Jews not have a place to go to, not have a nation that would receive them when turmoil stirred in the world. Marvin provided for Susan, an already wealthy woman; Eloweiss, through his half of the business profits he'd amassed; and David, through his gift of the mutual fund complex to make a living during his lifetime. Additional monies he left to several Plaintown synagogues.

He also made a map of where he'd placed the diamonds, with instructions that the safe deposit box into which the map was placed was not to be opened until fifty years after his death. He made provisions for a separate trustee of the safe deposit box and for successor trustees with powers to act and remove the locked box from within the safe deposit box should there be considered risk that the bank would be closed or liquidated, or should the government pass legislation or administrative orders to seize private property. Marvin wanted to be a step ahead of the next Hitler and the next FDR.

In a year when the stock market plunged to its depths in the mid-1970's, Marvin Sustak died. Eloweiss darkened her home and sat Shiva. She was comforted by her friends, relatives from out of town, and several rabbis. Susan wept inconsolably for several days. Her heart ached with her grief, which she shared with no one.

David grinned, ecstatic with joy. In his early fifties, he finally had the freedom to live life as it pleased him, no longer needing to be mindful of his father's standards, or demands. The freedom to operate the fund complex in any manner he chose enthralled his imagination. He felt the same euphoria as when he was a child pulling wings from flies.

ESTELLA'S SON

Soon after Nevin's death, for reasons never explained to Estella and which little Bobby would never know, the Bund relocated mother and son from the north end to the southeasternmost corner of town, the most isolated section. It was called The Heights because it sat on a bluff overlooking a beautiful stretch of the Sechewuekin, the Indian name for the Shohono River. From the back porches of the few homes at the edge of The Heights, as this duplex was, there was a grand view of the Shohono River as it coursed past the town, met its confluence with Cedar Creek, and flowed southward past Cedar Mountain.

Cedar Mountain was pine covered near the water's edge and raised steeply upslope from the south bank of the creek. The swampy north bank was overgrown with clumps of marsh grasses and cattails. It was home to numerous species of snakes, frogs, toads, beaver, muskrats, and waterfowls. Fox and coyote routinely patrolled these environs making meals of its varied inhabitants.

Mother and son lived in their tiny duplex, which shared its other side with an old Army veteran and his wife. The couple mostly kept to themselves. The husband fought in World War I and was poisoned by German mustard gas. His lungs were compromised and he coughed a lot, but he stayed fit by taking daily walks. He kept memorabilia in his house, including a captured Mauser infantry rifle, a Sig Sauer .38 caliber pistol, and a German officer's dress sword, all wall mounted in cradle holders, which made them easily accessible. He was a fixture on the Bund counsel, and his opinions were valued by many townsfolk.

War took a toll on the old man's psyche. He told Estella and young Bobby that he hoped someone would break into his home so he could shoot the no-good riffraff son of a bitch. The war made him used to killing people and he missed the action. He told Bobby that once someone's killed people, they kind of miss not doing more of it. Their home had numerous pictures of Germany on its walls, and featured many German Hummel figurines on knickknack shelves. The old warrior answered his phone by saying, "Sergeant Hoffman here."

The sergeant's wife was a plump, jovial woman, always cordial to the neighbors and agreeable to the opinions of her husband. She mostly stayed indoors during daylight hours, tending to her cooking, baking, and household chores.

In the early evenings, little Bobby would sit on his back porch and watch for her. Predictably, Mrs. Hoffman would venture outdoors at that time to sit on her back porch swing and stare at Cedar Mountain and the Shohono River. It was a peaceful, quiet time for both of them. Sometimes she'd talk to Bobby from porch to porch, and sometimes, when she'd been baking, she'd ask him to come over to see her. The excited boy would scramble down his own back porch stairs, then run across their two backyards and up her porch stairs. She'd reward him with a cookie or sometimes a piece of strudel. The two of them would talk about things little boys talk about.

He shared all his secrets with her, except he never told her about the beatings from his mother. He felt it was something she knew about without him saying anything. Mr. and Mrs. Hoffman both talked with his mother quite a bit. Bobby had the perception little boys sometimes have, that the Hoffmans knew just about everything about him and his mother.

Mrs. Hoffman was a good listener and never admonished him for the things he did. She heard all about the animals and the occasional people he saw in the forest. She listened to him tell her how he was trying to get across Cedar Creek and climb the mountain. Together, they watched fireflies glowing in their backyards as the sunset turned to early twilight, and they laughed together when rabbits came into their yards near dusk. The male thumpers would stand on their hind legs and box each other, and Bobby and Mrs. Hoffman would try to predict which rabbit would win the scuffle. Sometimes, actually quite often, two rabbits would begin copulating with the buck mounting the back of the doe. Mrs. Hoffman explained to Bobby that bunnies do that stuff when they like each other a lot.

The Hoffmans' backyard had several birdhouses mounted on high metal poles. Mrs. Hoffman explained to Bobby that Mr. Hoffman liked the little wrens that lived in the houses because they ate lots of mosquitoes, and fewer mosquitoes made it more pleasant to sit out at night. Mrs. Hoffman called them her precious little sparrows, although they weren't actually the same species as the common English sparrow. Mr. Hoffman put the houses on the high poles so the neighborhood cats couldn't climb up to the birds. Together, they kept track of how often the mother Jenny Wrens made trips to their houses, and they watched to see if the birds were carrying insects, which meant little baby birds were newly hatched in the houses.

The old woman and the boy became avid bird-watchers, waiting and watching night after night for the new chicks to appear. Bobby felt good and warm inside when he sat there on the Hoffman back porch with Mrs. Hoffman. This plain, uncomplicated woman seemed to have an answer for everything a boy could think to ask about, and she was always patient to explain things to his satisfaction. She was a good friend.

Bobby instinctively knew there was one subject that was off limits with Mrs. Hoffman. He never spoke with her about his mother. The duplex basement had a wooden wall partition separating the Hoffmans' from Estella's place, and the third floor attic wall had a crawl space that traversed the eaves frames around the units. Bobby discovered he could listen at the basement wall or crawl quietly through the eaves and hear what the Hoffmans were saying in their bedroom. On one occasion, he was in the eaves on the Hoffman side when his neighbors were speaking freely.

"It's not so good for her that she has no man. Shouldn't we try to arrange something?" Mrs. Hoffman was asking about his mother.

"I don't want to interfere. She is loyal to the Bund. She is raising the boy to be strong, to be ready to fight. As long as we see her mind is in the right place, we should let things alone."

"But a strong young woman like her needs a good rooster. She's lonely."

"Yes, but this is a special woman with a special task. Her duty is to the boy. She's sworn to that and we see her keeping her promise. This is not about her life. It's the boy. She's doing well by the boy. She had a man in Germany. He was SS. He loved her, bred her. That's enough for her. Stop your woman thoughts. When he's grown, she can have a man late in life. We get paid to watch them and report. We are not in the marriage broker business."

Bobby's truest and best adult friend was Arlene. She was a confidant he knew he could trust ever since she explained death to him. He saw her every day at school and stopped in her nurse's office to say hello to her. Bobby loved Arlene, and he was beginning to notice she was very pretty. The boy felt his heart throb for her. That day, he needed to talk with her.

"Arlene, what's an SS?"

"Where did you hear about that, Bobby?" Arlene seemed cautious.

"I heard Mr. Hoffman say Mother had a man in Germany who was SS. He bred her. Did he hurt Mommy?"

"Oh, those are just initials for sugar and salt. Mr. Hoffman was just talking about a huckster man who brought bread to your mother long ago before she met your father." Arlene was a quick thinker, but she hadn't covered all her bases.

"Where's Germany?" Bobby pushed his curiosity.

"Well, that's a place far away, and also a place nearby. Some people call it Germantown and some of the old people call Germantown Germany. I'm sure Mr. Hoffman was talking about a sugar man who got bread in Germantown and gave it to people to help them during the depression years when people didn't have any work. He helped a lot of people. You just keep your mind on your schoolwork, Bobby. I hear you're doing so well. Mrs. Dauxtator says you are the brightest one in her class, and Mrs. Rhonemus says you're her brightest also. I can't wait to see your report card grades. I'm so proud of you."

Arlene fast-pedaled to deflect Bobby's curiosity about things taboo. The boy left, his thoughts redirected for the time being.

When Bobby returned to class, he leaned over to Pamela, a pretty little girl who sat next to him. He liked her. She was pretty neat for being a girl.

"Do you know what an SS is?"

"SS? Like super stupid?" Pam was also a quick wit, even in first grade.

"Nope, it's a sugar and salt person who gave away bread in the depression." Bobby thought he had special knowledge and he passed it along.

"Do you like my hair in pigtails?" Pam had no use for sugar and salt that day. The two children talked about meeting on the playground for recess. They often played together after school and were each other's friends. Pamela lived close to Bobby, and she joined him on a moment's notice to go into the forest. There they lay on their backs and looked up at cloud formations and birds and squirrels in the trees above.

"Look, there's an elephant!" Bobby pointed to a cloud.

"I see a fish!" Pam pointed to another.

Girls and women were easy company for Bobby. They held a place of wonder and fascination in his heart. He liked Pam, Florence, Arlene, Mrs. Hoffman, and all his women teachers. As Bobby looked up at the clouds with Pam by his side, he had an odd sensation. Pam was soft, her cheeks were pretty, her hair was pretty, and he felt so happy being with her. He rolled over on top of her and gave her a kiss on the cheek. She turned her head away and wiped his kiss off with her sleeve.

"What are you doing?" She sat up, startled.

"I don't know. I couldn't help it. You're so pretty." They stared at each other. A long moment passed and neither child said a word.

Pam eventually broke the silence. "Well, just stop that mush stuff or I'll tell on you."

"Okay." Bobby lay back down and looked for more animal clouds. "Will you ever let me kiss you?"

"I don't know. Maybe I'll let you someday when we're older. It scares me. Mommy said bad things happen to girls who kiss boys. Mommy said I'm not supposed to kiss boys, that kissing boys is dirty, so I'm not doing it. Let's just be friends. We can promise to be best friends, no matter what." Pam took Bobby's hand in hers and squeezed it.

"Okay. Best friends no matter what." Bobby squeezed back. Lying in the grassy meadow holding hands, they resumed cloud watching and wondering.

Pam wore lipstick to school the following week, which caused a sensation on the playground. Her curious clique of girlfriends surrounded her, probing. Some wanted to judge her application and choice of bright red, but two others wanted to know why she did it.

"Why are you wearing lipstick? What made you do it?"

"I'm not telling." Pam pretended resolve.

"Oh, come on. We're best friends. You can tell us. Who are you looking pretty for?" This line of inquiry persisted, the girls' anticipation fevered, until Pam caved and spilled the beans.

"I've decided I'm going to kiss Bobby! I love him!" she blurted out. "Mommy said it would be okay if I just kissed him on the cheek!" She stared crying, embarrassed she'd revealed her intentions. Now she sat in judgment of her peers even before committing the daring deed.

Uproar and squeals burst from Pam's entourage. Some jumped up and down screaming.

"Pam's going to kiss Bobby. Pam loves Bobby! They're going to kiss! Hey, everybody. Come here. Pam's going to kiss Bobby!" One girl ran to a group of boys playing marbles. "Hey, you guys. Pam's going to kiss Bobby. She said she loves him! Go get Bobby. You have to see this!"

Soon, a posse of boys rounded up Bobby, who was brought to the girls' tribunal like a fugitive before a court. He stood before Pam, embarrassed. Then the taunting began. Alan, Warren, and Buzz, the schoolyard bullies, circled Bobby, pushing him from one to the other.

"Girl sucker! Sissy! Chicken! Pussy! Yellow! You're no man! You're a girl!" Bobby was subjected to a barrage of catcalls and shoving as the children looked on with glee. Pam was horrified, covering her face in shame. That intensified the taunting. Now Pam and Bobby were picked upon by boys and girls alike. The two were pushed and shoved to the center of the crowd until they were face to face.

"Kiss him! Kiss Bobby!"

The girls pushed Pam toward Bobby. Embarrassed, she resisted. Two girls pulled her by the arms, another pushed from behind. A boy broke sides and went over to the girls, helping push Pam forward.

"No! Stop! Please, stop!"

Pam shouted for them to stop. This was not how she wanted her special moment to be. She'd wanted to surprise Bobby, catch him in a private moment, but now her surprise was ruined. She was humiliated.

Bobby looked at Pam, the tears running down her cheeks. Her chest heaved from humiliation. That's when it happened. It wasn't getting pushed and shoved that detonated Bobby's fuse, nor was it the catcalls directed at him. Estella had conditioned him for this moment very well. When he saw Pam's tears, Bobby snapped. His blood boiled, his skin flushed from a testosterone surge. Blind rage overpowered Bobby's comportment as he turned on his tormenters and began swinging.

His burst of fists shocked the bullies. Girls ran for distance and then turned to watch the fury. The ring of boys backed off, their eyes widened and jaws dropped. Bobby was avenging Pam's hurt and he brooked no quarter. His fists connected to nose, then to jaw and eye. Warren, nose broken and bloodied, retreated and ran away from the battle crying.

"I'm hurt! He broke my nose!" Warren wailed for sympathy, but the onlookers only coped with their own shock.

Buzz, with blood streaming into his eyes from cut eyebrows, staggered in circles. "I'm blind. I can't see!" he screamed. A fist found his eye and knocked him dizzy. He turned away and sat on the ground, finished. The stunned crowd stood agape but feared to help one of their own. Alan, the biggest bully, was left to battle Bobby alone. He got the worst of it.

"Sorry, sorry" was all Alan could stammer as Bobby pummeled him mercilessly. He was so concerned with covering his face and head he never got off a punch of his own.

When Dr. Sensmaker, the elementary school's principal and only faculty male, finally got to the fight scene, he was horrified. Never had he seen such violence unleashed upon one elementary school child by another. Bobby was on top of Alan, who was holding his hands over his face in a vain attempt to ward off the blows. Alan's nose was broken badly, smashed into a pulp. His eye sockets were cut and his face suffered multiple bruises. Bobby alternated punching the hapless boy and lifting his head by the hair and slamming it back into the concrete. If the beating didn't stop, Alan might not live. Bobby, in his maddened rage, even fought against the principal. He wanted to continue beating Alan until he killed the bigger boy. Estella was called to the school.

Dr. Sensmaker implored her to instruct Bobby in non-violence.

"Your son must stay home for two weeks. Make him think about what he did, Estella. He might have killed the other boy if I hadn't stepped in. Do you have any idea how serious this is? He has a temper, an uncontrolled temper. You must talk with him and make him understand that he can't solve his disagreements with his fists. If he grows up this way, sometime in his life he's going to meet a situation where he encounters someone who angers him in some way. He could kill somebody. Your son is dangerous to other people. You must, for his sake, work to correct this."

Estella took measure of her son's performance from what she'd heard. "You said the other boys pushed him first."

"Yes, but the response he gave was way out of proportion, Estella. He can't just maim other children who tease him."

"And the children were teasing the girl, Pam, too?"

"Yes. The two of them were getting pushed together. It was something about Pam wanting to give Bobby a kiss."

"And you talked to the parents of the boys who were teasing Bobby?"

"Yes. I told them they needed to tell their boys it's not good to tease."

"I should think the boys found that out on their own, no? And the girls who pushed Pam, did you talk to their parents too?"

"Well, no. They were just little girls teasing on the playground. They didn't make Bobby hit anybody."

"They made Pam cry."

"Yes, but that's no reason to hit the boys."

"He did not hit any of the girls, did he?"

"No. Thank God."

"He's a good son, Mr. Sensmaker. He does as I say. He knows right from wrong. He knows not to ever hit girls or women. But he also knows to defend himself, and he is taught to stand up for girls and women because they can't always stand up for themselves. It's a man's world, you know."

"Yes, I know. Will you please teach him to be in control of himself?"

Estella sat in the principal's office, nodded her agreement, promised to get the boy "straightened out" and assured Dr. Sensmaker that Bobby would be well behaved in the future. Inwardly, she was gleeful. Bobby was Paul's seed and hers. He had the warrior's blood. In his wars, he would be successful. Her seed was growing.

"Arlene, I heard your project boy clobbered the stuffing out of three boys at school while I was up line. Is it true?" Morris Zippen sat at the kitchen table. He often heard Arlene extol how well Bobby did this or that, but the playground episode was out of character for the boy.

"Yes, it's true. I've talked to him about it. I'm working on him so it won't happen again." Arlene's frustrations tugged at her voice.

"It seems you may not be the only one working on him. How well do you know the mother?"

"I know her as well as anyone besides her sister. Yet, I can't say I know her all that well. She's a brooding sort, and secretive. She opens up a little sometimes, but just enough to give me what she thinks I want to hear. Maybe I'm in over my head."

"She was put here by the Brotherhood after the war, wasn't she?"

"Yes, you know that."

"Yes, yes. I just think you better be careful. If she's true to the old Nazi ways, she'll raise the kid to think he must fight the world and to distrust even you."

"I've never told her or the boy that we're Jews."

"Don't be naïve, Arlene. The Bund knows. Someone knows for sure. They all talk. What do you think? You've nurtured the boy for five years now, yet he did this. He nearly killed the one boy. Have you ever seen a boy from our temple behave like that?"

"No, of course not."

"Well, there's a reason, Arlene. You got him a woman to read to him. You spend time with him, but you are not his mother. You are not the dominant influence."

"But I thought I could sweeten him a little, make him less rigid, show him something better than hate."

"Oh, my love. My sweet, sweet love! Of course you thought so, and you did some good things with him. I'm sure you've had a good effect. I'm only saying the mother's influence is stronger, but it's not his only influence. You've done a very good thing."

Morris hugged his wife, embracing her for a long moment.

"But now, my dear, you must ease off some. I'm not saying don't talk to him. You should respond when he has questions, but you must not tell him this is right and that is wrong. That will put you at odds with the mother and you will lose your influence entirely. He's going on his own path now. He will always have your influence. He will not hate Jews as I believe his mother does. But you must never think you failed. You did not fail. Why, look at it this way. The boys he pummeled were all gentiles, weren't they?"

"Yes, he makes no allowances for like-mindedness. He is blind to differences. He only sees rights and wrongs!"

"Well, see! He's a warrior in the making, and he doesn't discriminate. He beats up on anybody!" Morris let out a chuckle.

"I love you, my wise husband. I'm glad you're home."

Arlene returned Morris's hug. She appreciated his insights and gave them the same respect she gave Rabbi Goldberger's guidance. She lost sleep that night thinking about Bobby. He was her personal project child and she desperately wished a good life for him. Perhaps she could do more; perhaps she'd overlooked something about Bobby that she could still correct. She worried that he would be in fights of one sort or another all his life. Her fears compelled her to make another appointment to see her rabbi.

Once again seated at Rabbi Goldberger's study, Arlene unburdened herself before the bearded wise man. He looked upon her sympathetically from his massive high-backed leather chair and listened carefully as she narrated the incident on the playground. Wiping her tears from her eyes, she asked the wise rabbi where she failed to keep Bobby on the right path.

"Arlene, my dear, you have not failed this boy. I believe you have done all that could ever be expected. You must not trouble yourself so. You must allow the boy to find his own way. You gave him excellent guidance and it will serve him well. You must trust your own work. These things take time."

"I don't seek your patronage, Rabbi. I just feel something is missing in him. I need to understand what it is and do my best to fill this void he has. Help me see it, please."

"Well, let me see. When you first told me about him, you told me he was a very beautiful boy, and you told me he was considerably larger than other toddlers his age. He had big hands and feet. Am I remembering well?"

"Yes, of course, Rabbi. You never forget any detail."

"And now you concern yourself that he got into a fight with other boys over a girl on a playground."

"Yes, Rabbi. I'm afraid he will always be in fights and be hurt some day."

"And why do you feel afraid for him?" The rabbi's eyes opened wide and his eyebrows lifted, revealing their unmistakable mischievous twinkle. A wise, knowing smile lifted his mouth.

"Because, Rabbi."

"Because? Because why, Arlene?"

"I don't know. I can't say, Rabbi."

"Which is it, Arlene? You don't know or you can't say?"

"I'm confused, Rabbi."

"Arlene, listen to yourself! You don't want him hurt. You don't know why. You can't say why. Arlene, you need to understand what is going on here. You have fallen in love with this boy."

"Oh, Rabbi. He's only a boy." Arlene blushed.

"Yes, but a beautiful boy, a very big handsome boy. He fights to protect a little girl. He is fearless and beats up many other boys who offend a little girl. Arlene, you are a woman and you have fallen in love with a boy whom you see as a knight in shining armor. It's nothing to be ashamed of. Women naturally love little boys. You want the best for him, just as you do for your own husband. You just need to understand why you feel as you do. You are afraid to see him growing up and leaving your influence because you know that someday he will fall in love with a real woman his own age and he will leave you forever. This is only natural in life, Arlene."

"But my fears for him are real, Rabbi."

"Yes, real fears, but misplaced feelings. Your real fear is that he will fall in love with a bad woman who will hurt him terribly and that he will have a miserable life. You love him and do not wish a bad woman upon him. You want him to find a good woman like yourself. This is all natural, Arlene. You have a true love for him."

Arlene was crying by that point. Rabbi Goldberger put the light of truth upon her feelings and she understood herself. "I see, Rabbi. I am only a foolish woman, aren't I?"

Rabbi Goldberger rose from his chair and went to Arlene, placing his arm over her shoulder to comfort her.

"You are not a foolish woman, my child. No good heart as yours can ever be foolish. You are the best trait of any woman, or any man. You seek the best for another and not for yourself. That is everything in life."

"What will become of Bobby, Rabbi? What do you foresee?

Rabbi Goldberger sought to comfort this good woman. "Ah, what do I foresee? I think your little boy who fights so well is like a colt horse that will grow up to become a big horse stallion that will have many fights in his life. His father figure left him in death, which is a major sense of loneliness and abandonment. His mother beats him terribly, which makes him reactive and well-conditioned to do battle. He has an inner resilience to adversity. She raised him as a female Hun would, to become a warrior, and he has already become a warrior.

"But then there was you, Arlene. You gave him warmth of the heart and showed him to care for another and another's needs. So, what I foresee for your little boy colt is he will grow to become a wild and ferocious warrior stallion. He will be sought after by many women and some may attract his interest for their own narcissistic needs, but because of you, Arlene, there will come along in his life one special woman who is like you in her heart. She will show your stallion what true love is, and she will guide him to a good and happy life with her. In his heart of hearts, he will know a good woman from a bad one and he will be open to the message of true love from a good woman. He will have a happy and long life. You may sleep at peace knowing you have set your little colt on the right path in life."

"And he will have fights?" Arlene had some residual apprehensions about Bobby's welfare."

"Yes, I'm afraid so. Many fights until he is settled."

"You mean until he is with the right woman?"

"Yes, Arlene. That is exactly what I mean. And now you need to let your little colt go so he can become a big stallion on his own legs."

"And someday he will find the right woman, Rabbi?"

"Not quite, Arlene. I meant until the right woman finds him. Women decide whom to take into their lives. Women and wise men understand this is the way of things. Now you must let him go to find his own way and be found. I insist. Set him free."

Arlene rose, thanked the rabbi, and promised to let go of Bobby. From then on, the boy would not be her worry. On her way out of the Goldbergers' house, the plump and ever cheerful Mrs. Goldberger hugged Arlene as a woman who shared her feelings for the boy and her newly felt measure of relief.

When the rabbi saw his tearful wife hugging the tearful Arlene, he thought to himself, *What is it with these women and this little boy? Are they all going crazy? I will never understand them and I have no one I can ask!*

To round out her son, Estella had him join first the Cub Scouts, then the Boy Scouts. Bob loved the whole program, memorized the scout's oaths and the lists of dos and don'ts. He learned the scout's ways. Instead of watching a feeble person try to get up from a bench or cross a street, he learned the civilized thing to do was to help those less able. He learned courtesy, kindness, goodwill toward one's fellow man, and self-reliance were the best measures of men. Estella was perplexed by these teachings. In Nazi Germany, handicapped and feeble people were burdens. They were eliminated.

The scouts taught Bob how to trap rabbits unharmed in big green boxes. He got fifty cents for each rabbit trapped, which were turned loose outside of town so they wouldn't eat the townsfolks' vegetable gardens. And hunters could shoot the rabbits in the fall. That was the theory, anyway. Bob never told his scoutmaster, but he was certain that some of the rabbits he'd trapped were the same ones he'd trapped before. He just didn't see a rabbit as a rabbit; he saw each animal as a unique animal and made a mental study of it. No two rabbits looked alike to Bob.

By the age of seven, Estella had Bob out selling. He sold magazines, Christmas and Easter cards, candy for Easter, raffle tickets, tickets to church socials—whatever a child could hustle door-to-door, little Bob hustled. She told him he was the man of the house so he had to bring in money. When he was strong enough, around the age of nine or ten, he shoveled snow from neighbors' sidewalks during winter and mowed their lawns with a push mower that had a revolving blade wheel in front and a catch basket behind during the warmer months.

Bob earned enough money to buy several sets of steel traps. Mr. Hoffman showed him how to set the traps to catch muskrats and foxes. By the age of ten, Bob was up at twilight to run through the forest to Cedar Creek's north bank and check his trap line. He never caught a fox, but he caught fifteen muskrats. He skinned them and received fifty cents a pelt from the man who ran the local hardware store. If his skinning was better, he could have a quarter more, the man told him. He checked his trap lines and skinned his muskrats before he went to school.

In the duplex at town's edge, near the forest, Bobby sat with head on folded hands at the kitchen table. He wore a frown and stared at the kitchen wall.

"What are you thinking about?" Estella asked.

"Nothing," Bobby answered.

"Tell me. I'm your mother." The prospect of a beating was implied in her voice. Bobby held back for a moment, and then he spoke.

"It's girls, Mom. I'm thinking about girls."

"What about them? Tell me."

"You wouldn't understand, Mom. You're different than girls my age."

"I was your age once. I know all there is to know about girls. You can tell me." Estella was now the reassuring confidant.

"Okay, well, it's just that girls are so soft and they're more fun to be with than boys. I like being with them. When I'm with the boys, I feel like I need to fight with them."

"Soft? How do you mean soft?" Estella's alarm bell went off.

"I mean up here, soft. Why are girls soft up here?" Bobby put his hands on his chest.

"How do you know they are soft up there?" Estella was alarmed. It was too soon for this talk.

"Well, a couple years ago, I rolled over on Pam. I could tell she was soft there."

"Why did you roll over on her?"

"I don't know. I can't explain it. I just felt like I had to and I wanted to kiss her. But why is she soft there?"

"She's a girl, that's why. We girls are soft there. We make milk there when we have babies and we need to be soft there for feeding babies, but you must not roll over on girls and kiss them."

"And I know girls are different down below too. Sharon and I showed our private parts to each other."

"I remember, and I gave you a whipping for that."

"I know. But why do I like girls so much and the other boys like to play with boys? Is something wrong with me?"

"Well, do you ever wish you were a girl yourself?"

"Oh no, not at all! I just want to kiss girls and see what it's like to put my thing into their thing. I heard it feels wonderful. I can't wait to do that."

Estella was shocked. "Listen to me. That girl part is not for you. You must concentrate on your studies, not girls. Girls will just get you into trouble and make you do poorly in school. You must do well in school, understand?"

Bobby nodded. "But is there something wrong with me that I like girls so much?"

"No, there's nothing wrong with you. If you liked boys and felt about boys the way you feel about girls, then there'd be something wrong, but what you feel is normal. Why did you hit those other boys that time on the playground? And why did you hurt them like that?"

"They were teasing us."

"Who are 'us'?"

"Me and Pam. The girls were pushing Pam toward me, especially this one girl, Janet. They wanted to make Pam kiss me. The boys were pushing me toward Pam. It was Alan, Warren, and Buzz."

"And you got mad because they were pushing you?"

"No, that didn't bother me much. But when I saw Pam crying and I saw they were hurting her feelings, I just had to hit them."

"But the boys weren't pushing Pam. The girls were pushing Pam."

"I know, Mom, but I can't hit a girl. I just can't do it."

"So, you hit the boys because the girls were pushing Pam?"

"Yes. I wasn't thinking. I just suddenly felt wild inside. Something happened to me. I just knew if I stopped the boys from teasing me that would stop the girls from teasing Pam too. I went crazy seeing her crying like that, Mom. I think about Pam all the time. I want to be with her all the time. I'm in love with her."

"Bobby, you're too young to be in love. It's okay for you to be friends with Pam, but you must not put your thing into her thing. You must not be kissing her either. You are much too young for that stuff. When you and Pam grow up, you can still be friends, but you must not expect any more than that. She will grow up and marry another man and you will grow up and marry another woman. You will grow up and discover a very special girl. She will be a good girl who loves only you, not some naughty girl who goes with all sorts of men, but a very wonderful and smart girl, and you will have children with her."

"But Pam and me, we want to be with each other. We don't want anyone else. And Pam is very smart," protested Bobby.

"Life has a way about these things, Bobby. It has a way of taking us away from those we love very much and there's nothing we can do about it." Estella sounded experienced and farseeing.

"You mean like when my dad died?" Bobby's thoughts were of Nevin.

"Yes, when your father died." Estella's voice turned wistful. She remembered being held in Paul's arms that last time before he left for the Eastern front. She looked far away and was silent, her eyes watering.

Bobby thought and wondered. He loved girls and women, but especially Pam. His heart jumped when he saw her, and he couldn't get his mind off her. He thought she was the most beautiful, most wonderful creature ever to inhabit the earth. Mom confirmed his feelings were normal. He was happy around girls and women, but gosh, they sure were complicated, and each one was different.

He loved when females hugged him, just not in front of other boys. He loved talking with them. He felt awed and safe with them, especially Florence and Arlene, with his teachers a little less so. But he felt combative toward other boys. And those feelings were normal too. His feelings toward boys and men were the same ones he sometimes had about his mother. But today his mother was more like a friend, more like Arlene. Women were hard to understand, but he loved them anyway, especially Arlene and Florence and Mrs. Hoffman.

On the day of fisticuffs, the injured boys were brought to Arlene's office. The bloodied faces of Warren and Buzz waited while Arlene put smelling salts under Alan's nose and placed a cold wet rag on his forehead. She thanked God the boy revived.

When she heard Bobby had visited this brutality upon his classmates, she felt failure as his friend and mentor. When Bobby returned to school two weeks later, she pulled him from classes for an official counseling session.

"Bobby, what were you thinking when you were hitting the other boys?"

"I told Mother and Mr. Sensmaker already. I was trying to stop them from making Pam cry."

"But, Bobby, the girls were pushing Pam, not the boys."

"I know, but I don't hit girls."

"What were you feeling inside when you hit the other boys?"

"I felt mad at them."

"After Alan was on the ground and he was covering his face with his hands you kept hitting him, and you lifted his head up and banged it on the ground several times. Did you know you were hurting him very badly?"

"Yes."

"Okay, why were you hurting him like that and when were you going to stop?"

"I wasn't going to stop. I wanted to kill him."

"Okay, now tell me what's really going on in your mind. Why did you try to kill him?"

Bobby blurted out the truth. "He always makes fun of Mom and me. He has a dad who makes a lot of money and he lives in a big house. He constantly tells me I'll always be poor and he'll always be rich. I hate him."

"But the two of you used to be good friends. I've seen you playing together many times. What happened?"

"Well, one day his dad bought a brand new car. It's a Chrysler Imperial with the really big V8 motor. Alan asked me to come see the new car and we went and sat inside of it. Alan got behind the wheel and pretended to be driving the car and I sat in the passenger seat."

"Then what happened?"

"Then Alan said we should switch places, and I was behind the wheel."

"And that made you angry?"

"No. It's what Alan said next. He said I should remember how it is to be driving a nice car like that because I was never going to be able to drive a nice car for real. He said my mom was too poor to ever have enough money to buy a car like that, and we would always have beaten-up used cars and we'd never have a nice house like his house and I'd always be poor like my mother and he'd always be rich like his dad."

Bobby looked at Arlene with eyes that implored her to tell him that what Alan said wasn't true.

"Bobby, let me tell you something. Now you listen to me and you listen well. You are a hundred times smarter than Alan. He does poorly in school, and you are probably the brightest boy in the entire school. He sees that, don't you think?"

Bobby nodded. "But is what he said true?"

"No. It's not true at all. Bobby, what Alan's father makes and what your mother makes has very little to do with what you will make and what Alan will make when you boys grow up. Let me tell you something. Many years ago, in a place called Europe, boys grew up to do the same things their fathers did. It was called the caste system. If your dad was a blacksmith, you'd learn from him and you'd grow up to be a blacksmith. If your dad was a stone mason, you'd be one too. The first boy of a family got his father's land and business when the father died, the other younger sons were sent off to join the Army. That's why Europe had so many wars. The ruling classes, the aristocrats, had to get rid of all the excess sons, so they got them killed off in wars. But, Bobby, this is America. You can study hard and work hard and grow up to become anything you want to become and you can make as much money as you possibly can. There's nothing holding you back. Do you know what we call that?"

"Yeah, we can say Alan's full of shit."

"There's a better way to look at it, Bobby. It's called progress."

"Progress?"

"Yes, progress. It means that the world and life moves on, moves beyond the petty thinking of people like Alan. People like Alan get left behind to wallow in self-pity. They look to things like what their daddies can do for them or give to them to compensate for the fact that they can't do well on their own. You see, Bobby, by doing what Alan did, he was admitting that he was jealous of you and he felt inferior to you. He couldn't help himself. He feels like you are superior to him, and that stunt he did in the car was his way of getting even with you."

"Are a lot of people like Alan?" Bobby was engaged. He asked questions and drew insights from her. That's what she loved about the boy.

"Actually, Bobby, there's only one Alan. A lot of people have thoughts and behaviors similar to Alan's and you need to understand it when you see it, but there's only one Alan."

"How do I know when somebody has thoughts like Alan?"

"It's something you learn with time and experience with people. It's a matter of listening carefully to what people say and then thinking about why they say what they do, especially if you find a pattern to what they say and do or if they break the pattern of what they normally say and do."

"I can't read about it?"

"No, not really. There are books called psychology books you can read, and some people study this people behavior stuff in college, but the best way is to think about the what and the why of what you're hearing people say and do."

"It sounds hard to learn."

"That's because it is hard to learn. Bobby, you've seen it when it snows, right?"

"Yes."

"Well, every one of those snowflakes is different some-how, slightly different from every other snowflake that falls or that has ever fallen anywhere on the Earth in the history of time. People are like that. Every person who's here today or who was ever here or that ever will be here is different from every other person who is or ever was."

"Even twins?"

"Yes, even twins. God made every person unique, different from all other people. That's why it's so important for you to understand what people are really like on the inside. On the inside, where their heart is, that's where you learn what a person is really like. When you understand someone, you'll know whether you want to be friends with them or if you want to do business with them."

"What do you mean by doing business with them?"

"That's like trading baseball cards. Do you trust the other guy to do an honest trade? It could be doing work in exchange for money, or trading a car, or trading where you do something now and he does something in the future. All that stuff is called doing business."

"Okay, Mrs. Zippen, can I go now?' Bobby squirmed in his chair. He wanted to go back to his classroom.

"You call me Arlene, Bobby. We've known each other too long for you to start calling me Mrs. Zippen. And yes, you can leave now."

As Bobby walked back to his classroom, he wondered if each and every snowflake was really different and who would know for sure if they were or weren't.

Estella was the most complex person Bobby knew. To cope with her moods, he needed elementary animal survival skills, honed by trial and error, combined with an understanding of Estella's aberrant personality. When his skills or judgment failed, he was whipped. When he succeeded, he had a day or more of tranquility. He learned when to listen, when to run, when to hide, when to confide, and when to conceal. He lived in constant danger with a mercurial mother roommate. She was not a mother committed to reading to her child or nurturing warmth between mother and son. Her singular pursuit was to instill obedience in her son. But with each passing year, she feared she was failing.

Bobby resisted her, evaded her, and often escaped to the forest. It was impossible to break his spirit. She wondered if he had outside influences which pitted her son against her. Estella was demented from her war years. She was obsessed to develop a protégé of her late SS husband without revealing her goal to anyone but Florence. Many nights she dreamed she was back at youth camp, pampered and cared for. She dreamed Paul returned to her and America was just a nightmare with its many freedoms and lack of structure. America was wearing her down, steadily eroding her preconceived ideas of superiority.

She expected America to change, to see the wisdom of German superiority, but the opposite happened. Black people were gaining more freedoms, not fewer. Handicapped people were respected, accommodated, and not shot. People didn't care about her superior command of formal German. Instead, they laughed at her, pointed her out as some sort of misfit. Her presupposed assumptions about how she'd be extolled and venerated by these Americans were completely wrong. She needed to compensate for America's shortcomings by working harder on her son. America was winning; Estella was losing. Perhaps if she worked on Bobby enough her boy could change America. She couldn't comprehend that Bobby liked America just fine. Bobby was on America's side.

Estella was misplaced, displaced, and disoriented in America, embattled by poverty, ogled and lusted after, and chronically tired. Her behaviors swung wildly between brief minutes of mania followed by hours, days, and weeks of dark depression. She was burdened with an obstinate boy and mentally self-saddled with her impossible dream. The Reich was dead and gone. Her son would never be a future Nazi leader. This was America. The Nazi party was finished. The return of her beloved Reich was only the pipe dream of mad men. She was getting older. The Broderbund reduced her payments to a charity pittance. The gloomy East Coast winters darkened her moods.

Coping with Estella required emotional awareness, escape and evasion tactics, and an ever present Plan B. Bobby became wily as a coyote and wary as a cat.

Estella's duplex had a bedroom for mother and one for son on the main floor. Sharing the floor were a bathroom, kitchen, living room, and bathroom. The kitchen centered the floor plan. The other rooms surrounded it, and the layout resembled a figure eight. The kitchen floor was linoleum tiled in a pattern that resembled red half-moons with black sticks coming out the bottoms, all on a beige background. The home had brown carpeting and beige wallpaper throughout. Each bedroom had two entrances with large floor-to-near-ceiling solid wooden doors varnished dark brown. The living room door opened to a large front porch. The room also had two interior doors, one joining Estella's bedroom, the other the kitchen. The kitchen joined the bathroom, Estella's bedroom, and the living room. Bobby's room was accessible from Estella's bedroom and the bathroom.

Bobby learned the floor plan. There were no dead-end traps on the main floor. The Coal Street row house had a linear floor plan. Whenever Estella wanted to catch him there, she could. Here, the layout was circular. Each room had two entrances, except the kitchen with its three—advantage Bobby. When he needed to escape Estella's wrathful beatings, he ran from her to another room. There, he listened attentively for footsteps or any slightest sound. Once he realized where she was, he ran to a different room, always keeping one room ahead of her.

From the age of four, he deferred corporal punishment by using speed, agility, and wits. Punishments deferred were sometimes more merciful than immediate beatings when Mother was in her rage state. Bobby ran. Estella chased.

Around and around the figure eight they ran until one of them became exhausted or until Estella tricked and trapped her son. As Bobby grew, catching him had less satisfaction for Estella. The boy fought back, punched her, and began landing hurtful blows. Her enthusiasm for the chase slackened and she resorted more to guile and treachery.

Estella developed tricks to catch her son. She pretended to come to hug him, but instead she grabbed him and beat him for an offense he did a day or week before. Bobby became wary of affection. Even while sleeping, the boy had escape routes in mind. Nighttime was usually a peaceful cease-fire, but not all nights. Estella occasionally woke him and beat him for an offense she'd neglected to punish for during daylight hours.

Bobby tried to understand the whys of behavior, like Arlene said. Was it all a game to her? Was she getting him ready for grown-up life? He wondered but didn't know. He just knew his life wasn't normal. Other boys were beaten sometimes, but none had it like Bobby. Mostly, other boys' parents stopped physical punishments by the age of seven or eight. He was almost ten and still getting hit for the slightest reason. But how could he end it? That required a plan and a great deal of thinking for a prepubescent boy.

But from his hellish experience, Bobby developed a valuable skill. He learned to listen carefully for the slightest subtle inflections of voice, the slightest change in the tempo of household routine. Was Mother's voice clipped or strained in pitch? Were her footsteps quickened? Did the sound of her calls come from a different side of an adjoining room? Was it payday or a day far away from payday? Was she wearing shoes or sneakers? Where was the beating stick she usually kept in the kitchen? Did she leave the groceries on the kitchen table or did she put them away first? Did she ask how his day was with Florence or at elementary school, or did she ask first where he was in the house? Was she late coming home? Did she leave her gloves on or did she take them off? These were the behavioral clues Bobby learned to read, clues that served him all his life.

It was time to end his punishments. Bobby reached the decision that his mother would never stop on her own volition. If the beatings were going to stop, it would only happen because he put a stop to it. He thought about the animals he trapped. Each trap had bait the animal wanted to eat. His mother was an animal, just like any other.

Mr. Hoffman often told him people were a lot like animals. People were predictable, needed food, and followed patterns, just like animals. Bobby thought about what his mother needed. She had food, so he couldn't bait a snare or steel foot trap for her. But by thinking about what his mother needed, Bobby came to the realization that the one thing in her life Estella needed more than anything was to beat him. Beating him made his mother feel she was doing something useful, made her feel her life had a purpose. That need to beat him, not the need for food, was the key to understanding the kind of trap he needed to make.

The punishment game ended with Bobby's plan. He got home from school a good hour before his mother and glued a block of solid oak to the back of his bedroom door. The block was precisely placed at the height of Estella's head. Then he waited.

"Where are you, Bobby? I see you didn't rake the leaves when you got home like I told you. Why didn't you?"

"Because I didn't want to. I'll rake on Saturday."

"You'll rake when I tell you. Where are you?" This insolence, this disobedience was not tolerable. Estella went into the kitchen. Bobby heard her pick up the willow whip from its corner by the stove.

"I said I'll rake Saturday. That's good enough. Everybody else rakes on Saturday. Nobody rakes every day. I'm not doing it!"

"You're what? What did you say?" Estella was boiling mad.

"You heard me. I said I'm not doing it! What's the matter? Can't you hear?" Bobby egged her on.

Estella took the bait.

"I'm going to get you, you little bastard! Where are you?" Estella was furious. Never had Bobby defied her like this.

"Leave me alone. I'm telling you. You leave me alone!" Bobby's tone was firm with a touch of warning.

Estella saw red. Bulls taunted by matadors were docile compared to her temperament. "Gotterdamn you!" she screamed in German and ran flying toward Bobby's bedroom, switch in hand. She meant to give her defiant ten-year-old son a whipping he'd never forget. She homed in on his voice, as he expected.

Sometimes Estella could use her speed to catch Bobby before he escaped through his other door into the bathroom. She was running at full speed when she entered the doorway to his room, as expected. That's all she remembered. When she revived she was lying on the floor with a broken, bloodied nose, the force of the door with its protruding solid oak block having multiplied the force of her forward momentum when Bobby slammed the door in her face. He kneeled over her holding a knife, poised to plunge the blade into her throat. She looked up at her son, alarmed, frightened. She couldn't comprehend what happened.

"Mother, I love you very much, but if you ever try to beat me again, I will stick this knife into you. It's time to stop, Mother. It needs to stop."

Estella's eyes focused on Bobby's. There was fear in hers. Bobby had never seen fear in his mother before. The tables had turned.

"You wouldn't dare use that knife." Estella summoned a measure of contempt for the smaller figure kneeling over her.

"Yes, I would, Mother. I'm not taking it anymore. I mean it. Now I'm taking your switch stick, see?" Bobby held up the stick she'd dropped when she hit the door. Then he broke it over his knee. "I'm taking your stick, Mother, and I'm putting it in the basement furnace. If you ever bring another stick into the house, I will hurt you badly. Do you understand me?"

Estella didn't know what to do. The unimaginable had happened—she'd lost her power over her son.

Bobby let her save face. "From now on, Mother, if you need something done, you will ask. You will not give orders and knock me about or hit me. I will obey you as long as you are reasonable and polite, but I am not here for you to beat upon any longer. I will listen to your advice about things, but I may or may not take your advice. Frankly, Mother, some of your ideas about the old days in Germany are crazy. Nothing like that Hitler stuff is going to happen here. I am sorry your life is so difficult. I will try to be a good son to you, but I am not here for you to beat anymore. Now, I'm going to put this knife back into the kitchen drawer. I just need you to know that I'm serious. Things are different from now on. If you come after me again, I will fight back, and I will stick this knife in you next time."

Bobby let his shaken mother rise from the floor. She quietly went to the bathroom medicine cabinet, held cotton to her nose, and tipped her head back to staunch the bleeding. Then she went into the living room, sat on her sofa, and cried for a very long time. She realized her son was right; her crazy behavior had to stop. And it did stop. She was ashamed that her son had to be the one to put a stop to her behavior, ashamed he had to be so cunning and violent to make her see what she'd done to him all these years. Estella's green whip stick burned into crumpled ashes and the smoke from it went up the chimney along with her vengeance toward her son. Her nose eventually healed with a slight bend in it, and her relationship with Bobby became her relationship with Bob.

For the first time since Nevin died, mother and son became friends who spoke as person to person instead of master to slave. Estella discovered admiring respect for her son when he left the house and ventured into the forest. When he was three, she only worried about his safety in the forest. When he was six, his absences annoyed her, but she was curious about them. By the time he was eleven, she saw he drew a measure of self-confidence from going to the forest, and she decided to go there herself. She saw many of the things Bob saw and gained her first appreciation for natural wonder. As her son opened her eyes to the beauty of nature, her personality mellowed and she saw humor in life and herself. Estella became a happier woman.

The lush green grass behind the duplex held two large maple trees, a weeping willow, and a row of beautiful blue lilacs along the western boundary. The maples and the willow were in a straight line running north to south, which was ideal for young Bobby From the back porch, with the trees leafed out, Estella couldn't see where he was. He hid in the trees for hours without fear of being discovered or beaten.

The backyard merged into forest, and the forest went on forever. It was mixed deciduous and spruce with smatterings of hemlock and blue spruce. In winter holly bushes sported bright red berries, and in summer purple-black choke berries, and deep red bitter cherries fruited for many species of ravenous birds. Winter was colored by bright red cardinals and blue jays; summer brought orange-breasted orioles, blue birds, finches, and red-throated warblers. Doves passed through and cooed love calls in the fall, but during the other seasons they were absent. Magpies, blackbirds, crows, and sparrows were ever present, and migrating hawks rested in the forest canopy above the gully on the north side of the Cedar, keeping Cedar Mountain in sight as they journeyed their migratory route.

From the duplex's yard a footpath meandered through tall sumacs and alder scrubs into Bobby's magical world. It opened onto a grassy meadow that topped a bluff, then dropped into a gully. There, pine trees and tangles of laurels and vines made the woodland seem as if it were interrupted by a jungle footed upon loose rocky shale.

Rivulets from the bluff above made the damp, mossy gully a great boy place, where Bobby pocketed frogs and toads. This portion of forest was home to skunks, possums, rabbits, ground hogs, and snakes, including copperheads, rattlers, kings, bulls, and occasional garter snakes. From Mr. Hoffman, Bobby learned the poisonous snakes and gave them wide birth. Other boys feared the damp gully and stopped at its edge. No one followed Bobby there except Pam. She and Bobby were unafraid of anything when they were together.

Several bird species dwelled in the trees above the gully. Bobby and Pam often sat at the edge of the meadow and saw blue jays, thrushes, sparrows, finches, and hummingbirds. In winter, cardinals appeared. Goshawks sometimes worked the bluff's edge, patrolling silently for wayward field mice, young rabbits or squirrels, and fledgling chicks still in their nests. Once, the two best friends saw a goshawk flying with a garter snake in its beak. It was Bobby and Pam's special secret place of discovery and wonderment.

The trail continued down a long winding slope below the bluff and gully. Through birch, maples, mountain laurels, and some oaks, it meandered through a tangled forest glen for about a half mile until it came to Cedar Creek. Just off the trail, the creek opened to a large expanse of water—at least it seemed large to a small boy. The expanse was Cedar's Dam, and the dam's spillway sent water plunging straight down a drop of about eighty feet onto rocks and some shallow pools, not more than two or three feet deep, below. Below the dam, the creek spread out widely and ran swift and shallow in places. Bobby made several attempts to cross the creek, but the swiftly flowing waters knocked him off his feet and dragged him downstream. He didn't mind getting soaking wet or getting his clothes muddied; he was determined to cross and undeterred by dangerous waters.

Eventually, after going to the creek for several days, he found a place where the water was just slow enough and only as deep as his chest. When he crossed the Cedar for the first time, he sat quietly on the mountainside shore. He looked at the creek for the longest time and wondered if he could cross back again to the other side and home. A thought arose that told him he didn't have to go back, that he could keep going. He could run away. But he wasn't ready to put legs under that thought, at least not yet.

He summoned his courage, re-crossed the creek, and went home, but after that first time, he came back often and crossed to the other bank. From there he climbed up the mountainside and, over time, he explored the entire mountain. He was only five or six years old and already going off for entire afternoons by himself. Estella knew he was out beyond the backyard, but she thought he was somewhere in the near forest, never suspecting he went so far away.

Bobby was six years old when he first discovered the Iroquois' caves. They were a series of natural tunnels that end in bedrock, similar to mine adits, with linked passages between them, positioned by some mysterious freak of geology below a subtle slate shale outcrop near the top of Cedar Mountain. They were located in an extensive grouping of very dense pines, far more vast than a mere copse, and distinctly apart from the nearby less dense forest. Likely the flora favored the soils and water flow on that area of mountainside.

It was doubtful that stretch of mountain saw a human more than one or twice over a ten-year span. Those who ventured there likely hurried to leave. Winds from the valley floor made the caves howl when there was an easterly storm, and prevailing westerlies caused the pine tops to whirr rustle and their trunks to creak and groan and rub eerily together. It was easy to slip and fall on the steep mountainside's loose shale, and the downfalls invited broken arms and legs for the careless. Bears, bobcats, and owls resided there. If one stopped and sniffed the air, one could smell them.

Bobby's secret place was spooky. He never even took Pam there. There were some things women just shouldn't know, Mr. Hoffman said, and Bobby thought the caves' location was one of those things.

There were drawings carved into rock inside the tunnels, animal shapes and strange symbols. When Bobby discovered them, he wondered if the Iroquois made them thousands of years before. Atop the caves there was a nearly flat place where he could sit amongst the pines and scrubs and look out over the entire Cedar Valley and Milltown. From that high perch, Bobby looked east to the Shohono as it flowed downstream past Milltown. He saw to the north the town's church steeples and the large clock face on the huge gray tower of Calvary's Church. Everything looked so small and far away. He saw tiny houses and watched cars move about, like they were faraway ants. And he wondered.

He sat for hours at a time and wondered about what life was like beyond Milltown, and why other boys had a dad and he didn't. He sometimes felt sorry for himself, as most everyone did from time to time, but his sorrows were blended with a touch of angry seasoning. When he felt dejected up there on his perch, he wished he had a dad to take him fishing and to baseball games like a lot of the other boy's dads did with their sons. He even wondered if he wasn't good enough to have a dad. Anger grew within him, but then he remembered the things Arlene told him about how every person was different and how life was what you made it. Then he felt resolute and strengthened.

"What if I showed the other boys and their dads that I was just better than the other boys? Then what?" He talked to himself up there on his mountain perch and questioned life and its mysteries. He wondered why he loved women and girls so much more than other boys did, or maybe they did but they hid their feelings. He didn't know the answers to his questions. He just wondered.

For years he went up to his place high up on the mountainside and wondered. Why did he have to beat the other boys in school? Get the best grades? Beat them in sports? Was it his way to prove he could be better than them despite their advantage of having a father, or was it his way of getting praise and recognition from teachers that he couldn't get from a father? These introspective ruminations troubled him and he wished he didn't have them. When they arose, he tried to brush them aside and just stay focused on whatever was the task at hand.

But he began to understand at an early age that he was not like other boys. He grew confident that he was smarter than most of them, and he often thought of them as animals to be observed. He liked observing. He liked abstractions and stayed detached from most of his peers, except Pam. She was special for him. Likely there wasn't anything he wouldn't do for her. He did not make friends easily, but he was intensely loyal to the few he had. And he enjoyed the adrenalin rush of the risk-taker. He learned how to hang by the joints of his legs upside down from tree branches, high above the ground, and he challenged other boys to beat his jumps from high places onto the ground, always besting them as the heights increased and they declined to match his jumps.

In winter months, when the creeks and the dam froze solid, the children of Milltown went skating. The Cedar froze a foot thick with a mirror-smooth sheen of green, glassy ice. Most kids were content to skate upon the creek or on the dam and never strayed close to the dam breast. The drop from the breast to the rocks below was about eighty feet, enough to break legs, skull, and backbone and drown a child who fell over the edge.

Bobby gained the awe and respect of the other children skaters. For reasons known only to a boy who sought adrenalin rushes and escape from Estella's tyranny, Bobby skated upstream fifty yards and then turned around and sped straight for the dam breast. As he raced toward apparent death, Bobby thought to himself, *I'll prove to all of them that I don't need a dad. I can do things they are too afraid to do. I am without fear. I have everything I need. I believe in myself!*

"Look! He's going over the dam!" screamed one of the girls as she watched in horror. All heads turned to see Bobby flying downstream as if his skates had wings.

It looked like he intended to lift into the air and sail over the dam breast, hoping to land on the frozen creek downstream from the plunge churn of the dam. Then, about twenty feet from the edge, Bobby lifted his legs into the air and turned his body to his left. A collective gasp rose from the children observers. A few long, agonizing seconds passed while Bobby appeared suspended in midair.

He landed hard with a force that tested the strength of the ice. Simultaneously, he dug his skates' edges hard into the ice and sent a plume of ice spray ten feet into the air and out over the dam breast. Then he stopped, six inches from the dam breast and certain death. He did it! And he'd lived.

He turned toward the other children and nonchalantly skated toward them. The boys who saw this feat of bravado were stunned. They knew Bobby had tempted death and won.

252

Afraid to try the daredevil stunt themselves, they were cowed by his bravado.

"Show off," said one.

"He's nuts," said another.

"He's trying to kill himself," said a third.

The girls saw the stunt differently. Bobby was their hero. He could do anything. They saw in that instant that he was different and special. He was fearless, manly, and skilled. They wanted to share his spotlight. Many wanted to become Bobby's girl.

He repeated the maneuver two more times, proving it was no fluke. Each time, he successfully stopped six to twelve inches from the dam breast's edge. No other boy attempted to replicate Bobby's feat. Fate wasn't further tempted.

When the Cedar froze, Bobby, now called Bob, skated upstream from the dam past the creek's rapids. His strong legs propelled him into the air from below the small waterfalls and his nimble feet dug his blade tips into the ice shelf above. He was unafraid of slipping and falling into the stream and being swept under the ice. No others dared to follow. Bob became a local legend.

As Bob grew older, there were fewer episodes when he would get hit for things he failed to do, like coming in late from playing, or failing to take the trash out to the curbside, or not timely raking ashes from the coal-fired stove, or not raking the leaves as ordered, or, heaven forbid, for playing in the leaves instead of raking them.

As he grew, he became bolder. The jump from the next highest porch step was symbolic of his physical growth, and destructive for Estella's plants. He was chastised for letting other children into the house, but no longer punished.

No subsequent punishments were as memorable as the ones he'd received as a toddler for entertaining Sharon, the little girl from around the corner who took her pants off in the basement to compare her anatomy with Bobby's, and the one he got for chasing an airplane on an active runway because he wanted it to stop and give him a ride. By the age of ten, he'd lost his fear of Estella. She stopped beating her son, dug up her peony bushes, and replaced them with rose bushes.

In her later years, Estella remembered her "straightening-out sessions" with her son. The first, when Bobby was three, amused her and she retold it to Florence and her girlfriends at the mill.

Estella caught the two three-year-olds together, hugging each other while naked from the waist down. She dragged the screaming little girl by her hair unceremoniously to her parents' home, sans pants, and threw her into their house via the front door. Estella, in rampaging mother mode, returned to gather up little Bobby and beat his bottom with a fresh-cut green switch until she exhausted her arm strength, screaming the whole while.

"That is not for you! Stay away from that. Girls are dirty!"

Other punishments seemed mild compared to the one for Bobby's first exploration of the opposite sex. He was whipped for taking a hot poker and carving his name on a wooden beam in the basement, and for making messes of sawdust and nails while building birdhouses and animal traps in the basement. The punishment years continued as Bobby passed the age of five. That year he and his mother were at the county fair. There was an air show, which gave rise to Bobby's second great straightening session.

Planes landed and took off on a long grass runway. They did loops in the sky and men walked on their wings. It was wondrous. Small boys gaped and awed.

"Can I ride in the airplane, Mommy? Please. Please!" Bobby was intent on flying that day.

"No. I said no. We can't afford something like that. You'll just have to stand here and watch. That's almost as good as flying."

"But other kids are flying, Mom. Can't I go up just once?"

"No, damn it. Don't ask again."

Estella squeezed Bobby's hand firmly. He tugged to escape, twisting his hand in hers. The crowd gasped at what happened next.

Little Bobby broke free of Estella's hand and chased a plane down an active runway because he wanted to go into the sky for a ride.

Women screamed, "Stop that boy! He'll get his head cut off by a propeller!"

Bobby's dream of a ride was not to be. A policeman chased him down, scooped him up, and returned him to a hysterical Estella. Bobby was taken home, stripped of his pants, and hit with the switch until his behind bled.

"You will obey me when I say no, damn you!" Estella screamed.

"I'm never going to hold your hand again, no matter how often you hit me. Never!" Bobby cried.

The stick lashed into his back and bottom side.

"You're going to learn to listen. Who in the hell do you think you are?"

Estella whipped furiously with the switch, oblivious to the psychological harm, mindless of the numerous cuts on her son's skin.

"Stop, stop! Please, Mommy, stop!" cried the helpless recipient of Estella's wrath, but she ignored his pleas and continued until her arms were too tired to hit him.

Bobby writhed in terrible, searing pain. The whipping stick left scars on his backside that stayed all his life.

His beatings were less frequent thereafter, and Bob never held his mother's hand again, not even on her deathbed when she begged him to forgive her for the way she'd beaten him as a child.

When Bob was older and physically able to perform a chore, Estella showed him what she wanted done and expected him to do it. She set her mind to raise Bob, insofar as possible, with the same challenging exuberance and willingness to work, as if he were, like her, a child of Hitler's Reich. She brooked no man into her life. American men were too casual, lacking in purpose, without much morality, and lacking any sense of urgency to sacrifice for a greater good. She viewed Americans as being unfair to Germans, even though people of Germanic ancestry were the largest ethnic minority around.

Americans were, in Estella's estimation, pathetic. Her surrogate husband was selected because he was convenient and because it was likely he wouldn't live very long after they "married." The poor fellow hastened his demise trying to please her, to win her love beyond the appearances of the Bund's arrangement. She believed his death happened for the best. Americans lacked the fierce, conquering, warlike qualities she felt coursing through the blood of every German SS officer she'd slept with. No, she would never allow an American milquetoast man to become involved with her or contaminate the mind of her son. She would raise him to become a man who would have made her führer proud.

Self-control, discipline, hard work, and honor were goals Estella established for he son. She strived in all her methods to instill him with those qualities, teaching him not to cry or complain when whipped or tasked, and always giving him more chores as soon as he could do them. She showed Bob little affection, reasoning a man's attachment to a woman, even a mother, softened his resolve. It was best if men and women mated like animals, as Hitler wanted. The state would raise people properly. It knew more than the family.

As she aged through the '60s to the '90s, Estella noted that America became more and more like Nazi Germany. The state gradually displaced the family as a child's most influential presence. She viewed that as a good thing. She raised Bob to overcome adversity, to work ceaselessly, to obey superiors, and to control his feelings. She did her best to impart her attitudes and prejudices to Bob, just as certain views and prejudices were imparted on her at Nazi youth camp. She fulfilled her duty.

Bob was developing largely to her satisfaction, but he was not blindly obedient as she wanted him to be, and he had an elusive quality about him that she could not undo. He questioned more of her commands as he grew. He'd ask why he couldn't wait to rake leaves until they all had fallen, and why she didn't wait to do laundry until there was sunshine and a breeze instead of always doing it on Saturdays, rain or shine. For these questions, Estella simply told him it was "because." However, Bob noticed after a time that his mother would do laundry more on sunny breezy days than always on Saturdays, and he wasn't summoned to rake leaves until all had fallen.

For some questions, like when he was only three and asked why he could no longer play with Sharon in their backyards, she had no answer. She eventually capitulated, allowing him to play with her as long as they stayed outside where they could be seen. When opportunity presented itself, Bobby and Sharon ran down the footpath at the end of the yard into the forest. There they tried to kiss like grownups did and marveled at the differences they saw when they took their pants off. These were fast trips, two explorer pups returning quickly to their backyards.

Elusiveness became Bobby's forte as he grew older. He often left the house and went into the forest, traveled down to the dam, and crossed the Cedar downstream. Then he'd climb up the mountain to places only a nimble boy could go. Some days he'd disappear for the entire day. He told his mother he liked being with the animals and that he could follow them around. He learned how deer patterned their lives, where they fed, slept, hid, and went for water. He studied how the wind made them uneasy when it rushed through the pines, and how flies annoyed them in the summer heat. He learned to be unseen when near them, and he noted their quickened gait as they neared a spring. Then they slowed to a cautious walk when they were close to the water. Their heads and eyes moved suspiciously as they drank, as if they were afraid of being caught by a passing black bear.

By age nine, Estella got Bobby active in the Holy Church of Bethany. He was one of the altar boys and sang in the church's choir. He tried to kiss the pastor's daughter, Dorothy, one night after choir practice, but was pushed away and rebuffed. She told him she didn't want to be serious about boys until she was finished with high school. His ardor cooled from that embarrassing encounter and he vowed to ignore her, pretty thing though she was, and try his luck elsewhere.

When he turned fourteen, Bob got a paper route. He delivered a morning newspaper for the Fortown Morning Bugle, the voice of the Shohono Valley. Through snowy, icy cold mornings and hot, sweaty summer ones, Bob delivered papers before he went to school. One Saturday each month, he went to his customers to collect their subscription fee for the month just ended. One such spring Saturday, happenstance dealt Bob a card that focused the boy's career path for the rest of his life.

His mind wasn't on anything in particular that day, one of those idyllic spring days in Milltown. Robins were hopping about, heads cocked, listening for worms, nests filled with fresh hatchling chicks that were screaming to be fed. Bees buzzed about the lilacs, irises, dandelions, and daffodils, and rabbits scampered upon the meadow like manicured lawns. Sometimes the rabbits stood to box others' paws and sometimes they took a moment to fornicate. The air smelled fresh and clean as it always did in Milltown. Young Bob didn't have a care or a thought in the world.

One customer was an elderly, reclusive man, a retired postal worker named George Meltzer. Usually he'd meet his paper boy at the front door, opening it before Bob had a chance to knock. Without saying a word, he'd hand the lad an envelope for the exact amount due. He never tipped. That spring morning, he was sitting inside his screened-in front porch on a swing glider, some books setting beside him.

"Hello, boy. How are you this fine day?" he asked Bob.

"I'm just fine, sir. Thank you. And you?" The Boy Scout manners were a part of young Bob and the old man noticed.

"Say, I see you about here quite a bit. Your mom sure keeps you working, doesn't she?"

"Yes, sir." The reply was cautious. Why did this old man notice him and his mother?

"That's okay. I don't mean anything by asking. I know your mom's story pretty well. Many years ago, I knew some of her family back in the old country. I'm glad to see you and her getting along so well. Word has it you're a smart boy and a good son to her. Too bad about what happened to your dad. He was a fine man and I knew him well."

"Thank you, sir."

He warmed to the man a bit. Mother told him the man had delivered mail for years. Perhaps he shared some empathy for a fellow deliverer of the printed word; perhaps he sought some camaraderie. It was heartwarming to hear a good word about his father, Nevin.

"Well now. If you have a little time, I'd like to show you something. Come here and sit on the side of the glider over there. I want to spread out some books between us."

Bob did as he was told, and the old man spread out a large Horsey Stock Chart book. There were stock price charts for hundreds of companies, simple arithmetic charts with monthly price ranges going back over a history of about ten to twenty years for each company. The pungent, sweet smells of cigar smoke gave credence to the old man. He smelled of wisdom and experience.

"Look at that page, boy," old George said. "What do you see?"

"Charts" was the quick reply.

"Well, look harder, boy. Tell me what you see."

Bob thought the old man was playing some kind of game, but he didn't understand.

"Charts, sir. There's nothing else to see on the page but charts." Bob was insistent.

"No, boy! You are looking at money!" George erupted with a raspy, booming voice.

Bob knew what money was; he toiled mightily to help bring money into the household. Still, all he could see was charts. He looked at George, puzzled and curious for the answer to this riddle.

"These charts show you stock prices." The old man went on for about an hour with the boy, showing him how stocks moved both up and down, and how different stocks in different industries could react to different business conditions during the different phases of their cycles. Young Bob's eyes fixated on the different charts. He was fascinated by what the old man knew.

"You see, boy, you work hard for your money, and you probably save it in the bank, don't you?"

"Yes, sir." He wanted the old man to tell him more, and he was not disappointed.

"Well, Bobby, if you bought a stock with your money at the right time and the stock went up, you could make a lot of money. You'd have your money working for you. Look at this one," he said, pointing to a stock in the chart book. "If you put a hundred dollars in it here, and you held it for two years, your hundred dollars would become a thousand dollars because it went up ten times in price. Let's look at some more."

And so it went, Old George kindling Bob's interest in investing. He explained how important it was to learn all you possibly could about investing, about each of your stocks and the company behind the stock price, and about all the reasons why it could go up and down. The old man and the boy talked for hours about the economy, the markets, the roles of banks and brokers, the different types of cyclical forces that businesses experience, and the reasons profits could rise and fall. Bob became a willing pupil of old George and would spend many an hour with him thereafter. He'd learn more from George in each hour spent with him than he learned in a whole week at school.

"Could I be an investor like you?"

Bob was ready to start investing on his own. He wanted to learn all he could about stocks and investing from that day forward.

"You most certainly can. Tell your mother to call me. If she agrees, we can get you set up with what's called a brokerage account. You can then call a stockbroker and buy and sell stocks."

Old George and Bob beseeched Estella to open a modest brokerage account at the Fortown office of Watson and Co., a New York Stock Exchange member firm. Estella put Bob's money in the account and her son began investing, having his mother phone the broker with his buy and sell orders. What began as a curious learning experience blossomed into a career. Bob became a stock market junkie. When he was sixteen, he started a mutual fund for students in his high school class, invested their money for them, and kept records of all trades and each participant's contributions.

One warm spring afternoon, during recess, young Bob received a second lesson. That one wasn't about money. Well, maybe it *was*, in an indirect sort of way, but it was better described as a lesson about cultures and mindsets and how their intersection barricades innocence.

Weeks before his investment lessons, young Bob noticed a girl who appeared in two of his classes. Her name was Rose Levine, and her girlfriends called her Rosie. Bob noticed Rosie and her friends often looked at him, then cupped their hands to their mouths and whispered softly before bursting out in laughs and giggles. In the school's hallways, some of her friends passed by and gave him a "Hiiii, Bobbyyy" elongated salutation, implying they knew something he didn't.

Shortly thereafter, in a hall passageway, Rosie herself passed in the opposite direction and lightly brushed against him. He wondered if the brush were accidental or intentional. It happened quickly and there were many students in traffic at the same time. The female organization knew how to plant a seed. Bob began thinking about Rosie during those lapses his mind had when it wasn't thinking about algebra, muskrat traps, stocks to buy, or chore lists from his mother.

Thoughts of Rosie drifted into his mind. She was the first girl who'd captured his romantic interest since he and little Sharon had scampered in the forest with their pants off, and his obsession with Pam. But this was different. Rosie was old enough for sex.

"Life isn't misery's soul mate, Bob. Life can be fun. Life is to be enjoyed, not something you fight against. Life is what you make of it." Pam's words often echoed in his mind when he thought of Rosie.

Pam once asked him if he'd ever considered being a farmer.

"Wouldn't you like to have a farm, a place of your own out in the country by a stream with your own orchards and animals?" She wanted to be married to a farmer and surrounded by children and animals.

"It sounds great until you try to live it. Do you really want to be mucking cow stalls, cleaning chicken coops, driving ten miles every time you need something? Do you want to be with your animals when they're sick?"

"Yes to all of it. And I especially want to be with my animals when they're sick. I love animals, and they need someone like me who cares about them. Most people just use them like they have no feelings."

That was Pam. Pam and her animals. Living in a city, having a business, working with people's money scared the hell out of her. She loved her Dutch countryside; a team of draft horses couldn't pull her away. But what she said about life rang true and helped Bob break the shackles of Estella's misery.

Pam knew what she wanted in life—that much Bob understood—and it wasn't a fit for him. It was a sadness to know they were parting ways, but Pam said life was what you made of it. The more Bob thought about her words, the more he thought about Rosie. Pam was in many of his classes and their friendship was strong. They often talked and shared notes about algebra problems. They even studied together and their childhood attraction never left them, but now she went on dates with other boys.

Things happened like Arlene said they would. He felt a little sad about losing Pam but saw they were taking different paths in life. He wanted to go into finance and business; Pam wanted to live on a farm, take care of cows, chickens, and pigs, have lots of kids, and become a school teacher. One particular boy she often dated stood to inherit his father's farm. He was a tall, freckle-faced country boy who doted on everything Pam said or did. When they were together, they laughed a lot, and Bob noticed Pam allowed him to carry her books for her. Bob watched with regret as his and Pam's childhood slipped away.

Years, families, and distance eventually separated Bob and Pam, but they remained distant friends all their lives. They exchanged letters with their goings-on two or three times a year until they were well into their nineties.

"Good friends need holding on to," Pam always said.

ROSIE AND PAPA

Whenever teenage Bob saw Rosie, he wondered what this pretty girl was like. She was enigmatic and alluring. Bob was shy around girls he didn't know, and he denied himself opportunities to make their friendship and company. Besides, Estella disparaged girls in general, telling him they were a needless distraction from his studies. He went along with his mother about that, figuring she knew best. He wanted to get into a good college, study to become a stockbroker, and then work in the investment business—which, he often reminded himself, left no time for girls.

But there was something magnetic about Rosie. She was very bright. Her mind was quick and she understood things without excessive study or memorization. She was near the top of their classes together. And she had a beautiful doll face with porcelain skin and dark, flashing eyes. She wore a bright red lipstick on lips that begged to be kissed. When Bob looked at Rosie, his eyes lingered on those lips, and when he closed his eyes, he imagined kissing them. Rosie laughed lots, with a genuine, rolling, mirthful laugh. She looked at life as an endless series of happy, wonderful party days, and she was first to find humor in many things. Rosie was Estella's opposite. Not dour, Rosie was joyful, full of life, and her happiness was contagious. When she entered a room, happiness arrived with her and everything became bright and wonderful.

Estella approached life out of a sense of fear and misery. She was one of life's downtrodden unfortunates by circumstance and her own choosing. She railed against those who lived better than she and raged over the slights the world dealt her. She also harbored the belief that her lot in life was Bob's fault. If she weren't tasked with raising him right, life would've been easier.

From Estella's perspective, she and her son should excel at toil, and somehow if they toiled and suffered enough, she's be vindicated and thus triumph over life. Bob was raised to see life through his mother's eyes. During his formative years, he never questioned her views, just accepted them. His life then was a chip off hers.

Now, he wasn't so sure. Arlene, Florence, George, and Pam had views that were shades of contrast to Estella's. Rosie's views about life simply brushed Estella's aside and ignored them completely. She had no room for misery.

Recess periods lasted twenty minutes, enough time for students to go to a neighborhood snack shack or bakery to fortify their tummies. Bob usually went west on Cedar Street to Fisher's Bakery and picked up a Persian donut and a carton of milk during these interludes. Rosie disappeared during recess hours, but that day, as fate would have it, they'd met. An ambassador from the female organization told him Rosie wanted to see him. She'd wait around the corner, about a half block east of Cedar Street. Bob knew the location. There was a family grocery store on the corner. Around the back of the store there was an alley, about a half block east on Cedar.

Excitement and intrigue made Bob's heart beat faster. Rosie wanted to see him! As he made his way through the throng of kids leaving the gray granite Milltown High School building, his thoughts were only of her. Everything about her was beautiful. He'd noticed her face, with its coy, flashing smile, inviting red lips, and shiny white teeth. Rosie's thick, lustrous brown-black hair accented her dark dancing eyes. She was incredibly seductive. Her breasts bulged against her blouses and her buttocks bounced when she walked in a natural sort of way, not like some girls who tried to exaggerate a cow's sway. Rosie was a bouncing package of life, the kind of girl who young boys prayed would magically appear in their bedrooms.

Rosie gave Bob a friendly wave and an open smile as he rounded the corner of Third and Cedar. She took him by the hand and led him into the alley. They were alone, no prying eyes able to see the two young heartthrobs. Once in the alley, Rosie put her arms around Bob's neck and pressed her body hard against his, her crotch into his leg. Then she kissed him full on the mouth. Her tongue darted into his mouth and probed his tongue, electrifying him. He'd never been kissed like that before. He pulled her even closer, squeezing her tight against him. Then they broke for a moment to speak.

"I think of you every day," Bob said. "You're very beautiful. I can't think of anything else but you. Do you feel the same way about me?"

"Yes. Of course I do. I love you. My heart beats like crazy when I see you. I want to be with you all the time. But we must be careful. We should not be seen together. We have to keep our love a secret."

"Why?" Bob couldn't imagine a reason not to be seen with a girl he loved. He even thought he'd like to introduce Rosie to his mother.

"I can't explain things to you now. I'll tell you later when it's time. You must trust me on this. Know that I love you, and that I want you very much, but we must be smart about this. I want to be with you for my whole life, but you must promise me you will tell no one. Absolutely no one until I tell you it's okay."

"I don't understand. Why must we be secret? Does that mean I can't be seen with you anywhere? We can't dance together? We can't have lunch together? I can't have you meet my mother?"

"No, we can't have any of that for now. There will come a time. I can't explain things to you now, but I will. Until then, we must meet in secret. We must plan times to meet. It won't always be this crazy, I promise you. It may take me a while before we can be open about our love, so for now, you must promise me."

Bob's head was spinning. There she was, this voluptuous, beautiful girl of his dreams telling him she was in love with him, but they couldn't see each other in public. It seemed crazy. He'd sensed from the first time he'd noticed her that there was something mysterious about her. This confirmed all those thoughts. He loved her too. She gave him no choice, so he played along.

"Okay, I promise. I'll tell no one. I love you too, Rosie. I'd do anything for you. It'll be our secret. Just let me know when and where I can see you again."

"I will. Just be patient for me, okay?"

"Okay." The two young lovers kissed some more. Rosie placed Bob's hand on her breast and let him feel her. She put her hands on his behind and squeezed him close to her. Bob was sensing nirvana and couldn't believe his great good fortune. He was lost in her essence, the smell of her hair and the taste of her lips.

Rosie broke it off quickly. "We have to go back to school now. Act as if nothing happened. Remember, tell no one. It's important. I'll get word to you where and when we can see each other again."

"Okay, I promise. It's our secret. I'll tell no one."

"Good. Now we must go. Good-bye for now." Rosie broke their embrace.

Bob left the alley first. Rosie followed later, straightening her hair and blouse and applying fresh lipstick. As he walked back to school, Bob wiped her lipstick off with a handkerchief. He didn't understand the need for secrecy, but most guys he knew said girls were just plain nuts. Based on what occurred in the alley, Bob figured they were right.

Rosie's secret Monday noontime rendezvous with Bob and their kiss in the alley caused her nascent love to burst into a hot flame. The flame was doused and guttered on Friday of the same week. Her plans to gradually gain her family's approval were crushed by her father. She began to feel uneasy at the dinner table.

It was Shabbat. Her mother lit the Shabbat table candles and invited God's spirit into their holy day. Her father said the blessings of the wine and the fruit of the earth. After they sipped their wine and Papa Levine pulled a piece off the challah loaf, her mother began serving dinner. Normally her three brothers, especially Dick, her older brother, would be engaging in lively tableside conversation with her and her parents. But this night was different. No one spoke a word, and that alone made Rosie uncomfortable. It meant that something was troubling the family in some way. Worse still, Papa Sam Levine just ate his meal and stared at Rosie the entire time, never once taking his eyes off her. The silence continued until Mrs. Levine brought out her creamy cheese blintz dessert tray.

"Rosie, I have heard you do more at school than study your lessons. Is that true?" Papa Levine got right to the point. Rosie knew the cat got out of the bag somehow. Maybe one of her girlfriends told a mother and that mother told her mother. Her mind raced. It was too late to come up with an excuse. She couldn't lie to Papa.

"Father, please don't be angry. He's a very smart boy. He's the smartest in the class and he is a gentleman. We didn't do anything except have one kiss, Papa. I was going to tell you about him and discuss it privately." It was the best halting retreat Rosie could summon.

Papa Levine just stared at his only daughter.

Mrs. Levine spoke up. "What Rosie says is true, Sam. I talked with Arlene Zippin about the boy. He is brilliant and very strong and handsome. Arlene took him under her wing when he was only two, and he's half orphaned, and she's made a lot of progress with—"

"Is he a Jew?" Papa Levine stared at Rosie, ignoring his wife.

"No, Father, he is Christian. He attends the Holy Church of Bethany. But, Father, he's not very religious. He works very hard and makes good money for a boy."

"Enough!" Sam Levine slammed his huge open palms down upon the table. The dessert dishes leaped into the air and landed again upon the table. Every other family member trembled from Papa's outburst.

"Papa, don't!" Rosie screamed.

"Silence!" he shouted at Rosie.

"No, Papa, please," Rosie whimpered.

"You are not bringing a gentile into this family. He may never come into this home. You may never eat a meal with him. You may never see him again. You will change your school classes so that you are not in any classes he is in. You will never kiss this boy or touch him in any way ever again."

"Papa, please! Papa, oh please, don't do this. He's a good boy, an honest boy, and I love him, Papa." Rosie was bawling and her tears streamed down her cheeks. Papa showed no mercy. She was not going to have her way about this.

"This is my family, my house. You live under my roof and you live with my rules. This is final, Rosie. If you see him again, you will be out in the street with no place to go. You will never sit at this table again. You will never go to temple with the family again. You will inherit nothing. You will never speak to your mother or me again. You will be out of this family and you will never be allowed to come back."

"Papa, why must you be so harsh? Please, Papa. No. No." Rosie was sobbing, pleading shamelessly. Her mother and brothers just sat there staring straight ahead. She received no sympathy. Rosie stood from the table and ran upstairs, crying and screaming "no, no, no" until she reached her room. She closed her door and threw herself on her bed, bawling like a wounded animal. Her feelings and her dreams of love were crushed.

Rosie's retreat didn't stop her papa. His deep voice boomed up the stairs after her. "And you will throw away your lipsticks and your tight-fitting clothes. You start dressing and acting like a lady. You go to school to learn, not to catch boys."

After a long ten minutes, her mother came into her room and sat on the bed next to her sobbing daughter. Mrs. Levine gently rubbed Rosie's back.

"Your father is right, you know. You know that because you tried to hide this matter from him. I know what young love is like, Rosie, but it passes like a bad fever. There will be lots of boys and men who want to be your husband. Father and I will help arrange for you to meet some nice Jewish boys from good families from the big cities. You'll go to college and have a wonderful time, and you'll marry and have children and you'll be very happy. Papa just wants you to have a good life, free of misery. He has his ways, but he loves you very much and he knows what's best for you. I know this hurts, but it is right. The gentiles' ways are not our ways. There's no good future with this boy. You and this boy have no idea how hard you'd be making life on yourselves if you stayed together. Papa is right to end this business before it gets serious, if you know what I mean."

"Mother, please let me be alone for a while." Rosie needed time alone to digest what her parents said, how something so wonderful and beautiful could be forbidden. She stayed in her room the rest of the evening.

A week went by with no word from Rosie. She did not come to her classes. Then, at recess, Bob was confronted by Dick Levine. He was a senior, much bigger and stronger than Bob, a mere skinny freshman.

Dick put his big paws on Bob's shoulders from behind. It was totally unexpected. Dick turned Bob around, facing him.

"I understand you like my sister, Rosie. Is that true?" Dick was formidable. Bob half expected a punch. He remembered his promise to Rosie. Not a word.

"Rosie? Oh, her. Well, I see her in some of my classes." Bob was as noncommittal as he could be.

"Look. I know all about it. I know how you two feel about each other. You're a nice kid and all, but you can't see Rosie ever again. You need to forget about her. Find yourself another girl. I don't ever want to hear that you even talk to her anymore."

There was a look of seriousness on Dick's face. Bob thought perhaps Rosie was dying from some terrible disease. He was worried.

"Is she all right? Is something wrong with her?" The young heartthrob was concerned for his sweetheart.

Dick smiled, even laughed a little. The younger boy's reply took him aback.

"Oh yes, she's all right. It's nothing like that. She just made a mistake when she kissed you in the alley, that's all."

So, Dick did know. He wasn't bluffing. How? Bob didn't tell anyone. Rosie must've talked, or maybe one of her friends. No matter. They were caught.

"So I'm a mistake Rosie made, is that it?" Bob was a bit miffed.

"Yes, Rosie's mistake. Not yours. You couldn't know."

Bob looked at Dick, puzzled. He deserved an answer. It was forthcoming.

"You see, Rosie is a Jew, as I am and our father, Sam, is. Dad will not allow Rosie to marry a gentile man, so he won't allow her to date any gentile boys either. He doesn't want her to learn any gentile ways or think any gentile thoughts. Your people are different from our people, and that's just how it is."

"And what does Rosie think about this?" Bob was perturbed.

"It doesn't matter what Rosie thinks. It only matters what Papa thinks. He's the head of the family and he makes the rules. If Rosie were to disobey Papa's rules, he'd throw her out of the family. She'd not be allowed to talk with him or Mama or me or her other brothers. She'd get no money from the family ever. She'd inherit nothing. She wouldn't be allowed to sit with the family at synagogue services, and we'd be ordered not to speak with her again."

"And you agree with this?" Bob was appalled.

"It doesn't matter whether I agree or disagree. It's what Papa says. That's it. That's final. Rosie is his daughter, and that's how he wants it. She's going to grow up and marry a Jew, and she's going to raise her children as Jews. It's Papa's way. Look, she made a simple mistake, that's all. Not much harm was done. I'm telling you, for her sake, to let her go. Do not see her again. Let her have peace in her life as a Jewess. Do not try to mix her up. If you care about her, let her go."

"And if I don't?"

"Then our papa will destroy her. He will! And I'll beat the living shit out of you every time I see you. She's my sister, and I don't want you seeing her anymore. We aren't kidding about this. You forget her."

Dick pushed his finger into Bob's chest, but it didn't hurt anything like the heartache the younger boy was feeling. He'd never be with Rosie again. He knew he needed to let her go. It was some religious cultural thing that he'd never before encountered.

Bob couldn't understand why Rosie's father wouldn't think he was good enough for her. He had the best grades of all the boys in his class, and he worked hard and learned quickly. He loved her with all his heart and would honor and defend her all the days of his life, he was sure of that. And she loved him. He knew it. She'd told him so, and he could feel it. The love seemed real, and he believed it was. He'd heard of puppy love, but he put Sharon in that category, not Rosie. The only thing about him that didn't measure up to her papa's criteria was that he was not a Jew. That seemed ridiculous to him. Also, he couldn't imagine Rosie being happy with another man, marrying some guy when she was older just because he was a Jew. It all seemed surreal to young Bob. He'd wait for a sign from her.

Rosie was out of school that following week. When she returned, it seemed as though life was drained from her. Her eyes looked duller than before, she wore no lipstick, and her clothes were much looser. She didn't look at him in class anymore, just stared at the floor. He continued to look at her regardless, hoping to catch her eye. Eventually she did glance up at him and their eyes met. She shook her head, and kept shaking it. Then her eyes started to tear. A few tears ran down her cheeks. Then she burst out crying, unleashing a flood of tears and sobs right in the middle of an algebra theorem.

The teacher stopped the class and asked Rosie if anything was wrong. She shook her head at the teacher and got up, crying noticeably as she walked from the classroom. Bob began to get up to follow, but she held out her arm and flared her hand toward him the same way a running back straight-arms a linebacker. Bob sat back down.

The next day, Bob learned that Rosie's classes were reassigned at her request. She would study algebra with section two students from then on and her civics class would be taken with the commercial class. Bob would never see her again, except from afar, and she never looked into his eyes again as she had in the past. He was left with the bitter realization that Jewish papas had long arms that reached out and controlled their daughters. The two young hearts were broken.

BOOKS AND HEDGES

There was something different about Bob that some boys in school resented. Many young boys in Milltown had no aspirations to ever leave town or to get a higher education. Why bother, they reasoned. College cost money, and when guys graduated, they didn't make as much as a boy who went straight to work for Big Steel in nearby Steeltown, or in any of the nearby factory mills. When these boys saw Bob going to the town library, taking out a stack of books to read, they felt uneasy, as if their premises about life were challenged. They were intolerant of Bob's unorthodox behavior.

One fall Saturday, some of the boys' tensions snapped. There had to be a reckoning. Bob walked on Third Street from the town library with a stack of books under each arm. The maples, elms, oaks, and birches that lined the streets were turning their beautiful reds, oranges, purples, and yellows. Maple nose pinch seedlings were occasionally twirling down like helicopters from their branches aloft. It was a peaceful, serendipitous, glorious sort of day, or so it seemed.

Suddenly, Walter and Warren, two thuggish boys from the football team, jumped out from behind a hedgerow onto the sidewalk in front of him. Trouble did what it intended to do sometimes, and this was one of those times.

"Whatcha doing, book boy?" Walter taunted.

"Ya don't need dem books, bookworm," Warren stated.

After the taunts came the action. The two interlopers knocked the books from Bob's hands and kicked them into the leaf-muddied street gutter. They began knocking the books around, soiling their pages as best they could. Bob watched Walt and Warren smear pages with mud. They disrespected him, but worse, they insulted knowledge. This happenstance summoned something within Bob. A surge of adrenalin flushed his face red, the same sensation he had when he saw Pam cry from embarrassment that day on the playground. It rose up the back of his neck and pulled his fists into clenches. He liked books with a budding reverence for their knowledge content, and he respected the tremendous work authors put into their writings. What these two thugs were doing infuriated him.

Walter got hit first. Bob threw lightning-fast punches. The fullback was not expecting the flurry delivered directly to his face. It was impossible to react. Bob beat him severely about his eyes and broke his nose, sending streams of blood from his nostrils down over his shirt. Warren's mouth gaped in disbelief. It all happened so quickly, a fast fury like nothing he'd ever encountered on the football field or anywhere before.

Warren panicked and froze, watching Bob unleash the same fury on Walter that he'd unleashed on Alan, Buzz, and himself years before. He was petrified, uncertain whether he should try to help his friend. He was a big kid, an offensive tackle for the Iroquois, but not very fast. Bullies tended to run when confronted and Warren ran for his life, but Bob ran faster than every other boy in the class. Warren had no chance. Bob ran him down and shoved him into a hedgerow, then dived in after him, landing on top.

Hedges have stiff, poking branches that jab and scratch their intruder, inflicting pain. Warren got the worst of the hedges, and also received the beating of his life from Bob, who punched him unmercifully about the face. Like Walter, Warren received battered eyes and a broken nose, and he also suffered a broken front tooth. Neither opponent landed many blows on Bob, and what few they did he scarcely noticed, too intent on engaging and destroying these Neanderthals.

In those fierce few minutes, Bob gained a reputation amongst his high school peers. He would not be intimidated or bullied. He did not back down from a fight, even two against one with boys bigger than him. And if someone did fight him, he could hurt them.

SALES

Marvin's will provisions regarding Israel and his bequeath of the Associates company to his beloved mistress, Susan, along with Associates' perpetual contract to provide services to the fund at exorbitant rates confounded David. He was trapped in a box created by his own father, controlled from the grave.

Susan's staff was all female, a sex David basically hated. He felt pinned down and trapped by Susan's staff. He was stuffed in in a box of Susan's office procedures and sacrosanct routines, potshots from females sniping at every move he tried to make and stymied by industry regulations whichever way he turned. Every idea he had, whatever move he tried to make, he had to first clear with Susan, and there was nothing he could do about it. He held ownership, but Susan held power. Marvin set up the company that way. He was technically the owner of the fund complex, but he couldn't sell it while he was alive and he couldn't even do as he pleased with his asset when he died. The rabbis would sue him for specific performance of Marvin's will if he bequeathed the complex to anyone but Israel when he died. It was predestined to go to Israel; David was just a caretaker. Marvin didn't think much of him; he was certain of that now. He was being given a living, and could earn more if he could grow the company, but the asset he lived off was not really his. He hated Marvin in death, and now he also hated Israel.

David often cursed Marvin under his breath for his entangled predicament and spared no venom in his thoughts of Susan. She controlled the service company, its employees, the fund's contracts for shareholder services, its transfer agent services, its attorneys, its litigation budget, its audit budget, and its regulatory filings. These agreements were effective for a period of thirty years and automatically renewed for another ten years if his father's mistress bitch was still alive after the first thirty. So, conceivably, Susan could live long enough to torment David until he died. She was still his babysitter.

David could manage the fund's assets, a chore he didn't particularly like doing. If he did well, he could make a larger income. He could also grow sales. His underwriting discount left plenty of room to compensate other dealers to sell the fund's shares, and there was another source of income in the portion of the underwriting discount that the fund's underwriter retained after payments of sales commissions to its own captive sales force.

The sales effort was meager. Insurance salesmen were not like securities salesmen, who sold hope for capital gain and yield for income. They were the racehorses of the world of sales. Insurance salesmen sold fear of death, fear of leaving behind the widow and the orphan. Thus, an insurance salesman was a curious sort of crossbreed between a ghoul and a blind squirrel.

Every once in a while, after religiously going to their churches and schmoozing with the leaders of their respective congregations, after going to numerous church socials, after giving endless seminars to yokels about how to keep track of their checkbooks, the squirrel would happenstance upon his acorn meal ticket. A fellow parishioner died. Now the squirrel was given leave to gather his nuts, or assets. He could be there, could rush to the funeral to be at the side of the aggrieved widow. He could tell her how lovely she looked beneath her sagging breasts and smeared mascara. He could portray himself as her substitute savior right here on Earth by selling her some annuities and mutual funds from the proceeds of the poor stiff's life insurance policies.

Aggressive squirrels would raid other squirrels' nests. They would read the obituary columns for every death within a hundred miles and would show up at funerals with their grieving acts about how they knew old Fred from years ago and how terrible they felt about not staying in touch. All this came complete with business cards and sales brochures in case the widow needed his help, or if she wanted to bed the out-of-town squirrel. Many squirrels offered such added services in exchange for annuity and fund sales.

Female squirrels also worked the graveyard business. Widower men could be especially vulnerable to a younger woman with a pretty smile and a willing disposition.

Through the world's tedious turns of sunsets and deaths, the captive sales force of blind squirrels brought the fund an occasional piece of new business, but it was an agonizingly small inflow. The widows and widowers didn't really have much interest in investing. They looked at their holdings the same way they looked at their bank checking accounts, outflows nearly equal to inflows. Money for trips, new clothes, remodeled kitchens, "investing" in the new boyfriend's nightclub or gas station idea, and sending the children off to wherever places for whatever reason all took priority over investing.

The administrative offices were more frustrating to David than the paltry sales effort. Run by Susan, administration was smooth functioning and efficient, but the fact that the employees were all women drove David to near madness. He was one of those few homosexual men who positively loathed women. David saw women as competition for the affections of males, and he was suspicious of their cliquishness. He harbored intense resentment of Susan that continually boiled within him. She constantly reminded him of his father, his father's control of him, his father's brilliance, his father's good looks, and his father's shabby treatment of his mother, whom he despised as much as his father.

David never confronted his feelings of animus toward Eloweiss. Mother was just the parent who was never there for him. But somehow, in David's mind, everything that was wrong with his life became Susan's fault. All the slights his mother gave him as a baby and young toddler were because of Susan. She was a woman too. That was reason enough.

Now Susan held him captive to her procedures and methods of running the administration of his firm. His version of an ideal firm was an exclusively male homosexual one, a big playpen for David. As matters now stood, he could not give orders to any female staff member. All his requests had to go through Susan. His father had made him a eunuch to these wretched cunts!

David never wanted to be in the investment business in the first place. All his adult life, he'd wanted to be a bureaucrat working in some government office from nine in the morning until five in the afternoon. He wanted nights and weekends off, vacation time, holiday time, overtime, and a government pension. He envied those in government. Unlike those in the securities business who worked the markets around the clock in a never-ending grind, government employees just sat around making petty rules to raise havoc with people who worked for an honest living. Government people also got to intimidate and play God with real working people, a benefit David envied. He fancied himself as a do-nothing, sitting at a desk with his feet propped up while collecting extortion bribes from the victims he regulated and writing occasional memos to justify his existence and request for a larger budget.

David was profoundly unhappy. He longed for male companionship. He wanted an all-male company so he could demand love from other men and have some measure of control over them. His life was a miserable shadow world of secret rendezvous, subtle signals in grimy bathhouses, and constant fears of discovery. He married a presentable woman whom he trusted with his secret. She was a religious congregant and a determined traveler, dedicated to month-long excursions with her girlfriends to faraway places. When in Plaintown, she spent her weekends riding horses in the foothills and shopping for Indian artifacts, but she was rarely with David. She was a willing bisexual woman who cared for her friends but had no particular loyalties to her husband.

David couldn't bring himself to have relations in the maiden position. He couldn't get hard that way. The one time they really tried to force matters, he threw up on the bed. He was only able to have sex with his wife by entering her from behind. After their third year of marriage, she noticed he stopped getting hard altogether.

For a time, she believed David was making some progress, but one day she smelled him when he came in from the barnyard. He carried the distinctive smell of semen, but there were no women on the property. It seemed at the time to be an unexplainable oddity to David's young wife, but she soon forgot about it. About two months later, she returned home from a three-week jaunt to Europe. She came home late that night and went straight to bed. David was sleeping and she did not wake him.

In the early morning twilight, the young Mrs. Sustack felt an overpowering urge to scratch her scalp. Her crotch also itched unexplainably. She turned on the light, now seeing the bedroom clearly. There were sheep droppings on the carpet on her side of the bed, and the stale smell of urine came from the rug. There was some foam residue around the urine patch, obviously from an amateurish cleanup effort. When she turned down the sheets on her side of the bed, she screamed.

"Fleas, David, we have fleas! There are fleas in our bed!" The young wife was screaming hysterically. "And lice, David. There are lice in the bed! AHHHH! AHHH!" she screamed even louder, grasping the extent of the infestation. Her mind raced with thoughts of horrible diseases and a horribly mistaken marriage. David just rolled over slowly, still in a sleep stupor. He didn't react to the filth. That's when it dawned on her that David was excited by the sheep. While she was away, David brought animals into her bedroom.

The bedroom and adjoining rooms were professionally fumigated. Carpets were torn up and destroyed by fire, all bedding and closet clothing removed and burned. The distraught wife set up her own sleeping quarters in the guest room on the main level and decamped permanently from David's upstairs bedroom. She withdrew from him sexually, and they never had relations thereafter. They then developed the perfect marriage of two people who each preferred solitude. They lived apart from each other under the same roof.

She threatened David with divorce if he ever brought one of the barnyard animals into the house again. He just laughed at her turmoil and said nothing. His gambit succeeded. She stayed married to him, even after subsequent animal episodes and follow-up fumigations.

David often thought of selling the business, but Marvin's will provisions thwarted his hopes. He'd also have to overcome Susan's contract and the rabbis. Maybe he could persuade the rabbis to reach a compromise, but Susan would likely accelerate his payments and litigate against him tooth and nail. After years of deliberation, David decided he would fight Marvin's graveyard grip, somehow outwit his nemesis father.

David would find a way to thwart Marvin's will. Israel would never get the companies. He'd get revenge on his father by destroying his father's mistress. He would plot and scheme until one glorious day when he would unchain himself from Marvin's golden handcuffs. He'd show the world and all his father's crony watchdog friends that Marvin could not control him! Marvin handpicked his advisory board, old codgers all of them. Each was once successful in his own right, but now they were retired executives, community gadflies, and club-goers. They were not liable for the fund's investments as they were an unaffiliated board, and David's personal travails were of little concern to them. Their main concern was that the companies or the proceeds of their sale would be left to Israel.

All the same, David resented their presence because they reminded him of his father. Still, he kept the board. It was nice public relations window dressing that masked a deep internal division between David and Susan. David was consumed with an inner rage toward his late father. Marvin, from his grave, had the two adversaries tied together with an ingenious Gordian knot.

Susan had her own share of frustrations. Her handsome Marvin, love of her life, was gone, replaced by his implacable, slovenly, aggravating, toady son. At every opportunity, David tormented her staff girls with lame pretexts. He asked them to leave the office to run the most ridiculous errands. He sent them to buy a certain type of paper or pencil, or to plug a quarter in his curbside parking meter while he had free garage space a block away. He asked them to do nonsensical things like look up the times for shows or movies, all of which he should do himself. He deliberately hindered the staff and accidently spilled coffee on their desks and clothes all too often. He cleared his nose obnoxiously in front of them, and he belched and passed gas in the front office where Mrs. Rodriguez worked.

David often arrived at the office without bathing. His body odor was blended with the obnoxious smells of animal dung which clung to his cowboy boots. He leered at the females in the office, pretending to be heterosexual or possibly trying to become so. He asked girls to climb the file room shelf ladders to the very top, looking for some mysterious file he said he thought was up there, all the while standing at the base of the ladder looking up their dresses. Susan caught herself thinking about David more than was healthy. She referred to him as the little chickenshit son-of-a-bitch bastard.

Though David was a committed homosexual, female anatomy did attract his curiosity. He'd had few real encounters with women, having tried them out of frustration with his own self-loathing and resentment of his homosexual stereotype. But, he could only mount women from behind because facing a woman during sex brought back memories of his mother. His vaginaphobia stemmed from an incident he witnessed as a three-year-old. Unable to fall asleep, he went to his parents' bedroom and unbeknownst to Marvin and Eloweiss, David knelt down next to their bedroom door and watched. Once each week, at his appointed time, Marvin serviced Eloweiss. David observed closely while his dutiful father took the deep breath which enabled him to tresspass the stench of his mother's unwashed vagina. David watched as his father wedged his magnificent head between Eloweiss's massive ham hocks and began to fulfill his mitzvah.

This was not to be an ordinary evening for the married couple. Eloweiss felt deeply betrayed by Marvin's tryst with Goldie Blinkly. She'd given Marvin her family's money to manage, all her family's friends' monies, the Temple's money, and a great deal of money from her cousins in Chicago. She'd also given Marvin the ultimate sacrifice. She gave her own flesh and blood and labored for three hours to produce his miserable little shit of a son. Marvin begged her to get pregnant and she did. She never promised Marvin she'd do that. David wasn't part of their deal, but she relented and had the boy as an extra favor to Marvin because she loved him. She gave Marvin a son!

What more could a good Jewish wife possibly do for her man? How ungrateful could Marvin be? She earned her right to indulge her cravings for blintzes and chocolates. She could still fuck good enough for Marvin to get off. Her body fat was still manageable. How dare he insult her by bedding that smelly ash tray of a woman? What could Goldie offer him besides a pretty face and a spunky body? Goldie's family had little money, few connections, and few successful professionals. It was time to bring Marvin back to reality. Tonight she would meet out her punishment to Marvin because she knew she could. Her family's money and their social connections formed the core asset base of Sustack Associates' investors. Marvin and Eloweiss both knew many of Marvin's assets would flee to another firm if he ever divorced her. She figuratively held Marvin's balls and his business in her hands. Tonight she also held Marvin's head between her legs and she intended to make him pay for his indiscretion. She saved her bladder for this moment.

Little David didn't understand what he saw. At first his father's head was nodding between his mother's legs. Her massive pelvis was propped up upon an overstuffed stadium pillow. His mother's hands were behind her head and she looked down her abdomen at his father's nodding head. Then his mother suddenly clasped her legs tightly around his father's head. Her ankles held the back of his head in place and pressed it into her vagina. Little David thought his mother's pee place was swallowing his father's head. Then, his mother released a spurt of urine into his father's face. His father struggled to pull away, but his mother held his father's head tightly to her vagina and continued pissing in his face until her entire bladder emptied. The bed linens were flooded with his mother's urine pool. The bed spread, the mattress cover, and the mattress itself were all soaked with his mother's urine. His father finally escaped his mother's leg lock. Marvin ran to the bathroom and gagged into the sink. Then he repeatedly washed his face with soap and his mouth with mouthwash.

Mother Eloweiss lay in her urine pool and laughed vindictively. She shouted at his father from their bedroom. "You stop seeing that Blinkly whore! You hear me, Marvin? *YOU STOP SEEING HER!*" She screamed hysterically. "Tonight is just a sample of what I'll do to you if you don't drop that whore. The next time we see her at a function, you ignore her. You don't take her home in your fancy new car. You don't fetch her drinks like you're her little puppy dog. You stay away from her. If you see her again, I'll know, Marvin. I'll *KNOW!* She can't keep her big mouth shut. She brags about fucking you, Marvin. She brags about fucking you to my friends. *SHE HAS TOLD THE WHOLE COMMUNTIY SHE'S FUCKING MY HUSBAND!* You thought you could sneak around on me and I wouldn't find out. *HA! WELL, FUCK YOU TOO, MARVIN! TASTE MY PISS, MARVIN! MY PISS IS TOO GOOD FOR YOU! NOW YOU KNOW HOW I FEEL!*"

Little David was shocked by what he witnessed. His mother was screaming hysterically. His father ran away to save his life. It was all very terrifying for the child. His mother's female part had the power to hurt his father in some way he couldn't understand. He went to his own bathroom and threw up, terrified that women could somehow hurt him with a deadly weapon they kept hidden between their legs. From childhood to adulthood, David stayed intimidated by the thought of frontal sex with a female. For his rare episodes of heterosexual sex, he carefully mounted prostitutes from behind.

When Castro was about to come out of the mountains to take control of the Cuban government, David took full advantage. He flew to Havana because it was said the prostitutes were desperate for business. He spent a week there, and each day he had several different young men. He also mounted one female prostitute from behind. David fantasized he was living dangerously and helping stave off communism while he advantaged himself of the desperate plight of social outcasts gathering money to escape Castro's clutches. He boasted about his Cuban conquests for years afterward, carefully omitting that, with one exception, they were younger men.

Susan had her own frustrations. Besides Marvin's absence and David's behavior, she was also heartbroken over the antics of her daughter, Marty.

Marty grew into a stunning woman with a full figure and a winsome porcelain doll face. She had lustrous black hair with a slight tinge of reddish brown that emanated from a cowlick plug on the front left side of her head, just a half inch behind the facial juncture with her scalp. Everyone who saw Marty for the first time took a second look. Some thought the hair streak was an artful dye job by a skilled hairdresser, but it was real and it resulted in an unusually stunning appearance. Her eyes were a deep, radiant brown with a tint of green.

Many men lusted for Marty from first sight. She recognized that and parlayed men's desires into considerable financial success. Susan saw her daughter's career plan was much like her own, maybe even more so. She was nagged by a premonition that the path of promiscuity would be her daughter's ruin, but given her own history with Marvin, she was frustrated and powerless to restrain Marty. The possibility of being in closer contact with her gave Susan some hope.

Marty arrived in Plaintown after her education in eastern Ivy League schools, quickly becoming the personal secretary to the board chairman of Plaintown's largest bank. Her duties were merely perfunctory, her main talents deployed after business hours or on jaunts out of the office. But there arose a messy problem with the man's wife when Marty and her chairman were caught in a compromising situation. There followed a scandal that made her position at the bank untenable. Their dalliances and waste of corporate assets were collateral damage to the man's divorce, their affair cause enough for the bank's board to remove them both.

Marty was very bright, educated at the best schools, but she had limited practical skills. She was also scandal-tainted goods and badly in need of employment. Susan's empathy for her daughter-protégé prompted her to seek a compromise with David. She went to his office, something she did as little as possible. "David, I'd like to hire a new employee. Our contracts require us to agree on it."

"You need another clerk?"

"No. This position would be in marketing."

"That's my department. I don't need anyone."

"It's my daughter, Marty. She needs a job. She'd be good in sales." David sensed an opportunity. Susan wouldn't come to him asking for a job for her daughter unless there was an element of desperation.

"But Marty is highly educated. Why can't she get a job in some big company?" David knew about Marty's scandal, but feigned ignorance.

"Well, she's been in a bit of a situation, and she needs some time to get past it." Susan was both diplomatic and honest.

"I'd be her supervisor? You'd let me supervise your daughter?" David felt like a fox that was placed in a henhouse.

"Yes. I think marketing is her best place. In administration she wouldn't fit well with Barbara and Mrs. Rodriguez. She doesn't like strong women and does much better with men. I believe Marty would thrive in a sales setting. I think she'd be a huge asset to the firm."

David thought for a moment. "We'll hire her, but I want a favor in return."

"What?"

"You know I would like to see more males in the office. I've told you that."

"You want me to hire a man, a man for you. You want a man for you in exchange for Marty for me?"

"Two."

"Excuse me?"

"I want to hire two men of my choosing and put them in your department under your supervision. They are not to do any serious work, but their pay will be the same as Barbara's."

"But, David, Barbara is valuable to me. She's paid well for her skills. I can trust her. How will I be able to supervise two men who have no duties? How could they be good for the firm?"

"What's good for me is good for the firm. Look, do you want your daughter hired or don't you?"

In an agreement born of mutual human needs, Susan agreed that David could hire two men of his choosing, provided they would not interfere with her administrative staff, and David agreed to hire Marty for marketing. Thus the fund complex charted a new course to become a front for a combination playpen and whorehouse. Neither Susan nor David saw that as a problem; after all, investors had no idea who their fund managers were or what went on at mutual funds' headquarters offices. The fund's investors absorbed the added expense of the two male fixtures. Marty was expected to earn her income through sales. Susan hoped David would become preoccupied with his playmates and interfere less with her staff.

Finally, Susan would be reunited with her daughter. Her life was lonely without Marvin, and her hope was that Marty could help fill an aching void in her life. Mother and daughter could have lunches together and often visit each other in the office, and hopefully Susan could influence Marty to curb her promiscuous inclinations.

The day Marty was hired, Susan showed her around the offices. In Susan's, Marty stopped to stare at the portrait of Marvin. "Mother, why do you have Marvin Sustack's portrait in your office? Why not hang it in the hallway or the conference room?"

"Oh, we had this blank wall here and David wanted the halls and conference room decorated in western art, so here it is. Do you remember Mr. Sustack?" Susan hoped Marty would recall her childhood days when she bounced on Marvin's lap. Perhaps there'd come the perfect moment to tell Marty that Marvin was her true father.

"Barely, from when I was a little girl. I remember I sat on his knee a few times."

"He was very smart. Can you remember his voice? He used to talk with you." Susan wished to talk about Marvin, but Marty had no interest.

"Look, Mother, I have a hard time remembering my father. I often wonder how he could lose control of the car and go off Independence Pass up by Aspen. I miss all the times he played softball and waffle ball with me. Remember how Dad and I used to play monopoly and checkers? You never wanted to play with us. Why do you now want to talk about dead Mr. Sustack when you hardly ever mention my father?"

"Well, it's just that you'll be working here. I thought you should know about the founder."

"Let's go to lunch, Mother." Marty didn't want to hear any more about the dead founder of the firm.

Susan's hope to introduce Marty's paternal connection was quashed for the time being. She decided to let Marty go on believing that Joseph was her father; after all, she did carry the name Maloney.

Marty got herself securities licensed. Then David tasked her to accelerate sales of the fund and gave her free reign to choose her methods. Her modest base salary was augmented with a commission bonus for increased sales. Marty was soon out on the stump, calling on stockbrokerage branches. After a few short days, local salesmen began calling for her.

"Could she please come at such and such a time to such and such a place to help make a presentation to a client? Could she go along on a road trip to Greely or Durango or Aspen for three days to meet some large clients?"

Suddenly the fund was getting big-ticket sales. Marty was single-handedly producing more than the rest of the entire sales force. There were ranchers, doctors, and businessmen to sell and to bed. As prospects decided to get into bed with Marty, they also got into bed with the fund, and sales doubled from the single-minded dedication of one determined woman. Her results put the entire blind squirrel sales force to shame. Marty was on a mission to fuck her way to wealth and power.

Susan stopped by Marty's office after a $2 million order was posted on her sales blotter.

"Can you tell me the secret to your success? I mean, are you romping at will out there?"

"Mother, don't tell me you've never had a dalliance."

"Yes. I've been in the corporate world, and I know about having an affair or two, but Marty, the way these sales are pouring in here has me worried about you. Do you even know some of these men who are asking you to go out on sales calls with them?"

"Mother, please. I'm a big girl now. I'm just taking your good example and upping your game a little." She looked at her mother in a matter-of-fact, "take it or leave it, like it or lump it, but I am not changing my ways" expression.

Susan wasn't stupid; she knew the sales surge involved extras from her daughter. She listened to Marty's phone conversations in the office and they made her cringe. Marty promised to fuck and suck off every salesman who could deliver big-ticket sales.

Years before, without David's knowledge, Susan had installed a telephone surveillance system. She could monitor internal intercom conversations, as well as calls to and from outside the firm. Her secret system was securely locked away in her credenza behind her desk and concealed by a matching false-wood front. It looked to the world like a harmless end panel.

Susan heard salesmen arranging with her daughter to slip away to clandestine places. Marty's Grand Junction trips ended instead in the Mountain Top Lake Lodge; her trips to Durango went no further than The Broadmoor Resort in Colorado Springs. Although she was somewhat envious and filled with memories of her own times away with Marvin, Susan simply could not stand her daughter becoming Colorado's premier traveling working girl, no matter how much money she was bringing into the firm, no matter how much Marty was earning, and no matter how many romantic sights Marty was seeing while fucking her brains out.

Susan insisted on making changes and went to David.

"I want Marty off sales."

"But it was your idea to put her on sales."

"Yes, but not that she'd be fucking every mutual fund salesman in the state!"

"So what? No one's getting hurt."

"Marty's getting hurt! She's out of control. Someday she'll get a disease or some jealous wife will kill her. It needs to stop."

"You're being too protective."

"Listen. If you don't stop this, I'll start busting sales. Not every investor is suitable for this. I'll sit on every sale and I'll reject orders. I'll have the regulators in here. What's it going to be?"

Susan cowed David as only she could. She stood tall over him, next to his throne chair, ignoring his pretense of superiority. She was in babysitter mode once again; she gave the

THE SECRET AND THE BUTTERFLY

orders when it was time for David to stop what he was doing.
When she squinted and her lips pursed, David knew from
childhood days he could get spanked. Now that they were
older, Susan wouldn't spank him, but she was capable of
slapping him down, and she never made an idle threat.

David backed down. Marty was yanked from her fieldwork
and confined to office sales support.

As the new director of sales and marketing, Marty hatched
a scheme to ramp sales. She interviewed a number of female
models with hot bodies and loose morals. In actuality, she was
looking for freelance types with massage escort experience who
would be willing to do sexual favors for tips. Marty contracted
for six of these eager beauties and outfitted them in skintight
leotards and blouses that accentuated their cleavages.

Marty didn't bother to get the girls their required security
licenses; she had no time for annoying details. They were
contracted to simply deliver sales literature to every security
firm's branch office in Plaintown. Brazenly, the girls would
walk into an office, blow past the receptionist, and declare that
they were delivering sales literature to John, Peter, and Bill, who
were all waiting for it. For the most part, the girls got away with
the scam, dropping fund sales literature on each man's desk
along with their personal cards. Salesmen who bit on this hook
were treated to time with their hooker delivery girl, expenses
paid for courtesy of the fund based upon sales achieved.

Marty's move into mutual fund sales and prostitution
services was wildly successful. Sales rose fourfold in the first six
months of the new campaign, surpassing her solo efforts of the
year before. Alas, all successful sales campaigns have their
potential foil.

By the mid-1970's, many brokerage firms were discovering
that women were better management administrators than men.
They tended to follow rules better than the men and they kept
their branches running relatively clean and ethical. Marty

referred to these women as anal retentive, uptight spoiler bitches. One of Marty's girls ran afoul of one of them and was threatened with jail for prostitution. The girl spilled her guts on Marty and her sales methods.

As a result of the squealer in their sales ranks, securities regulators came to the fund and ordered Marty's sales operation shut down. Fines were levied against the fund's broker-dealer for unlicensed sales activities, and offers to rescind sales were sent to all the johns. The mayor of Plaintown summoned Marty to his office to personally lecture her. She had given the town's mutual fund sales the reputation of a seedy, slimy business, and many Main Street firms were viewed by the public as notorious snake pits.

"Young lady, did you realize salesmen's wives were complaining? Did you know customers' wives were in an uproar? Honestly, Marty, decent people find better ways to make a living." The mayor was speaking as if the town were without sin before she arrived. "Why, I, your mayor, even got a call from my wife about your sex-for-sales scheme and she demanded I put a stop to it! What do you have to say for yourself, young lady?"

"Well, Mr. Mayor, a girl has to find a way to get along. This is a man's world she finds herself trapped in. I've just done what comes natural and what I enjoy. I like to make men happy."

"You feel no shame for what you've done? Look at the marriages you've damaged. What about these women and their children?"

"Well, if the men's womenfolk kept their beds warmer for their men, we wouldn't be having this discussion, would we? I just try to do my part to keep half the population happy."

The mayor rose from his desk and came around to Marty, putting his arm around her. "Look, young lady. Marty, isn't it?"

"Yes, sir." Marty felt him squeeze her waist and thought, *He's just like all the others. He'll drop his line on me any minute.*

"Well, Marty, I know how tough things can be out there, competing with men in a man's world, so I'm going to go easy on you. You just promise me to be a good girl from here on out and I won't have anyone press charges against you. Frankly, Plaintown needs young women with spunk like you have. If you ever need my help, you just call me. But I want to hear only good things about you from now on. Agreed?"

"Yes, sir."

"And if you want my help, I'm sure I can find a place for you. Okay?"

"Thank you, sir." And, that was the end of that. She got the signal that the mayor would find a place for her in his administration if she asked, but as he was only going to hold office for another year, she decided to let the overture fall silent.

Curiously, no one took up the firm's rescission offer, all assets staying with the fund. The girls went their way without prosecution, and Marty was returned to sales support under the watchful eye of Susan.

David made a few faux passes at Marty, but she found him ridiculous and repulsive. She rebuffed him, as he expected, with her best good humor, reminding him that he wasn't really her type. He always gave up easily when it came to the feminine pursuit, and he was forever cowed by Susan. Now that sales growth had stymied, he thought of Marty as an overpaid clerk and a liability to both the firm and him.

David set aside his thoughts about Marty for the time being though, instead spending many of his office hours studying his stock index charts, hoping to discern a way to grow the fund through improved performance. Results were never David's forte, yet each day he meticulously plotted daily price ranges and the closing prices of the Dow Jones Industrial

Averages and the Dow Jones Transportation Average on a huge scroll chart upon a massive table, along with the volume of the Dow Industrials. After his scribe work, David stared at the charts for hours, hoping they'd reveal their secrets.

Marvin developed the charts initially as a tool his son could easily follow. They were kept in a room by themselves and no one except David was allowed to enter. For him, the chart room was analogous to the Holy of Holies at temple where the Torah scrolls were kept hidden behind a partition and accessible only by rabbis.

When an infrequent visitor came to the fund, they were taken by the chart room and the receptionist whispered to the fund's guest, "It is in this hallowed, always locked, top secret room that the fund's top secret charts are maintained."

In truth, the fund's charts were published on a smaller scale in every daily issue of almost every business newspaper in the world.

Marvin introduced David to the Dow Theory, a concept that helped one know the true direction of stock prices. The theory was developed by Charles Dow and written about extensively in a book about the theory authored by a man named Robert Rhea. David had a copy of the book, which he read and referred to often. By following the book and the charts, he robotically managed the fund largely by being totally invested in the market or being partially in cash when the theory indicated the market was declining.

The rest of David's time was taken up by long lunches with his new male hires. The men would disappear for three or four hours at a time, often for entire afternoons. David was enthralled to have two male employee playmates. His favorite was a young, muscular specimen with extremely short-cropped hair, earrings, and tattoos on his arms and forearms. He was a smoker, the only one in the company. His smoking was terribly offensive to the women employees and several took their complaints to Susan. He was stinking up their clothes, leaving his ashes in the trash cans, blowing smoke in their faces, and refusing to empty his ashtrays or trash cans. He turned their tranquil lunch room into a pigsty. They demanded a no-smoking policy for the firm. A turf war between David and Susan ensued, David supporting the smoker and Susan supporting her girls.

"The situation is intolerable, David. We need to get rid of him or I could lose staff. Can't we find you a playmate who doesn't smoke?" Susan was at her wits end.

"But I like him. I need him," David moaned. "Can't you just lease another space for him somewhere?"

"Sure I can. But his space goes on your marketing budget, not on my administration budget."

"Agreed."

Ultimately Susan and David compromised. The firm leased another office space and made it into an office exclusively for the smoker. He was forbidden to smoke anywhere else in the firm's offices. The compromise didn't entirely remove the stench of the cretin, but it helped some.

The smoker's job description, for fund expense accounting purposes, was to operate an aging Burroughs card fed computer for about two hours each month. The machine was an ancient beast of an apparatus. It could have been replaced by a modern personal computer that would have cost less than one month's salary for the smoker, but the Burroughs got lucky—David adored the man.

The other new male hire was a youthful, twenty-something, pimple-faced, skinny man-child who rarely bathed. He was required to work one hour each day in the mail room. If there was no mail to go out that day, he did nothing. If there was more than an hour's work, one of the women from the reception office was required to assist him.

The two new drones in this female beehive whiled away their days in the company nonsmoking lunch room, reading comic books, lifting hand weights, and listening to rock and roll music. The only time the newly leased smoking office was used was when "The Muscle" needed to take a puff. The duo was a constant source of agitation for Susan's staff girls; the women all worked hard for their money.

Resentments built and staff jokes flourished. The girls ascribed nicknames to them, calling the muscular one "Will Eyesuck," and the skinny one, "Jack Meoff." One staffer, Lucinda, when passing either of them in the hall, would hold her hands up to her mouth as if she were holding a giant cock. Then she would bob her head up and down over her imaginary prize while moving her tongue in and out of her mouth like a dog does when it laps up water. Soon, the males complained to David that the women were making fun of them and the women were complaining to Susan that the men were ridiculous wastrels. Susan thought the situation was deplorable and maddening. David thought it was hilarious.

The fund was at a standstill. Caught by the market decline of 1973 and 1974, the death of Marvin, the regulatory wrist slap, and Marty's absence from field sales, the firm's assets were dropping fast. David hired salesmen to go on the road and talk to his quasi sales force, but the effort showed meager results. The company was like a sinking ship stilled in the water, with no prospects of fresh winds for its sales. The business was going nowhere.

MEETING

Change happens. Meteorologists say weather in America can be altered by a butterfly flapping its wings in Japan. Amongst millions of Japanese butterflies, some climate modelers assert that one maverick butterfly doing an unexpected flap of its gossamer wings could drive their static, predictable weather equations into wildly erratic behavior. This explained cyclones, tornadoes, snowstorms, lightning, high sea swells, and mudslides they didn't predict. A faint breeze may set strong winds into motion, relieving a ship becalmed. Until forecasters could model butterfly wing flaps, their models would be suspect.

Like legions of butterflies flapping their wings, investment research firms and newsletter writers sent forth blizzards of written epistles called research reports to investment advisors and fund companies. This blizzard of reports contained a smorgasbord of information about companies, industries, economic and demographic trends, charts of all sorts of things, banking and money issues, and many things beyond bizarre and crackpot. Mostly the missives were received, sorted, stacked, perused, and discarded. Rarely did a piece of unsolicited work evoke a response, but occasionally a piece would cause an eyebrow to raise and a reader's curiosity to ignite. Then, with luck, the reader would be enticed as a cat lured to catnip, and a call went out to the report's author.

In the investment world, that was big business. Calls to analysts were paid for, either in cash or in chits promising a certain volume of commission trades to the firm that housed the analyst. Those sums could run from small ten-thousand-dollar retainers to millions per year in commissions to the broker dealers in firm-to-firm arrangements. Calls cost.

David read a research report one hot summer's afternoon that sparked his imagination. If the analyst was correct, the idea he wrote about could be that fresh breeze he'd been waiting for. It had the potential to move the fund from the doldrums and propel its assets to new heights. David placed a call to the analyst author and invited him to the office.

The floor of offices that housed the fund complex seemed otherworldly to David's guest. When his elevator opened, the guest was face to face with an expansive wall of thick glass, behind which was a huge lobby area with two reception desks. At one desk sat a portly Hispanic woman. The guest could see under the portal in the desk that she was wearing a pants suit. The other receptionist was a remarkably comely woman.

She had high cheekbones and wore her lustrous dark hair braided tightly behind her. Her face had a luminous amber quality about it, and a radiant glow lifted from her skin. Her native Cherokee bloodline was blended with tastes of the Levant, where her maternal ancestry fused Macedonian conquerors' blood to Bedouin royalty. Her eyes and flared, uplifted eyebrows bespoke her royal lineage. When her eyes lifted from her desk to gather in the appearance of the visitor, there was majesty about her and the way she slowly raised her head. She looked up at her visitor as if she were inspecting a morsel of food offered on a tray. Blue turquoise earrings framed the beautiful, dazzling face. She wore a conventional pleated black skirt and white silk blouse, buttoned up to her neck. Under the portal of her desk was a pair of shapely nylon-sheathed legs, crossed, with her skirt tipped just below her knees. There was a mesmerizing beauty about her overlain by a prim and professional bearing that signaled she was off-limits to male curs.

When Bob first saw this composite woman, a rush of saliva came to his mouth. His visceral reaction flooded his thoughts with an instant desire for her. He was stunned to see a woman so beautiful doing office work, or work of any sort. She was misplaced. She belonged on a throne in a palace somewhere. He blinked rapidly, thinking there must've been some mistake at what his eyes beheld. Her photogenic face belonged on the cover of a beauty magazine or in the movies, not hidden away in some obscure office. Bob's head lifted slightly and he gasped a quick, short breath as he beheld this girl-queen model-woman. The Romans had a word for his temporary disassembly. They called it the "thunderbolt moment," the moment when a woman's beauty struck lightning into a man's heart. She was a beauty worth dying for.

A few passing seconds seemed like an eternity. Bob imagined her standing in a canoe, clad only in a thong with a scant frontal cover barely extended an eighth of an inch beyond her vagina. She glowed in the moonlight beneath a star-filled sky. The goddess princess wore a single eagle feather in a simple red headband. She was poised bare breasted with a drawn bow and arrow, about to shoot a duck sleeping on a predawn lake. A gentle wave lapped against her canoe, and she stood in a sensuous, undulating rhythm with the wave motion, aimed her arrow, and then released it to take the mallard's life.

Bob sensed his heart was that envisioned duck. Without speaking a single word, she'd taken his heart for her own. He imagined holding her close and kissing her tenderly. He would protect her and never let her go. His blood ran hot and his desire flared. Flames of red shot up his collar into his neck and face as Bob hoped he'd have the chance to talk with her. His eyes were glued to her while he waited to be received.

Both women sat there stoically and stared at the visitor. Bob guessed it was normal for them to appraise newcomers before taking the slightest action. Neither greeted him, neither stood up to come to the door. They just leveled a steadfast stare at him. A lone frontier horseman riding into an Indian village received that same look from the assembled squaws. Bob was being scrutinized with a female microscope.

Barbara, the beauty, narrowed her eyes to a slight squint. Her head lifted higher to fully measure the interloper. Intuition told her the man wanted her. Somewhere within her womanly senses, a spirit told her this man came here to come into her life. She noticed he was awestruck, his gaze on her face in an unmistakable, unrehearsed look as his jaw gaped for a brief instant. He held her gaze too long for a simple recognition gaze. The old tribal chiefs termed it the "Look of Awakened Spirit" or the "First Spark of Life." It was the look of a man who wanted a woman. This man was not there a minute ago; now he was. He stood there like a big horse waiting for her, and she wondered if he could be gentled and ridden. He seemed like a well-mannered horse. She thought he had possibilities. Barbara was intrigued by how he looked at her. He seemed to want her to be close to him. He could be a good horse.

Barbara studied him, looking him up and down. Bob thought for an instant she might be carrying a concealed weapon; after all, it was a mutual fund company, accessible from street level, and there was no visible security. Then Barbara slowly turned her head toward the Hispanic woman, revealing her stunning profile. Bob couldn't take his eyes off Barbara. He again thought she was terribly misplaced. She belonged on a runway as a top model, not behind a desk hiding her attributes.

Some sort of meaningful silent communication passed between the two women followed by a grunt and affirmative nod by the older one. They'd decided Barbara should greet this visitor. She rose deliberately from her desk in a smooth, graceful standing motion, all the while maintaining eye contact with Bob. Her braided hair reached the halfway mark between her waist and knees. A raucous thought fled through Bob's mind when he first saw Barbara's proud hair. *If only we could be transported back to caveman times, I'd drag her lovingly by that inviting hair into my cave, ravage her immediately, and make her my woman.* Wisely, he did not voice the thought.

Barbara opened the front glass door and stepped into the hall, her eyes riveted on Bob's. Deep, mysterious pools drank in the man standing before her. Bob felt her scour his mind looking for his soul. She assessed character with that look. It was beyond attraction, though it was not an invitation; it was a look into his heart. Bob wondered what she was like. Would he see her outside of this formal business meeting? He thought to say something of a personal nature, but her look disarmed him. Before he found his tongue, she spoke.

"You are…?"

"I'm Bob Burke, analyst. Here to see David Sustack."

"Follow." The beauty spared words. She did not reveal her name. She turned her body slowly until she faced the office at the far end of the corridor, revealing her trim, shapely profile. Bob caught her scent. It was understated and alluring, a blend of sandalwood, oleander, and sage oils.

As she led him down the hall to the corner office, her braided hair stayed in a straight plumb line, obedient to her perfect posture, while her trim buttocks rippled against the constraints of her skirt. The heavenly motion took Bob away from his usual analytical thoughts. What was her name? Was there a man in her life? Would he have a chance to talk to her? Would she give him an opening to ask her out?

Wait, what am I thinking? This woman has a white-hot body wrapped in emotional ice. She's probably protected by a tribe of warriors who'd kill me if I even touched her.

Walking in front of Bob, Barbara had thoughts of her own. *This man is like a big, strong horse that needs the love of a good woman. I hope I will see him again. He is a very handsome horse. I would love to tame him and ride him. He would be a good partner and a great help to me and father, Big Chief, and the people. And I think life with this big horse would probably be a lot of fun.*

As she walked down the hall, Bob saw himself wrapping her in his arms from behind while cuddling and caressing her, nuzzling her neck and nibbling on her ear. He imagined they were in bed about to make love. He forced his thoughts back to business with difficulty.

Barbara opened the door to a cavernous office, walked inside, and pulled out a black leather chair on roller castors before motioning him to sit. She didn't look Bob in the eye, but as he seated himself, she noted his muscular arms and shoulders. She thought, *Someday these arms will hold me,* before she turned away and left silently. The door closed without a sound.

Bob sat at a large, angled desk made of a light blond wood. On the other side of the desk was a huge throne chair with its back facing him. He assumed he was alone in the room but quickly learned it unwise to assume.

"Did you write that report yourself?" spoke a voice from the sitting side of the throne chair. The chair sat on a raised platform. Bob felt odd staring at the back of the chair. *David must have some sort of power complex,* Bob thought . This was all eerily like the final scene from *The Wizard of Oz* where the wizard stayed behind a curtain.

"Yes," Bob answered.

There was a long silence. Bob began to wonder if David had an inferiority complex or if he was playing some sort of mind-control game. Bob looked around the office. There was a credenza behind the throne chair and a second behind him against the opposite wall. Four other chairs on rollers attended the angled desk. There was also a weird piece about seven feet long, padded in black leather and sitting about a foot and a half above floor level. It was big enough for a person to lie upon, but why do that? There was a large leather sofa along the far wall.

"Yes? That's all? You didn't copy some of that report from somewhere?" the voice spoke. Then the throne chair swiveled around. The man in the chair was small, leprechaun-like in appearance. His graying, wavy hair was slicked back. Bob thought he must use hair grease. David stared Bob in the eye as if trying to make him uncomfortable. Bob wondered about his host, a bit perturbed. No hand was extended to him and no water was offered.

"It's my work. It's original. No one helped me with any of it." Bob returned David's steady gaze.

"I see you have a wealth of knowledge about African gold mines," David said. He broke the stare, looking down at the opened report he held in his hands. "I'm interested in them myself."

David was less than forthcoming. His interest was more in the morbidity of the miners than in the profitability of the mines. He got a ghoulish pleasure imagining the mineworkers in the African Rand crawling on their bellies three miles below the surface, perspiring in one-hundred-twenty-degree heat, chipping away at tiny half-inch-wide veins of gold-bearing ore. These black laborers had great mortality risks because of rock bursts, heat stroke, and accidents involving explosives and equipment. David was fascinated that for each miner who died twenty others were eager to replace him, having entered apartheid South Africa illegally seeking this dangerous work.

"How can it be that an analyst in Plaintown knows so much about African mines?" David sought to verify this analyst's veracity.

"Before I worked at my present firm, I worked at another firm and a bank. I've specialized in gold and silver mining for six years." Bob's reply was matter-of-fact.

"I see. But how did you come to know so much about the Kaffirs? The unit labor costs, the ore grades, recoveries, mill capacities, run rates, depreciation schedules, reserve life, capital spending by mine section, and dewatering costs? This is voluminous data you've got here."

Bob recognized the slur word for the mines and their black laborers. If he wanted to keep the conversation on a professional level, he'd need to nip this derogatory colloquialism in the bud.

"They are black men, not Kaffirs. Mines worked by black labor are called miners, not Kaffirs"

There, he'd set a tone that he wasn't going to slum. This was business. Bob waited for David's reaction. There was a pause. David was a measured, calculating man.

"We can get back to that," David said. "What I want to know is how you came up with this information."

"I called them."

"You called the mines? They're on the other side of the world!" David thought he had the young analyst pinned.

"Africa has phones."

"There's a time difference."

"Yes. I call them from 2:00 a.m. until 5:00 a.m. here. It's afternoon there. I talk to the officers, directors, and mine managers of the companies. Then I put it all together to estimate my earnings and cash flows."

"They tell you all that information?"

"Yes. They're pretty open. They rarely hear from Americans, so they're happy to talk about what they're doing."

"So, you are confident in your estimates?" David sought certainty.

"You need to take them as base estimates. There's a matrix of gold prices and costs based on each mine's assumptions and operating plans. If you're going to use the stocks, you need to have my updates on each mine."

"How much?"

"Ten thousand cash or thirty thousand commissions up front, three thousand cash or six thousand commissions monthly for the updates."

"That's not cheap." David expected room to negotiate.

"Original work isn't cheap." Bob didn't blink.

"Done. Now, can you give me the updates? This data is three months old."

"Trades first." Bob held fast. David respected the younger man's chutzpah.

"Before you leave, what got your back up about the word Kaffir?" David asked.

"I just respect people who work hard, and I bristle a little when I hear a derogatory term."

"I feel the same way you do. I was simply using the term the Boors and Brits use for the mines, not the workers. I think those men are the salt of the earth."

"Maybe I just misunderstood and overreacted." Bob wanted to leave now that business was concluded. David kept him there.

"You see, the African black man who works in those mines is far better off than many American black men, even though the African black only makes a few hundred dollars a month. The reason is the African black man has a life worth living. He has a purpose, and because he has a purpose, he has dignity. Dignity is what makes a life worth living. Dignity commands respect. Respect is everything. Many American black men have bought into the socialist idea that the world owes them a living because their ancestors were slaves. Many of them got this line of bunk from their parents or a parent, and they got it from the Democrat party."

Bob had no idea where this was going or why David wanted to talk about it, but he was going to be a paying client. Bob listened to David's opinion.

"The Democrats sold blacks up the river. They promised to give the blacks welfare, food stamps, housing assistance, affirmative action, and program after program ad infinitum ad nauseam. They built a race-hustling industry and a bought-vote constituency. It's a great human tragedy. It destroys the ambition of many black men, and thus destroys dignity. In a perverse sort of way, the blacks have gone from being slaves of yesterday to being today's entitlement class, which is a form of slavery. The upshot of it all is many have lost dignity. That's the tragedy of many of America's blacks. And it's not just blacks who fall for the socialist bunk. More and more whites are succumbing to it now.

"The day will come, mind you, that the socialist programs hit the wall because the government has to inflate the money supply to fund an unsustainable circus. When that happens, those blacks who bought into the 'give it to me' mentality will tear America apart because many never took education, family, work, marriage, integrity, and character seriously. I see a schism in the population. There are those who expect the government to take care of them. They've lost dignity, the very thing that makes life worth living. There are others, and I hope their numbers will grow, that see the beauty of self-reliance. They have that work ethic, that sense of family, marriage, and character. They have dignity, and they are the black people who are truly beautiful."

"Eloquently said, Mr. Sustack. If my reaction to your choice of words offended you, then I apologize. I see you have

310

a great compassion for the plight of many of our fellow men. Good day."

Barbara magically appeared as if her ears never left David's office, opening the door without summons. Then she led Bob down the hall to the elevators, her braided hair vertically suspended behind her beautiful derriere. She walked like she floated on air. Halfway down the hall, her pace slowed slightly and she walked beside him. It was a perceptible change from the way she'd first marched him to David's office. Then, as if by accident, she brushed her hip against his. When she didn't apologize, Bob knew her touch was intentional.

Barbara thought, *That should confirm for him that I'm thinking the same thoughts I think he's thinking.*

Bob thought, *Something about her tells me she doesn't do that with just anyone. I am a lucky man.*

When the elevator door opened to take passengers down to the lobby, Bob turned to face Barbara and extended his hand.

"It's been a real pleasure to meet you," he said with utmost sincerity.

He didn't have to offer his hand, thought Barbara. *He wants to touch me.* Barbara met Bob's inquisitive eyes and held them. *With others watching from the front office, I can only say to him with my face what I feel in my heart.*

Bob thought she possibly guarded her actions because she was in view of the others in the front office. She kept her back to her coworkers and continued to stand facing Bob. The elevator started making growling noises. It wanted someone to either get aboard or release it to another floor.

Barbara's eyes held Bob's. It was an awkward moment. She wanted to talk with him. She wondered how his meeting went. Would he come back? She couldn't ask what was on her mind. He was a very handsome man. He had a chiseled body and a handsome face. And that hair! He had the wildest, fullest head

ROSEMARY LIGHTFOOT NESS-BITNER

of hair she'd ever seen on a man. Maybe he really was part horse! She felt like a little girl and she wanted him, but all she could do to signal she was interested was give him a faint smile. Her face lifted, her eyes brightened, and her nose flared as if she were drinking in his essence. If he didn't understand her look, then he was a big stupid horse.

Barbara declined to shake his extended hand, but gave Bob a slight bow of her head instead. He knew she liked him; he had to satisfy himself with that. He suspended thoughts about getting to know her for the time being, but he knew she'd visit his imagination. The elevator gave an angry ring. Bob departed.

On the ride down, he thought he'd just visited a most intriguing place. He wondered how he could see Barbara socially and not risk disturbing his new client.

Barbara went back to her desk, returning to an open file as if her encounter with the guest had no effect on her. The old Hispanic woman, Mrs. Rodriguez, suspected otherwise.

"Handsome, that one," she mentioned matter-of-factly.

"I didn't notice," Barbara fibbed. She didn't want to engage in speculations.

"Him tall, strong, and handsome." Mrs. Rodriguez sounded like she could have been auctioning off a prized rooster at the county fair.

"I didn't notice." Barbara sounded less convincing.

"He was interested in you."

"I said I didn't notice." Now Barbara felt embarrassed. Her protest was hollow.

"You said you didn't notice he was handsome. I said he was interested."

"You say. You don't know."

"I say what I see. I say you're also interested."

Barbara blushed. The old woman had good eyes. Barbara thought she'd concealed her interest perfectly, but Mrs. Rodriguez knew people. The slightest variation from the norm did not escape her notice. They'd taken too long to say good-bye at the elevator.

"Nothing will happen, Mrs. Rodriguez. We'll likely never see him again."

"You'll see him again."

"You can't know that." Barbara's face betrayed her hopes.

Mrs. Rodriguez could read faces. Barbara wanted to see Bob again, of that she was certain.

"I know that. I know his eyes. He'll be back. He's interested." With that conclusion, the old woman sought to reassure her younger friend and coworker.

Barbara chose not to respond to Mrs. Rodriguez's forecast, but that night, in her apartment, she sat alone in her armchair remembering and thinking, wishing she were in the arms of the one she thought of as "Big Horse."

The next day, Susan called Bob and opened several accounts for the firm and the fund.

What soon followed were a series of luncheon meetings between client David and broker-analyst Bob. They first got together weekly, then two or three times each week. David belonged to two luncheon clubs, both exclusive watering holes for men only. Both clubs were opulent and boasted magnificent panoramic views of the majestic Rockies to the west. In those opulent settings, David encouraged his guests to relax with a cocktail and talk freely. Bit by bit, he pieced together a composite résumé of his young guest.

One afternoon, looking out at the snow-capped Rockies set against a brilliant blue sky, David probed Bob about his childhood. He noted Bob's quest to earn income. David was particularly intrigued with Bob's trapping adventure. Trapping and skinning animals fascinated David. He listened attentively while Bob explained the procedures he used to remove the pelts from the animals' bodies.

"How did you come out with your trapping business?"

"Not great. It was terrible work. Often the muskrats were still alive and I had to club them to death. Sometimes I'd catch a possum and those things were really nasty, trying to bite. The muskrat skinning was tricky work. I was just a kid and was in a hurry to get to school, and sometimes I'd get nicks in their pelts. Fur buyers would pay two dollars each, but the guy I sold them to only gave me fifty cents a pelt because of the nicks and the banged-up heads. He 'Jewed' me down." Bob chuckled as he reflected upon his childhood moments. David's eyes widened and he gave a knowing smile.

"Well, you've certainly come a long way from skinning muskrats!" David said as he raised his glass in a toast to his young guest. He pretended not to hear the anti-Semitic comment and made no mention of his religion at this time. The young man unwittingly dealt him a card that he would play at the time of his choosing.

David noted the man had lost his father at an early age and didn't have a strong male influence in his life. He visualized the dim outline of a plan to harness this young Bob's talents and put them to considerable advantage. After several months of meetings, he believed Bob was confident in their friendship.

"What sort of deal do you have at the firm you're with?"

This was clearly an invitation to dance, to see if the client and analyst could come together on a deal that would be advantageous to both.

"It's a salary plus commissions deal. I head the equity research and corporate finance efforts. I have my own clients for commissions on my research."

"So, when you get an underwriting, do you get part of the underwriting discount as well?"

"No. I get some of the deal for my clients. That's all."

"Last year, how much did the firm make on the deals?"

"We did five million, plus another five from the follow-on commissions."

"You know, I have a broker-dealer who distributes fund shares, but it could do corporate deals as well."

"Why aren't you doing them already since you're set up for it?"

"I would if I had someone like you to head it up."

"Can your sales force sell anything besides mutual funds?"

"Sure. They're great salesmen. They need more products, but they can sell."

Negotiations followed, the outcome being Bob joined David's firm and they split profits on corporate underwritings fifty-fifty. Bob's income doubled.

The underwritings required exact record keeping. Shares or bonds issued by underwriting agreement needed to be confirmed to the participating dealers and settled into the proper accounts. The escrow of monies into the firm's bank account needed exact tracking until the offerings were sold. Then funds needed disbursement to the issuing company.

LITTLE SPARROW
AND BIG CHIEF

"For the underwritings, I'm assigning Barbara to work with you. She's a very fast learner, very high IQ. She doesn't say much, keeps to herself. She's all business. I think the two of you should be able to handle all the work involved without additional assistance. I like keeping costs down, which is why I'm having Barbara work with you as a team person. She's the company Cracker Jack. However you two divide up the work is up to you. I don't expect you'll need me to get involved. Just make the money."

Barbara worked closely with Bob to execute the underwriting functions. The work flowed smoothly. Deals were landed, negotiated, and closed. The shares went out, the money rolled in. The two of them became a perfect combination of mutual respect and professionalism, and more.

Barbara noticed Big Horse was extremely competitive. He fought hard for every deal and fought even harder to get the terms he wanted. She admired that quality in him. He was also considerate of her. He got her coffee, always asked if he could get her anything when he went out of the office, and he'd go out of his way for her. He was also protective of her, a very unusual trait for a man. He shielded her from David's pranks, even telling David that she didn't have time to be bothered with doing some things he demanded. She no longer plugged David's parking meter or called around for movie times and appointment times at his manicurists. She felt secure with Big Horse. She believed he would always protect her and be there for her. And she could tell he would also be a good friend.

Barbara thought, *I work with my Big Horse. I see him every day. We work well together. I like Big Horse. Yes, I could easily love Big Horse. If he asks for me, if he wants me, what should I do? Father Chief has plans for me. My heart and my mind are going in two different directions. What happens next?*

Bob thought, *I'm almost losing my mind here. I come in every day and sit at a desk across from her. If I ask her out, that could upset David's office. I need to stay focused on business, but damn, it's so hard to stay focused when I want to make love with her. I want to take her in my arms. What would she do? Wait, stop thinking those thoughts. But I can't stop thinking those thoughts. My God, she is so beautiful. Every day she looks beautiful. I'm trying to stay professional, but she's all I think about now. I think about her when I go home, when I wake up, when I go to sleep. Hold yourself together here. You don't know much about her. Who's this Chief fellow she mentions? Take cold showers. Go for short walks. Don't be stupid.*

During her evenings alone, Barbara knew something inescapable was happening. She was falling in love with Bob. She felt his warmth when they sat across their desk from each other syndicating the underwritings. Her heart fluttered when he touched her on the arm or shoulder. Her heart leaped when Bob opened doors for her as he always did, and her imagination soared when she visualized him as her future husband. He would sire beautiful children and be a very good father and defender of their family. She'd found the right man, she told herself.

The more she thought about Bob and the longer she worked with him, the more she accepted Mrs. Rodriguez's initial assessment. The two of them fell in love at first sight; there was no denying it. Now, Bob and Barbara sometimes had lunch together. It was all about work, they told themselves and their colleagues, but they both knew that wasn't completely true. Their eyes knew what their hearts felt. In the evenings, before she fell off to sleep, she imagined holding Bob in her loins and falling asleep in his arms. Perhaps his love would come to her. Perhaps he would love her as her father loved her mother. Perhaps.

Barbara recalled the time her mother died and the years she'd lived alone with her father, the chief. Her mother was beautiful and very good to her father, and in his time of grieving he was lost without her. Chief and Barbara grieved her loss together, and father and daughter grew close during those years. They still were and would always be very close. Her father was always there for her. He was protective, and Barbara had complete faith in his wisdom and judgment. They were each other's closest confidants. He'd raised her to be an extraordinary woman.

Chief brought Barbara up as if she were a son to him, the heir who would someday lead his tribe. She was his only child and he conferred upon her all his wisdom, pinning his hopes for the future of their people upon her. Chief told her she must strive to accomplish great things. She must deny herself an ordinary woman's life. She must learn to succeed in the white man's world and become a business woman. She must lead by example and help the others, showing them strength and perseverance. She must show them it was possible to rise to the top in the white man's world. She must be ascetic, must shun alcohol, and must even deny herself earthly pleasures until she was ready to lead. Her mate must be the right man. She must not make a mistake here. Not just any man would do.

With her father's molding, Barbara set out to conquer the world. She drove herself physically. Each morning when she lived on the reservation, she arose in darkness and ran for miles in the morning twilight and into the rising sun. She climbed all of Colorado's fourteen-thousand-foot mountains, and mastered technical rock climbing. Barbara loved the outdoors and her mountains. And she was a huntress, skilled with rifle and bow. She learned the ways of the elk and deer, and of all the predator animals—the fox, coyote, wolf, bear and grizzly bear—and of all the lesser animals and waterfowl and birds of prey. She learned to survive on her own in the forests and plains.

She immersed herself in her school work and read prodigiously the books in the tribal library. She learned the languages of the Lakota, the Cherokee, the Northern Cheyenne, and the Mohawk. She also learned English, Spanish, and Italian. Her goal was to be able to communicate in nuanced terms with all those she knew and worked with. She attended tribal meetings with her father and sat with him at chiefs' councils. She asked many questions, and as years passed, her questions became better, and as her questions became better, her father knew it was time to send her away to learn better answers. Chief and the other elders recognized Barbara as an information sponge and a doer. She was the most outstanding student in her graduating high school class. She received a full scholarship to Colorado University in the infamous city of Boulder, nationally known for its development of fruits and nuts.

At college, when the other students partied, smoked marijuana, and drank alcohol, Barbara studied. She made acquaintances with several of her professors, and she asked them questions. She was a knowledge-guzzling machine. She understood the needs of her people and became an extension of the chief, committed to the betterment of the tribe.

The reservation children had little chance for a good future off the reservation, and reservation life was a dead end for a young person in the modern world. The young people needed more than handouts from government programs, more than old folks smoking the pipe and telling them about buffalo hunts of years gone by. Learning the tribal dances and costumes, language, and lore was all well and good, but few could make much of a living from it.

Father said what was needed was leadership that understood both the white man's world and the Indian world, and the leadership had to be so knowledgeable that it could compete and succeed in the white man's world. Tribal leaders had to be examples of exceptional achievement, living inspirations, and in their heart of hearts must always be fiercely loyal to the needs of the tribe and willing to put their hearts and souls into bettering the tribe. Business, investment, and technical knowledge were keys, decided Chief, so he set Barbara on her path.

And Barbara excelled. She graduated summa cum laude with degrees in business and psychology. She networked with her professors and had a reservoir of good contacts she could call upon to ask her endless questions. But lately she'd wrestled with a question of a different sort. It was the question her heart asked. "Is Bob the one?"

"Father, I need your counsel." Barbara began with some trepidation.

"Of course, I am here." Chief knew from his daughter's wavering voice on the phone this was not a usual call. He was wary.

"It's not about business or policy, Father. I need your thoughts about a man. I believe this man loves me."

There was a long silence from the chief. He knew this moment would come one day. He had a beautiful daughter, a prize many men wanted, but all these years he'd managed to scare them all away. He was an imposing giant of a man, standing over six feet five inches and weighing over two hundred eighty pounds. He could easily have played professional football in his younger days, but his interests were to develop businesses that benefitted the tribe. Regardless, his physical presence and stature scared away many a young buck from courting his precious Little Sparrow.

Now, a young buck readied to fight him, take his daughter from him. His feelings divided. Was he about to lose her from his life, from the tribe? Who was he to deny her the life every woman needs? Was the man a good man or a bad one? How could he know? She was the glow of pride in his heart, his joy, his precious little girl and the very reason he lived. He loved her and wanted the best for her. How could he ever let her go? Was he about to become a relic, a useless old man? Did this young buck seek to dethrone him?

He knew he must be a wise father. He must listen. He summoned his best counsel.

"Tell me about him, and tell me how you feel, Little Sparrow." This was one of those times when he called her by her tribal name, the name he'd given her when she was first born.

Barbara told Chief all about Bob's qualifications and skills, his ability to make money, and his investing experience. That was all well and good. Sparrow did her homework on this man, recognized Chief, but what of his character? What sort of man was taking a place in his daughter's heart?

After listening to Sparrow's praise of Bob's résumé, it was time to be her father in the most important way. Above all other considerations, Chief wanted his daughter to have a happy life. He wanted to know how serious his daughter felt about this man. "Little Sparrow, I ask you again to tell me how your heart feels when you think of this man and when you are in his presence."

"I love him, Father. My heart beats faster when I think of him. I am certain I love him. I've never felt like this about any man before. I even have a secret name for him when I think of him. I call him Big Horse."

"And you said he was a white man."

"Yes, Father. He is white, but I see no prejudice in him. He treats me like a perfect gentleman at all times."

"And have you and he…?"

"Oh no, Father! We have not even kissed. I wanted to seek your counsel before I allowed any sort of courtship from him."

"But you believe he is ready for courtship?" Chief felt a measure of relief. The man had not bedded his daughter.

"Yes, Father. I sense it. He just waits for me to allow him an opportunity. So far it is strictly a business relationship."

"I see." Chief sounded relieved. Then he continued. "You know, Sparrow, our people haven't been treated well by whites. You know there are many in the tribe who will question your allegiances if anything should come of this. His people may also wonder about a relationship between you and a white."

"I understand that, Father. I also understand whites no longer kill us with guns and diseases, and many whites love our wonderful culture and our wild spirit. I also know that there are many different personalities within the whites, just as there are many different individuals within the tribe. What would you advise me, Father?"

Again, there was a prolonged silence. Chief never hurried, as he was deeply thoughtful and a profound respecter of time and thoughts. He believed as time unfolded it always revealed answers to the most vexing questions; therefore, he always allowed his mind time to think.

"My advice for you, Sparrow, is to proceed with great caution. Be true to who you are above all else. Know that many whites have broken Indian hearts in love as well as in war. You must be painstakingly certain that whatever test your Bob encounters in life that he will remain true to you in his heart. You must be certain that when matters of importance are tested he will come to his center, and that he knows you are his rock and his center. You must know his loyalty is to you. That is the measure of love."

"How can I know his heart, Father?"

"Time, Sparrow. You must give this matter time. Time will tell you everything about him. Allow time to reveal him to you. In time you will see if he wants your world to become his world and if you want his world to become your world. You must find the truth about this. When you feel you know these truths, I'd like you to bring him to me. I should like to meet this Big Horse. And, Sparrow, it is never wise to hurry time."

"Thank you, Father."

"You are welcome, Sparrow. Does he want children with you?"

"I don't know, Father."

"That's also something you must know, and you must have understandings with him about all that comes along with children. What paths will you set them on, what will they know of The Great Spirit of all Living Things, and what will they know of right and wrong? You and your man must have agreement about such things. Children are big responsibilities."

"Thank you, Father. You are most wise."

"You are welcome always, Sparrow. I am here whenever you wish to talk."

With that, the chief hung up his phone and silently thanked the Great Spirit that his daughter talked these matters over with him. He'd raised her well. She was unlike those who ran off with a man, got pregnant, and became single mothers struggling to make ends meet. He knew too many stories of such unfortunate women and their children.

Barbara decided to follow her father's counsel. She and Bob would wait and let time unfold the mysteries of love.

MONEY

Word traveled. Women gossiping over a backyard clothesline couldn't hold a candle to the whisperings and boastings of stockbrokers. Underwriting deals were an open book. Tombstone advertisements, actually block ads with brokerage firms' names in them, named the issuer of the security sold, the lead underwriter(s), and then, in descending order in bracket groupings based on selling group participation, the names of the participating firms. The tombstone was the security firms' way of saying to corporate America, "We just raised money for these guys, and we could raise money for you too, so give us a call!"

Within this proper country-clubby teacup world, each firm jealously coveted the positions of the firms higher up in the pecking order of the tombstones, and every firm's underwriting personnel knew or knew someone who knew the underwriting personnel in all the other firms. These people were constantly on the phones with each other, testing, probing, checking and double-checking the demand for each offering. When preliminary prospectus, or "red herring," demand was strong and easy to sell, each firm sought to wheedle its way to an upper bracket by being allocated an overstuffing from the lead underwriter. Favors were called in, Super Bowl tickets promised, invites to exclusive happenings with beautiful Hollywood types were offered, exclusive whores and exotic vacations were procured, and old friendships were constantly tested.

When demand was soft, a smaller spoonful of bitter medicine was preferred. There was always the next deal, which made it consequential to break a relationship by declining to take down the underwriter's allocation and refusing to "push out" a tougher sale, or if necessary to "eat" the deal, which was to own it in the house account until demand appeared or sufficient time had elapsed since the underwriter's stock price support operations had passed, at which time it was fed to the open market. It was analogous to the baker marking down day-old bread. The constant ebbs and flows of demands in the market overall, and for a given deal in particular, gave rise to "the buzz."

Buzz was the constant beehive din amongst this small, highly compensated clique of white-shoe prima donnas as they tried to assess which deals were hot and which were cold, and which firm would be in which bracket when tombstones were published. Buzz included which firm's personnel negotiated the deal with the security issuer. Some underwriter employees had reputations for being astute, others not so much. Buzz included how much "grease" or compensation each deal carried.

During a time when most underwritings greased 10 percent, there appeared in quick succession eight tombstones. The dealer doing these offerings was an odd duck in the underwriting business. It was a mutual fund broker-dealer, a fund distribution firm. Normally fund distributers only underwrote shares of the fund they distributed. Fund offerings were continuous; unlike a corporate underwriting where the deal was closed and the proceeds given to the corporation in exchange for the company's shares, or bonds, fund offering proceeds went into the fund in exchange for fund shares and the offering never closed.

These eight deals were peculiar. They didn't have co-underwriters or white-shoe members listed. When the tombstones appeared, there was a flurry of buzz about them. Was this some *Little Red Hen* tale where the chicken did it all herself? And gasp! They were all done "best efforts," meaning the underwriter didn't pledge the firm's capital firmly to the issuer, but simply sold the deal to investors without any loss of capital risk to the firm. And gasp again! The grease in all these deals was 13 percent! These guys made a lot of money! They kept lots of the deal themselves and just listed in alphabetical order the firms that got a piece. Word was the deals were tight, hard to get, and other firms only got a sniff. The deals flew off the shelves. Who were these guys?

The buzz soon learned these guys were one guy, Bob Burke, and one girl, Barbara Lightfoot. Bob found the deals, convinced the issuers he could raise the money, negotiated the terms, and sold the shares, and he did it all without risking firm capital. Barbara made sure the entire process ran smoothly and seamlessly. Bob and David split four million dollars evenly based upon a handshake, and Barbara was paid a bonus equal to triple her annual salary. What the two did was a notable feat and it resulted in calls. Soon, three midsized firms were talking with Bob about leaving David's firm and coming to work with them. They were offering more attractive compensation packages and a greater sales force capability, which would enable Bob to push through bigger deals.

WAIT

All the while Bob was doing corporate deals, he worked closely with Barbara. She assisted in allotting dealers their share of underwritings and monitored the interest levels in the firm's deals as well as competing firms' offerings and how they were selling. She was integral to the entire process and had great aptitude for syndication and distribution work. She played her cards close and never gave away information. She didn't suffer small talk or fools. Demand moved along, deals were closed, companies got their money, the bank arrangements were always clearly understood. Everybody involved looked to Barbara to make sure they knew where things were in the different deal pipelines. She cooled heated egos and kept the waters smooth. If Bob received an attractive offer from another firm, he determined he'd take Barbara with him as a package deal. He felt a professional bond with her, and a personal one.

One night when Barbara and Bob were working late, he tried to get to know her better on a personal basis. "What is it that you do at night when you're not working?" He was fishing for an opening.

"I'm home studying business matters and investments. Why?" Barbara's guard went up. She sensed a pass coming her way.

"It seems unusual that you have no outside interests." Bob thought, *Oh please, you gorgeous goddess, just let me pry open that closed door just a little.*

"I do have an outside interest. My people need me to learn all I can about investing and the business of running a firm so I can help them someday."

"But surely there must be more to your life than work?"

"Yes, of course. I love the outdoors. I mountain climb and rock climb. I also hunt and fish, usually with my father. I also run every morning to stay in shape." She let Bob know she was a busy girl. The door stayed closed.

"That's it? No man in your life?"

"Yes, there is a man in my life. I just haven't told him yet."

Bob hoped she was thinking he was that man, but he was frustrated. *She's testing me. She wants me to feel like a cat who seeks a bag of catnip. She keeps that bag of catnip just beyond reach. Maybe she just likes to tease.*

Bob's desires for Barbara approached vexation, and vexation approached madness. She put off his advances, requested him to restrain his demands for a personal relationship. She could drive men crazy with desire without making any effort to interest them. With Bob, it was different. She'd alluded to her interest in him, but then put his feelings under a cold shower of postponement. She didn't give hints about her reasons or timetable. No poker player held his cards closer. Chief was her romance coach.

"So when will you allow us to have a relationship?" Bob was direct in his frustration.

"When you are ready and I am ready. We must wait until time lets us know."

"Why must we wait? Who in the hell is time anyway?" Bob wanted her. He swam and lifted weights to ease his frustrations, but he was trying to tell her that wasn't enough.

Then Barbara rose from her desk and went to Bob's. She told him to stand up, and then she put her arms around his neck and drew him close to her. She gave Bob a bear hug and held his body against her for a long ten seconds. Then she gave him a sincere kiss on his lips. Their eyes were inches apart when she broke the silence and said, "We will wait."

Bob's blood raced. He wanted her so badly he thought he'd lose his mind over her. In those ten seconds, Little Sparrow sealed his heart to hers and held it for all eternity. He loved her. But now he was more frustrated than ever. "Why?" He couldn't make sense of waiting for what they both obviously felt.

"Because I said we must wait, that's why. I can't tell you more than what I have told you, except to tell you everything is worth waiting for."

Bob felt like he needed to take a cold shower, but he just stared at her as she returned to her desk and resumed checking her numbers. "That's all? It's worth waiting for? I need to live with that?"

"Yes. You must. I will tell you when the wait is over."

"Until then, what am I supposed to do?"

"You are a man. You must be a man and do those things that men do. Just remember I've told you it's worth waiting for."

She didn't look up and showed only stoicism. She didn't threaten him to avoid other women; that was not her way, nor the way of her people. But for what really mattered, for marriage and children, they needed to wait. She didn't elaborate that, in her culture, sexual experimentation among young people prior to marriage was accepted and that she herself had experiences. Her reasons for restraint were born of practical business considerations, but she was not ready to reveal those considerations to him. She'd made her point well. That should satisfy his inquiries.

Bob wanted to run through a wall to ease his frustration. He hoped Barbara would invite him to climb a mountain with her or go along for a morning run, but Barbara offered nothing.

"Would you like to go to a movie or something?" Bob was flailing, desperate.

"Yes, of course, Bob. There are many things I would love to do with you, but this is not the right time to even think of such things. I have desires too, but it's too dangerous. You must trust me about this."

Barbara thought to herself, *I would love for him to know about the conversations I've had with Chief about our situation, but Chief said that would not be wise. That could only hurt Big Horse and me. Chief said he could foresee that this union I desire with Big Horse will work, but only if I wait until after David reveals his own plans for Big Horse, which Chief believes won't be too long. Only then will we have our time together.*

There was a hint of exasperation in her voice. Surely he knew her well enough to understand when she told him something he needed to take it at face value. Surely Bob knew she also had her share of frustration with their situation.

Bob finally understood. It was hard to get logic through the hormone barrier, but he did it. Barbara was aware of something, some sort of disguised venue or hidden agenda within the firm. She was ultracautious for a reason and wanted to give no excuse to David or Susan to dismiss her. She was, after all, an Indian, and she likely believed it would be difficult to gain a top job elsewhere. Perhaps she was protecting him. Out of such revelations, respect was born. Their working relationship took on a deeper meaning. They had camaraderie.

Asking as a comrade, Bob queried Barbara about Marty. "I can't help but notice that all the women in the office seem to confide in you and seek out your advice and help when they have decisions to make, corporate or personal. But the woman in sales never speaks to you. There seems to be a chill between the two of you. It's like when she's in your presence the temperature of the room drops. Is there some reason for the distance between you two?" Bob opened the window of conversation.

"Marty and I are different, that's all." Barb's tone was clipped. She wanted the subject dropped.

"Come on, Barb. Tell me why you get ice cold around her. In what way are you different?"

"In every way." Barbara shot Bob a look that said to back off.

"Look, we're friends. Enlighten me. All I see is two women who try to avoid each other. How are you different, exactly?" Bob's palms opened and his eyebrows went up, along with his shoulders.

"It's just that I have certain principles and Marty has other values. Does that help you, most curious friend?" *I wonder where this is going. Is he getting interested in the company slut? Is this something I should worry about?*

"Well, like what, for instance?"

I'd better throw him a bone to shut this down. "Well, here's a for instance. Marty wears a gold bracelet, a big thick one with flames of red running through it. That symbolizes, to me, all the pain and suffering Native Americans have endured since your Columbus arrived. It represents, to me, the ongoing genocide that the white European culture has inflicted upon my people. It represents destruction of the land, the insult to Mother Earth, and for what good reason? She flaunts that bracelet as if she's the only one who could afford it, and that misses the point. She has no sensitivity to the hurts of others."

"But surely that genocide stuff was generations ago, with the smallpox blankets and the killing of the buffalo. How can you get that frosted over a gold bracelet?"

"Genocide of Native Americans continues to this day, Bob. That's why. It just takes a different form. Now the whites have advanced their methods to make our people wards of their trusteeships, like we are helpless children. Then they take our land, like good trustees, and put it to the highest and best use. This means they will drive us off, kill our cattle and horses, and run them through barbed wire fences to injure them, to drive us off when they want to get at the gold or the oil on our lands. It's a subtle form of murder." There was pain in Barbara's voice.

"Why don't you talk to Marty about how you feel? Maybe she'd stop wearing the bracelet."

I need to tell him in a way even he will understand. "It wouldn't do any good to talk to her, Bob. She's not the kind of person who concerns herself about sensitivities of others. Besides, it's common knowledge amongst the women here that she earned that bracelet and she's proud of what she did to earn it. Does that help you?" Barbara was clearly annoyed with Bob's questions about the other woman.

"Sorry. I didn't mean to step on your toes. Let's drop it." Bob got the message Barbara delivered in girl-speak terms— Marty was an easy lay, a punch bag.

He retreated, and drop the subject they did.

RIDING THE TIGER

While Bob was doing the corporate deals, David stuffed the fund with Bob's gold stock ideas. By investment company rules, a diversified fund may have no more than 25 percent of its assets in any one industry and no more than 5 percent of its assets in the securities of any one issuer, based upon the initial investment made. But hey, what's an industry anyway? If the rules left a loophole, David was willing to drive a truck through it.

Convinced by Bob's research on gold, David put one quarter of the fund into African gold stocks, defined by David as an industry. Another quarter went into North American gold stocks, defined as another industry. A third quarter went into diversified mining companies that had large gold holdings, again defined as a separate industry; and the final quarter into silver and platinum companies, again a separate industry. Having totally perverted the concept of diversification, David was riding a boom time in precious metals. David was all in, in gold.

David often asked Bob about events in the gold patch and the companies that mined it, and Bob continued his research. Taking measure of the fund's massive gold holdings, Bob asked David where he'd first become interested in gold. After all, had David not taken the time to read that first report, they would not have gotten together.

"Actually, it was my father, Marvin, who first explained gold to me." David recalled a lesson from the great master. "Dad studied the Great Depression of the 1930s and knew everything about central banking and the Federal Reserve. He understood how the financial system worked, which was how he became so successful. He believed gold was the best wealth protector for the next depression because in times of depression, people stop trusting their government, and they stop trusting the government's paper money as well. They stop believing the government will stay solvent. They think government will collapse and default on its treasury obligations. Counterparty risk, Dad called it, meaning the government's money is no good.

"U. S. government's securities are used for loan collateral all over the world. Could be a bank in South America has U.S. treasuries, and then that bank makes loans in its local currency. The buyer of those loans, or if the lending bank keeps the loans, depends upon the U.S. Treasury security collateral not going into default. The risk the South American has is that the U.S. Treasury security becomes worthless because, in a depression, the U.S. cannot suck in enough tax money to service and repay debt as it comes due. The counterparty risk is that the original collateral, the U.S. security that the South American bank trusted as a good asset enabling it to make a loan, is not a good asset.

"Dad said the U.S. was taking risks with the entire world, that the government debt would just get larger until there could be another collapse and depression, and that the next one would be worse than the depression of the 1930s because the dollar was backed by gold and silver then, whereas now it's backed by the promise that the government can collect taxes to service the debts it has.

"When the hard times come again, dollars will not be accepted for goods and services because people the world over

THE SECRET AND THE BUTTERFLY

will know the U.S. does not have good gold- or silver-backed money. Those people will always take gold and silver though. The metals are 'honest' money. They stand alone, worth their buying power based on the value of the coins themselves. They don't depend upon a government backing their value with tax dollars that fall short of government spending, thus the metals have no counterparty risk. If that South American bank had gold as its asset instead of U.S. treasuries, it would not be subject to counterparty risk, which is the ultimate worst risk any entity can take on, be it an institution, a country, or an individual. It's really the risk of default of a country, the risk that the country's money becomes worthless as well as its bonds. It's the risk that you work all your life for a retirement and you wake up one morning and have nothing. Gold and silver avoid that risk."

"What did Marvin think of the Federal Reserve?" Bob asked. He'd studied its operations extensively in school and wanted to know the Great One's take on it.

"Oh, Dad thought it was a mistake. He considered it a self-perpetuating money monopoly contrived by the nation's elitists in 1913."

"So Marvin was a gold bug?"

"As opposed to a fiat paper-money cockroach, yes."

"What was his outlook for the Fed and the fiat dollar?"

"Both doomed to fail, likely in your lifetime. 'Without honest money we have a dishonest society,' Dad used to say. The nation had better prosperity and morality with honest gold and silver than it has with the Fed.

"Wilson destroyed prosperity and the honesty of the society. Ben Franklin and the other Founding Fathers knew it was vital to the longevity of the Republic to have honest money, controlled by the people with no counterparty risk. If the president or Congress wanted a war or a social program, they'd have to go to the people and put it to a vote. They couldn't just pass some spending authorization bill and sell some bonds to the Fed and have the Fed print the money to pay for it. That puts the cart before the horse. Since Wilson, the nation has had the cart before the horse."

"But if the Fed can manage credit creation well, what difference does it make?"

"That's just it. The Fed can't manage credit creation because the politicians over the generations always vote for more than the country can afford. Social programs and wars will not stop until the country bankrupts itself and the money is worth nothing. It's become a system where cronies and oligarchs get close to the lawmakers and president. They get the programs and sweet deals they want and the other 99 percent of the people get screwed."

"For sure?"

"Well, likely. There's always the chance we'll avoid the worst. Freedoms have vestiges. People remember honest money, and those who can still read after the teacher unions have destroyed education can still learn about honest money.

"Silver was the last honest money. Kennedy first pocket-vetoed the Patman Coinage Act of 1969 back in 1963. It was going to take silver out of the coinage. You've seen those movies of Kennedy getting his head blown off, then all those people crying. Well, they weren't actually crying because Kennedy was killed. They were crying because he was a decent guy and was trying to prevent the government and the Fed from taking silver money away from the people. People were crying because, deep down inside, in a place they don't like to think about things because they'd need to turn their brains on, they were crying because they knew that somehow they were getting screwed.

"LBJ completed the screwing of the people. He signed the abominable Coinage Act and took silver away from Americans. Then Johnson had the Great Society and the Vietnam War simultaneously. He caused all the inflation he needed for his war because the people could no longer take worthless paper dollars and swap them at face value for silver coins.

"Johnson hurt the country two ways. The poor got their welfare programs, which destroyed their work ethic and made them dependent Democrat voters, which doomed America to become a worthless socialist mess. Then the right-wing Republicans in the military industrial complex got a lot of money to piss away on a war in Vietnam we didn't want to win and got fifty-eight thousand Americans killed, and probably millions of Vietnamese killed.

"Conspiracy theorists can say what they want about how many bullets shot Kennedy, who done it, whether it was Russians, Cubans, the mob, or just a one-man nutjob. The result Dad took away from the assassination was honest money was taken away from the people. Dad believed the government sent a message to the people when they coined a commemorative Kennedy half dollar that was only 40 percent silver.

"Dad said the message was, 'Your government has the majority of the power now. You, the American people, are our slaves. All you peasants work for the government now. Just to prove we have control over you, we're minting this coin that has only 40 percent real money. That represents your share of power. The other 60 percent of the coin is worthless base metal. We're putting your nose in it. We're showing you that we can make you work for worthless money.'"

"We're five or six generations past Wilson now. What did your dad think would happen when the system ran out of control, past the point of possible recovery?" Bob was probing the thoughts of the great dead investor through the memories of his son.

David chuckled. "Well, Dad used to say he hoped the public would not turn to the Madam Defarge treatment."

"The what treatment?"

"He was referring to one of Dickens's characters, Madam Defarge, in his book *Tale of Two Cities*. She was a tavern keep's wife who minded her knitting, and during the time before the French Revolution, she kept a record of all those who were wealthy and big shots in government and who were collectively screwing the people. She turned her list over to the revolutionaries after they sacked the government. Then she went each day to watch the executions at the guillotine. When the blade came down and cut a head off, she'd cross that name off her list, and all the while she kept on knitting. Dad worried that when the day came that the system couldn't correct its imbalances, people would get overly emotional."

"Come on. Did Marvin really believe something like that would happen here in the United States, in our modern times?"

"He didn't know. No one can know these things." David's thoughts trailed off. He was remembering things he'd heard long ago.

"Dad said there's a natural order of things in human nature. Whenever a populace is taxed without representation, without voting for the tax, like the Molasses Act, the Stamp Tax Act, and the Townshend Acts in the colonies, it gives rise to voices that more represent the will of the people, men like Sam Adams, Thomas Paine, Patrick Henry, and the like. Dad took to his grave his belief that the Federal Reserve System is a modern form of taxation without representation. He always prayed that our nation's leaders would act wisely and change the system peacefully, held out great hope for the American people to reason and compromise and change gradually. He wished the Fed system would get torn up by its roots. Dad loved America and the concepts of its Founding Fathers.

"Neither the elite nor the peasant can change the system as an individual. Change comes about like a breeze that can grow to gale force, and then it becomes a whirlwind from which none can escape. Dad feared change could come upon us that way. He worried it would start with rumblings of discontent, like a far-off thunder rumble from darkening clouds over the mountains, and then there would follow isolated incidents of civil strife with protests, confrontations with government law enforcement, and shootings of police and government people and bankers. He said I'd be able to feel it coming, like a gathering storm has flashes of lightning you can see arcing through the dark clouds. As a storm approaches, people can sense a change in the air. There is an eerie stillness, where even the birds stop singing and the ground animals seek cover and hide away.

"People can sense change coming also when the economic system sputters and casts a pall over human activity. They'll scurry to the stores to stock up on essentials like ground animals acting out of instinct, and they will sense fear they can't identify or voice. Then the fury of pent-up frustrations unleashes from its social moorings. Powerful keepers of the status quo are ignored, brushed aside. Crowds become angry, and their vengeance boils up and gives no quarter. Mercy is closeted and afraid. Grace, goodness, and decency go into hiding, afraid of the crowd.

"We are now where we are. We are the generations left to live through the storm those men who lived long before us set upon us. They were sinister men, selfish, unscrupulous men. Dad believed we are predestined to suffer the consequences of the decisions of those who died long ago. He believed we must keep living the doomed experiment that is Keynesian economics until we fling ourselves into the abyss with our own profligacy."

"Profligacy?"

"Yes, profligacy, spending by borrowing and going into debt, depending on a house to appreciate so money can be borrowed on it and spent, social payments for non-workers, idiotic politicians who promise idiot voters they can have more if the country borrows more, bread and circus shows like *Dancing with the Stars*, the National Football League, rock concerts, and the like. It's all a giant distraction from the serious problem, which is the country imports more than it exports, spends more than it saves, has lost the moral moorings of family with a father in the home, and basically has gone soft and immoral. The United States is ripe for the picking.

"Dad said all that's about to befall the United States is preordained and unstoppable, like a train going off a bridge, because the status quo never willingly changes the status quo. How often does a billionaire give a million away to a less fortunate without a favorable tax benefit? Do you ever expect a news pundit who spews the nonsense that the solution to the problems caused by too much debt is to issue more debt will admit he is completely wrong? Of course you won't. He has too much invested in his own dogma. Near the end times, Dad believed elections would become meaningless media shows because all major political parties become corrupt. They agree to get along to get a lot for themselves. Peaceful change becomes illusive, requiring a true statesman because honest money is gone and no longer available to use in honest compromises.

"Dad worried the Federal Reserve System would resist compromise. He feared a bloodthirsty Madam Defarge type person would arise, purge the established order, and settle things. He thought she was waiting for the system to collapse, waiting for her moment and watching our economic circus. Dad feared she was making her lists and waiting to reappear in America's future."

"But," Bob protested, "the Revolutionary War was a break from England. The French Revolution was internal to France, a revolt against monarchy. What made Marvin think that something like that could ever happen here? I just don't see an analogy."

"Sure you do. Just look closely. The Founding Fathers of the United States had very serious intent that the government should always work for the people and not the other way around. That's why they passed the Coinage Act of 1792. That act provided punishment by death to anyone who debased the nation's gold or silver coinage. They were clear that freedom of the people depended upon the people having honest money."

"But the Patman Act superseded that. Silver isn't money anymore and gold is only the reserve of central banks now, upon which they heap their paper."

"Dad knew all that, but he was unmoved by it. He said you can be sure that silver would be money again and the people's constitutional right to real money would be restored, possibly after the people suffered the storm of a systemic debt write-off. He believed that the current system is on a quickening timeline, just like the taxes on the colonies, just like the burdens of the French monarchy. The Federal Reserve System is today's greatest problem for the country. Dad thought the Fed was riding on a hungry tiger. He believed all the Fed governors were just a bunch of pompous dummies that spewed hot air. Dad believed the regulators of the commodity markets, the Commodity Futures Trading Commission members were riding the tiger as well."

"Why them? They just govern trading rules."

"Well, not exactly, according to Dad. He always thought their rules determine position limits on futures contracts traded. They allow outlandishly huge short positions on silver in particular, as much as two hundred days of world production on open interest shorted. That holds the price down artificially low. The same dealers who hold the paper shorts have a smaller number of long contracts that stand for delivery of the physical metal."

"What's wrong with that?"

"It's monopsony power in the marketplace. It violates antitrust concepts. It's the opposite of monopoly power, where the seller restricts supply to get a high price. In silver, the buyer restricts demand to get a low price. It's a way to separate real wealth from the people and dupe the people into thinking everything is fine so they take on even more debts. It's transference of risk to the public and transference of wealth to the very rich. Holding down the value of real money artificially props up the value of paper currency. It breeds complacency."

"How does it all resolve?"

"Dad would never say for sure. He said it's never too late to change the current system if the political leadership would wise up and begin truth-telling and phase in gradual change. Gradual change is always possible if leaders will tell the truth. Dad believed that people's feelings today are similar to people's feelings in 1773 when the Tea Party Indians threw tea into Boston Harbor. He thought we were getting dangerously close to that same mindset. He especially believed that the moods of people today are the same as those of people in the past. Group moods are like cattle in stampedes. People don't think when they're in an angry group; they just act.

"Dad often said the people of yore didn't revolt against George the First, as he was already dead. The people couldn't revolt against Louis the Fourteenth, because he too was already dead. But those revolutions came to pay a visit to their successors. Americans today cannot revolt against Wilson or John Maynard Keynes because it is now in their long run and they are indeed dead, but their successors carry on in a system that needs to end. Those successors to the status quo, the bankers, academics who propagate Keynes's brand of economics, media people who mindlessly push it down the public's throats are all going to wake up one day soon and find out they are on the wrong side of history. Political leaders, regulators, media people, academics and bankers are all riding a hungry tiger. The people are the tiger. The tiger wants change and he will have it. The riders are trapped where they are, riding the system. They need to get off before the ride ends or they will be eaten.

"So, he believed we'd have honest money again?"

"Yes. He thought it would likely be forced upon us from usage in another country. He remarked often that silver was money under Peter the Great. Dad believed Peter was the greatest Russian ever, the best man for that country and its people ever. Dad also noted silver has a three-thousand-year history as money in China, and he thought the Chinese would make it money again to throw off the yoke of the paper dollar. Silver also has a long history as money in Latin America, Arabia, and in the United Kingdom, so Dad believed it was likely that people would once again clamor for honest money as the way to get their power back and it would stage a powerful come back worldwide."

"What could ensure a peaceful resolution to the debt problems?"

"Well, if the nation had a debt jubilee that could work."

"What's a jubilee?"

"It's debt forgiveness. All debtors default without penalty and society starts over. We Jews do it every fifty years." David accidently revealed a small part of himself.

"You're a Jew, David!" Bob was shocked. "In a whole year of knowing you, you never mentioned that." His voice faltered. "I apologize for that slur I made when I was telling you about my muskrat pelts." He was sincere, offering a real apology.

"Oh, that's okay. Forget it. It never happened." But David knew it happened and would not forget it. He remembered it as if it were yesterday. Besides, had Bob apologized for being anti-Semitic? Not really. He apologized for saying something anti-Semitic to a Semite, so was he sorry he said it or was he sorry he was caught saying it? These questions about Bob stayed fixed in David's mind. He vowed to destroy this anti-Semitic gentile and make him rue the day they met.

DOLLY

David lived on a small gentleman's farm on the outskirts of the city, complete with a menagerie of barnyard animals. There were sheep and goats, a compliment of geese and guinea hens, a barn to shelter them, duck ponds to water them, and two dogs to protect them. One sheep was David's favorite. She was a black sheep named Dolly, and David held monologue conversations with her as if she were a human who understood every word he said. Often when Bob dropped by to talk about the business, David sat in a recliner near the barnyard with a dog by his side and Dolly grazing near him on the lawn outside the barnyard. Dolly always stayed close to David.

The time arose when other firms' interest in the team of Bob and Barbara became serious. They were prepared to offer a significant boost in compensation and greater opportunity as well. Bob wanted to take Barbara with him and leave David on good terms, so on one lovely Saturday morning he went to visit his friend to tell him that he needed to advance his career. It was time to say good-bye. As Bob got out of the car, he could hear David's wife screaming hysterically from inside the house.

"I told you! You keep that sheep out of our house! You keep her out of your bedroom! If I ever see her in the house again, I swear I will kill her! I mean it. Don't ever bring that filthy animal into the house again!" Then the distraught woman began screaming and wailing hysterically. Suddenly, a sliding glass door opened on the ground level and Dolly came trotting out. David followed shortly behind Dolly, calling after his sheep.

"There, there, Dolly. It's all right. She's not going to hurt you. Come here, Dolly. I'm going to put you in the barnyard now."

David was wearing a bathrobe and slippers. He was startled to notice Bob was there observing the scene. "Hello, there!" David said cheerily, quickly regaining his composure. "The wife just gets a little hysterical sometimes. She doesn't relate well to animals like I do. I like to have them around me because they relax me. Most people wouldn't understand it, but they have a calming effect on me. Don't pay any attention to the wife's screaming. She just needs to do that sometimes to get it out of her system. She'll get over it and she'll be a love-dove again after a few hours."

After the awkward incident passed, Bob let David know his intent to leave for another firm. David's response came quickly.

"I'd like you to hold off on your decision for a while. Give me a couple weeks. There might be a way to find room in the firm to give you more compensation and access to firm capital so you could attract larger deals. Let me first talk with the firm's bankers and attorneys to see what arrangements I can make."

David knew he'd earned Bob's trust by splitting their corporate underwriting profits fifty-fifty based upon a handshake deal. Otherwise, Bob would have simply accepted a deal elsewhere. Obviously the young man valued the friendship.

After a couple weeks' time elapsed, David called Bob over to his farm and the two men met in the barnyard. With sheep milling about them, David opened the discussion.

"Well, I've talked to the bankers and the lawyers," he began with a lie. He'd neither spoken with bankers nor lawyers during the elapsed two weeks, but it was a useful ploy of feigned sincerity. There was always the chance that the other firms would lose interest and pull their offers if they thought Bob was stalling them. "It seems that risking our regulatory capital by pledging it to firm commitment deals would jeopardize our representations to the Securities and Exchange Commission that we are capable to meet large-scale redemptions from the fund out of our capital should the need arise."

In actuality, this was a misleading representation because every fund has the right to meet redemptions by issuing shares in kind during times of great market stress, but Bob had no reason to doubt the veracity of David's representation. He had no experience with mutual funds, and no occasion to study the rules governing their operations.

"But I have given your situation a great deal of thought," David continued. "It seems to me that you have so much energy and talent that you need to be doing underwritings constantly. You just don't have the patience to wait for the next right deal to present itself, a deal we could do best efforts. So you see, if you can look at your problem from a behavioral viewpoint, what you really need is a situation where you can be doing an underwriting all the time." He was artfully planting the seed of a thought that he would nurture into a return for himself. "Well, we have that right here in the fund itself. We've got a great track record, thanks to your research, and now you could go out to all the dealers all over the country and raise a ton of money for the fund. You could make a fortune doing that."

Bob balked at the idea. His whole career to that point was about raising money for corporate America, deal by deal. Find the need, create the deal, match its terms to where the market would be when the deal hit the marketplace, check out the issuer thoroughly to make sure there were no misrepresentations, understand the issuer and its competitors and the risks it faced, explain the deal to Barbara and the other firms' syndicate people, sell the sizzle of the deal to the syndicators so they could sell it to their sales forces, and carve out the best possible compensation terms for the firm. He wasn't about to change careers to sell a mutual fund.

Bob enjoyed matching investor appetites to issuers' needs for capital. It was more than just making money to him; he was helping America grow, helping companies and investors succeed. It was difficult to wrap his mind around the idea of pushing a mutual fund all over the country. It sounded like a dull gumshoe chore. He knew fund wholesalers made a good living from it, but the field never piqued his interests. "I can't see myself doing that, David. I'm just not interested."

"I can tell that you can't see the potentials and that's understandable." David picked up a rubber ball from the barnyard floor and threw it far away. One of the dogs gave chase, gathered up the ball, and brought it back, wagging his tail. The dog dropped the ball at David's feet. David picked it up and threw it again. The dog was thrilled to serve his master, which was obvious. David continued, "You can't see it right now, but the beauty of a continuous offering is that it's not like a corporate deal.

"After each corporate deal, you have nothing to do. You have to start all over looking for the next one. Maybe it will come, maybe it will never come, or maybe it will take a long time to come. You just never know. The public can be hot to buy new issues one year and the next year can be stone cold. Then you just starve. Firms lay you off when they don't need you. It's not always big money this year and every year. With the continuous offering of a fund, it's like building a snowball. It's some work to put it together, package it just right, and shape it the way it'll roll, but when it's ready, you just start rolling it downhill. It picks up more snow and becomes a huge rolling juggernaut. Salesmen are just like snowflakes. They see one salesman selling a fund, and that it's an easy sale with a good commission, and then they want to sell it too.

"Most salesmen have customers they don't really want. That's just how it is. These are the small people who want to save ten or a hundred dollars a month or people who have a couple thousand dollars to invest. The brokerage firms lose money just opening accounts for them. So what's a salesman to do with them? Well, he can't just tell them to go away because a friend or relative who has money probably referred them to the salesman. Turning them away is an insult.

"You like to help people, and these people need help. You pack them all together and soon you've got a snowball. You get big orders also, but you get steady money coming in all the time. What do you say you give it some thought? I know this area really well. I've done it myself some and I can show you the ropes." This was a shaving of the truth. The only fund marketing David did was when Marvin presold the idea to his contacts in the Jewish community and David went to the family's home to fill out the paperwork.

Bob was nonplussed. He had his contacts in the corporate world. He understood financial markets well. Even in hard times, firms kept their core corporate people. Besides, he figured he'd make enough in the good times to last him through the lean times. Besides again, what was to say a fund wouldn't fall on bad performance years and see its sales dry up and its redemptions rise? There were no sure things in either endeavor. Another few days passed as Bob agreed to give David's proposition some serious consideration. He then called David with his decision.

"David, I've made up my mind. I've decided to leave Plaintown and take a job in Dallas. Barbara will be going along with me. It's a team deal. I hope there are no hard feelings."

David felt an air of desperation similar to the fisherman who played a fish almost into his net, but helplessly watched it throw the hook and slip away into the deep. The fisherman knows he's lost, but David was not a fisherman and Bob was not a fish. "Before you go, I'd like you to come by the barnyard tomorrow. I have an idea about this whole matter I'd like you to consider, and I'd like to talk about it with you face to face." There was a sense of urgency in David's voice. Out of a sense of obligation, Bob acquiesced.

Once again the duo returned to the barnyard. It was there amongst the animals, with the dogs at hand and Dolly grazing close by, that David felt most at home in this world. It was one of those lovely Colorado days with wispy cirrus clouds above drifting above on a downslope breeze in an azure sky. On days as these, one could actually look above the blue dim reaches of sky to the stratosphere and the tinges of black endless space far above the atmosphere. David wore a huge straw hat because of the ever constant danger of skin cancer at high altitude and bright sunlight. As Bob approached, David turned toward the north where there were empty fields that stretched to the end of the property.

"Come, walk with me a while," David said.

He put his hand on Bob's shoulder and squeezed it softly.

"You know, I have no children. My wife and I just can't make that happen. I've always wanted a son, and I've never had one. That's always been a void in my life, a terrible loneliness I have never been able to fill. I had a wonderful relationship with my father. He was my partner in business, and my best friend as well as my dad. Until you came along, I never thought having a relationship like the one I had with Dad would ever again be possible for me. But you did come along, and I've come to think of you as the son I've never had. You're already prepackaged. You know investing, you've got the education, you love what you do, and you work very hard at it. I know your dad died when you were very young and I'm sorry that happened. It must have been hard for you as a child. But from now on, I'd like you to know that I think of you as if you were my own son, and I'd like you to think of me as if I were your dad."

As they walked through the barnyard, Dolly followed closely behind. Those who knew David and Marvin's relationship understood it was strained. Neither father nor son could stand the other. David was a perpetual source of disappointment to Marvin, chaffing at his father's controls over him until the day Marvin died. That was a day of rejoicing for David, but his joy was short-lived. Even now, David smoldered under the controls Marvin had bequeathed to Susan. He could not be his own man until she died or quit the firm. He omitted all these material truths in his talks with Bob.

While David set the father-son hook, Bob's mind turned over his words, wondering if all this was preordained in some way. Could it be that this reclusive gnomish man with all his behavioral quirks was somehow destined to be a father-like personage?' It was late in life for both men to even think that way. Parental imprinting took place well before a child became an adult. That personality was set for life and not easily unlearned. *How bizarre this all seems.*

Here was a Jew twenty years his senior telling him, a gentile from an anti-Semitic mother, that he wanted to be like a father to him. Still, despite all the trepidations, there was a powerful tug on the half-orphan's emotions. David expressed some deep feelings to him. All the heartaches he'd felt as a boy growing up echoed through his reservoir of manly strength. They pierced the competitive fortifications he'd hardened over the years. Bob was humbled and shamed at the same time. The dimension he'd never had before in his life, the missing father piece was suddenly offered him by his quirky business partner, but a partner who'd kept his word without fail in the year they'd worked together. He respected that.

David continued, "I've had time to give my life a great deal of thought, and I've decided that I'd have no greater joy than to see you build the firm into a huge success, and I'd have even a better feeling about what I've done with my life if I left the business to you when I die. You see, I have no one to follow me. No one! It's a terrible feeling to work all my life and then know it's all going to just disappear into nothingness. When I'm gone, I'd like to know the firm will continue forever." David placed his hand over his heart and looked Bob in the eye. "I promise you, here and now, if you will change your career to work with me to build the fund, then when I die, you will inherit all the common stock of the underwriting company and all the common stock of the investment advisor, free of any estate or inheritance taxes." David was mum about his pledge to Marvin that the companies would go to Israel.

There it was! He'd made his best possible offer. He was not about to let a prized catch get away. He pulled hard on the pole of emotions and firmly set the hook of visions of grandeur.

Bob believed he now had a father-like older man solidly in his corner. He set aside their different cultural backgrounds, blocking them out of his mind. Differences didn't matter. He was bestowed with the gift of a dad!

He received assurance from David that there would be plenty of money to provide for David's wife should he predecease her. Besides, David told him that, as his son, he should know where there was a hidden cache of diamonds that Marvin had amassed while working with the Roosevelt administration, and that these diamonds were untouched since Marvin and David hid them away in a secret place. David told Bob he would take him to the secret place when the time was right, closer to his death, and that then Bob would become the guardian of the vast fortune of diamonds that made it out of Nazi Germany.

Bob was simply overwhelmed by his sudden good fortune. He pledged to David that from then onward, until David's death, he would set aside his career in investment banking and work to build the fund. Just like their previous underwriting deals, the two men shook hands on their new venture. Bob put aside all his corporate underwriting work and set out upon his new career path of building the UGGA Universal Fund. As the two men left the barnyard, they walked through the gate to go toward the farmhouse, Dolly following behind. As David closed the gate that kept Dolly in the barnyard, the sheep let out a sharp bleating sound in protest.

"Not now, Dolly," David said as he closed the gate behind him.

PURGE AND LOVE

David knew the best sale was the one that left the buyer with a strong sense of satisfaction afterward. He was not someone to give away anything, always thinking five chess moves ahead of those with whom he negotiated. He delighted in corrupting others and mocking their sense of morality. His genius was his innate ability to wring the greatest personal benefit from the talents, foibles, and weaknesses of others.

He hatched a devilish plan. An executive order was promulgated to all employees from David, their president:

From: David Sustack, President
To: All Employees

Subj.: Romantic relationships within the office

1. Based upon recent government studies, it has been determined that romantic relationships within office workplaces between co-workers damages workplace productivity.
2. Henceforth, it is company policy that all company personnel shall refrain from romantic relationships with other company personnel.
3. Any person(s) found to be romantically involved with any other company person(s) will be required to submit their resignations to the president.

It was hard for the employees to take the memo seriously. After all, hadn't Marvin and Susan carried on a tempestuous love affair for over twenty years? Wasn't David himself having sexual encounters with "Muscle Man" and "Man Child"? And hadn't the firm actively promoted prostitution with local brokers, even going so far as to recruit call girls? The memo was met with guffaws, derision, and the rolling of eyes.

A few weeks passed. It seemed to all employees that David himself was spending considerable hours away from the office with "Man Child." They were seen going into seedy bathhouses and gay bars together. With the lapse of time, most employees dismissed the memo as some sort of whimsical joke. It was a policy that was completely incongruous with the mores of the firm.

But there was one employee who recognized there was some sort of political game afoot. Barbara was initially crestfallen when she learned her move to Dallas with Bob was dashed. She knew the Sustacks' deep commitment to Israel and when Bob told her he would inherit the business, it raised a question in her mind: Would David, a deeply committed Zionist, actually leave his businesses to a gentile? She discussed the new development with Chief.

"Is it possible, Father? Do you believe a Zionist would leave his business to a gentile?"

"Yes, it is possible. Anything is possible. He is an old man and perhaps he wants a son, even at this late age, so these two with odd backgrounds may fit together. But you say he also likes bathhouses and has troubles with his wife. That makes it less likely, but still possible. Now, as to the Zionist question, I can only answer it this way. Would Crazy Horse adopt a white man for a son and leave him a parcel of the Black Hills after his death? It's possible also."

"So your advice would be what?"

"Tell me, when you look into his eyes, do his eyes tell you he loves you?"

"Yes, Father."

"Do you feel the same about him?"

"Yes, Father. I cannot deny my feelings. I love him. I love him with my whole heart."

"Now, Sparrow, this is important. Tell me, when you look into David's eyes, what do you see?"

"I see an evil presence. David chills my blood when he looks at me. He makes the air cold around me when he is near me. He is like a kind of death that has not yet died."

"Then you must allow for more time."

"Why do I need more time?"

"You don't, Sparrow. Bob does."

"Why?"

"He will be tested in ways you cannot see at this time. He must learn his own heart and he must decide your place in his heart."

"So, I must wait?"

"Yes, Sparrow, you are a woman. You wait."

"Will he survive his challenges?"

"That depends on his heart. You will learn of his heart."

"I believe in him. He is a strong Big Horse. I believe he will overcome his challenges."

"When the time comes, I believe he will need you, Sparrow."

"What is your thought, Father?"

"When a man comes face to face with certain truths, he needs a good woman. I think the time will come when he will need you, Sparrow."

"Will I know when he needs me?"

"When the time is right, you will know."

David decided Bob should first get his feet wet selling mutual funds to local representatives who were already familiar with the firm. Many of these men already knew Marty, but now that she was pulled off sales and moved into sales support, it was David's goal to transfer their loyalty to Bob. To facilitate the transition, David directed Marty to accompany Bob and visit the local brokers. She arranged the sales appointments and introduced Bob as the new representative. He then dutifully gave his presentation. After each presentation, Bob and Marty stayed to answer questions.

Naturally enough, the men, several of whom had previous trysts in the hay with Marty, gravitated to her to ask their questions. Often enough a salesman would claim he had a big sales prospect, but needed to take an officer of the fund to close the deal. And, of course, he insisted that the officer to accompany him be Marty. He was told, politely, that Bob would be the sales closer and that Marty was confined to home office sales support duties.

Local sales took a nosedive. These same eager salesmen who were chomping at the bit to go afield and afar with Marty suddenly found reasons not to make any effort to sell. They told Bob their client prospect decided on a different investment, or his wife decided the money was needed to buy a second home, or the prospect simply died.

"What are you doing to sabotage my sales?" Bob confronted Marty.

"Nothing! Why would I do that?" Marty shot back.

Marty's temper flared. She wasn't doing anything to kill sales. What was killing sales was David's reordering of the sales effort. She could no longer go on the road, but she couldn't tell Bob the truth about how she'd previously gotten sales.

There was a stalemate. The brokerage firms' sales reps position was no blow jobs, then no sales; no fucks, no orgies, then no big sales. Marty's position was, if she couldn't make the big bucks in sales, she wasn't about to help Bob make the big bucks either. His impression was that she and her sales support staff were too slow and too sloppy with their responses to sales aids and supplies requests, and that somehow her presence at sales meetings was impeding sales.

"I don't want you going along to sales meetings anymore. You stay in the office and get your department running more efficiently. I'll make my own appointments and let your staff know what I need for sales aids." Bob unilaterally changed Marty's role.

"Yes, sir, yes, sir, three bags full!" Marty snapped. This upstart pissed her off. Now he was completely removing her from contact with salesmen. She was furious at being relegated to sales support like she was stale goods.

And Bob went forth sans Marty to the local sales outlets. After a couple months, sales picked up some, but they were only running at one-fourth the level Marty previously achieved. Bob reasoned the local market for the product must be largely tapped out. He was partially correct, but he didn't understand the real reason for it.

He went to David. "I want to try a new distribution idea. The local market seems saturated. I want to go on the road, get new dealers, introduce the fund broadly into many more states and make presentations to new faces. Sometimes the guy who shows up from out of town is regarded as the expert. I want to see if that will make a difference."

"I like the idea. Go for it," David approved.

When she was told of the new plan, Marty's reaction was like a teakettle set to boil. She barged into David's office when she knew Bob was already there. She caught them both unawares.

"You guys are brilliant. Instead of figuring out why you aren't getting local sales and fixing the problem, you're going to send your problem nationwide. Don't you see you could be making a nationwide mess that will be impossible to fix after it's made? Can't we slow down and take some time to rethink this?"

Marty's ploy was to get Bob canned and never reveal to him that she lifted her skirts for sales, and that her own past methods were the cause of the sales' previous spike and subsequent drop.

Bob shot back, "Are you afraid that an idea not your own will work? It's a test. If it doesn't work, we'll try something else. Turn down your thermostat."

Marty looked at David for support.

"I think we should try Bob's idea." David smiled at her and Bob.

Marty's support evaporated. She seethed with anger, realizing she was little more than a glorified clerk now.

David ground a little salt into her wound. "From now on, when Bob needs something from sales, I expect your department to get him whatever he needs and get it promptly. And I want the both of you to stop your petty feuding and get along. I want to see office morale high, and it doesn't help the staff to see officers behaving badly. Am I understood?"

"Yes, sir," Bob replied.

"Yes. certainly," Marty replied.

"Now, I want to see the two of you shake hands, right here, right now. I want to see you getting along from now on."

Bob extended his hand to Marty. She shook it with reluctance, but forced a smile. She'd never been so humiliated in her life. Bob was David's fair-haired boy. She was a used toy, thrown into the corporate dust bin. She retired to her office to lick her wounds, figuring the new plan would fail and somehow she'd get back to her former glory. She'd bide her time.

After six months elapsed from the time David promulgated his "no romance" memo, he called Marty into his office. She was dressed in a no-nonsense blue business suite complete with pinstripes, a white shirt, and a stylish feminine necktie. That attire on a woman annoyed David to no end. He preferred female employees in dresses, especially revealing dresses on the off chance he'd get a look up their thighs. He liked their blouses unbuttoned with some cleavage showing, something that suggested vulnerability and invited voyeur impulses from every red-blooded man.

Every time he saw Marty in one of her successful business woman outfits, he needed to suppress the urge to throw a paperweight or stapler at her. She was one of the firm's greatest assets for what she had wrapped up inside those ridiculous cocoons, those Malloy "Dress for Success" sacks. David wished he could order that Malloy book banned so women couldn't read it. For his money, tits and ass would always trump the female penguin look for women who wanted to advance in a man's world. Now she stood before him in her most proper penguin attire, as summoned.

David began the conversation on the cheeriest note he had in his repertoire. "Hello, Marty. I've called you in to compliment you on the fine job you're doing. I hear lots of positive things about your efforts in the sales support area, and I want you to know that your tremendous personal efforts in direct sales were very much appreciated. You are an extremely valuable employee." David rubbed his hands together. As he spoke, he visualized Marty fucking three salesmen simultaneously. He knew he'd allowed six months to elapse without putting her greatest talents to use.

"Thank you, sir." Marty's head drew back and her jaw gaped slightly. The compliments were so unlike David.

"David! Marty, call me David. We're all in the same family here." His tone had an air of veracity to it.

"Okay, David." Marty flashed an impish grin and wiggled her ass like an insect in a mating rite. *Same family, did I hear that correctly? We're the same family. What's going on with David?* No matter; she was willing to play along.

"There's something I'd like to talk with you about. It's a little delicate, and maybe it's asking a lot of you, but I believe you could be of tremendous help to the firm."

"How, David? What do you need me to do?"

"Like I said, it's delicate, but the way I see it, you are the perfect woman for the job. You are extremely intelligent, you have an impeccable résumé of accomplishments, you have exemplary ethics, and exhibit the very highest, most outstanding moral standards of our firm. You are widely regarded for your professionalism and righteous conduct. In so many ways, you represent the very best traditions of UGGA Universal. Why, sales executives all over this state respect your ideas and hand over client assets based upon your excellent leadership qualities. There is no equal to you in our business, Marty. You represent the highest goals, the highest standards we have here at UGGA. That's why I've settled on you to help the firm with a very special mission. I know you're a true-blue company gal, Marty. I'm counting on you. My concerns are unique. They have to do with Bob."

"Bob? You mean, the new executive vice president Bob? I'm already helping him. We're doing absolutely everything he asks of us and doing it quickly."

"I know that, and I'm extremely proud of you. But there's something more I believe you could do. I believe you are not being used to your fullest capabilities."

"More?"

"Well yes, you could do more. I'd like you to help more by helping him keep his mind on this firm and on building the firm."

"David, you don't need to worry about that. The guy is focused like a laser beam. He lives and breathes sales. Bob's a sales machine."

It was apparent to David that Marty was not on his same wavelength.

"Yeah, I know all that, but he's on the road a lot. There are a lot of women out there and he's a very good-looking man, and there's always the chance that he'll get distracted or another firm will try to steal him away from us."

"Well, that's just life, David. What could I do about that?" Just as the words passed her mouth, Marty had an inkling of exactly what she could do about it. She sensed a scheme was brewing.

"Marty, I just believe if a ravishing beauty like yourself were keeping Bob blissfully occupied while he was in Plaintown, maybe even keeping him occupied while he was on the road, you know, during his off hours, then I believe he'd work that much harder building the fund. I just think if he were occupied with Marty full time in the evenings and the fund full time during the day, his mind wouldn't stray from his mission in the slightest. I guess what I'm asking, Marty, is would you be willing to be 100 percent committed to the company? Will you be a good company girl and go the extra mile? Will you do whatever it takes to keep Bob committed to a career at UGGA Universal? Will you give of yourself a 100 percent effort, and give Bob whatever it takes to keep him happy? Can I count on you to sacrifice body and soul for the firm, and I'm saying your *whole* body and soul, Marty?"

Marty cleared her throat. It was clear David was acting as her pimp. He wanted her to seduce Bob, which titillated her imagination. "Well, David, there's the matter of that policy memorandum you sent out a while ago. You know, the one about employees not having romantic involvements with other employees. I have concerns about how that might look. Besides, I have no idea if he'd even have any interest in me. My woman's intuition tells me he's interested in Barbara, if he has interest in any woman at all. They seem to have pretty strong feelings for each other."

"Oh, Marty, don't you give that policy memo any further thought. Put that out of your beautiful head. That's just for the little worker bees, not for you or Bob. You two are officers of the company. You are both special. Besides, I'm sure you know how to be discreet. I wouldn't expect to see the two of you kiss in the lunchroom.

"No, what I'm talking about is giving you a special entertainment expense account that you can use to entertain Bob. Just tell him it's a secret benefit, or better yet, don't even tell him where the money is coming from. After all, he's the number two man in the organization. He's worth some extra expenses. Marty, if you'll keep him focused on you and the firm, I promise next year you'll receive a huge bonus. And don't give the skinny Indian girl another thought. I see how she has eyes for him. I'll warn Susan to keep her from giving Bob any smoke signals. I'll make sure she stays out of your way. You'll have Bob all to yourself. Just leave her to me."

Marty's grin widened. Never in her wildest dreams had she ever imagined that her subsidized official duty would be to fuck her way to the top of the company, especially since there was a longstanding tension between David and her mother. This was quite the breakthrough. David had loosened her reins. Even Susan couldn't keep tabs on her—not that Susan could do anything about her sales activities before. This was unprecedented freedom in her corporate career. It would be all play and no accountability. She was ecstatic, so thrilled with the idea that she began salivating. She agreed to David's plan and promised him she would do her very best.

As she left his office, he rubbed his hands together, pleased that Marty's libido overcame her capacity to detect his mendacity. The plan he'd discussed with Dolly was successfully set in motion.

The next day, David closed the office that Bob and Barbara shared. The underwriting files were sealed and sent to storage. Bob's office was moved to the fund sales floor and located conveniently across from Marty's office. Barbara was moved back to her old reception desk next to Mrs. Rodriguez in the front office. David snipped the bud of their hopeful romance and crushed it. They had no business reason to spend time together anymore. David's actions proved his good faith to Marty, as he'd sidelined her competition.

Days later, her wit and wile engaged, Marty asked Bob to show her on the conference room's whiteboard how regression analysis worked amongst multiple data series, so she could understand correlation coefficients better, as that knowledge might be helpful to her when it came to explaining to salesmen why the fund was positioned the way it was for their current strategy.

Wearing a short, pleated, black skirt and black nylons attached to garter belts, her below-the-waist attire sharply contrasted to her white silk blouse worn opened three buttons down, revealing a black laced-bottom brassiere. Her tits lifted beautifully. She was magazine-cover gorgeous. She wore Chanel No. 5 perfume, applied strategically between her breasts, about her neck, and inside her upper thighs. Marty also wore a home-blended gardenia-based fragrance to her uppermost thighs and liberally applied this same aphrodisiac to her openly exposed butterfly pussy. Her panties stayed home. It was their day off. Her dark brown eyes were accented with a deep taupe eye shadow and black eyelashes, complimented with irresistible pink rose lipstick.

No burlesque queen or movie siren was ever more alluring or sensually packaged than Marty that fated day. Seated upon a raised student's chair with skirt lifted slightly above her knee, Marty faced Bob who stood with his back to her while he faced the whiteboard, colored markers in hand.

After a proper interval, once Bob finished writing the equations for standard deviations, Marty sensed the time was ripe to present an out-of-left-field six sigma deviation of her own. She flipped off her shoe from her extended leg and gasped slightly, pretending to be a maiden in distress. Her casual slipper fell to the carpeted floor with a soft thump. Her foot flip cast her lure to perfectly just beyond her reach.

It was a Ferragamo, black leather, solidly made, classily styled. To any cultured man, it signified the woman wearing it wasn't cheap. Bob heard the light thud and turned from the whiteboard. He noticed the shoe and looked at her to see if she'd like him to retrieve it.

"May I return this to you?" he asked, revealing his uncertainty about whether her act was accidental or intentional.

Men are so like dogs or fish to be reeled in. Bob's bewilderment was her cue. "Oh, I'm terribly sorry. I was so into what you were saying I forgot to mind my silly foot," she said in her most disarmingly helpless, damsel-in-distress innocence. "Yes, please, Bob, could you pick it up for me? And would you be so kind as to slip it onto my foot?" It was a page right out of the "how to drop your handkerchief so the man will pick it up for you" chapter of the female playbook.

Bob complied. As he picked up Marty's lure, she reached out and tugged ever so slightly on his ear, lifting his head until his eyes were parallel to the floor and level with her knees. Never was a trout's lip more subtly pierced with a sharpened fly hook. Bob was hers. He was solidly on her line. Now all she needed to do was play him in slowly, not too hard or fast. Let him dance on the hook, but don't let him panic and run. Don't let him break off the line and run away.

Her fragrance was intoxicating and her message was unmistakable. Marty was naked beneath her skirt. Her butterfly tattoo's wings were wide open, ready to receive Bob's penis and take flight with it to a land of sexual nirvana, far, far away from his whiteboards and regression equations. Bob scented a waft of her gardenia aphrodisiac simultaneously with a glimpse of her offering.

No battleship beating down a channel at flank speed with eighty thousand horsepower straining mightily to reach open ocean could match the unbridled power of a virile male's testosterone surge sparked by a woman's beckoning invitational. Bob was helpless to resist the urge of his penis. He welcomed Marty's gentle touch as she guided him into her net. He felt a tinge of self-doubt about whether he should resist Marty and hold out hope for Barbara, but Barbara had him on some kind of "danger hold," and she did tell him he needed to do what a man must do.

Marty's pheromones knew their business. They vanquished equivocation and drowned deep thinking, bearing proof that women decide who beds them and when. As Bob willingly surrendered, the thought flashed through his mind that he could be on an irreversible course, away from Barbara and into Marty's arms.

Marty wasn't just another woman in Bob's eyes. When he first met her as he was introduced to the employees of the fund complex, he did a double take. He hoped she hadn't noticed. She resembled Rosie, the girl of his high school dreams, the girl he couldn't see because he wasn't a Jew. Now, fifteen years later, there was Marty, who could have passed for Rosie's twin. She looked so much like Rosie he thought they must have the same bloodlines. Marty was perhaps an inch or two taller than he imagined Rosie would be now, with fuller breasts, but her face was nearly identical to Rosie's. Marty made Bob wonder what became of Rosie. He figured she'd married some man her father chose for her, likely a Jew from a wealthy family. He imagined Rosie had two or three children and that she was happy with her brood and her father was happy with her. Yet, Bob always chafed at the thought that some man he never met could prevent him from being with the girl he fell in love with, that first love that could have gone the distance.

"Come see me after work today. I'll be waiting for you at my place. I'll have something very special for you." Marty handed Bob her card with her home address and phone number on the back. "I'll leave the office shortly. Maybe you could come by around five?"

Bob wondered if this just a business appointment for Marty. She acted like she'd done this before. He brushed aside concerns about her matter-of-fact, clinically sounding tone. No doubt Marty had some experience with men, but what could that matter? It was only an impromptu date. Bob looked into her eyes in a way that the woman had to know the man was all hers, that he wanted her, that nothing would stop him from coming to her.

When they left the conference room, Marty went straight home.

Bob went to his office, leaned back in his chair, put his hands behind his neck, and stared at the ceiling with curious wonder. He imagined Rosie had come back to him, indirectly. Marty had that same alluring, irresistible confidence about herself that Rosie had. She was unashamed and direct. Yes, she was direct all right. Only this time, unlike Rosie, Marty had no daddy obstacle to foil her desires.

Bob heard a few office hints about Marty. When he first went out with her to a local sales meeting, Barbara stopped him in the hall.

"You're going selling with Marty?" Barbara asked.

"Yes, why?" Bob detected she was trying to warn him.

"Be careful." He was duly warned.

"What do you mean?"

"I mean be careful." Barbara looked deeply into his eyes and past that day to many days in the future. It was a profound look that said nothing but tried to say everything. She felt like she was saying good-bye forever to the only true love she'd ever felt. She sensed he could be slipping away from her, going out of her life forever.

Bob knew Marty was no virgin, but what woman over twenty was, and who was he to judge or care? He'd bedded a few women in his past. Why would any woman he dated be any less experienced? Besides, Marty could probably have practically any man she chose, but she'd chosen him. Why? He could only wonder. Maybe there was something about him that attracted Rosie. Maybe the two femmes were genetically wired so similarly that whatever attracted Rosie to him was the same thing that attracted Marty. It was puzzling stuff, women's stuff. His mind raced ahead and wondered.

What was Marty like? Would she kiss like Rosie? No woman kissed like Rosie. No woman generated the heat within him like Rosie did, except for that brief hug with Barbara. What would Barbara think about him seeing Marty? Well, she told him to be a man. What could she expect?

Bob once thought there would never be a woman who would reach into him and hold his heart in her hand like Rosie could, but there it was again, almost that same feeling. He definitely rediscovered the feeling with Barbara, and now he had something close to it with Marty. It seemed more superficial than his feelings toward Barbara, but the sexual attraction was definitely there. He thought between Barbara, untouchable Barbara, and Marty, who obviously wanted to have sex with him, he could possibly lose his mind. He instinctively knew Barbara was the higher quality woman, the better but unattainable choice.

When Bob looked into Marty's eyes, he felt the pulsing beginnings of an erection. He wondered if she could tell he was sex-starved. It'd been over two years since he'd been with a woman. Bob wanted her so badly he could barely wait to leave the office. By making him wait a few hours, had she calculated he would explode into her like a bull moose in rut?

Bob stared at the ceiling, shaking his head as if trying to shake his feelings loose from his antlers. He told himself that mixing with Marty could be a huge mistake in his life, and could even lower David's opinion of him. The notion of getting involved with this sex symbol couldn't possibly be sensible. *Where is Mr. Sensibility when I need him?* But Mr. Sensibility took a vacation from Bob's conscience that day. He packed his bags and left the moment he looked up Marty's skirt. Bob gave up on Mr. Sensibility; he could talk with him later. For now, he wanted to fuck Marty. Nothing else mattered.

He turned Marty's name over in his mind and wondered. What did she like? What did she think about? What made her happy? Had anyone ever hurt her? Wow! He suddenly felt protective of her and he hadn't even kissed her. He put his hand to his chin as if to bring his thoughts back to earth, but he was stymied. Marty was on his mind and he had to have her. He wondered if he could be her man, her only man, or at least the first man in line for her. He knew he was completely irrational now. This was not love. It was lust pure and simple. He knew it, but it didn't matter. He wanted to get laid.

What time is it? Marty left two hours ago. I shouldn't be early. Give her some time. You don't want to seem too anxious. Just hold off an extra half hour, hope the phone doesn't ring. Hope David or one of the sales reps don't need something.

"Tick tock" went the time clock in his mind.

Marty was home making preparations, going through her checklist. *I douched myself and applied a fresh concoction of my most exotic perfumes to my pussy. I slathered Chanel No. 5 around my upper thighs and rubbed my gardenia and lavender oil blend around my outer vaginal lips. To give him my welcoming velvet feeling, I fingered a dab of KY jelly into my inner lips. Bob's entry will be smooth, wet, warm, and wonderful. I have my favorite music selections on my CD player. I've fluffed the pillows on my bed, and picked up things that seemed out of place in the house and threw them into the garage. Let me double-check the rooms. Yes, all magazines, old shorts and sweat tops, old sneakers and my travel guides are all in the garage. Now, I must do my mouth. He must love my mouth.* She brushed her teeth, swallowed some peppermint herb capsules, and for a final touch of irresistibility, she added dabs of Chanel behind her ears and on her cleavage.

Bob is going to have the greatest sex he's ever had in his life. If there is anything going on with him and Barbara, I'm just going to shove her out of his life tonight. I'm going to be so good in bed, he'll always want more of me. I'll show him I know music and the arts. I'll give him a taste of what it's like to be with a real woman. I'm going to fuck him all evening and on into the night. He's going to spend the night in my bed, and tomorrow he's going to want to be with me all the time. Fuck that skinny Indian bitch and her righteous, know-everything bullshit. Fuck her! I'm going to have her man's face in my cunt, eating me. I'll imagine her watching us while I come on his face. I feel delightfully wicked about what I'm going to do to her dreams. Tonight she's going to lose her man. He's going to forget she exists.

The interminable madness of Bob's waiting hours finally passed, and he drove to Marty's house. She lived in a chichi East Side bungalow halfway between Plaintown University and Goldstrike Creek. It had one of those curving brick walkways with two levels of stairs and sat high up on a bank. Irises and tiger lilies lined the walkway to Marty's door, lovely innocence on one side, radiant seduction on the other.

Bob wondered which flower symbolized Marty. Their petals opened fully in the warm afternoon sun, bees rubbing their stamens with pollen and buzzed softly. Bob mused as he approached the walkway steps. *Bees and flowers don't hurry sex. They just do it and don't think about it. But I'm not a plant or an insect. The hell I'm not. Something happened when I looked up Marty's skirt. I'm no better and no different than a bee. I want what's inside that girl's flower. I want to put my dick deep inside her butterfly. I want sex with her and I want it bad.*

Marty's front door was a huge solid oak, arched entrance portal with a barred view slider at eye level. Her home had a bay window that accented its brick walls and red tile roof. As Bob walked up the second set of steps, he was thinking of what he was going to say. He was naturally shy around women. His mother intimidated him all his childhood, then cautioned him endlessly about how women can ruin your life, but there he was. All he knew about this Marty woman was from hearsay. The drift of the hints he got was she knew her way around a bedroom. He realized he didn't know anything about her. He considered whether he was even in his right mind coming here, but he simply couldn't turn back now. He raised his hand to knock on her door, but before his knuckles could rap upon the oak, Marty opened it.

She was stunning. The only thing she wore was a sheer, see-through, light green nightgown. Nothing underneath. Bob was mesmerized by the most sensuous, shapely woman he'd ever seen. No woman in real life, in pictures, in movies, or imagination compared to the package standing before him. Marty smiled and told him to come in, but he was entranced. He couldn't comprehend what he saw or her invitation to enter.

Marty took control. *This is going to be easy. He's almost a baby. I'm going to make him want me. Barbara, you're not going to have any chance with him after tonight.* She took Bob's hand, gave him an inviting tug inside, and then closed and locked the door. "The neighbors will do too much thinking if we stand in front of the open door. Come in, be comfortable." She unbuttoned his shirt and deliberately rubbed her palm on his chest while removing it.

"I like the feel of your chest," she said. You're very hand-some and strong. I've noticed you from the first day we were introduced. I've hoped this day would come for a long time. I really want you. I think you know that."

Then Marty gave Bob their first kiss. It was full on the mouth with the same deep soulful French tongue that Rosie kissed him with years ago. Everything about Marty reminded him of Rosie. He let his curiosity get the best of him.

"I need to ask you something. Don't ask me why. I don't want to tell you why. Are you by chance somehow Jewish?"

Marty burst out laughing. "No! I guess I might look a little Jewish, but no. My dad was Irish. He died in an accident when I was just a little girl. I didn't see him much, barely knew him. Mom is, you know, Susan. She's Irish too. I've wondered sometimes how I got the dark hair and eyes, with Mom and Dad being light-haired, but people say it happens sometimes. Okay? So now I have to know. Did you have a Jewish girlfriend once? You did, didn't you?" Marty had terrific instincts when it came to men.

Bob nodded.

"And she kissed you like I did, right?"

Again, Bob nodded.

"Well, did she kiss you like this too?" Marty opened Bob's trousers and unzipped his fly. Kneeling down, she lifted his penis into her mouth and began to perform a deliriously sensuous act of fellatio, with her mouth and hand working in concert.

Bob whispered softly, "No, she never did that. She didn't—" Bob's words were cut off. He'd never started a first date with a blow job before. Marty stood and put her arms around his neck before she French kissed his mouth again. Somewhere between the first and second kiss, Bob stopped thinking of Rosie or Barbara. There was a change. Whenever he'd been with another woman, whether he was romantically involved or just talking with her, his mind would drift in and out of his involvement or his conversation and he would think of Rosie. He'd often ached for her over the years, and lately he ached to be with Barbara. But now, between Marty's kisses and being there with her pressing her flesh closely against his, Rosie was gone. Marty had vanquished Rosie from his mind. The memories of her, her brother Richard, and father Sam vexed him no longer. The bitterness suddenly melted away.

And Barbara had him on hold. What did she expect from him? He wasn't some court eunuch, and she wasn't Cleopatra. He was a red-blooded male. He loved her and she loved him. He wanted to be her man, her life partner, but she kept putting him off and playing some kind of mysterious game with him. What did she expect would happen?

The tinge of regret Bob felt for not being patient, for not waiting for Barbara, was crammed down into a tiny little corner by Marty. Then, as Marty began rubbing his cock with one hand and stroking the back of his neck with the other, she figuratively picked up Bob's little tinge of regret, deposited it into a mouse jar, and locked it away from his conscious thoughts in a closet of his mind. He surrendered, spellbound, to the gorgeous, irresistible, wanton whore he held in his arms. Marty was eager to fuck, and he'd be an idiot not to welcome her overtures. He wanted to take her into his life, like a fool blindly rushing in and not caring about the consequences. In the space of minutes, he'd gone from being an apprehensive novice to a man consumed by lust. His blood ran hot with passions he'd never felt before. His heart pounded and his penis swelled full. The organs were charged up. They knew intimacy was in their future.

Marty pervaded Bob's mind. She didn't allow room for another woman to stay in a man's mind once she was there, evicting all traces of them. Marty was the femme fatale, the siren nonpareil. All other women—mothers, lovers, wives, yesterday's loves—were shoved aside. When Marty was with a man, there was only her. She smothered her quarry with unbridled insatiable sex.

Many men who'd known her and loved her couldn't shake their thoughts of Marty. She stayed around in their minds because she put her whole soul into her lovemaking, even if was only going to be a one-night stand. She prided herself on leaving an indelible impression with a man. She still heard from old castoffs she had no use or time for. They sent their little notes and cards, and some die-hard hopefuls occasionally even sent her flowers. Men clung to their dreams, but Marty was discerning and coldly calculating. She had to be that way. Sex was business; falling in love wasn't a luxury she could afford. Men were toys to be used, nothing more. "No pay, no play" was her credo.

Bob was totally different. He came with a first-class ticket and full-time exclusive services paid for and he didn't even know it.

"Come with me," Marty said to Bob as she led him into her bedroom. "Let's make our first time together something we'll always remember. Let's make it sweet and wonderful."

Marty's bedroom had a soft and inviting décor with spring green walls and taupe drapes. The effect was to draw her guests' attentions to her almond-shaped brown eyes. The allure of those eyes captivated Bob. He watched as she went to the stereo system on her dresser. She pushed a button on the disc player and "Ave Maria" began playing sweetly, softly, sung by a female soprano. The song made Bob feel what was about to happen was holy.

The soprano sang in German. Marty knew the words and whispered their translation into English. The lovely melody strengthened. "Safe may we sleep beneath thy care, though banished, outcast, and reviled," Marty spoke softly as she came to Bob and opened her light green gossamer nightgown. She was a stunning woman. Seeing her fully naked while hearing her erotic words and the spiritual music hardened Bob's member. Marty pressed close against him. "Let's make our first time together something sweet and holy. Let's make it last forever," she whispered.

With that stated goal, she guided Bob's penis tip into her while they stood upright. Her message was electrifying and erotic. She was wet, slippery wet, and warm. She wanted Bob now, right now. They climbed into her bed, she propped a huge feather pillow under her pelvis, and then they began making love in the maiden position. The soprano's voice strengthened as their movements quickened and their passions built.

"We bow us to our lot of care, beneath thy guidance reconciled," Marty whispered as the soprano shifted into her most comfortable tessitura; she now sang the Latin version of "Ave Maria" in coloratura soprano.

Marty whispered to Bob, "Hail Mary full of grace, blessed are thou among women" as their closeness became intense. They were as one body and one being, held together by the magical forces of music and spirit. Then, as their passions heightened to peaks neither had before known, Marty again spoke softly. "Pray for us sinners now and at the hour of our death. Hail! Mary!"

She adored those passages from the prayer song. Simultaneously she believed she was chosen to be blessed among women and, although she was a willing unrepentant sinner, the Virgin Mary was praying for her while she fucked to her heart's content.

Marty was the first to orgasm. It was a continuous, sweet, unhurried, long-lasting release, like a flowing river of euphoria. She continued rubbing her clitoris over Bob's still rock-hard cock, like her love organ was an endless river flowing softly over a smooth boulder in a stream. She became heady and slightly dizzy. Her clitoris swelled to near bursting with the excitement and rapture of fornication with its newest lover and his considerably oversized, stalwart cock.

I can't believe this guy. He has more stamina than my black lovers. He's incredible, even as enduring as my vibrator, but more pliable, more real. Oh God, I love the feel of his cock inside me. Judith said he spent some time in the Army. Now I finally understand what they mean when they say "Army Strong"! I could rock this cock inside me forever. I'm like I was when I first fucked the twins! I could do this forever. Oh geez, he feels wonderful in there. I hope he likes sex as much as I do.

That was the first time in her life her orgasm happened that way. Usually, the man came and she didn't orgasm at all, or the man came first and she would, with the considerable effort of rubbing against a wilting penis, come later and only for a small release. Of course there was oral sex. She could come easily then. With man or woman, Marty responded fully and uninhibited to oral sex by released pulsating gushers. With many men, Marty preferred oral to straight sex because those men were so patient and loving that they could continue stimulating her long after she began to orgasm. Those who loved performing oral sex with Marty's clitoris were her treasured, long-standing lovers. They could drive her into a frenzied state of wildly uninhibited, continuously gushing orgasms.

She loved continuing to gush that same way with a penis rubbing her clitoris, with the penis continuing firm long after it had ejaculated inside her. It was imperative that the man stay hard after he came if she was to have an elongated, gushing release. Such men were rare, and she treasured those who could sustain her release. To her happy wonderment, Bob was the best of these men. The very first time they made love, he stayed firm until she completely released her own orgasm. She was awed and deliriously joyful to be so wonderfully fucked on a first encounter like that. Others needed her alcohol kisses to harden them, but Bob stayed hard for her entire duration. It seemed miraculous, almost as if he'd been trained to satisfy women. However he was able to do that, she didn't care.

And I'm going to be paid to get wonderful fucks like this as my full-time job? I am beyond thoughts to describe my good fortune. He feels so much at home in my cunt!

She mentally separated oral from regular sex. Oral was wonderful and she loved giving it and receiving it, but it wasn't a holy thing to her. It wasn't a "God wants us to be together this way" kind of thing, like a man and a woman fucking intimately while listening to the Ave Maria prayer. Marty believed oral sex lacked the romance that made love sacred and blessed, although some of her lovers were completely in love with her clitoris and totally absorbed themselves in the intimacy of their oral sex with her. The way they tenderly tongued her clitoris made her euphoric and wildly orgasmic.

Perhaps Marty would have had the same religious thoughts about oral sex that she had about copulation with a penis if Susan had shared with her Marvin's explanation as told to him by a rabbi. Susan learned that oral stimulation was a Torah mitzvah, and it was meant to first bring the woman to orgasm before she was asked to receive the penis. The act was ordered by God and meant to make sex highly pleasurable for the woman, and it was the man's duty to orally bring the woman to orgasm. The act of oral sex and the woman's response through orgasm was the bringing of God's blessings to the vaginal portal into the woman's womb.

A small tremble coursed through Marty's entire body. She felt more alive in that moment than she'd ever felt in her life. What was it about this man? He was handsome and intelligent, but so were many men. He was uncomplicated; perhaps that was it. He took her at face value, didn't ask questions about her past, and he didn't try to control her. He didn't know in the back of his mind that she was fucking for sales now as she'd done so often with so many others. Bob willingly became one with her, without conditions or caveats or quid pro quos. It was simple and elegant to be with him. Bob made her feel good about herself. And his cock was positively incredible. He was stronger than a horse.

When they changed positions, Marty atop Bob and his cock deep inside her, she looked closely at the man in her bed. He had a gorgeous body. He was like a god, with well-sculpted muscles and a firm stomach, a magnificent chest, and broad muscular shoulders. His hair was a golden blond and his face was like a cherubic angel's with its soft, loving eyes, handsome cheeks and forehead, and perfect white teeth. And again she marveled at his hair! How often had she seen him in the office and held back the urge to run her hands through his hair? She wanted to hold his head in her lap and twirl her fingers through his hair.

She stared at Bob, who had his eyes closed. He was fully engaged in making love with her, for the third time. He had such amazing stamina. He had a golden bronze body that was so perfectly muscled she thought he must work out daily. She must be dreaming. It seemed like Christmas when she was a little girl and her father sat watching her open a dozen packages. He spoiled her every chance he could. Now she was being spoiled again. How could she be so lucky?

There she was, astride the most beautiful, strongest man she'd ever fucked. His cock was deep inside her and he loved her enthusiasm for fucking. He didn't slow down or tire as so many men did. She could pinch herself to see if it was all real. She was having the time of her life with this man and she was being paid for it. It all seemed too good to be true. She could feel herself falling in love with him. She couldn't wait to explore him fully over many lovemaking sessions. She always put her heart and soul into her lovemaking. She would lovingly take his balls into her mouth and tease them with her tongue. She would suck him ever so lovingly and patiently until he released his cum into her mouth. She couldn't wait to taste his cum and swallow it.

She loved this body beneath her, and she loved his smile when she rubbed his massive chest with her hands. More than anything, she loved his splendid cock. He was so strong! He kept it rock-hard for her without any extra stimulation or prompting. Bob was a wonderful man, and his cock was beyond words. She wanted to keep this newfound treasure inside her that entire evening, savor it in her pussy and permanently imprint her pussy's memory with the sensation of this amazing cock. She wanted to keep Bob's cock locked in her pussy all night long while she glided up and down his marvelous shaft. While she gently rocked it back and forth and squeezed it with her Kegel muscles, she savored each moment this remarkable, magnificent cock was within her.

Oral sex will have to wait. I'll have his face in my cunt another night. I think the skinny Indian would be shocked enough with what I've accomplished this first time with her man. I'm going with straight fucking all the way tonight. Oh, my sweet darling. You and I are going to have so much fun together. You have no idea. Oh, keep fucking me, darling. I could even fall in love with you.

Except for some brief recesses, she kept Bob's cock inside her that entire first evening.

As she dozed in and out of sleep that night, Marty dreamed of a lifetime with Bob and his astounding organ. *Perhaps this is a cure for my nymphomania? I've never known a man who could stay hard like him. It's like I have a swollen meat Popsicle inside me that never softens, and every so often it shoots a wad of creamy cum goo into me, like it's a vanilla custard dispensary. I can't wait to have it deep in my mouth, tickling my tonsils while I lick its underside and suck its head with my lips and tease it with my tongue. I love the way he makes love, the way he holds my hips so firmly and gently with his huge platter paw hands, how he gently lifts me up and down on his ever-pleasing cock. He's not as big as Carl or a few others I fuck, but he's by far the most enduring and endearing. He's staying hard all night, and whenever I urge to have him push hard into me, he keeps responding. I've got to keep him interested. Barbara has no idea what she's missing. He told me she wasn't interested in dating him. She's the most foolish woman ever. No woman would pass up a man who is this tender, this loving, and this amazing with his cock.*

Bob spent the next twelve months meeting with brokers and financial planners all over the United States. Marty arranged her office work so she could join him for long weekend stretches, usually meeting him for three or four nights each week. Bob arranged his schedule so that when Marty joined him, they would be close to an area she referred to as a "playground." They saw many of the most romantic places in the country together, from Hawaii's Maui coasts to Florida's Sun Coast, from the Big Sur Coast to New Orleans, New York, New England's Maine coast, and many places between.

Marty excelled at making their byway excursions interesting and memorable. At the Kahala Hilton on Oahu, she donned a seductive grass skirt and performed an erotic hula wedding dance for Bob. In Natchez, Mississippi, she costumed herself as a southern belle complete with corset, breast lifters, and sun bonnet. In New York, she danced to "Respect" sung by Aretha Franklin while wearing her seductive black skirt and an inviting pink blouse.

Sadness settled over Barbara during this trying time. It was incomprehensible to her that Bob couldn't see Marty for the incorrigible whore she was. Were all men so stupid? Did they all think with their penises? She saw Marty's expense reports. She was both dumbfounded and deeply hurt. She could just imagine Marty fucking and sucking her Bob in every position and situation possible in every romantic location in America. What was David thinking when he turned the company whore loose on Bob? Why would he pay good money to subsidize debauchery? What was wrong with this picture?

Chief had told her to give Bob time, but now she needed to resign herself to possibly waiting years until they knew time made them ready for each other, not merely weeks or months. She yearned to have Bob in her life, in her arms. She rued the day she told him they needed to wait. It took all her willpower to believe Chief knew what was best. She prayed to The Great Spirit of All Living Things that Chief could see her future clearly and that her trust in his wisdom would not waver.

One night, while Bob and Marty were traveling on the East Coast, Barbara lay in bed crying, thinking vengeful thoughts of killing Marty, and becoming more and more frustrated and angry at her situation. How could she go through each day at the office knowing Bob was somewhere out of town with Marty? How could she control her emotions knowing he was fucking Marty every night, probably telling her he loved her, kissing Marty like Barbara wanted him to be kissing her, holding Marty close like she wanted to be held?

How could her heart bear this steady diet of emotional pain? How could she hold her head up in the office and pretend nothing was eating her guts out? And when Marty and Bob were back in Plaintown, how could she keep from gouging Marty's eyes out? How could she not lower herself to Marty's level? Why shouldn't she pull her pants down in Bob's office and spread her legs on his desk in front of him and give him a comparison look? Why not be as base as Marty? Maybe she could give Bob an unmistakable message of her displeasure if she just punched him in the balls!

Men! Damn men! Sometimes men can be so stupid! Men know how to piss a woman off without even trying to piss them off. They are just stupid jerks! It comes naturally to them, just by being men!

Barbara pounded her pillow with her fists, wishing it were Marty's face. Then she lay there and cried some more. Her heart ached. For several days after she learned of the new marketing plan, she could barely summon the will to eat. She never expected this turn of events. The office whore was going along with Bob on the road! She believed it was a crazy idea from its inception and it made no business sense. It was plain crazy!

Barbara sought Chief's counsel the next day. If she didn't talk with him about her feelings, she feared she would lose her mind. She heard from others that a whore could eat the guts out of a good woman, but she never thought it could happen to her.

Marty was stealing her dream life from her. The woman was a shameless interloper and an unprincipled harlot. How dare her! Barbara wanted to claw Marty's eyes out and bite her nose off, at the very least. What she was doing was beyond insulting. That slut had to know that Barbara had eyes for Bob. Marty had to see that she and Bob were falling in love, but Marty didn't respect boundaries. There should have been an unspoken understanding that Marty respected, but she knew no respect. She only did what pleased her fuck-crazy cunt. She just saw Bob and dug her evil claws into him.

Barbara thought to herself that calling Chief about a woman's matter was selfish of her. He had many other duties that affected so many people, but who else could she turn to? Her mother was gone, she had no sisters or aunts, and confiding with any of the office girls for advice would surely be a mistake. They were all whites, and likely many of them would like to see Bob's interest in her wane so they could try for him themselves. There was only Chief. He would understand why she needed to turn to him. He would not disparage her if her heart was true. He was so wise in so many things, but was he also wise to the ways of women? She screwed up her courage and called her father.

"Father, my heart aches for this man. I know he is making a terrible mistake with his life, and I know my love for him is true, but he is spending his time with this seductress and I fear he is falling in love with her. What should I do?"

"Sparrow, my dearest child, you must first know yourself and your feelings well. You are a beautiful woman, more beautiful than the most beautiful of the entire world's Cleopatras, and you are highly intelligent. You are the natural first choice of any man with eyes and judgment."

"But he told me of his interest, and I held him away because I need to learn so much more. I told him I was not ready."

"Then he should understand that and you need to trust his heart."

"But this seductress, she is so skilled at tempting men."

"Sparrow, these things tend to run a natural course. You would be wise to allow nature's spirits to work their magic for you."

"But if they marry, Father, what will become of him?" Barbara felt the anxiety rising in her own voice, but she did not restrain her emotion.

"You do not know that they will marry. Usually worst fears do not happen. Tell me, when you look into his eyes, what do you see?"

"Oh, Father, I see sunshine and happiness. I see the warmth of life in his eyes and goodness from his eyes into mine. He looks upon me with a lift in his heart."

"And how do you feel when he sees into your eyes?"

"My heart leaps and my breath hurries. The blood rushes to my face. I want to hold him in my arms. I feel this way about no other."

My loins ache for him. I want to hold him tightly in my arms and within my loins and never let him go. I want him to fill me with his seed so I can bear his children. I often think of nothing else. Barbara thought it was best not to tell Chief all her thoughts.

There was a pause before her father answered her. His silence told her Chief knew her thoughts as well as her words. He had understandings about people she couldn't fathom.

"Sparrow, since we last talked, have you noticed any change when you look into David's eyes?"

"Father, I feel the same cold chill in my blood. Evil comes from his eyes as before. There is a difference though. There is a feeling that he has an inner confidence, that he is more in control of something. I see self-assurance now. I didn't see that before."

"Tell me this, Sparrow. Do you sometimes look into the eyes of the Marty woman?"

"Yes, some few times we have held eye contact."

"And what do you see when you look into her eyes?"

"I see coldness and hatred, and yes, even a danger from her to me. I see her eyes shooting the venom streams of a diamondback rattlesnake into my eyes as if to poison me."

"And your feelings when you see her eyes?"

"I don't know how to describe my feelings, Father. I believe what I feel is a kind of deeper sorrow for her than I feel anger toward her behavior. I feel she is somehow very sick in her soul, and what might have become a beautiful, loving woman somehow became a twisted, vengeful temptress. I feel I look into the eyes of a soul that has departed this woman. There is a certain hollow evil about her. Evenings when I am alone, I think angry thoughts about her, but I keep them to myself, and when I see her, I then see only sorrow, not anger."

"Very good, Sparrow. What you have told me is that they will not marry. They are different in their souls and her soul will try to reach out to his, but it will never escape the prison of its base behavior and it will never have him. David will play some role in their relationship."

"How do you know these things, Father?"

"I spend many days with the other elders in many coun-
sels. I listen as many tell of feelings they hear about from tribal
members. Your circumstance is not new to the spirits. It is only
new to you. Understand, your apprehensions are heard by the
spirits and they will guide you to the right outcome with your
Bob."

"So what can I do to understand the will of the spirits
better? I have nowhere else to turn."

"First you must take each fact, examine it carefully and
with great thought, Little Sparrow."

"What's there to examine? He is with her night after night,
day after day, week after week. He hardly even sees me
anymore. I fear I have lost his love and I will never get it back."

"You overlook the most important fact."

"Which is what, Father? I am too beset with my heart's
feelings to think clearly!" Barbara's pouting went unseen by the
chief, but not unnoticed.

"Sparrow! I command you now. Hold emotions and
answer! Who decided Marty should travel with Bob as his
assistant?" Chief rarely raised his voice to her, but he did then.

"David did." Barbara's anxiety lowered slightly. She sensed
Chief understood something she could not see.

"And does Bob need an assistant for what he does? Do his
competitors in sales take assistants with them?"

"No, Father."

"Does David spend money foolishly, Sparrow?"

"No, Father."

"Then you have nothing to concern yourself with, Little
Sparrow."

"I don't understand."

"You will in time. David put the two together for a reason.
It is not for you to know the reason at this time, but eventually
you will. It will be revealed to you."

"But he makes love to her, Father. I am certain he does. I don't know if I can live with that."

"Are you sure you love him, my child?"

"Oh yes, Father. I love him with my whole heart. I want no other."

She felt the maddening rush of emotions as she again confessed her feelings. *If only I could hold him within my loins just one time, he would never want to be with Marty. He would know love with me, and after that, her vile whore box would only repulse him.* Her desire for Bob was driving her crazy.

"Then you must be patient, Sparrow. It is normal for a strong brave to know other women before he settles to marry his true love. It will have no effect on him after he decides to be with you."

"But, Father, what if he falls in love and marries the woman named Marty?"

As soon as she spoke the words, she realized she'd challenged her father's judgment. *My, how far off the deep emotional end you have gone. It's a wonder Chief has any further patience with you.*

"Then he does, my child. But I do not think that will happen, and I don't believe you should think any more on the matter. Before that happens I believe it will be revealed to you why David paired Marty and Bob together. Until then, have patience. I think you should not overly concern yourself with what a man feels or does when his sex organ is in control of his mind. Men are that way sometimes. It is like a bad cold, but in time it goes away. Give him time, Sparrow. Think of him as a horse that has been left free on a trail. Do not worry yourself about the horse. It always finds his way back to the village. Like the horse, your Bob will return to you."

"Father, you are most helpful and wise. I will wait for this horse to come back to me. I still think of him as my 'Big Horse.' Right now, my Big Horse is my Big Stupid Horse."

"Yes, Sparrow, but you must also be sure when Big Stupid Horse comes back to you that he has a good heart, that his spirit is a good spirit and that you still want to keep your Big Horse."

"Oh, I will, Father! I will take Big Horse back and I will love him and he will know what true love is." Barbara's heart was lifting.

"Then you do truly love your Big Horse, my dear Little Sparrow, and your heart is pure. Now you must get some sleep. The best thing in life is a good night's sleep. Big Horse will find his way home to you. Good night."

"Thank you, wise Father. Good night." Barbara would wait. Chief always knew best. There had to be a way to get Bob back, and she needed to trust her father that the way would be revealed to her in time. She told herself she must not dwell upon this matter. In time she would see the way. She just knew it.

Barbara lay in her bed staring at the ceiling. She turned the words of her father over and over in her mind. Her heart swelled with hope that Bob would return to her, while her mind tried to comprehend that he was making love to another woman. She thought of the mustang stallions she'd seen on the prairie, how they fought each other and how the best stallions had many mares. She felt smaller than she'd ever felt. Her mind was swimming with emotions. But she was a woman, not a mare breed horse. She didn't like sharing her Big Horse with another. Hope and belief in Chief swirled and danced around the misdeeds of Marty and the stupidity of her Big Horse Bob. As she lay there, she closed her eyes to see the spirits of her people and all the animals dancing in her mind.

Her tears streamed down her cheeks and she sobbed quietly into the lonely night. *Why is love so hard?* she silently asked the Great Spirit. *Why are men so foolish? How could Big Horse fall for a woman like Marty? How many roosters does Marty need, anyway? Why can't men see things as clearly as a woman sees them? Why have I fallen in love with this Big Horse? Are all men so foolish, or have I just been the fool to choose a fool to love? Why, Great Spirit, did you choose me, of all your people, to torture my heart this way? Oh please, please, Great Spirit, please give Chief the wisdom he needs to guide me correctly, and please give me the patience to learn Chief's wisdom. Please, Great Spirit, come into my heart and let it always be a good heart, and let me not wish evil thoughts. Please, Great Spirit.*

Then she fell into a deep sleep and dreamed of her father's ranch and his sitting teepee, and little children playing, the children she would have with Big Horse after he stopped being Big Stupid Horse. And she would love her Big Horse with such a true and honest love that he would never want to leave her again for another. Big Horse would be hers forever. She dreamed these things, and in her soul she knew that these dreams would come true.

MONOGAMY

During their weeks on the road, Bob spent his days in brokerage offices selling. Marty didn't go along for those sales meetings. He thought she'd likely be too much of a distraction from the sales message he was trying to deliver. This arrangement left her alone for the day.

One week, after two days reading books and watching television in their hotel room, Marty stared at the ceiling, miserable with monogamy. Her bedside radio was playing a sixties tune about a boy not being able to understand that a girl like her wasn't able to love just one man. She made up her mind then and there that she had to go where she wanted to go and do what she wanted to do. She slipped into her black lace camisole and teddy, put on a skirt and blouse and heels, and walked to the hotel on the next block. Concealment and misdirection were Marty's allies in masking her indiscretions. Deception was one of her well-developed art forms and it traveled well with sex. She approached the concierge.

"Excuse me, would you happen to know where your local motorcycle gangs hang out?" she inquired in direct fashion.

"Yes, ma'am, but I don't advise you going there. Those aren't the places for a lady like you." The concierge looked her up and down. Marty wore a tight black skirt with a slit up one side, black silk stockings, and spiked heels. Her blouse was low-cut and revealing. Her hair was perfectly coifed in flowing curls and her makeup was perfect.

THE SECRET AND THE BUTTERFLY

"I'm only going to look for a story I'm working on," she lied.

"Uh-huh." The concierge smiled a knowing smile. Her yearn to fuck was written all over her like a neon sign. The concierge gave her directions to the seedy part of downtown.

Marty craved action, so she sought out the bar where the local bad-boy bikers hung out. It was a dark dungeon with dimly lit yellow lights, and the place reeked of dank smoke and stale spilled beer. She made a mental note to send out her clothes for cleaning and to shower thoroughly when she returned to the hotel.

The men at the bar were coarse hombres. They obviously handled women rough, and wouldn't know any other way. She needed that. She needed to feel debased, humiliated, even roughed up a little, but most of all she needed to satisfy her nymphomania. Marty needed a hard, merciless, multiple-men fucking. She craved to get slapped on her ass, to have her tits squeezed and nipples pulled until they hurt, and she wanted some big cocks to pound her pussy and ass until she was sore inside. She couldn't control her craving, regardless of how often she promised herself she would and how much she deluded herself into believing she could.

"Who's the classy bitch sitting at the end of the bar?" The biker wore an open leather jacket over a tattooed chest. He had a three-month beard, huge hands, and an insignia on the back of his jacket that said "Animal." The bartender had never seen Marty before. The biker and one of his friends, a slimmer man of the same height who wore similar garb and a baseball hat backward, went over to Marty and stood behind her. She was sipping a martini.

"I think we just found ourselves a lady," said the first biker to his sidekick.

"Whatcha doing here, babe? You slumming?" the second asked.

Marty welcomed the hit. "I'm just passing time, boys. Passing time and looking for someone."

"She's looking for someone!" the first biker sneered to his friend. "What does someone look like? Does he wear suits and ties? Is he your big strong man?"

Marty pulled her head back and gave the biker a look that told him she wanted him to cut the crap. The biker pulled his face close to Marty's. "Is he man enough to handle you, Miss Fancy Lady?"

"It takes more than one man to handle me, boys." Marty smiled at the bikers but gave no information about Bob. She put the palms of her hands against the big biker's bare chest and rubbed him seductively.

"This lady acts like she wants to play with some real men. Do you want to play with us, fancy lady?" asked the big biker loudly. He was speaking more to his friends than to Marty. The bikers guffawed at her bravado, but she called their game.

"You want to show me what big men you are? Come on." Marty beckoned them with her index finger to follow her. She slid down from her barstool, took the hand of the big biker, and led him to the pool tables. The second biker followed, and when the others saw something was going to happen, three more moseyed over to the tables. The messaging preliminaries were finished.

Marty chose a table that was illuminated by a recessed ceiling light. She casually, seductively, removed her clothes—blouse, camisole, and bra first, then skirt, teddy, and panties. She positioned herself so her body was in a spotlight with her head on the raised lip of the table in the light's penumbra. She was about to perform salacious sex acts on a stage of her own making. She outstretched her arms and became a woman transfixed. Her body imitated a Christian cross. She was the holy symbol, welcoming all sinners, eager to relieve their sexual burdens.

The bikers were awestruck, momentarily frozen and speechless. This was no ordinary woman, not some piece of meat for rough bikers. This was a special, divine, beautiful creature, a rare goddess who ordinarily would not give them the time of day. They looked at each other, as if ashamed to violate the beauty of this magnificent woman by putting their rough hands on her. In an odd sort of way, they were momentary gentlemen, empathetic and puzzled by her obvious needs.

"It's all right, boys. I came here because I need you. I need each of you to fuck me hard and long like only real men can. Pretend I'm the only woman you'll have for the rest of your life. Pretend your other woman died and I'm all there is in the world. Don't hold anything back. I want everything you have. Don't be shy. Let's get started."

Marty assured them their good fortunes were for real with her winning smile. She was all about having pure, uncomplicated sex. She spread her legs open wide, her butterfly inviting them to fly away with her.

The big biker kneeled over her on the pool table. She rubbed her saliva into her pussy and on the tip of the biker's cock, and then she guided him home. Her butterfly tattoo fluttered as she feathered her thighs, widening and closing her opening as the big biker thrust his cock repeatedly into her opening. Her motion was seductive, something the bikers had never seen before. Her fellow fornicators were stimulated, all pricks at full alert and rock-hard. She was Marty, glorious butterfly sex goddess. From her resting place on the table edge, she rolled her tongue over her lips, signaling that she wanted to suck off a penis. The second biker stood next to her head and placed his cock in her mouth. She was in heaven, now getting fucked and giving a blow job at the same time. She was now the real Marty being true to her deepest nymphomaniac needs. Soon her outstretched hands held the balls of two more bikers, kneading them, squeezing them, and readying their hardened pricks to fuck her every orifice.

Marty felt an inner nirvana as her thoughts took her back to another time and place. Once again she was the little girl on the playground with her friends and her daddy. For these precious moments while she was getting fucked by multiple partners, she imagined her friends and father never left her. Mother Susan never sent her away. Now she could feel her friends close to her. They were with her, inside her, giving all their friendship, all their loyalty to her. With each thrust of a prick deep into her pussy, she believed her friends were proving their love to her. She felt so wonderful when she was loved.

"Fuck me. Fuck me. Oh please, fuck me some more. I want more of you. Please give me everything, all of you. Oh that's so good. Keep coming. I feel you now. You're shooting inside me. That's wonderful, baby. Oh, I love how you make me feel. You're doing so well. I want more. Fuck me harder! Give me more!" She managed a brief interlude from the blow job she was giving to exhort her fornicators to fuck her harder before she returned to concentrate on the cock in her mouth. Both men answered her plea for more intensity. She succeeded in making them focus only on pleasing her and ejaculating their cum in her.

She felt the big biker's semen squirting into her pussy at the same time the biker she was blowing his wad into her mouth. She savored his taste and silently congratulated herself on her glorious performance. She loved the thrills of whoring.

Three other bikers joined in the activity and all five men took turns fucking her until she was exhausted. While the bikers banged her like she was a piece of raw meat, Marty felt acceptance. When fucking, she glimpsed her escape from her mother's rejection. Her inner sadness fell away. These clandestine rendezvous were her escape and nirvana. Perhaps

THE SECRET AND THE BUTTERFLY

that's how it all started, back when she was in boarding school. She rationalized that was what caused her to lust after cocks in the first place, but now the turmoil she felt as a young girl was supplanted by a stronger need. Now she just needed to fuck because she loved it so much she couldn't get it far from her mind. Fucking was now her addiction.

When each biker shot off his wad, Marty squeezed his balls and continued sucking his cock with a splash of gin in her mouth. Their cocks stayed hard and continued flowing semen. Her anxious tongue savored each offered stream momentarily before she swallowed it. She sucked all five bikers dry and exhausted them.

The bikers offered to pay for her martini in return for her favors. Not to insult them, she accepted. Her thirst for cock and cum was slaked for the time being.

She didn't want pay. She was the one with the insatiable need. She didn't expect them to understand it or how impossible it was for her to control it. She could only surrender to it, feed it. Getting a cock into her pussy was the only way she could satisfy herself. As she rose from the table, one of them put his hands on her waist.

"You're a genuine nymphomaniac, ain't you?" This curly haired biker looked at her with sincerity, trying to understand the source of his good fortune. In a different life, she could have gone for him. He was cute.

"Yes. I am. I am an unrepentant nymphomaniac."

"How long are you in town?"

"I'm here for two more days, boys."

"Well, you come back and see us. We'll fuck you real good. We promise."

"I'm glad you asked. I'll come back. Just promise me no nasty stuff. I've got to look good for my man, and I can't be going away with you on your bikes. Do we have a deal?"

"Deal."

Biker George stared at Marty's ass as she walked out of the bar.

"What's a nymphomaniac?" he asked curly biker Jeb.

"You know those girls who ride with us, the ones we calls the mommas or the sluts?" Jeb replied.

"Yeah."

"Those girls are just what you call cunts or whores. They fuck like pigs in the barnyard. What that woman just did was classy, almost religious. Nymphomaniacs are classy like that. They fuck because fucking for them is a divine art form. They love their artwork. They're like artists who can't stop painting. They can't stop fucking. They live to fuck. Whores just let you ride on them because they have to or they don't get food and drink or a place to stay. And when you shoot off with your momma, she just pushes you off or rolls over."

"She's not like that?"

"Hell no, you saw how beautiful she was. You saw that body and that face. Biker whores don't look that good. And that ass of hers! Whew. You noticed how her ass was puckered up, nice and plump and firm. It didn't sag or have any flab on it like our whores' asses. You saw how she moved her hips and that beautiful ass. That woman is a fucking machine, like a high-end classic bike we can't afford to buy. Her ass was the kind you want to grab with both hands while you pull her tight and fuck with her.

"Fucking her was like being in rhythm with beautiful music. You know how our hogs just lay there and grunt and take it until we get off. You can tell they don't like it, but this lady loved it. Hell, you got your cock into her too. You never had any women who fucked like that. It was like a once-in-a-lifetime experience, like looking at the Mona Lisa picture or the Sistine Chapel or seeing the sculpture of David's dick. You don't forget an experience like that. I'll always remember the way her pussy smelled. Hell, her pussy smelled better than my bitch's perfume. Remember how she smelled?"

"Did she smell nice?"

"You dumb fucktard! That was the smell of top pussy. Her pussy smelled better than those lavender juices my bitch rubs on her tits. That nympho's cunt still smelled great after she finished fucking all of us. That was one hell of a woman. That woman can get any man she wants and sleep wherever she wants. That's the difference. We just got lucky she had her pussy itching today and we were here when she came in to get it scratched."

And Marty went back to the biker's bar two more times and fucked her brains out. On her second day, she brought a cassette tape of a mellow saxophone tune and a husky woman's voice singing, "All of me, take all of me." The music set her mind raging for lust.

She eyed a stanchion pole that propped up the sagging corner roof of the pool hall, went to it and spread her legs parallel to the upright pole. The bikers obliged her. One supported her torso while another held her uplifted leg. Marty was suspended naked in midair with her pussy open and thirsty for penetrations. Each biker took turns fucking her in this upright position, each thrusting deeply into her with his full eight or nine inches of hard cock. And the song played while they fucked. When the tape ran out, the bikers rewound and replayed it.

Marty spurred her champions onward while the music played.

"Fuck me harder. Oh yes! Fuck me, fuck me. Oh yes! That feels so good, baby. Fuck me some more. Faster, now, stroke it faster. That's it. Ooohhh! That's good, baby." Then Marty squeezed her pussy muscles hard on the cock inside her. Her squeeze stole the life forces from the compliant cock and it sent a hot stream of cum shooting deeply inside her, thrilling her.

"Oh, baby. That's so wonderful. I loved it so much. That felt so good in me. I loved that warm cock shot. Now who can give me another one like that? Who can fuck me really good like that? I need to be fucked some more, so please get another cock inside me. I need it inside me. I need it now. I love that feeling. Come on, boys. Give me another cock. I have to have it."

Another biker stepped up and slipped his penis into her. He began to thrust savagely. He was rock-hard. "Oh, my, that's sooooo gooood! Keep pushing hard into me, sweetheart. Keep on fucking me hard. That's it. Oh, how I love this cock. It's so big and so hard. Oh, keep going, baby, keep going. That's it. Ooooh! I feel you shooting now. Oooh. I feel you. Come deep into me, baby. Keep spurting, keep pushing. You feel so big and strong. Oh, how I do love fucking you. You are my lover man. Ooooh that was soooo soooo gooood."

Each biker took a turn at the torso and leg position and each of the five shot a huge wad of semen into Marty. Each shot brought a faraway messianic smile to her face, and tears of joy and sadness rolled down her cheeks as semen trickled down her leg. She'd found the love she needed but never received from Susan. The cock was her mother substitute and she loved it more and more.

When she walked out of the bar the second day, while waiting for her cab, Marty reflected. *I want you to know I love you, Bob. Monogamy is wonderful, but I must go out for recess and play when I need to. Will you understand my feelings when you learn about me? Will you still love me as before? It's just sex. It's not the same as being in love. Will you understand that about me, Bob? Will you accept my addiction and still love me as I love you?*

Will you come with me and watch me while I have orgies with others? Will you join me and the others and fuck me while I'm giving another man a blow job and will you let me suck your incredible cock while I'm fucking another man? Will you do that for me? Will you do that to please me?

Will you try to understand how special I feel when I'm being fucked by several partners? Please tell me you won't be ashamed of me. Please tell me you want to see me happy and please tell me you feel desire for me when you watch me fucking other men.

Bob, please understand this about me. It's not a choice for me. If I can't be a complete woman, I can't be completely in love with you. I think I'll die if I can't be in love with you. I need you, baby. This part of my life means so much to me. When you find out about me, please don't say no to me or be angry with me. It's my addiction, sweetheart. I don't smoke or do drugs, only sex, darling, only sex.

When she returned for her third and last day, Marty sat on each of the biker's faces, let them each lick her pussy, and leisurely sucked dry all five of their cocks for two full hours while Bob worked sales. The bikers were perfect gentlemen and honored their understanding. On her third day in the bar, five of the bikers' women came along to watch Marty perform. They were dumbstruck seeing a dedicated sexaholic seduce their men's cocks. Marty was proud of herself. She knew each man would compare his biker bitch with her the next time his bitch fucked him, and she knew the biker would find his bitch inferior and wanting. She raised the bar for the bitches that afternoon and took the hearts of their men with her when she left.

Marty kept Bob in the dark about her compulsion to fuck total strangers. She often searched out biker bars and sailor or soldier bars wherever they traveled. Never once did her daytime romps interfere with her evenings with Bob. In fact, her day dalliances made her evenings with Bob more titillating. Her sexual energy was more than ample to please him. And she began to notice a subtle change within herself.

Two months passed since she'd been with the bikers. Marty went out while Bob sold in the Washington, D.C. area. That week she decided she would give monogamy an honest try. While Bob was out, she went to museums and looked at exhibits of items from ancient Egypt, South America, and Europe. She shopped and window shopped, and walked the parks in the nation's capital. She stood and reflected on the passions of the Union and the Confederacy at the Lincoln Memorial. She walked the length of the Vietnam Veterans Memorial and remembered the horrible scenes of that war playing across the television night after night, watching men with their guts shot out and their heads in bandages. The visions of that horrible carnage overcame her. She sat down in front of the wall of names of the Vietnam dead and bawled her eyes out. So many boys gave so much for the country. The least she could do was be a good citizen and an honest, decent woman. *I don't know myself any more. I don't want to be a nymphomaniac anymore. I want to be a good woman and a good wife for a man. I need to change. I need to become a better person than I am.*

She made up her mind to make a fresh start in life. Perhaps she could become a good suburban housewife. She thought about taking her little girl to a soccer game and her boy to his baseball practices. She imagined her and Bob living in a suburban home with a beautiful yard and a patio and a pool. They would hold pool and barbecue parties for neighbors and friends. They'd go to concerts and dinner parties and sports events with new friends. Maybe she'd learn to play bridge and even volunteer to make sandwiches at some sandwich line for the homeless. She'd deliver meals for the shut-ins. Yes, that was the life she really wanted. She wanted to get away from her sex addiction and have a wholesome attachment to one man. She wanted to have an honest partnership with this man she was with. Bob was the right man; she knew that with every fiber of her body.

That night, after the memorials, Marty waited for Bob in their hotel suite. She had two large bouquets of red roses placed upon the nightstands of the bedroom, and a blanket of rose petals covered the bed. She refreshed herself with a warm shower and perfumed and oiled Gloria. When Bob came into the suite, she was waiting. She wore a sheer silken nightshirt that reached barely below the tops of her thighs and nothing else. She only had one of its middle buttons fastened.

I am going to be Mrs. Burke to Bob from this night forward and forever. I will love him and cherish him as if there never was nor will ever be another man in my life. I will be monogamous.

Bob's male instincts took over when he saw her. He couldn't get enough of her, ever. He always wanted her and always responded to her slightest hint for attentions.

She put her arms around his neck and pulled him close, then slowly removed his jacket and untied his tie. She nuzzled his neck while she unbuttoned his shirt. As the shirt came away, she kissed his huge, manly chest and drank in his smells. He was so masculine, so handsome with his flaxen golden hair with its slight curls along his temples. *Yes, this is what I want. This is what I need for me, forever and ever. I have my life right here and I will never let him go. I will never do anything foolish again. I will never let my impulses fuck this up.*

She took Bob into the bedroom and pulled him down onto the bed with her. They made sweet, long and slow love on the rose petals. When he released his semen into her, she thought, *This is happiness and contentment. This is marvelous, magnificent monogamy. This is what happily married couples do.*

She held him close after he finished. "Don't go. Please stay inside me. I want you inside me," she whispered.

Bob didn't go. He lay upon her, his weight propped by his elbows on the pillows. His penis stayed in her until he fell off to slumber. She laid there, one hand rubbing his massive back and shoulder muscles, the other softly stroking the back of his neck. Her thoughts were only in the present, on what she had and held in her arms.

I will be true to him and love him all the days of my life. I will be the best woman any woman could ever be to any man. This is all the love and attention I was cheated out of when I was a child, and now I am restored and fulfilled. I am so happy. This must be happiness.

Marty fell off to sleep herself.

The next morning when she awoke, Bob was gone. He'd risen, showered, and left without waking her. A hot room service breakfast sat on a tray by the bed with silver covers over the offerings of eggs, bacon, breakfast cinnamon rolls, fruits, coffee, and orange juice, as well as a note.

"Good morning, love of my life. I didn't want to wake you from your beauty sleep. You are divinely beautiful, sexier than Aphrodite, and the most wonderful woman ever. I love you. Bob."

She read and reread the note as she ate her breakfast. Then she began to cry. She was happy and guilty all at once. He was so sweet to her, so good, but was she? Was she true to herself or was she just pretending to be something she wasn't? She kissed the note. No man had ever left her a morning note before. She thought about the previous night and about her time with the bikers. Sex with Bob was different than all the other men she'd been with. He had a reverence for her. No other man ever felt like that about her. She felt her emotions going around and around in her head. *What is going on with me? Am I head over heels in love or what? Am I this lucky? I have a new life now, don't I? Can I live up to his expectations?*

He wasn't rough with her. He never spoke a word of coarse language. He was tender and, yes, reverential with her body. He didn't slap her ass or pull on her tits. He touched her with loving hands and softly rubbed her forehead and temples. And he massaged her neck muscles, held her hands in his, and rubbed her feet and her toes with deliberation, never hurried. He performed oral sex beautifully and took a great deal of time with her. He was inordinately patient and focused on giving her pleasure. He never rushed her. It became apparent to her that

Bob enjoyed cunnilingus more than even she did. He was so committed to giving her pleasure.

How many women have a man who worships them like this? How many men care more about giving their woman pleasure than they care about their own pleasures? How fortunate am I? How can I be this happy?

Her orgasms were so soft and continuous, like they would last forever. He was so in tune with her. They were so united when she came. Sex with Bob was a total "feeling like a woman should feel" experience. It was never in any way degrading or belittling of her as a person or a body. Bob worshipped her and her body. Other men just fucked her, and yes, sex was wonderful, but with the others it was all impersonal. It was just fucking for the feeling of the moment, just a temporary emotional reunion with those wonderful feelings she had when she was a little girl with her daddy. Bob was altogether different. He treated her like she was a goddess. He made love to Marty the person, not Marty the sex siren. He was a friend in bed who earnestly dedicated himself to pleasing her. Bob could only make her feel the way she felt if he truly loved her. She got that. And she was thankful for it.

She knew what happened to her was special and blessed by some mysterious goodness. But she kept asking herself if that was how she really wanted to feel about herself. She felt like a beautiful goddess after sex with Bob, but not receiving rough, hard sex and debasement was a strange differential. *Couldn't Bob be a little sadistic, just once? Couldn't he manhandle me and abuse me just a little bit now and then? Couldn't we have a "Me Tarzan, you Jane!" romp in the grass somewhere? Couldn't there be a balance between sweet sex and rough sex?*

Tears welled up and her chest became heavy with a burning sensation. Her feelings all jumbled together in a confusing blend of joy and sadness. She felt wretched and guilt-ridden. She didn't deserve such happiness... or did she? Had she earned his trust and love? No, she hadn't, but maybe she could. But did she really want that, or did she want to be the old Marty?

Who am I really? Can I be a monogamous woman? Is there something wrong with me if I crave feeling abused, fucked hard, and debased? If I don't feel like an exhausted piece of pulsating meat afterward, does that mean I'm not a normal?

And what's normal, anyway? What woman wouldn't kill to have the man I have? What woman wouldn't kill to be treated as well as Bob treats me? What woman wouldn't leap at the chance to be his woman? How can I even question or think for a moment that his love isn't enough for me?

She went to the hotel room window and pulled back the drapes. There was a road across from the fountain in the hotel's open plaza, but where it led to she could only wonder. If she took a cab along the road, would it lead to a bar with bikers playing pool? Perhaps she could take a cab to a bookstore and then hang around the romance section trolling for a lonely male?

What am I thinking? Her tears rolled down her cheeks. She finally had what she'd set out to capture. Did she want the catch she netted? She thought of her many orgies and how she seduced her partners with her opening invitation. She'd lay her hips canted upward on a huge pillow, spread her thighs wide open, and then sing her little ditty. "You won't find God up in the sky. She's right here in my butterfly." She'd flash her winsome, iniquitous smile and hold her pussy open widely. Then she'd beg them to start fucking her with her irresistible plea, "Please come inside me and fuck me. I'm ready!" She'd open wide and partly close her legs and open them again. Her butterfly rippled and no man ever resisted her. Every cock wanted inside.

Could she live knowing she would never again experience the thrill of conquest she felt when a fresh cock entered her for its very first time? Could she live socializing with another married couple and not signal the other woman's husband that she wanted to fuck him? Would she make a total mess of married life for herself and for Bob? Would he eventually make her wear a chastity belt, or would he understand what she desperately needed to do if she couldn't control her needs? Would he stop loving her if he knew how badly she was addicted to conquest through sex?

She cried openly, her whole body trembling as she was torn between two conflicting desires. She missed her orgies terribly since she'd been with Bob. She told herself she could do without them, but how could she be sure? She told herself again and again that she would succeed, that she could change. She would be a one-man woman.

She fell back onto the bed. Who was she? Who was the real Marty? Was she Aphrodite, femme fatale, seductress extraordinaire, or was she a silly school child tumbled head over heels in puppy love, her heart pierced through by Cupid's arrow and her head filled with music from his sweet beckoning lyre? *Would I rather have him come home to me tonight, here in this room, or would I rather have five handsome, black, muscular studs from a professional basketball team coming here for an orgy with me?* Her thoughts swirled around and around. Her past deeds and constant yearnings collided and mingled with her dreams of future bliss, like separate fruits spinning in a blender.

Marty curled up on the bed in the fetal position with tears streaming down her cheeks. The part of her inner conscience that challenged her assumptions spoke to her. *He's going to find out all the truth about you sooner or later. It will happen at a cocktail party, or some angry woman will make an anonymous call to him, or a discarded jealous lover will meet him somehow and tell him all the sordid details. Then what? Will he leave you for Barbara? How can you, the modern-day Aphrodite, fall victim to the love barb of Cupid's arrow? Could you take Cupid's arrow out of your heart and go back to whoring again? Would David even keep you in the firm if Bob rejected you? How could you and Bob work in the same office? How could you live seeing him with Barbara? How did you ever let yourself fall so hard for him? What else can you do now except go on concealing your past life, pretending everything about you is legitimate?*

She turned to the part of her conscience that pleaded with her mind to understand itself. *I wish so much that my daddy was here and I could talk to him like I did when I was a little girl. I wish I was that little girl again. I'm still and always will be my daddy's little girl at heart. Someday I'll meet Daddy in Heaven and he'll make everything all right again.*

Marty took some comfort from her last thoughts. Then she fell back asleep and didn't awaken until mid-afternoon. She promised herself she'd be a good girl, a faithful girl, every day of her life from that day forward. Then she put on fresh makeup, dressed for dinner with Bob, and waited for him to return to her.

With each passing week, Marty found she loved Bob more and more. He was pure, wholesome fun. She relished creating new ways to keep her man interested. Soon she wanted to be with him all the time, not just on weekend rendezvous. Her pulse quickened when she thought of him, and he was never far from her mind. She became deeply in love and decided to go with her feelings, which was so unlike her. Before, men were just expendable, throwaway items, like tissues. Men used her and pounded her body. She wanted them to fuck her until she was near exhaustion, but she gave it back to them and more. She'd always considered herself the vamp, the user of men, but now something had changed.

I feel like a lovesick schoolgirl. I must give these feelings serious thought and not try to rein them in. I need to understand where this is coming from.

She thought back to when she met Bob. It was love at first sight when David took him around the office and introduced him to everyone. She noted he was startlingly handsome with bright blue eyes, a winning smile, and gorgeous tumbling blond hair. Her heart fluttered and her pulse quickened. He had that massive chest and commanding presence. He was a man's man, a natural leader, a man women wanted to get into their beds. Those initial impressions stayed with her, but she blocked out her thoughts of seducing him. She wanted him but made no signals to him about getting together outside of work because she didn't think David would appreciate it. When Bob moved to fund sales, she thought it was even more important to stay hands off because David wanted them both focused on bringing in money.

With his six-foot-three frame and broad shoulders he could have been a male fashion model, but there he was, eye candy in a largely female office. He'd held her eyes with his that first time they were introduced, staring too long to fix her name in his mind. She knew instinctively she'd registered an impression, but he made no effort to get to know her. She was baffled.

The gorgeous hunk either holed up in his office or was out on the road pushing his deals. Now he pushed the fund. He worked his ass off, his behavior bordering on workaholic mania. He was too quiet, too focused.

She'd checked with Judith, his secretary, and asked discreet questions. "What is Bob up to?"

Judith's response was the same. "Like I told you before, he just works. He's always working."

"Does he have a wife?

"No."

"Does he have any kids from a once-before, long-ago wife?"

"No."

"Are any women calling him?"

"No. I told you, he's just all business."

"Is he gay?"

"No, no way!" Judith opened up a little with that one. Bob was definitely not gay nor, was he a eunuch.

"Tell me how you know he's not gay," Marty implored.

"I've caught him staring at the Cherokee girl's ass as she walked down the hall." The secretary dropped her discretion. After all, Marty feigned no interest in her boss, so this was just girl talk back then.

"Barbara? He's hot for Barbara?" Marty knew many men ogled Barbara. The girl with mixed blood was slender, beautiful, mysteriously sexy, and very private. A lot of men liked a challenge, but Marty knew she was the more enticing, voluptuous woman, even though Barbara was more nubile.

"He stared long at that Indian's tight ass. You know how Barbara bounces it. It ripples and jiggles when she walks. That was no gay guy looking at that Indian ass. It was a man looking at an ass with an 'I really want to fuck it' look. Some men are drawn to tight ass like bees to honey. I think he likes her, but she doesn't let him get personal. They used to work together doing those corporate deals. They're friendly toward each other, but I don't think they do the dog, if you know what I mean. I'm sure Barbara doesn't let him have any. I'm real sure he isn't gay. No gay man looks at girl ass like that. No, ma'am, that's a real man, all man, in that there office," she said, pointing to Bob's door.

"Ever smell booze on him?"

"No. He never goes to bars. The dating scene doesn't interest him, but there is one real special woman he talks with for about a half hour every day."

"Who is she?" Marty craved information.

"His mother."

So that was it! Bob was a momma's boy. He talked to her every day. A guy couldn't be bad or inconsiderate if he thought of his mother every day. Marty's curiosity spiked. She thought about the mama's boy angle. *Maybe I should bake a cake and take it to him. No, that's too obvious. Sex always works for me. Why change what works? I'll bide my time.*

Then, when she least expected anything, there it was! David gave her a chance to be with Bob anytime, all the time, away from the office, on an all-expenses paid silver platter. Suddenly she was transformed from in-office schoolmarm into hot-to-trot kitty on a mission with the catnip placed right in her paws. David gave her nirvana. She had the golden opportunity to become a respectable one-man woman with a wonderful, decent man. Over a year elapsed since her eyes first met Bob's and several more months since David first ordered her to pursue Bob.

Now she thanked her lucky stars. She wanted a life with him. She knew that more than she'd ever known anything. She couldn't just go on being a nymphomaniac for the rest of her life. She envied respectable women. They had homes, children, friends, and social lives. Now she had a chance to become one of them. Besides, when she got the itch for sex, she could always watch a reality TV show and work a dildo along with her imagination.

The Bob and Marty relationship turned serious during a side trip to Bar Harbor, Maine. They sailed around one of the offshore islands and later ran across the bar when the tide went out. They were happy; being together felt right. By that point they'd made love over a hundred times. They'd frolicked in the surf together, hiked up mountains together, made love on a Colorado mountaintop and on Welches Beach in Barbados. Marty decided it was time to let Bob know her intentions.

They awoke at 4:00 a.m. that day, which they'd later call "Serious Day." As they hiked to the top of Bar Harbor's Cadillac Mountain to see the first rays of sunlight touch the first patch of land in the United States, she thought, *Today is the beginning of my new life. He'll love me in my powder blue cashmere sweater, no bra, and pink pedal pushers. I look the part of a happy new wife.*

On the mountaintop, in their own space on the rocks away from other lovers, Marty nestled in Bob's arms and pulled their blanket up to her neck. He held her with his arms wrapped around her stomach. He nuzzled her neck, taking in her scent of Chanel No. 5. Her hand played with her pearls, an accessory she always wore when they hiked outdoors.

"Why do you always wear pearls when we go hiking?" Bob asked.

"Because if I'm ever eaten by a bear, I want Mr. Bear to know he's dining first class. You like my first-class taste, don't you?" she purred in his ear.

"You know I do." He kissed her cheek.

"Well, you wouldn't want poor hungry Mr. Bear to have anything but the best, would you?" she teased as she rubbed his leg.

"Mr. Bear will have to wait his turn because I want to eat you first." He kissed her cheek again.

She took Bob's hands in hers and slowly pushed them under her cashmere sweater to her breasts. She put his thumbs and index fingers on her nipples. She loved it when he teased them with his fingertips. As Bob softly rubbed her nipples, she felt more at peace with a man than she'd ever felt before. It was time.

"I want you to eat me every day. You wouldn't let Mr. Bear eat me, would you? I want to spend the rest of my life with you," she said. There followed a quiet ten-second interlude during which Bob hugged her close to him.

"I want to spend the rest of my life with you also." He squeezed her tightly, the sincerest bear hug she'd ever received from any man. She knew he loved her. Bob was her keeper man.

Just then, the sun's first rays peeked above the ocean's surface. At sea, the lobster boats were silhouetted in the distance and the wave caps of white foam were just barely visible. It was a glorious moment, one of love's triumphs over all life's complications. It was one of those glorious shared moments only lovers know. They were behind a cluster of scrub pines and alone. Marty rolled over on her back, slipped out of her pedal pushers, and spread her legs before the morning sunrise. She felt the cool sea breezes touch her pussy. Everything was right and wonderful.

"Kiss my pussy, darling. Make me wet just a little and then come into me for a visit. I want you inside me," she whispered to Bob. He readily complied and there, under their blanket, they made love on Cadillac Mountain. Marty's orgasm arrived just as the sun leaped above the Atlantic's horizon. It was a glorious moment for the two wonderstruck lovers, a new beginning of lives joined in unity. They said nothing more of future plans that day or all the following week. They savored the wonder. By their silence, they both understood the special nature of what they'd spoken on Cadillac Mountain.

The following week, they were camped on Assateague Island off Maryland's mainland. That morning they surf casted for sea trout and had good luck. Marty landed a big one, which Bob filleted and broiled for their dinner. They lay camped in their tent atop a large sand dune overlooking the wild Atlantic. Seagulls hovered, eyeing the surf for morsels churned up by the crashing waves.

The surf surged forward on the incoming tide. Bob rubbed Marty's back. She was facedown, chin on folded hands, bra off. Bob's palms slipped into her underpants and rubbed baby oil on her buttocks. He squeezed her ass and she flexed to his touch. She felt tranquil and serene.

Marty's inner conscience spoke to her. *This is how monogamy feels. It's an eternal feeling. It will make up for all the neglect you felt as a little girl. Drink your feelings. Drink deeply of this man's love. Drink in all of it, hold onto it, and never let it go.* She was serene. She loved how Bob touched her, how he rubbed her shoulders and back with baby oil, tenderly and caring. Her thoughts mingled with the sounds of the surf and the gulls. She was absorbed in this transformative experience. Her nostrils savored the ocean smells as she breathed deeply, taking in the sea air fully into her diaphragm.

The warm afternoon sun on her back caressed her newly discovered happiness, and the deep blue Atlantic expanded forever before her eyes. There was endless promise in a life with Bob, a promise as deep and wide as the ocean that stretched its vast mosaic of blues, grays, and whites before her. She alternately opened her eyes to watch the surf, then closed them so she could concentrate on hearing it while relishing the thought of a life with Bob. Her hair lifted gently in the offshore breeze, like it could fly away with the gulls. Bob fulfilled the love she'd never received from Susan. Maybe true love was displacing her nymphomania. Maybe she was beginning to love herself. They didn't speak for the longest time.

Bob wanted to know all about her feelings. What made her so accepting and uninhibited? He spoke softly, not to change her mood but to understand her deepest feelings. "Does the surf inspire you as much as your church music?" he asked.

"They're both inspiring to me, but in different ways," Marty replied after a thoughtful pause.

"Help me understand what moves you." He was intimately sincere.

"I'll try. It's not complicated. When we make love indoors in my bedroom, I love to hear 'Ave Maria' when my mood tells me to cherish the special wonder of the moment. When my mood is to praise God and be glorious in lovemaking, I feel I can express it best if the 'Mass of Saint Cecelia' is playing."

Bob interjected. "Is that the one where the cymbals clash, the one that sends you into an orgasmic frenzy? I never heard it before I met you. Where does it come from?"

"Yes, love." She laughed. "That's the one. It's from Plaintown's Holy Mary Catholic Church. They make a recording of it and sell the copies. It's so powerful, so beautiful. They cram the Plaintown Philharmonic Orchestra into the organ balcony of the church and perform the entire mass from the balcony. It's so beautiful I cry every time I hear it. The sounds are like a perfect opera, and the music resonates from the organ balcony to the pulpit and the nave and back again. Then, when the cymbals clash, I shudder as if the presence of God is electrified within me and permanently impressed in me. I feel God's holy presence in that church during that service like I can feel nowhere else."

"It sounds beautiful." Bob was wistful.

"It is. I'll take you to that mass. You'll hear for yourself. Many women and some of the men get tears in their eyes. It's that beautiful, it affects people so deeply. That's why I play the recording of the mass sometimes when we make love. It makes me feel our love is glorious to God and a holy presence in his world. When the cymbals clash, you noticed, I come then. It's like my orgasm is a complete acceptance of God's blessing upon you and me, and we're together worshiping him. I just explode inside. I can't help myself. I can't hold anything back. That's how I feel. It's from my heart. I love you so much, Bob. It's my way of sharing my love for you with God."

"There's another one you play."

"Yes. That's Handel's 'Messiah.' It's a powerful inspiration. When we make love to that song, I feel as if we are forever protected from all evil, that evil is being driven away and nothing can ever come between you and me, no evil presence can ever harm us for all eternity. I feel safe with you and with God, no matter what evil comes in this world. And I come easily when I feel that way. I feel joyful and unafraid. I surrender to my feelings of safety."

Bob lay there looking at the ocean, pondering this woman who wanted to spend her life with him. Neither spoke as the sun began to set behind them, casting a long shadow from their tent toward the ocean. A mare and her foal from the island herd moved past them on the beach and turned inland to the dunes to bed down for the night. Bob squeezed Marty's hand as the equines passed. She knew his signal without either of them saying a word. He wanted children with her.

Two more weeks passed and the lovers made their way to Virginia's Shenandoah Valley. Their little pup tent was pitched at the high end of a broad green meadow. It was a gorgeous summer's night. They'd made love earlier, and now were lying in the tent with its front flaps open, looking up at the stars in the Milky Way. Marty's head was on Bob's arm. The evening fireflies lit their green glows in the darkness, and the din of crickets and the occasional hoot of an owl were the only sounds. Then it happened, the words tiptoeing softly from Bob's mouth to Marty's ear.

"Will you marry me, Marty?" he asked.

She rolled over on her side and ran her finger down his nose. Her inner voice took her by the shoulders and shook her into a wide-awake consciousness. *You've got him! You've done it! You can now be a respectable woman with a family and a wedding ring, and kids and a house in the suburbs, and girlfriends to go shopping with and play bridge with. You might even become a soccer mom or a Little League mom. You'll see your kids grow up and get married. You'll have grandchildren!*

"Yes, I will marry you, Bob. Will you marry me?"

"Yes. I will marry you."

Then Marty offered the clincher. "I'd like to have your children," she said.

"You will, my love, you will."

That evening the night was still. Marty awoke as Bob slept with a soft, purring snore, at peace with her and his world. *How can men sleep like that and I can't?* She pouted silently to herself, looking out the tent flap at the stars.

Then her inner voice answered. *Because they're different from you. They are men and you are a woman. It's as simple as that. And by the way, do you really believe you can be a monogamous, loving housewife to this man, or to any man for that matter? Right now, tonight, it all seems so dreamily wonderful, but how will you feel when he has bad morning breath, or when he doesn't pick up after himself, or when he forgets what you told him you needed at the store? How will you feel when he sits in front of the TV watching football and ignoring you, huh? Are you sure you can change yourself, or is this just some mood swing you're having?*

And what will you do about your wonderful orgies? Have you forgotten about them? You know you love going to them. How will you feel when Rita calls you and tells you there's eight knock-down, drop-dead gorgeous black studs from an out-of-town basketball team who are begging Rita to include you because they all want to fuck you? Huh? Will you sneak away to play with Rita and her friends, or will you tell Bob the truth, or will you say no to Rita? How will you deal with that one? Huh? Huh? How are you going to feel months after you turn Rita down and she stops calling you for orgies? How will you feel being left out of all that sex, never again having eight black studs fucking you into a mindless frenzy with their beautiful cocks?

Won't you miss having those glorious black cocks shooting cum into your mouth? Won't you miss the taste of them? Won't you miss multiple streams of hot cum shooting like the Kongou Falls of Gabon pouring out life from all directions into your welcoming mouth and craving pulsating cunt? Won't you miss their spent, heaving hot bodies lying on you, kissing your tits, biting and pulling your nipples, telling you they love you, telling you that you're the greatest fuck they've ever known? Your ego will miss those compliments and you know it! You live to hear those words. You know deep down inside yourself that you'll go out of your mind without that hot sex. Admit it! Think about what you're doing, girl! Can you really become something you're not? Do you want to exchange a dozen hands stroking and petting every inch of your body for one guy? Will you be happy when you can't have some afternoon cock in your cunt because you need to stay home and change diapers? Or do you think you'll take your toddlers with you to an orgy party so they can watch you fuck your brains out? Do you think they wouldn't tell Daddy about what Mommy does when he's not home? You have no idea about the life married women have, do you? You have no idea how they dread their daily drudgery, yet you want to dive into that lifestyle! Are you crazy? Don't you think you'd better drink some hot black coffee and gulp down some shots of white cream before you decide this? Don't you think you better think about what you're doing?

Marty pulled her head back into the tent. Bob was still sleeping. She settled into her blankets and laid there looking up at the tent ceiling. It was dark and she saw nothing. She closed her eyes and imagined herself in an orgy with eight black lovers. She was kissing the heads of their beautiful penises, taking their cocks into her mouth, stroking their balls and cocks, inserting one cock after the other into her pussy, taking into her pussy and her mouth all the cum these male Adonises had within them, all the while feeling their loving touches on her sides and chest. She squealed with joy as they pinched her nipples and spanked her ass, arousing her senses to euphoria. She French kissed one after the other while each took his turn licking Gloria's playful clitoris. They succeeded in swelling Gloria to her state of otherworldly ecstasy, and she came and came in what seemed like a never-ending orgasm.

She rubbed Gloria's clitoris and imagined herself in her other world, her world of wanton nymphomania. Then her real orgasm came. It was a gentle, steady release that accompanied her trembling body and deep breaths. Her final imaginations were of a handsome young black lover pressing his body close against hers, squeezing her ass hard with his massive hands and plunging his steel-hard, swollen cock deeply into her welcoming cunt. She was French kissing this imaginary adorable male specimen, her tongue deep in his mouth, wishing the moment would never end as she fell off to sleep. She moaned softly. Bob was still snoring.

The next morning at daybreak, Marty tossed out her birth control pills with the trash. She steeled her mind to relegate her nymphomania to the past and never breathe a word about those episodes or her longings to Bob. From now on, whenever she spread her thighs, it would be only for him, only to invite his sperm to spark life into one of her yearning fertile eggs. She clenched her fists and swore to herself that she'd have the will to resist temptation's flare-ups.

It was Bob who brought up the subject of David. It felt to Marty that wherever they went, David was somehow there with them, as a silent unseen chaperone, making sure everything was going according to his plan. She often wondered if Bob had the same feelings about David, but said nothing. Now Bob wanted to talk about their mutual friend and father figure of sorts.

"Marty, you never speak of David. Is there a reason why he's never the subject of our conversations?"

Marty grew nervous at the question. *I can't tell Bob about my arrangement with David. That could ruin everything. I'll just deflect any inquiries about what my deal is with him and keep the conversation focused on his strange personality.*

"Well," she began, "what is there to say about David? He's rather secretive. I'm sure you've noticed that. He loves to spend time in his barnyard with his animals. He doesn't seem to have any friendships outside the business, and he's always guarded about his privacy."

"Yes, I've observed those things myself and I've wondered how he got to be such a recluse. Did Susan ever give you any insights about what makes David tick?"

"Mother was his babysitter, you know. Mother and Marvin were more than just two people in business together, if you know what I mean. Mother doesn't like to say much about that, so I don't push it. She doesn't talk much about David either, except one night when I was at her house. She'd had a couple of martinis and she loosened up a little. She told me when David was a little boy, his mother, Eloweiss, and Susan had to keep a close eye on him when he played outdoors. Mother said David liked to hunt down insects and torture them. He especially liked to pull legs off ants and wings off flies. Mother thought he did that because he didn't get much love from Marvin or Eloweiss."

"Kids will do the strangest things. I used to run away and hide myself in the forest and watch the animals, especially the deer. I liked to go where my mother couldn't find me. She beat me terribly when I was a little kid, and the forest was my escape."

"I did a weird thing too, when I was a little girl. I remember I was mad at Susan for losing my dad, Joseph. I subconsciously blamed her for his accidental death. He drove a car off a mountainside and died. I went through this phase where I peed outside in a corner of Mom's backyard. I thought by doing that I was defying her authority over me and she had that punishment owed to her for somehow being at fault for Dad's death. It was crazy, mixed-up logic, but I was just a kid."

"I guess all kids have issues they outgrow in time, but I wonder if David ever outgrew his. He seems so lonely and isolated."

"I'm not sure why he isolates himself like he does. Maybe his Jewish religion makes him feel he needs to keep a distance from everyone who isn't a Jew, I don't know. He practically lived with rabbis when he grew up. Maybe he's got that complex about being a chosen person and the rest of us aren't good enough. Who knows?"

"Has he ever tried to get you interested in his religion?" Bob thought Marty might have an insight into David's personality. Perhaps he was shaped by more than his parents and childhood days.

"No. Well... yes, just once. He asked me if I knew the significance of the story of the time God spoke to Moses through the burning bush. I didn't know, but David thought he knew. He said it was the first time God spoke to Moses, the last guy God talked to, and God tells us when he thinks something needs to get done, like getting the Hebrews out of Egypt."

"What do you make of that?"

"What, that David mentioned this to me?"

"Well, yes. And what do you make of his reasoning?"

"I have no idea why he brought it up, unless David thought God was going to talk to him personally, or maybe he hears voices and he thinks it's God talking to him."

"And what about his reasoning that God speaks to people to give them messages?"

"I'm not a religious person, Bob. I just try to think about what makes sense. For example, I have a hard time believing a burning bush talked to Moses. I think it could all just be a made-up story from thousands of years ago. In my mind, it's just as likely that Moses was up on a mountain away from his wife looking for a lost sheep and along came a Hebrew girl who told him they were having trouble in Egypt and they wanted Moses to come down and help them.

"Maybe the Hebrew girl was hot for Moses and they did the deed on the mountaintop. Maybe the Hebrew girl promised Moses he could have her as a side deal if he saved the tribe from the pharaoh. Maybe Moses went back to his wife and told her he was talking to a burning bush. Moses maybe meant a burning bush was a hot pussy, but everybody else took Moses's story literally. I have no idea how these stories get started. If someone is religious, I guess they have to take it on faith that God was talking out of a bush. I just have a hard time buying into it. Moses was a major alpha male, a leader. Lots of women go for a man like that. It's easier for me to think some woman with the hots for him banged him on a mountain than some burning bush talked to him. Bushes don't talk. And if a bush was burning and it could talk, it would more likely tell Moses to call the fire department.

"There's another thing about Moses's story that doesn't fit either. When he went down to Egypt, he did not take his wife, Zephorah, along, but she joined him after the tribe escaped into the desert, and she had two kids. Now, it takes some time to have two kids, so the wife wasn't just a one-night stand. Then the wife, kids, and father-in-law go away and nothing more is ever mentioned of them. It's really weird. Maybe Moses fell in love with his side dish and chucked the wife and kids. Lots of men do that, you know. Then, after he turns his back on his family, Moses goes up on Mount Sinai and gets the Ten Commandments. What's interesting about this, to me, is that the Seventh Commandment, the one that says you shall not commit adultery, is given to Moses after the burning bush and after the separation from his wife. And God didn't let Moses cross the Jordan because Moses sinned, but what sin are we talking about? It was fine by God to let Moses lead the people out of Egypt after he killed an Egyptian guy, really? Killing was okay and he could lead the people after killing, but now, long after the killing, Moses can't cross the Jordan? Maybe Moses really was the son of the pharaoh's daughter. Maybe he wasn't even born a Hebrew, so the tribe wouldn't let him cross the Jordan.

"I don't think the Torah tells the whole story about Moses. Maybe he committed adultery with a Goyim girl and had two children with her. Maybe his Goyim wife was the original burning bush and he had a Hebrew wife who the Torah doesn't mention because it doesn't fit the story. Lots of Jewish men have shiksas. Just look at Marvin and my mother. The Hebrews didn't want a non-Jew in the tribe, so the wife and his kids were kept out. To send the tribe a message, God threw in the adultery commandment, which was a new wrinkle from the

Noah-era laws that governed the tribe up until then. So the adultery commandment is the fault of Moses. Maybe he did those stone cuts on Mount Sinai by himself. Maybe he decided to atone for his adultery by not crossing over Jordan.

"Maybe this exodus story is a guilt trip. Maybe Moses was actually an Egyptian, actually a son of the pharaoh. Maybe he was a son with a rebellious streak. He killed one of his dad's overseers who whipped a slave because he liked Hebrews, probably Hebrew women. He ran away from his dad, the pharaoh. Either he was already married to an Egyptian and they had two kids, or he met a shepherd girl after he ran away and had two kids with her. Something has to explain how Moses sired two kids that weren't allowed in the tribe.

"Next he's on a mountain and meets a Hebrew girl. She's beautiful and has a hot pussy for him. He's hooked by her hot burning bush. He wants her, but she first requires him to set her people free and join the tribe. The story that says he doesn't know how to speak so he takes Aaron with him is a cover. Moses couldn't speak Hebrew. Anyway, the tribe won't have his wife and kids because they aren't Hebrew, so he leaves them for his hot pussy. It's a reverse shiksa tale. The mistress kept her man and the wife lost him.

"Possibly his ex-wife was the hot pussy on the mountain and he had to leave her and his kids to go to Egypt, but that leaves an unanswered question. Why would he go back to his wife and tell her about a burning bush if she *was* the burning bush? Which way was it, I wonder. The questions kind of fit, don't they? The burning bush story seems like a cover-up. After all, it's not unusual for two women to want the same man, is it, Bob?"

Bob caught Marty's veiled reference to Barbara. He didn't protest what he knew was true.

"What best explains Moses's burning bush is there was another woman involved. There's more to that bush than meets the eye! I get hot in my sex spot when I think about you, Bob. That burning bush passage describes a real feeling. You just didn't connect the feeling with a bush because I keep mine shaved. I burn hot like fire for you, and I want you inside me. I'm so hot to get you into me, I nearly go nuts. Maybe Moses also had a woman hot for him. Maybe sex compelled him to do what he did. Here you have a guy separated from his wife and kids. He's a Hebrew and his kids are not Hebrews because their mother wasn't Hebrew. He had guilt about not raising those kids. That's how Jewish guilt originated.

"Another thing that fits is that Moses spent lots of time away from Egypt before he met Hebrew hot bush. He knew the desert. She got involved with Moses because she needed a trail guide to get her tribe out of Egypt. She was the tribe's desert 'in.'

"My interpretation explains the kids, but it blows a hole in the concept of a chosen people. I don't believe God chooses anybody over anybody else. I believe God loves everybody equally, unless somebody is a mean person. Even then, God must love everyone or there wouldn't be any sin. God could just abolish sin, but he doesn't do that. Maybe adulterous sin is a good thing. It keeps the world interesting and it produces lots of kids. God wanted us to multiply, so adding adultery to the mix sped up his multiplication plan. God must like kids."

After mentioning children, Marty remembered the times at orgies when she sacrilegiously chanted to her lovers, "Do not look for God on high. She's here inside my butterfly!" She recalled her signature welcome when she spread her thighs widely and canted her hips skyward upon her pillow. She remembered the many times she'd held her wicked cunt widely open with her fingers, flashed her winsome smile, and said, "Please come inside my butterfly and fuck me. I'm ready!"

There are suggestions—like having children—Bob should hear, but there are things he must never know.

"I don't know either, but I have run into some who take religion very seriously. Religion can lead people, even nations, to go out and kill other people. It confuses me." Bob wanted to change the subject.

"Well, I have this thought. Maybe it'll make sense." Marty held both Bob's hands like a schoolgirl about to reveal a confidence. "I think David likes the two of us very much. He treats us special because he felt the same sorts of pains we felt as kids growing up. I missed my father's love because he died when I was only five. You missed your father's love because he passed when you were only two. David empathizes with us. He didn't get much love from his dad or mother. We are kindred spirits." Marty looked at Bob for agreement with her analysis.

"Maybe, but I'm not sure it's the same with David. He told me that his mother wished he hadn't been born. He told me Marvin and Eloweiss always sent him off to camps and programs. He basically lived with rabbis or stayed at summer camps and schools. Come to think of it, he told me his father was his best friend, but he never said that he felt love from his father. Maybe you're right. Maybe he didn't get much love from his dad. I don't know, it's complicated. David's complicated."

"Well, he's highly educated. He can't say he didn't get every advantage in life." Marty shrugged.

"But maybe he didn't get the greatest advantage, maybe he didn't get love."

"Who does get enough love in this world?"

"That's not what I'm talking about. You knew your dad loved you, but he was gone from you. That hurt. I knew my dad loved me, but he was gone from me. That hurt me too. But in David's case, his dad was there, and his mom too, but they pushed him away. In a socially acceptable way, they rejected him. We weren't rejected by our fathers. He was."

"Well, I felt rejected by Susan for quite a while."

"Yes, but deep down inside, you knew she really loved you, didn't you?"

"I came around to knowing that, but I had to work through some issues first. I searched for my identity."

"Well, that's okay. I understand and I believe you put your issues behind you. I had issues with my mother, but I worked them out and now we're on good terms. Actually, she's my best friend, along with David. But David only knows a lifetime of rejection. I think that explains the insect issue when he was a kid. He hated himself and he took it out on the bugs. He couldn't fight back enough to get the parental love he needed, and the bugs couldn't fight back either."

"You think he just kicked his misery downhill to the bugs?"

"Maybe it's something like that."

"Have you ever noticed how he looks at you?" Marty wanted to probe David's psyche a little deeper.

"What are you getting at?"

"Well, sometimes he'll finish a sentence and then continue to stare at me. He seems to lose his present train of thought and drift into some other world of thinking. It's weird. It's as if he doesn't see me, like he's looking through me. I feel like I'm dead in his eyes. It's hard to describe. I don't think he knows he does that. Sometimes when he does it, he chews on his necktie. I swear he doesn't realize it."

"Yeah, I've seen him do that. What does it mean?"

"I can only go by that look when he has a tie in his mouth. It's so distant. He looks through me into another world or he escapes to some other part of his mind, like I don't exist. He's not in the present world, or he's two different people and one of them checks out."

"Yeah, I've seen that look. I think his mind flits off to somewhere else and he doesn't realize he hasn't disconnected his physical presence from where his mind ran away to. I don't know the significance of it." Bob rolled his eyes away from Marty and shrugged.

"Bob, we're lucky. David treats us special. We have freedom to do whatever we want. He wants us to be happy. I think he loves us."

"I don't know, Marty. This is psychobabble and I'm not good at it. Maybe he just wants to fuck you, like every other man on the planet!" Bob grinned at her.

"Maybe he wants to fuck you, Bob! Did you ever think of that?"

"Jesus Christ, no, Marty! That's crazy. He's told me I'm like a son to him, and he tries to be like a father to me. Father's don't fuck sons!" Bob was taken aback. His inner reference frame was jolted.

"Probably not, but he never spends time with his wife and he likes your company a great deal."

"Business, Marty. All business."

"Are you sure?"

"Yes. If David has desires like that, they'd be for you, not me. I've never had a hint of homosexual interest."

"Well, I believe he's happy we're together." Marty hugged Bob and nibbled his ear while she caressed the back of his neck. She felt his instant erection. The little head told Bob it was time to stop talking.

"Yes, and we're going to keep it that way. Agreed?"

"Yes, of course."

Marty sealed her promise with a kiss but wondered if she could possibly keep it. Even as she kissed Bob, she imagined herself at an orgy, about to suck a cock while another lover was inserting his penis into Gloria's opened butterfly. *This will be hard, but I can do it. I can be true to him and love only him. I'll get there. I will!*

Even as Bob pinned her back to her sleeping bag and pushed his leg between hers, opening her to a delightful fucking, she saw dancing in her mind the images of multiple lovers taking turns with her as she encouraged them to be unafraid to surrender to her. But Bob's lovemaking was real and different from her carnal romps. He nuzzled her about the ear and neck and gently kissed her over and over again on every inch of her neck and her chest, down to the upper reaches of her cleavage.

He makes me feel different. He wants me. My body knows it. He sends goose bumps down my arms and legs and tingles through my spine. Every cell in my body is screaming this man really loves you for who you are, just for you. He wants much more than sex from you. He wants to hold you in his arms in the mornings and closely spoon you in your bed when it's cold outside. He wants to know how you feel about things, what you'd like to do or not do. He wants to laugh with you, be with you a lot. And he loves you enough to give you your own personal space. He's always a gentleman to you. He respects you and doesn't look for faults in you. He is an honest friend to you. You feel warm and safe with him. This is what love is, girl. Hold on to it. Hold on to him.

As Bob's thrusts came faster and pressed hard against her clitoris, Marty felt it come. It was like a trickle, and then it swelled to a flood that wouldn't stop. She gushed and gushed and writhed with honest lovemaking. Her heart beat faster and her breathing quickened. She didn't want to stop. The awareness she felt nearly drove her insane.

He held her close and kissed her softly about her face, gently caressing her hair before he kissed her eyes. He didn't want to let go of her, ever. She could feel it. It was the bond of true commitment. *Oh, how I've wanted this! Oh, how I treasure this wonderful feeling!*

After they took down their tent and wrapped it in its cover, she went to Bob and kissed him again, full on the mouth. There was one detail she needed to lay to rest. Call it a woman's inner gut check, or call it insecurity because she worried that, like her, Bob had thoughts of others. Well, maybe only one other woman.

Marty had a curiosity about Barbara. She'd worked with Bob for a year before he worked on the UGGA Universal Fund. They'd put deals together and syndicated them and laughed when they were together. They both said they were good friends, but was that all?

Barbara was a stunning woman. She had a brilliant mind and quick wit. Marty asked herself, *How could he not fall in love with her? How could he not be human? Surely he must have compared me to Barbara. Surely he noticed that I'm five years older and not as supple as she. So far, I've kept him close with sex. My experience helps—I'm sure no other woman ever gave him this much pleasure—but all I've done can be easily learned. Even inhibitions can be unlearned, and bedroom seduction tactics can be mastered.*

Marty took Bob's hand and bid him to sit on the ground with her.

"Bob, I'm curious if I'm enough for you. Tell me about how you feel about being committed to just one woman." Marty looked deeply into his eyes. How he felt about commitment was important to her, regardless of how she might behave within a marriage.

"Of course you're enough for me. I love you." Bob seemed perplexed at the inquiry.

"But I wonder if you've had thoughts about Barbara, the Indian girl." Marty smiled a slight upward-curling smile. She gave Bob a coquettish look. Did she tempt him more than her nemesis? She wanted the truth.

Bob's head lifted slightly at the implication Marty suggested. He looked up, reaching for a thought before his eyes met hers. "Barbara and I are friends. We worked together. We get along. There's nothing personal between us."

"That's a little surprising, speaking as a woman about another woman. Most men find her captivating and stunning. Didn't you?"

"Well, I can't deny that. She's hard to overlook." Bob was blushing.

"Don't you feel anything for her? I see how she looks at you. She holds a torch for you. You worked in the same office for a year. Surely you had a personal interest in her."

"No, you're mistaken. In fact, she once said she was off limits to any personal relationship, something about her professional goals, her commitments to her father and her people. There's no opening there for any man."

"So you did angle for an opening?" Marty was slightly alarmed, but not surprised.

"Yes, long ago, but nothing came of it. Relax, baby. I'm all yours. I don't want to talk about other women when we're together. I love you. Let's forget what ifs. Okay?"

"Okay, future husband, I will never mention it again, I promise. Just write it off as crazy woman thoughts. Forget I asked."

"I already forgot, babe. I'm thinking about how the local football teams are going to do this weekend. That's on my mind, not girly-swirly stuff."

Marty was relieved. Bob didn't lie to her. Of course he had thoughts about the Native girl. She was a mesmerizing, exotic beauty. She was close to the earth and her people. She had morals, smarts, goals, and determination. And she had a steady inner strength and pride about her. Just looking at Barbara gave Marty envious thoughts. *I wish I had her qualities and her incredibly firm ass! If I went to the gym every day would I ever get as firm as Barbara? What man wouldn't want her? Bob's reassurances make sense. Surely he won't wait an indefinite time for an unknown reason with an uncertain outcome with a woman he's never dated. I'm a fixture in his bed. Have some self-confidence, girl! No man ever threw you out of bed!*

426

Bob felt like he'd dodged a bullet. In truth, he sometimes longed to be with Barbara. He missed talking with her. She knew such a wide range of topics, and she was plugged into world events and markets. He missed their give and take, but the barriers she placed to a personal relationship were insurmountable. He exhaled in relief. *I'll never understand women. They're all crazy bundles of insecurities and hormones! It's a miracle that they somehow raise kids! Thinking about women is a recipe for insanity. Football, now that has better possibilities. I'm comfortable thinking about football. At least it's understandable. Will my team use a nickel defense? Will they play their opponent's receivers man to man or will they play a shifting 3-4 zone? Will the offense run from the quarterback under center or shotgun, and will they go with two tight ends or three wide outs? And, if they get behind will they run no huddle? It will be good to be in front of the TV for this one, and good to get my mind off whatever might be on a woman's mind. Why did God make them so impossibly complicated?*

Six months elapsed from Marty's shoe drop to Bob's proposal. After the proposal, they returned to Plaintown. Word traveled faster than light in their small office, and secrets slipped their leashes. Maybe it was Marty's telling giggle when Bob's secretary asked her how her travels were going, or maybe it was the serene look on Marty's face when her mother asked her how she liked assisting Bob, and Susan's follow-up question.

"Are you two getting serious?"

Marty smiled as she nodded. She looked like a little girl who'd just received a puppy for Christmas.

It was body language from daughter to mother. They were happier together than they'd been in twenty years. They hugged and swayed from side to side as only mothers and daughters hug. Then they beheld each other at arm's length and came back together and hugged some more. They even hugged in front of the front office staff one afternoon. Everyone soon figured out Marty's secret. Something made mother and daughter way too happy. Girl world has a high IQ for matters of the heart, unlike boy world which concentrates mostly on cars, trucks, rifles, hunting camp, fishing holes, football plays, and NFL draft picks.

David found out via the office grapevine.

THE PRIEST

Barbara took an unscheduled three days off. The women talked. They speculated she was upset at losing the man she'd set her heart on. Likely she was nursing hurt feelings.

When she returned, she went straight to Marty's office. She was unafraid of confrontation. She wore a black choker top, brown skirt and no makeup. She mourned lost love.

"Oh hi, Barb. How are you feeling? I heard you were out sick." Marty pursed words of officious sympathy.

Barbara barely stood inside her door. Her eyes telegraphed her thoughts. *You no good, base whore, how dare you smite my heart! How dare you corrupt Bob! You are vile and despicable. I have nothing but contempt for you.*

"I'm okay, Marty. It's only a tummy upset. I'll get over it. Thanks for your concern."

Barbara continued staring. *You're almost six years older than me, but still peddling sex like a promiscuous sixteen-year-old. Your face may be fuller, rounder, and angelic-looking. And your lips may be fuller than mine. And you've mastered the allure of your two shiny almond pools by how you accent them with taupe eye shadow. You have a more voluptuous figure than me. I have to give it to you, whore. Your sex appeal overwhelms men. But I don't envy you or your morals.*

How many men have had their cocks inside that mouth of yours? How many knew the pleasures of your hips and legs while you cradled them and guided their pricks into your fuck-crazy pussy? You're just a worthless punch bag. You're lucky I don't play on your level, you slut. If I fucked Bob, I'd take him away from you in one night. He'd understand the difference between a woman and a pig. You don't know how lucky you are that Chief wants me to wait for Bob. Chief thinks there's another shoe to drop in this story. You're lucky I trust his judgment; otherwise Bob wouldn't give you the time of day.

For a moment, Barbara considered her approach to Bob might be totally wrong. Obviously, whoring got fast results. Men really did think with their dicks! Barbara felt a jealous impulse but masked it.

"What's on your mind, Barb?" Marty had an inkling why the Native girl was there and she wanted to get past the perfunctory pleasantries. She smiled broadly. Her uplifted brow gave the impersonation of a cat that just swallowed Barbara's canary.

"I came to wish you well, Marty. Congratulations on your engagement to Bob." Barbara held back tears of bitter hurt the best she could, but saying those words made them form in her eyes regardless.

"Why thank you, Barb. That's very thoughtful of you." Marty prolonged her thoughtful gaze at the girl-woman. *She looks like she could still be in high school. That face! What I wouldn't give to have a fresh angel face like hers! I see her chest heaving slightly and her short breath. This must be painful for her.*

Marty felt a pang of regret and guilt for interjecting herself between two searching lovebirds. She realized Bob should be Barbara's, not hers. He deserved the better woman. Barbara was more intelligent and witty. They were better matched. Barb's love was genuine, while hers was opportunistic. *This lovely girl can't hide her feelings. Her heart is right out there.* For the first time in her life, Marty felt some sympathy for a woman whose man she'd taken.

A knot twisted in Marty's stomach. She'd stolen Bob's affections and did it in the seediest way possible. Barbara was a virtuous saint. That knowledge gnawed at her gut. She envied

Barbara's lithe, supple figure and age advantage. She looked like a Mediterranean beauty queen. Marty coveted her understated beauty. If she had Barbara's looks and body, there was no telling where she could go with it. Possibly she'd be married to a senator, or she'd be an exclusive escort for billionaires. Marty resented Barbara's employment in the company. She didn't need a constant reminder that there was a rival with superior morals, looks, and intelligence. It grated on her self-esteem and reminded her how loathsome her tactics were. Marty made a mental note to lobby Bob and David to get Barbara out of the company immediately after she married Bob.

Marty feared Barbara was more sensual in the bedroom than herself and likely able to perform with greater grace and stamina. Barbara likely didn't know half of Marty's bedroom tricks, but in the back of her mind she knew any woman could replicate her performances if she cast off her inhibitions and practiced technique. There was the Kama Sutra, books on props, scents, oils, creams, toys and crops and whips for sadists, and countless romance novels to help women with seduction plots and male bagging tactics.

Marty's worst fear was that if Barbara and Bob ever had sex, she'd lose him. But Marty intuited that Barbara planned more noble pursuits for her life. More than anything, Marty respected Barbara's professionalism and high moral standards. All she could do was bide her time until Bob married her. But she wished her aggravation would end. Barbara boiled her jealousy. She wanted to pull the Indian's hair out, plunge a knife into her, and push her off the building roof. She wanted Barbara to return to her father's place in Montana or somehow disappear.

"Marty." Barbara broke the silence. She saw Marty was off in thought somewhere.

"Yes, Barb?" Her answer was clipped. Now Marty wanted this awkward scene ended.

"Don't you dare hurt him." Barbara stared at her like a wolf might stare at a prey animal. Her jaw slackened as if her lips were about to reveal fangs. The stare had an element of a threat behind it.

There it was! Barbara had revealed an uncharacteristic show of emotion. She let slip her professional mask. There was an element of danger in that look. Marty liked the sense of pushing her chances to the limit. Maybe Barbara would try something stupid, like shooting one of her Indian arrows at her. Hah!

Marty sensed her opportunity to crush another woman's love and dash Barbara's hopes and dreams. She felt herself becoming moist, relishing the thought of taunting the younger woman, feeling the vicarious thrill of knowing Barbara felt defeat every time Marty and Bob left town together. Barbara obviously loved Bob enough to issue her veiled threat. She wanted "her man" handled with care. If Barbara knew how Marty plied him with sex and false promises of fidelity, and the money David gave her to spend on her conquest, she could lose this game.

But wait! Marty realized that Barbara saw all the firm's books. Maybe David hadn't masked her seduction payments well enough. Maybe Barbara would comb the books and start asking questions. Maybe this silent, witty Indian already knew how all this came about. Maybe she loved Bob so much she chose to stay silent out of respect for his choice, willing to let him later discover what a whore he married on his own. Marty perceived, dimly, that she could possibly be in over her head, that her whole scheme could be turned upside down. She stared at Barbara's mouth. A danger lurked behind those lips. It was palpable. For a brief second, Marty feared she might be bitten. A primal instinct cautioned her to not underestimate the Indian, but to fear her and stay away from her. Marty's confidence slid downhill.

"You love him, don't you?" Marty's question was sincere, and she expected an honest answer. There came a long pause where neither woman spoke. Marty sensed it was time to declare victory.

I can't be timid. I can't second-guess myself or worry about what if this or what if that. When I was only five and Mother dropped me off at boarding school, she told me to always believe in myself. Miss Shameless told me when I seduced Darren to never apologize for what I was, to never feel self-conscious or embarrassed about my whoring, to never feel sorrow or remorse for those I hurt, but instead to have an inner joy and self-confidence about my behavior. Now here's my chance to be true to myself. Fuck this Indian bitch! I'll send a thousand daggers into her aching heart right now.

Marty cocked her head as the nonchalant adult looking at a novice. Miss Shameless controlled Marty's every thought and deed now. She became a marionette performing a rote pantomime. The young girl in this audience of one was not the first to have her high-minded morality foiled by Marty's promiscuity.

Miss Shameless spoke to Marty. *I brushed away the dart of remorse that but a few moments prior briefly pricked your heart. I scrubbed away all your thoughts of guilt for our scheme that snared Bob's love. I purged all memories of your wrongdoings forever because you are entitled to take whatever you wish in this world. It is the end that matters, not the means. What we did is done. Now you must nip the budding flower of Barbara's searching love. Take it from her and hold it in your hands. Hold it out of reach from her and make her watch you devour it like a reptile swallows a hatchling. Crush down on her hapless chick of new love with merciless skeleton-crunching jaws. Pulverize the love chick's dream life and grind into your mouth this maiden's furtive hopes. Let her know her dreams as well as her intended's cock are gone forever from her, engulfed and held captive by your wanton cunt.*

Miss Iniquity seconded Miss Shameless's hurtful intentions. *When you taunt her, also mock her with the look on your face. Enjoy the warm radiance of sustaining evil in your stomach and the thrill of rapture in your breast as you vicariously shove this skinny bitch off a cliff to her death. Smile a contemptuous smile as you twist your poisoned knife in her heart. Enjoy your triumph over this fool. Make her surrender to the reality that your heartless, iniquitous cunt devoured her ridiculous life goals and her childish dreams of love. Make her want to throw up.*

Marty, with slow deliberation, raised her left hand across her chest and placed it over her right breast as if to scratch an itch near the top of her tit. Brazen and perceptively obvious, she scratched her imaginary itch with only her ring finger while keeping her thumb and other fingers motionless. As she attended her imaginary itch Marty imagined all the future times she would fuck Barbara's heartthrob. She smiled the self-congratulatory smile of a lizard that seized a chick. Her message was unmistakable. *The game is over for you, Barbara.* The diamond solitaire was a full three carets. It sparkled with rays of brilliant white with a tinge of blue. It was obviously an expensive stone. Marty flashed her victory smile over heartbroken Barbara, her eyes opened wide and brightened. She gave a nod to her rival while continuing to flaunt her engagement ring. Misses Shameless and Iniquity cheered her perfect performance.

Barbara's face registered dismay blended with tinges of remorse and concern for Bob. Miss Shameless saw Barbara's heartbroken expression and filled Marty's ego. *Yes, I am a promiscuous whore. I got what I wanted. Thank you, Miss Shameless, for bringing my thoughts back into focus. Thank you, Miss Iniquity, for returning me to my core personality. Soon I will own her man like I do so many others. I will fuck him at my leisure. I will use my new status as a married woman to make him do my bidding, and I will bring him around to the same debased lifestyle that I crave. He will join in my orgies and worship me like the others. You helped me remove my last barrier to his heart and soul. Bless you, Miss Iniquity. Oh goodness, I already feel moist just contemplating the future with Bob's cock in my pussy. Barbara, you're no different than those stupid virgins at boarding school. You lost him, kiddo. That's too bad for you. Now go away and cry somewhere else.*

"Is there something else, Barbara?" Marty donned her mask of office formality.

"Just don't you dare hurt him!" Barbara thought her emphatic repeat was all Marty was entitled to hear. *My breast aches from a scorching pain. I feel she has stuck a burning stick into my heart, but I must not show weakness to this incorrigible slut.* Barbara's face and jaw hinted of a dangerous wildness that concealed her inner anguish, but her underlying threat was unmistakably repeated. She abruptly turned her back to the whore fiancée and walked out of the office, disrespectfully leaving Marty's door wide open behind her. *Marty, you and I are mortal enemies now.*

While staring at the open door through which Barbara departed, Miss Iniquity voiced a retort to Barbara's admonition. *Just you wait, bitch. When I have my gold wedding ring I'll shove it in your face. Better yet, I'll get one of those wide band designer rings with etchings and inlaid platinum. Then I'll take a picture of it floating on top of Bob's cum pool in my cunt. You'll know whose ring it is. I'll ask you if it looks better in my cunt or on my ring finger. I'll make you want to retch up your lunch, and then I'll tell you I'm sorry that I didn't mean to upset you. I thought you'd enjoy some girl talk, that's all. Indian bitch, you're not going to tell me what I can or cannot do with my man!*

That night, Sparrow knelt by her bedside and prayed for a vision of wisdom from Jania, her departed mother. She closed her eyes softly and listened and waited. In her mind, she asked the same question over and over. After each asking, she waited and listened.

"Mother, Father says I must wait for Bob and give him time. Is there anything more I could do? He is engaged to marry another. Mother, speak to me. Please, Mother. I need you now, and I need your wisdom in the ways of men."

Finally, after hours of prayer, she could hear her mother's voice and the advice from her mother's spirit came to her.

"Daughter, Little Sparrow, hear my words from my spirit to yours. Chief's advice to you is true. You must wait until Bob sees the errors of his ways and returns to you."

"Mother, did I make a mistake when he wanted me and I did not give myself to him? Please answer me, Mother."

"Does he know he holds your heart, Little Sparrow?"

"Yes, Mother. He knows that he does. I am certain."

"Then you did not make a mistake. When a man knows a woman loves him, he will not stray far from her love. He will return to you when he is ready. And, Sparrow, do not pray that harm befalls the Marty woman. The spirits know she is hurtful to you, but it is not your place to wish harm upon her. It is not our way."

"But isn't there more I can do?"

"Yes, Little Sparrow. You must have goodness in your heart and you must continue to pray."

And Little Sparrow did pray. Each morning before sunrise, she awoke and went to The Church of the Risen Christ, lighting a votive candle for Bob in front of the statue of the Virgin Mary. She knelt for a moment and said three Hail Mary's. Then she went to the second row pew, pulled down the kneeler bench, and knelt in prayer. Each morning, fair weather or foul, mild or cold with snow, Little Sparrow prayed for the soul of the man she loved, prayed that God and Jesus and the Holy Spirit and The Great Spirit of All Living Things and mountains, plains, and waters would help Bob find his way to her, that he would turn away from the sins of debauchery and the whoring of the disgusting slut Marty and find the good life she offered him.

After noticing this devout Indian maiden praying so fervently each morning, a priest sat beside her in her pew. They were alone in the church.

"You are troubled about something, aren't you, my child?"

"Yes, Father. I am troubled for the soul of the man I love. He is a good man and he has strayed from God. And I want him to return to me. I need him. My family and my people need him. I want to bear his children." Barbara told the priest everything about Bob, David, Marty, the history of the Sustack firm, and her working experiences at the firm.

After a few silent moments while the priest and Sparrow sat together, the priest spoke. "You are a beautiful young woman. Why must it be this man?"

"Because with this man beside me, I can complete my purpose in life, and because I love this man and only this man." Barbara held back tears.

"And your purpose?" The priest was consoling and gentle of voice.

"It is to meld my people and the white people to greater harmony and understanding and respect and love, Father. My people need good examples and strong leadership. My father, Chief, provides that, but he is getting old and he looks to me to stand for him when he leaves for the Happy Hunting Grounds. I don't expect you to fully understand our ways, Father; but we need to bring this man into our tribe. We do not have his skills."

"Then this is business for you?"

"Yes, but also no. I am very deeply in love with this man. I have searched my heart and I know this truth like only a woman can know. I love him so much. Oh Father, my love for him is so deep. I love him with all my heart. I will be incomplete in my life if I cannot be with him."

"I see. So you come here each morning and pray that God will give him to you?"

"Yes, Father."

"Well, maybe it was God's will that I stopped to visit with you. May I make a suggestion that may be helpful to you?"

"Of course, Father."

"You are an exceptionally beautiful woman. You could help him find his way to you if you helped him notice you more."

"Are you saying that I should stoop to Marty's level? Are you saying the only way a man can think is with his penis?"

"Oh no, my child, nothing like that. There are other, better ways to help him notice you more."

"Such as?"

"Just be in his life, my child. Just go into his life with your help for his needs and with your love in your heart. He will not send you away. And you must continue to pray. Your parents called you by the name Little Sparrow, didn't they?"

"Yes, Father, how did you know that?"

"Perhaps all things we must know are also God's will, Little Sparrow. Now go into the life of your man and continue to pray."

And Sparrow continued to pray.

BUZZ

When the office buzz about Bob and Marty's engagement reached David, it aroused the archenemy of love and matrimony. He had a hard time containing his fury. He kicked Marvin's low bench and hurt his big toe. Then he swept his arm across the credenza on the wall, scattering reports and research papers all over the floor. When his blood pressure eased and he regained some semblance of control, he called Marty to his office and confronted her about her engagement.

"Are you and Bob engaged? Am I hearing grapevine talk about you two?" David's voice was clipped, sharply pointed.

His interrogation was unexpected and the opposite of graciousness and well wishes. Marty saw he was pissed. She tried to attenuate his wrath, backpedaling hastily.

"Now, David, don't get excited. Everything can work out." Marty tried to quell his rising anger, but putting the anger genie back into its bottle wasn't possible.

David's face was beet red. He wasn't about to hear anyone tell him how things could work out in his department.

"You saw my memo about office romance. We discussed what you were supposed to do!" David raised his voice to shouting. His teeth clenched. "I wanted you to keep him occupied, away from other women and away from other brokerage firms. I didn't want you to go pouring your mushy female ways all over him and seduce him to the point where he wanted to marry you. You know I think of him as a son. You know I have big plans for him. I don't want to hear any female excuses for what's happened here. I don't want to hear any women's speak that it just happened. This is fucking horseshit! I trusted you as an executive of this company. Instead you peddled your cunt and you've ruined a great salesman."

David's eyes bulged. He was about to blow a gasket.

"Can't I explain?" Marty sounded like a pathetic schoolgirl trying to explain romance to a mindless, bellicose reptile. Horseshit meant something was unacceptable as opposed to bullshit, which meant something wasn't quite as represented. Marty shuddered at David's word selection.

"No! There's no need for that. We're finished here." David slammed his palms down hard on his desk. "I want your resignation on my desk in the next ten minutes. Get your things and get your slutty ass out of here immediately. That's all!"

And just like that, Marty was out of a job and into an impossible situation. How could she tell Bob that she took company money to seduce him? David placed her in a terrible position and left no room for compromise. Now, if she told Bob the truth, she risked losing him. He'd likely think she was a common harlot. Maybe she was. She thought Bob would be right to think the worst of her. Love was confusing.

She thought it best to resign, giving no reason, and deal with the aftermath later. Crisis rocked her sensibilities and her trust in Bob's love for her. It occurred to her she wasn't being logical, that she should fight back instead. There were lawyers for this sort of stuff, but David had more money. She'd used company money. Her name would be smeared everywhere. She thought about those things, but decided to react to David's demand instead. She took her resignation letter to him, returned to her desk, cleaned out her personal effects, and left the building.

When Barbara heard of Marty's resignation, her heart leaped. Was it possible that her prayers were being answered?

For months since the priest spoke with her she'd tried to follow his suggestion. She baked cookies for Bob and made sandwiches, always leaving them on his desk. When she saw him in the hall, she made a point of standing in front of him and not getting out of his way. When she delivered his weekly sales reports, she sat on his desk and handed them to him personally, not saying a word. Her tactics were starting to take effect. Bob asked her out for coffee again to see if there was anything in the sales reports that showed a pattern.

"Yes, I see a clear pattern to your sales," Barbara said. "The more time you spend with Marty, the more your sales decline. I think the correlation is the higher your prick rises, the more your sales drop. Does that explain things for you?"

Bob was stunned at Barbara's new comportment. No longer the demure, meek supplicant, she was taking charge of her own destiny and making Bob up his game. There was a new camaraderie brewing between them, and it felt good for both of them. They were together laughing again. The office rumor mill noticed.

One morning after her prayers, Little Sparrow saw the deacon of the church and inquired after the priest who spoke with her months before. She described him to the deacon, but the deacon averred there was no such priest associated with the parish and there was no visiting priest during the month she had her conversation. That same evening, she called Chief.

"I heard your mother's spirit voice talking to me a few weeks ago. She told me she sent a priest to help you find your way, Little Sparrow. I hope the priest she sent was helpful."

Sparrow looked far away into an imaginary world she could never understand as her father could. She knew he had great powers, that he communicated with the spirits. But was the priest a spirit dressed as a priest or was he a real priest? Did Mother's spirit send him? Did Mother's spirit speak through

Chief and did Chief send him? It was all so confusing and mysterious, but she knew she'd talked with a priest.

She laid her head on her pillow that evening and thanked God and the spirits for the wonders of this world and for her place on this Earth and in her father's tribe. Then Little Sparrow slept a good sleep for the first time in many moons.

Even though Susan was in charge of the office staff, technically Marty worked in sales, under David's supervision. Marty knew running to Mother would not change things. David had manipulated her into a corner. She needed time to think.

Three days passed. Marty heard from Bob the previous two nights asking what was wrong, but she told him she wasn't ready to talk about it. He told her he'd be patient and would wait to hear from her. Marty thought her world was collapsing around her. Bob would ask her more questions. Barbara would comb the books, would figure out that Bob was scammed into a romance based on falsehoods. She would win Bob's heart. David had already fired her; could anything possibly get worse? She could only wonder.

She needed to find another job somewhere, probably in another town. Too many people knew about her fling with the bank chairman. Salesmen and wives all over Plaintown knew she was a tramp. She'd need to sell her house and leave, probably go to one of the coasts and start over. Who'd even give her a reference? Perhaps Carl or some of the men from her orgy parties would say good things for her. But just as likely they'd clam up or say she's just a punch bag for sales. Would her priest whom she hadn't seen in years help her? That seemed like a stretch. Besides, priests didn't understand business, except for getting money laundered through the Vatican. She needed to find a solution to her nightmare fast. She was half crazed and desperate.

On the morning of the third day, there was a knock on her front door. She was shocked when she opened her window slider and saw it wasn't Bob, whom she half expected. It was David. *What more could he possibly want from me. He knows I'm desperate. What is he up to?*

"Hello, Marty." David spoke in his most cheerful voice. She thought he must be bipolar.

"I've thought about things. Maybe I've acted a little too harshly. Anyways, I've brought you a little peace offering." He held up a strand of beautiful black Mikimoto Pearls. They were exquisite.

Marty opened her door. David wore a green leisure suit. She smelled barnyard dung on his boots. She wondered if this was the proverbial Greek bearing a gift, or if it was her resurrection after her third day in purgatory.

"I feel badly about the way I treated you, Marty. Sometimes I get a little carried away with my own emotions and I just can't help myself. I didn't mean to be so harsh with you and I don't want your mother upset either, so I thought maybe you could come over to the barnyard tomorrow. I'd like to talk with you about rehiring you on even more favorable terms than before, and I have another gift I'd like to give you. I didn't bring him with me, since he was just born four weeks ago, but I think you'd like him, and he could be a peace offering from me to you."

"What is he, exactly, David?" Marty was skeptical. *Here is this toady, erratic man coming to my home unannounced and totally unexpected. And now he's telling me he wants me back and he's bringing a peace offering? Is this David's version of the passion? Am I being resurrected from the dead?*

"I wanted him to be a surprise, but if you must know, he's a floppy-eared rabbit."

Marty's defenses melted at the thought of having a floppy-eared rabbit. They were so cute! David couldn't be all bad. He was just erratic. She relaxed her guard and agreed to meet him in the barnyard the following day at 10:00 a.m. to discuss her return arrangement and to get her rabbit. David requested, and Marty promised, that she'd tell no one of their impending meeting because they had to work through some of the details of her return first. He assured her she'd fall in love with the rabbit.

As he left, David turned to Marty and said, "Wear those pearls tomorrow when you come to the barnyard. I'd like to see how they look on you."

GLORIOUS BUTTERFLY

Promptly at ten the next morning, Marty drove up to the barnyard gate. She wore a pair of loose blue cotton shorts with a yellow cotton blouse that day. Her shoes were a pair of cheap flats made from hemp and canvas.

David was in the barn, looking the part of a gentleman farmer in his dungaree coveralls and straw hat. Marty lifted the pearls with her finger and gave them a little twirl to show she'd complied. He smiled in approval and motioned her to come into the barn.

"Be careful not to go too close to the goats in that outfit," he said. "They eat organics like you're wearing. That outfit is cotton, isn't it?" Marty affirmed David's assessment of her attire. "And those shoes, they're made of canvas and some kind of fiber, aren't they?"

Again Marty told David he'd guessed correctly. *Is he concerned about the constitutions of his goats? Does he actually believe they'd try to eat my shoes?* With David she could only wonder.

"Well, just watch yourself if a goat gets too close. They'll eat the clothes right off you if you let them. Just smack them on the nose if they bother you."

Marty laughed. "I can take care of myself."

"Of course you can. Of course you can," David said. He had a hint of mocking in his tone, but not enough for Marty to detect. He was just being a sweet, older gentleman.

"I'm willing to reverse my decision about your employment, Marty. I've thought long and hard about this, and I think I've been too harsh with you. You've been a good employee. You always did what I asked of you. You've been a real company gal and I like that. It's as much my fault as yours that you got carried away with Bob. So, I'd like to make a proposal. I'm willing to rescind my memo about romantic involvement as it pertains to you and Bob. After all, you're both company officers and I can make an exception because you two are special.

"I'd like to hire you back with a 20 percent pay raise, and just to prove to you I harbor no ill will toward you or Bob, I'd also like to give you this diamond necklace. You'll need a nice accessory for your evening wear. Maybe you'll even wear it on your wedding day. Pearls are nice for every day, but diamonds look best in formal wear. With you getting married to Bob, you'll have many occasions to dress formally."

With that preamble, David held up an exquisite three-inch-thick diamond choker necklace with a diamond pendant dropping down about four inches to the top of her cleavage channel. Marty gasped. The necklace had to be worth at least a half million dollars.

"David, I don't know what to say." Marty was speechless. His behavior was always unusual and unexpected. She'd never known him to gild a lily before. The pearls were an ample peace offering.

"Well, there are just two little things I'd like to ask of you in return before I give you the diamond necklace. First, I'd like you to help me understand you better. You see, Marty, I think in a certain way you and I are very much alike, and that fascinates me. You've always fascinated me.

"When I was a child, I used to hurt insects. I don't know why, but I kind of enjoyed it. I pulled wings off flies, I burned ants under the focused rays of sunlight through an eyeglass, and

I tore wings from butterflies to watch them struggle. It gave me a sense of power and I liked that feeling.

"I know from the way you went about getting sales that you must have thought about the effect you had on the lives of those men. I'd like you to tell me what thoughts you had when you were with those men, and especially explain the thoughts you had about the effect you had on their wives and families."

"You mean when I was being intimate with them?"

"Yes. I'd like to know what went through your mind when you were involved with them, and especially what your thoughts were while you were fucking them. It's important to me that you don't hold anything back. I believe we're so alike in our feelings when we are hurting others, and I deeply admire that about you. In fact, your feelings toward the women you've crushed excite passions in me about you. I promise you, everything you tell me will stay right here in this barn. Bob will never hear a word of it. You fascinate me, Marty. That's why I want you to have the necklace. It'll signify the bond we have between us, that we know we have power over others. So would you please tell me your deepest feelings?"

Marty thought this was bizarre, even crossing a boundary into the perverse, but after hearing David reveal his childhood feelings, she felt a kindred urge to share her feelings with him.

"Okay, David, but it has to stay here. You promise?"

"I told you. It stays here. I promise you."

"And you want all the details, even the lurid ones?" Marty felt nervous about revealing her innermost thoughts and her sexual exploits. Did David really understand what he was asking of her? Would he understand and accept the cravings of a nymphomaniac on his marketing team?

"Yes, I especially want to hear those details. Don't hold anything back. Like I said, you fascinate me. You're a true professional, and I'm extremely proud of the work you do for the firm. I know you must have some trying moments, especially when it comes to handling men's wives, and I'd love to hear every minute detail of how you manage to do so well. Oh, and there's another something else I'd appreciate your doing for me."

"What, David?"

"Please try not to laugh at me, Marty. I want to understand what attracts men to you. I mean, men go crazy after you. You have a rare talent. I am homosexual. I have no particular interest in women. You probably knew that."

"Well, I thought there was something like that with you, but I was never sure. You are married."

"Yes, but you know my wife is almost always away on a trip somewhere."

"Yes, that's well known."

"Well, I'm a lonely, short, ugly man."

Marty was silent for a moment before she spoke. "David, I find a way to see something beautiful in every man. You're not ugly to me. You just need to be open with your feelings. You keep so much of yourself hidden."

"That's because I'm afraid to trust anyone. It comes from my childhood. Mother hated me. Father ignored me. I grew up a tormented child knowing I wasn't loved. I guess that's why I became a gay man. I hated Mother and resented my dad. But Marty, all my life I've wanted to change. I've tried to find a woman attractive. I mean, attractive enough to me so I could make love to her."

"And you want to make love to me? Is that it, David?"

"I'm not sure. I don't know. It would be hard for me. I'm afraid to even try. Perhaps you could help me feel less ashamed of myself, less inhibited."

"What do you have in mind, David? I'm willing to help. I do care about you. Honest I do. Tell me what I can do to help."

"Promise me you'll never say a word of this. Not even to your mother. I need you to promise."

"Okay. I promise." Marty placed her hands on David's shoulders and looked deeply into his eyes."

"Well, I'd like you to help me become unafraid of a woman's female spot."

"You mean my pussy? You think you're afraid of my pussy?"

"Well, yes. I guess I am. That has to do with my mother. When I was a boy she shamed me constantly, always embarrassed me, and I got to where I believed the female part dominated the male part. Once I was old enough to jerk off, I decided I didn't need to ever take abuse from a woman to get sex from her. Then when I got older, I discovered my friend Hirsch felt much the same way I did. He hated his mother too. We began jerking off together. One thing led to another, and soon Hirsh and I were giving each other blow jobs. We formed a pact to hate women. Then one day to seal our pact, we trapped a little girl and held her down on the ground, and I bit her leg up close to her pussy. We were trying to let her know that we didn't need her pussy. We had each other. Hirsch and I have been gay men ever since." David was morose, seeking pity.

"That's terrible. What a shame your mother treated you that way. Sex between men and women is beautiful, David. Neither sex organ dominates the other. The two parts work together in unison. They make beautiful intimacy together. It's wonderful and liberating."

"I know. I understand that. But I need to be set free of my fear. I've had this fear of your woman part, or 'pussy' as you call it, all my life. That's the first thing I'd appreciate you helping me with."

"Okay. How would you like to go about losing your fear?"

"Could you sit on the hay bales and lean your head back? I'll put blankets down so the hay won't scratch you. Then could you take off your shorts and spread your legs out widely and let me look at your pussy and rub your legs? I think that might help me."

"You just want to look at my pussy and rub my legs?"

"Yes. And while I'm doing that, I'd very much like you to tell me about your sexual exploits, especially the way you've dealt with married men and their wives. Do you think I'm being kinky to ask these things of you?"

"No, David! You're not kinky in the slightest. You're not asking me to let you whip me or hit me or put ball bearings in my pussy. You're not going to deliberately hurt me while you fuck me so you can dominate me. You just want to get over a psychological hang-up that you have over a woman's pussy. There's nothing kinky about what you're asking, David. I'm here for you. I want to help. This is just something we'll do together, and we'll try to get you over this fear you have.

"You put down the blankets while I take my shorts off. I'll spread my legs out for you and we'll just talk. I'll tell you about my sex life while you rub my legs. There's nothing kinky about this. I'm a company girl, David. I'm very happy to help you through this."

David arranged the blankets and Marty assumed her position. Her long legs were widespread and her pussy was arched upward about a foot in front of his face. He began rubbing her legs.

"Is this what you wanted, David? Does this help some? You can see there's nothing to be afraid of, can't you? It can't hurt you."

"Yes, this helps a lot. I've never had this sort of chance to just feel natural about a pussy before. Now, could you tell me about your sexual encounters, how you came to be the glorious femme fatale that you are and how you discovered you had nymphomaniac tendencies?" David began softly caressing Marty's legs, alternatively looking into her eyes and at her pussy. She had a butterfly tattoo that straddled her uppermost thighs. David enjoyed this new experience. He succeeded in getting her to believe she could help him, but had no intention of having sex with her.

"The key to gaining a man's loyalty is to make him feel appreciated. When I'm with a top salesman, he'll often give me extra gifts, tickets to shows, trips away with him, all those things a girl likes. I always make sure to tell him that he's the most wonderful, thoughtful man in the world. That makes a man want to please me more. That's how I gain power over him. I feel like he'll do just about anything to please me.

"If I want, I can get him to walk away from his wife and children for me. I can make him desire being inside my pussy more than being with his children. I know by fucking him, I'm actually destroying his peaceful life with his wife and kids. I get pleasure out of knowing I'm causing that. I know my feelings are wrong, but I can't help myself. I feel wonderful being the evil temptress who steals away his goodness and his family life. I have some kind of deep-seated need to reassure myself that I'm an all-powerful evil vixen. It's a fun game for me, and I enjoy playing my role."

"When did you first realize you were okay with being a whore, Marty? And how did it all get started that your life took this path? Was it as a young girl?"

"Oh, I learned early in life. My experimentation with sex started way back in my boarding school days. When Mother dropped me off, she told me it was the best thing for me. I was going to get a terrific education and worldly experience. I believed her and accepted what she said. Mother hugged me and told me she loved me and that she'd always be close to me. I believed her and I had confidence I'd fit into the school and the routine.

"But after I was there for about three or four months, Mother stopped calling me every week like she first did. Then she stopped taking my return phone calls. The office staff told me she'd call back. At first she called back, but after a while, she'd wait a few days until I was in class and just leave a pathetic message with the dorm mother. She'd say she'd call again and we'd catch up, that sort of thing. I got used to crying myself to sleep. My father died, my mother didn't love me, and I was so lonely my guts hurt. Then I started feeling angry inside. I didn't do anything to deserve being treated this way by my own mother. When she played phone tag with me, I played phone tag back. I learned how to play phone tag from my mother.

"By the time I was there two or three years, the only time I'd see or hear from Susan was when I went home for Christmas and Easter vacation. I started to call her Susan instead of Mom because she didn't act like a mom anymore. By the time I was ten, she told me she couldn't even see me over Christmas or Easter breaks. Each time I had a vacation, she had an excuse not to see me. She always had to be away on a business trip with Marvin, or she had to be at a meeting at a resort with clients.

"Mother wrote me during my early years at boarding school, at first weekly then monthly, but by the time I was about ten, she even stopped writing. Can you imagine how it felt as a young girl to not hear from your own mother or even get a postcard from her? I felt terrible, abandoned and useless, like I was some piece of trash in Mother's life that she wanted to throw away."

"That must have been terrible. You felt rejected, didn't you?"

"Yes. It was awful. I figured out that she was seeing Marvin a lot. She always had time for him, whatever he wanted or wherever he wanted to go, but she never had time for me.

Initially, I told myself Mother was seeing Marvin for my own good somehow. I wanted to believe that.

"Then I started paying attention to when the older girls in the dorm talked about sex and how much it changed their relationships with boys. That's when I realized that Susan was having sex with Marvin and that she was doing it for herself. She wanted him more than she wanted me. That's when I started resenting Mother and feeling angry about my situation. I was two thousand miles from home and no one cared about me. I decided I had to figure out life for myself.

"My interest in sex started with normal pre-teen, pre-puberty curiosities and evolved in phases into a full-blown obsession with nymphomania. I had a lot of positive reinforcement about my choices every step of the way. Let me start by telling you about my experiences at boarding school.

"The girls there were all cliquish and I didn't feel I fit in. I was from out west and a boarder. Most of them were locals who went there for the education during the day and then went home at night.

"One day identical twins from the local school, Donny and Billy, asked me to a movie. We sat in the back of the theater in a corner. I sat between them. They bought my ticket and gave me a box of popcorn. In the middle section of the theater, down in front of us, were some girls from my school. They saw us and started whispering like girls will do when talking about another of their own. During the movie, Billy put his hand on my breast. I had my period three times already and my breasts were getting like a woman's.

"I started to push his hand away, but then I thought about it. The twins paid my way and I should show my appreciation. I relaxed and let Billy fondle me. I liked his touches; they made me feel appreciated. He was frustrated that he couldn't get my bra off. That's when I made a life-changing decision. I muzzled Miss Modesty, pushed her into a closet, locked the door behind her, and threw away the key. I opened wide another door and welcomed Miss Promiscuity, my new best friend. Together, Promiscuity and I reshaped my dour life to unrestrained happiness. I decided to be bold. I removed my bra for Billy.

"The girls in front sneaked looks at us, but I didn't care. After I got the bra off, Billy rubbed my tits. He put his other hand up my dress and placed it on my pussy. I didn't object. I liked the attention and the new feeling of being appreciated. I liked his hand being there and I felt a stirring sensation in my pussy. I wanted Billy to keep his hand there and touch me more. Promiscuity embraced me. I loved her. She opened the world of lust for me. I felt passion for her and the possibilities she offered me. I decided she was good and wonderful. I made up my mind then and there to introduce her to lots of boys. The boys would love our company.

"Maybe I craved the attention Billy gave me because Mother pushed me away. I remember feeling close to him like I once felt close to Mother. I liked the attention he gave me. I felt important. Then he put his finger into my pussy and rubbed it around inside me. I really liked how that made me feel. I felt stimulated. I sat with my head on the back of the theater seat looking up at the ceiling, savoring my feelings.

"I stopped watching the movie. The girls were giggling. Every once in a while, I looked down at them. They'd turn around to look at us, and then they'd put their heads together, whisper, and giggle. They were definitely monitoring the scene. I knew they were talking about us, but I didn't give them a thought. Miss Promiscuity had introduced me to Miss Shameless, another of her wonderful friends.

"Then in walked another of Miss Promiscuity's friends. She introduced me to Miss Superiority and another feeling. Miss Superiority complemented Misses Happiness, Passion, and Lust. Miss Superiority made me feel special knowing I was doing something the others weren't. I enjoyed my experience while they only imagined how I felt. I was the object of curiosity and envy. I was inwardly pleased that they couldn't see what Billy was doing to me. I knew their imaginations went wild.

"Then Donny joined Billy and did the same things with me. He rubbed the palm of his hand all over my pussy, massaging the crown very caringly and lovingly for a really long time. Suddenly a warm rush came over me. It was like thousands of tiny fingers tickling my skin all over my body from the inside out. My pussy got very hot and wet and my face flushed. My forehead began to perspire and my breathing quickened. Promiscuity introduced me to yet another feeling, the feeling of wantonness. What the boys did with my body in that theater felt wonderful. Their hands caressed me everywhere. I was touched all over my torso and stomach, my thighs, my breasts, and around and inside my pussy. I reveled in the stimulation. I wanted them to keep going and never stop. I knew I wanted more.

"Donny French kissed me while his hand rubbed my pussy. By the way his tongue touched mine, I could tell he put his whole heart and soul into that kiss. I knew at that moment Donny loved me. His feelings were completely honest and he felt no shame expressing them to me. He didn't care what the girls saw or thought. He held me in his arms while we shared long, deep kisses. Promiscuity introduced me to love, a tender, reverent feeling for the boy I was with. Promiscuity showed me I could love the boy I was with even if I didn't know him very well.

"One of the girls saw us kissing and let out a muffled squeal, but I didn't care. I loved how I felt. I also imagined the love Donny was feeling toward me, and I was happy that I was helping him find happiness. I was so into the moment, I blocked all other thoughts from my mind. We weren't dirty. We were beautiful. I sensed intimacy was in my future. Promiscuity promised me intimacy. Love I couldn't have from Mother, I could have from boys. That's when I knew I could survive life without Susan's love.

"I enjoyed what the twins were doing with my body. I felt like they worshipped me. I became wet inside and I wanted them to fuck me for my first time. I wanted to express my love and gratitude to them for the feelings they helped me discover. I'd heard and read about sex. Now I wanted to find out about it firsthand. I'd hoped they'd ask me to fuck them. I waited anxiously, wondering whether they'd ask.

"Then, as we left the theater, Billy asked me, 'Would you like to go all the way and let us fuck you?'

"'Yes. I'd like that,' I told him. 'I'd hoped you would ask me. I want to find out what it's like. Let's go someplace where no one will catch us.' I couldn't wait to know what sex was like. A lot of girls talked about it, but only a few of the senior class girls in school did anything about it.

"It was late afternoon when the three of us walked into an open field. Billy had a rain poncho in his backpack, which he spread over the ground. I told them about my hymen. I still had it, and I told them I wanted Donny to be my first because he was the gentler of the two boys. I loved how I felt when Donny massaged my pussy.

"Billy sat upright and acted as lookout. I lay down on the poncho and spread my legs for Donny. His penis was very hard. He let me touch it and rub it before he pushed it into my pussy. It was his first time too, and he was excited. He pushed and pushed until his prick finally burst through my hymen. I felt a little pain at first, but then this wonderful sensation overcame that initial pain. I was finally getting fucked. I was finally a total woman and no longer just a girl. Fucking felt wonderful! I loved having Donny's cock inside me. If I hadn't agreed to fuck Billy too, I would have told Donny to keep fucking me because it felt wonderful. I tingled all over with the excitement of that first experience. I remember thinking to myself that I could go on fucking like that for many years into the future. I was so happy to discover that I liked fucking as much as I did.

"I bled some and Donny's penis got all red. He was scared, but I told him it was going to be okay. I wiped him off with his handkerchief and cleaned myself up some. Then the boys reversed roles. Donny stood lookout while I fucked Billy. It hurt me some more because Billy wasn't gentle, but even with his hard, rapid thrusts, I knew from that moment on I very much craved the feeling of having a penis inside me.

"That's when Promiscuity introduced me to another feeling. While I was fucking Billy, I saw Donny's face. He looked hurt and wistful that his brother was fucking me while he had to watch. I felt a small tinge of happiness when I noticed that. I realized that my having pleasure with his brother was causing Donny hurt because he couldn't have me all to himself. Suddenly, I understood that my intimacy with someone could cause another person pained feelings. I thought to myself, *If fucking Donny's brother causes him to feel badly, just imagine what another girl or woman would feel like if I fuck her boyfriend or man.* I felt a naughty, evil thrill knowing I was hurting Donny by fucking his brother, and I got some measure of sadistic pleasure from it.

"I held Billy close to me and kissed his ear while he fucked me. I told him I loved him and how wonderful he was. I knew I was hurting Donny even more and making him jealous of his brother, but I loved what I was doing. I felt powerful and in control. I discovered I liked hurting other people by placing my feelings for gratification above my other feelings of love and happiness, and above empathy for anyone else. I opened my eyes to behold my new feeling. She was heartless, cruel, and bloody, Miss Iniquity. We embraced each other tightly and kissed each other full on our mouths. I loved her more than all my other feelings. We swore an oath of evil to each other that we would be inseparable. We loved hurting others. We reveled in the pain we caused the innocents. She set me free of all my inhibitions. Iniquity became my best friend.

"Over the next few months, the twins sneaked me into their parents' house on Saturdays and Sundays and the two of them often fucked me for hours. It was a perfect situation. The parents were antique dealers and they were at their store on weekends. The parents had a brass queen-sized bed.

"We tried lots of positions on that bed. My favorite was to stand over one of the twins with my back to the headboard. Then I'd hold onto the brass head frame and lower my pussy onto the erect penis. While I bounced up and down on the twin who was lying under me, the other one slipped behind me and squeezed my tits while I fucked his brother. Then they exchanged positions. I loved fucking them while sitting on their laps on their parents' bed. It was so intimate! We held each other closely and rocked back and forth until they shot their semen into me. I sometimes dug my fingernails lightly into their backs, and I discovered their penises responded by getting even harder. My iniquity swallowed both of them. They became obedient servants to my experimentations and my lusts. I dispelled Donny's hopes of ever owning me. He kept his cock hard for me always. I expected and demanded that he please my lusts while forgoing any hope of my fidelity. He and his brother became my sex slaves.

"By that time, I craved sex and experimenting with positions. The twins were perfect for my lustful passions. A boy of sixteen can fuck several times in an afternoon, shoot off his semen each time, and return to full hardness shortly after. With two sixteen-year-olds, each craving sex with me, each obediently trying every position I desired, I was fucked nonstop every weekend. I absolutely loved it! All my new friends rejoiced and romped freely in my mind. Promiscuity,

Shameless, Superiority, Happiness, Wantonness, Passion, Lust, Love, Intimacy, and Iniquity were each a beautiful feeling in their own right. Now, inside me, they became beautiful women, near mirror images of myself but each slightly different. We all stripped naked. We hugged each other tightly, kissed each other's mouths and nipples and cunts, and we loved the new woman we'd made me.

"I don't know how word traveled, but one day I was at a drugstore sucking a vanilla milkshake through a clear straw when Jerry, one of the older boys from the local high school's football team, asked for a date. He had a car. We went to a movie, and after the movie we fucked in the backseat of his car. Soon, I got dates from Jerry, Jason, Jeffry, and Jimmy, all boys on the football team. I called them my four J's.

"I fucked them on every date when one or more of them took me out. Why not? I had the most beautiful face and the most stunning body around, and I craved having a cock inside me. Boys flocked to me like fish to bread on water's surface. I became boy bait.

"Other girls sat in the dormitory at night while I had endless attention lavished upon me. Soon I had date requests from over a dozen boys. I obliged all comers as long as they were good-looking and had cars. My room was on the ground floor, so I had no difficulty slipping out the back door of the dorm. I'd walk down the school's gravel driveway and hop into a boy's waiting car.

"It wasn't long before the other girls were immensely unhappy with me. They claimed I stole their boyfriends, but I didn't care how they felt. The way my mind worked, they never accepted me anyway, just like Mother. The boys accepted me, so I was always eager to go out with a boy, or even two or three. Whenever a good-looking boy walked past me, I gave him a sweet, welcoming smile and batted my eyelashes to get him thinking about me. I did that even if he was with his girlfriend or his parents.

"If I saw a boy I craved to fuck, I waited until we were in close quarters at a sporting event or a shopping mall. Then I rubbed my tits against him or brushed my hand over his ass. My method worked. I was more than a good Catholic girl. I was also a Methodist! I struck up many conversations that way and got dates with the boys I wanted most. It's true when they say it pays to advertise. I was the most popular girl in the local high school, even though I wasn't a student there.

"My friend Promiscuity was ready to advance to professional status. One of the J boys, Jason, paid me a hundred dollars in advance to reserve me for his date. He wanted me for an entire Saturday night, no double dating, and no second date for me that night. I agreed to be bought. I knew I'd crossed over the bridge to whoredom, and I welcomed my special status. None of the other girls got paid to date. I took Jason's money. We went to a motel and fucked all night. I was the go-to girl for the local high school boys who had good looks, cars, and money. I became their queen.

"Some of the dorm girls started fucking their boyfriends to try to win them back from me, but they weren't like me. I heard about their botched efforts. They'd promise their boyfriend he'd be their only lover, they'd be true to him, stuff like that. Their problem was they had all sorts of mental issues about fucking before they got married or engaged, or they expected the boy to prove his loyalty to them somehow. They didn't love fucking like I did.

"They'd often cry and feel guilty after they fucked a boy. They'd try to make the boy promise he wouldn't tell anybody about what they did, and generally put up mental roadblocks to a great time. I was their opposite. I laughed about fucking my boys. I complimented them on how hard they got, how big their pricks were, how thrilled I was to have their pricks in my pussy, how delicious their cum tasted, how handsome they were, and how I couldn't wait to fuck and suck them again.

"I liked boys. I belonged to them mentally and physically. My date calendar was always full. When I wasn't at the dorm, other girls got calls asking where I was and would I please call the boy back. The girls began to openly call me names like slut and cunt and whore. I thought their attitudes were ridiculous. I just thanked them for their compliments.

"That's about the time Jimmy, one of the football players, took me to a pornographic video store. He bought several videos of porn queens giving blow jobs. We went to his house and studied the films carefully for many hours. We still-framed the videos while I studied each frame of every sequence, from the basic stimulation moves all the way to the ejaculation of the semen. I practiced those moves on Jimmy many times until I became outstanding at cock sucking.

"I learned a lot from those films. What sets me apart from other women, even most porn stars, is that I naturally love sucking cocks. When I see a cock, I instantly fall in love with it and I want it to love me too. I learned how to quickly take any man's penis from its limp state and make it a rock-hard, throbbing column. I learned how to tease a cock with my lips and my tongue and stroke it perfectly with my fingertips. I make the man forget everything else in the world except how much he loves only me by making his penis love me first.

"There's a meeting of the minds that takes place in a magical way during my fellatio, where I love the man and he loves me, and the penis knows it's receiving genuine, unbridled love. Then the little penis head throbs and opens its channel. I can feel that happening in my mouth and with my lips. I make a soft kissing movement with my lips and tongue around his blessed little head. I let him feel how important he is, and then at just the right instant, he relaxes his semen channel and the valiant little gentleman surrenders to my love for him. He shoots his semen into my mouth.

"Unlike the porn stars, I learned that to really give a man pleasure, it was important to savor the man's semen and taste the flavor of his sperm in it. Each man has his own distinct taste, and all semen has a wonderful, acquired taste, kind of like the different tastes in wines. Also unlike the porn queens, I learned with Jimmy's help that to leave the man craving to come back to me again and again, I needed to suck all the semen out of him after he came into my mouth or onto my lips. I learned to use my fingers while sucking on the penis head to bring up a whole column of semen from deep within his scrotum. That leaves a man feeling delirious with happiness and he never forgets the experience.

"To be a successful whore, it's vital to have repeat customers, so I did all I could to encourage boys to keep coming back to me. Promiscuity introduced me to yet another friend, Miss Determination. She was strong and resolute and beautiful. When she made up her mind to capture a heart, she was relentless. She taught me to never waver or retreat from a challenge and never allow a distraction to come between a cock and my pussy. And she taught me to persist in my exploratory tactics until my man capitulated to my seduction. Her motto was to suck every man dry of his last drop of semen. I owe a lot to her.

"Promiscuity next introduced me to Miss Curiosity. She told me it was important to understand my market, to position myself to best serve it, to promote my service, to price my service properly, and to please my customers with a wonderful experience. I compared notes with a few other girls and was amazed at my discovery. Most girls didn't give blow jobs at all. They thought fellatio was dirty. The few girls who did suck cock mostly only sucked their boyfriend. The ones who sucked made their boyfriend shoot his cum onto their chest or face or into their hair. They watched him shoot, and then they wiped and washed themselves off to clean up. That was the end of his experience. I gave my research a great deal of thought. There was an untapped market just waiting for me.

"I wanted my blow jobs to be a wonderful, unforgettable experience for the boy. I wanted to make my blow jobs so memorable that the boys would put me on a pedestal in their minds, above all other girls. My goal was to become the queen of cocks, and I took my quest seriously. I wanted to look like a movie star goddess for the boy both before the blow job and after, so I didn't want the boy's cum shot all over my face or hair. I developed an acquired taste for male cum. It's actually delicious, slightly tart and acidic. It can be watery or thick and creamy, depending upon how long it was since the boy last shot off and his diet. But I soon discovered that cum has a velvety substance that slides smoothly down my throat, kind of like liquid ice cream. After savoring semen, I loved swallowing it. I figured since it's a form of human protein, it had to be the best protein I could get. I felt like a complete woman when I swallowed it, knowing I wasn't wasting anything. I told myself I was recycling life. I was in the recycling business! I also felt united with the boy's life force when I sucked him off. It felt like I was doing something holy. Sucking a cock made me feel religious.

"When I gave a boy a blow job, I took my time. I never rushed him. I'd suck him on his penis head, lick his shaft, and suck his balls too. When he did eventually come, I made sure all his cum went into my mouth and sometimes directly down into my throat if he had a huge load. I didn't get cum on my face and in my hair. It's very distracting to the intimacy of the experience for the boy, it's unprofessional, and it ruins makeup. When the boy comes into my mouth I take it as a signal to start, not stop. I squeeze his ass and pull his cock into my mouth as deeply as I can.

"Then I make the extra effort for the boy. It's the little things, the attention to detail that make my blow jobs special. I'd suck the boy's cock like it's a soda straw while I gently squeezed his balls. That way I drain all his cum from him. He'd feel that final rush of semen shooting up his shaft from deep inside his reservoir. That's a wildly sensational feeling for him. I've sucked that way ever since.

"All the time I'm sucking a cock, I'd stop for a brief few seconds and tell the boy, and now I tell the man, how wonderful his cock is and how much I love sucking him. I understood how important it was to mentally fuck his mind as well as suck his cock. I visualized myself taking his life essence from him and into my innermost self. I believe the boys appreciated the positive mindset I had about my blow jobs. I made sure to communicate clearly and unambiguously that I absolutely loved what I was doing, that I loved sucking their cocks more than anything else in the world. When my partner finished, I congratulated him on giving me a wonderful mouth full of cum and assured him I was anxious to suck him off again, whenever he wanted me. I told him his cum was delicious and I could hardly wait to swallow more of it. I gained his loyalty through my tactics, my work ethic, and my sheer love of sucking. Once I had a boy's cock in my mouth, his girlfriend became ancient history. He became my repeat customer.

"I built up a terrific business by giving wonderful blow jobs. I didn't need the money. As you know, Susan is filthy rich, but I took special pride in getting paid because that was money the boy wasn't spending on his girlfriend. Getting the boy to give his money to me was my way of feeling I'd achieved something special, that I came first in his life. Miss Iniquity was my conscience.

"Jimmy and I started charging his friends for a half hour blow job with me. We were soon making over a thousand dollars a week each. Jimmy found a compliant motel owner who rented me a room for a cheap hourly rate. We sometimes booked the room for an entire weekend. A new boy came for a blow job every hour. We spaced my calls by a half hour between boys so they wouldn't see each other or get possessive or embarrassed. We paid the motel operator cash, of course.

"The other girls at my school despised me. Very few of them talked to me, but they'd never included me before, so I didn't lose anything important. I could tell they were envious by the way they looked at me. I was the one with the beautiful clothes and more date offers than I could handle. I loved who I was. I was accepted by the boys. I belonged to the boys. I was their cock-sucking queen. I joyously skipped along, sucking, fucking, and reveling in my experience as I traveled the road to perdition.

"I learned a great deal about the way other girls think in my junior year. Jimmy introduced me to friends of a boy named Darren. He was going steady with a girl named Carol. She was a very pretty girl, but very uptight. She didn't let Darren do any more than feel her, but he wanted to go all the way. Darren's friends asked if I'd help give Carol a wake-up call. I agreed to their naughty plan. Miss Iniquity rubbed her hands together in anticipation. Miss Determination promised Carol would not deter her. Misses Wantonness, Lust, Shameless, Passion, and Love all chimed in and agreed they'd do their best to rescue Darren from his miserable circumstance.

"By that time in my development, I was aware that a boy needed a memorable sexual experience. At high school age, men are easily repulsed and naturally a little skittish about lovemaking, so I determined to give them all the help I could. I thought about sex from their perspective. Miss Promiscuity introduced me to Miss Freshness and Miss Cleanliness. They told me a big key to a successful experience was to ensure nothing about me grossed them out.

"I started with my mouth, the boy's first contact point. I went to an oral hygienist monthly to have my teeth cleaned. I didn't want any lingering bacteria to cause bad breath. I also scrubbed my tongue with a hard toothbrush twice daily, again to remove bacteria. I always carried mouthwash and breath freshener. I also ate a healthy sprig of parsley twice daily to make sure my body odor was nonexistent. My lymph nodes, adrenal glands, and sweat glands all had internal deodorizers constantly working for me, so when I French kissed a boy, he got a taste of heaven. He could subconsciously imagine his penis entering my mouth, entering a place that was clean and wholesome, and the perfect home for his penis. I did everything I could think of to make myself a delightful-smelling and tasting whore. I wanted the boys to identify me with fresh flowers and mint and running mountain streams. Olfactory senses are even more important than visual ones, Miss Cleanliness told me.

"By that point, Miss Freshness had helped me develop my butterfly pussy blend, my special secret concoction of perfumes and oils that I rubbed on my upper thighs and around and inside the outer lips of my pussy. I also rubbed it on my chest, between my breasts. I wanted boys to become enraptured by my aphrodisiacs. Miss Freshness and I designed an irresistible scent that gave boys the urge to lose themselves in me. The scent attracted a boy like a bee to a flower.

"We rented an upscale hotel suite. Jimmy and I discovered by then that if we went upscale we could charge more. These boys didn't care about costs. At age sixteen, I had already arrived as an accomplished upscale, high-class whore!

"I prepared extensively for my rendezvous with Darren and Carol. I got to the hotel first, as a great hostess should. I thoroughly cleaned my mouth and pussy. I refreshed my mouth with mint mouthwash and anointed my pussy with her special perfumes and oils. My scents were exotic and irresistible.

Darren arrived next, as scheduled, slightly after I finished freshening myself. I invited him to sit in a chair by the bed.

"I wore black nylons, black silk panties and teddy, and a matching black silk lace bra under a loose, cotton print polka dot dress. My front dress buttons were opened down to below my cleavage. I was almost fully developed. I had beautiful cleavage for a girl my age. Darren and I waited and exchanged pleasantries before his friends brought Carol. I told him I'd make sure he'd have a wonderful time. I liked his looks. He was handsome, tall, and muscular. He began to relax.

"The other boys and Carol arrived next. They told her Darren had something special he wanted her to see. They kept her guessing about what was so special to lure her into the room. When they came into the suite, they locked the door behind Carol. They brought her into the bedroom and sat her down in a chair in a corner of the room beyond the bed. They held her arms and restrained her in the chair and told her, 'You're going to love seeing what Darren and Marty are about to show you. Just watch.'

"Then Darren and I rose from our separate chairs, walked over to her as planned, and stood together, next to the foot of the bed, right in front of her.

"She said, 'Darren, what do you think you're doing with this girl?' He didn't say a word. He just lifted my dress over my head, dropped it on the floor, and stood there facing me.

"Carol gasped. She feared the worst. She said in her most authoritarian voice, 'Darren, don't you even think about touching that girl. Anyone can see she's just a slut. Guys, let me up. I'm leaving. I don't want to look at her.' But the other two boys just continued holding her down. The boys were all first team football players for their school, all offensive linemen, and all strong and virile. Carol wasn't going anywhere. She initially put up some resistance, but seeing that was futile, she sat back in her chair and assumed a look of disgust. I think she tried to convince herself this was all just a joke.

"Then Darren put his arms around my neck and I put my arms around his waist. We closed our bodies together and French kissed long and slow.

"'Jesus Christ, Darren, what do you think you're doing with that ho? You stop kissing her or we're through. Stop this minute.' Carol became alarmed. She seemed repulsed by anything erotic.

"The boys continued holding her down, and Darren and I didn't stop. He competently, deliberately unfastened my bra. I was impressed by how smooth he was. Then he kissed my nipples while I rubbed my fingers through his hair and held his head close to me, pressing his face into my beautiful tits with their upturned nipples and my special secret scent.

"Carol screamed, 'Stop, Darren! That's enough. I order you to stop. If you care about me, you'll stop this right now.' At that point, I unsnapped my teddy and slipped out of my panties. I undid Darren's belt buckle and pulled down his pants. Then I put his cock into my mouth. I started sucking Darren just three feet in front of his steady girlfriend.

"Carol pleaded. 'Darren, don't. Sex is special and beautiful. It's not something you do with just anybody. Darren, don't do this. I want you to stop. She doesn't love you like I do, Darren. Stop!'

"Then I stood up from sucking Darren's cock. It was already rock-hard. I could tell this was going to be a wonderful experience for him and for me. Miss Passion surged hot in my loins, Miss Shameless felt a tinge of joy to have her naked ass in front of Carol's face, and Miss Iniquity gave a lift to my heart knowing I was trampling the feelings of this ridiculous prude. I French kissed Darren long and passionately and held his body tightly against mine. Miss Love entered my mind. I adored this boy and wanted to give my whole self to him. I rubbed my

THE SECRET AND THE BUTTERFLY

pussy against his leg, and then I kissed him softly on his forehead and on his eyelids, gently squeezing his balls with my hand. Miss Lust began to salivate. I could hear Carol squirm in her chair, but the boys continued holding her. She was going to sit there through the whole show. The thought flickered through my mind that Carol had the best seat in the house. I felt very naughty, but wonderfully sensuous and very sexy. Miss Determination entered my mind and told me I was doing everything right. She told me to do more of it and not allow myself to be deterred from seducing Darren.

"Miss Iniquity teased Carol while I held him in my arms and swayed my body back and forth, rubbing my pussy against his cock. I said, 'Darren, sweetheart, Carol wants us to stop. Would you like me to stop?' I gave him another deep French kiss and rubbed his cock suggestively with my hand, softly stroking it and gently pulling on it. I spoke again, mocking Carol. 'Your girlfriend says we need to stop, Darren. Should we listen to her?'

"I French kissed him again, holding the kiss for a long time while I took a deep breath and shoved my chest hard against his. I continued stroking his cock. Then Darren squeezed my ass with both hands and I began softly kissing his eyes. Then I put my tongue on his nipple and followed that by kissing him on his neck. I whispered to him, a low, lusty whisper that Carol could hear. 'Carol says we need to stop.' Miss Lust was in my mouth at that point and she had no intention of stopping.

"I dropped to my knees, took his cock into my mouth again, and began sucking him off. 'Carol says we need to stop,' I said playfully as I fondled Darren's balls and continued sucking his cock. Then I spoke to his cock. 'You don't want this naughty girl to stop, do you? I bet you'd like to find out what it's like inside this naughty girl's pussy, wouldn't you?'

"Darren's cock was incredibly hard. I stood up and gave him another French kiss before I asked him in a teasing way, 'Do you want me to stop, Darren? Maybe you need to obey Carol. If I'm not what you want, Darren, I can stop.'

"Carol screamed, 'Take me home, please. Take me home now. I don't want to be here. Don't make me watch her kissing him. Please let me out of here.' That's when Miss Iniquity and Miss Determination instructed me. They told me not to pay attention to that stupid bitch in the chair. They told me they felt wonderful when I hurt her feelings and told me to stay focused on making love to Darren no matter what she did or said.

"Then I French kissed him again and squeezed my body tight against his while I fondled his testicles. 'Should I stop, Darren? Should we stop for Carol?' I laughed a little from my belly and smiled my most inviting smile. Misses Happiness, Iniquity, Lust, Superiority, Intimacy, and Love all became dancing nymphs in my imagination. They skipped and frolicked naked in a circle around Darren, kissing him, teasing him, touching his cock, pinching his nipples, rubbing their fingers in his hair, and putting his tongue into their cunts. They all wanted Darren.

"Darren said, 'No, don't stop.'

"'Carol,' I said, not looking at her, but continuing to fondle Darren's balls while I rubbed my pussy against his leg. 'Darren doesn't want me to stop. I think Darren likes what I'm doing. I believe Darren is falling in love with me, Carol.' I went back down on Darren and sucked his cock again, all the while kneading his balls softly, lovingly. Miss Promiscuity introduced me to Miss Touch and her sensitive fingers. She was happy to join us and fondle Darren's cock and balls.

"Then I stood and rubbed Darren's cock against my pussy while Carol looked at the two of us, horrified. I guided the head of Darren's cock into my inner lips. My cunt was hot to receive his cock. She was so slippery and anxious to get Darren's cock inside her, it took all my willpower to hold myself back and complete the entire routine I'd planned for Carol. She started crying and begged Darren to stop. But, of course, we didn't stop.

"I moved to the nightstand at the head of the bed and lit three aromatic candles. They had the scent of lilacs. I love lilacs. Then I pushed the Play button on my CD player and turned the lights out. My naked body was silhouetted by the glow of the candles. I went back to Darren, embraced him tightly as if I were holding my grand prize, and French kissed him again, long and slow as Bette Midler's 'When a Man Loves a Woman' began playing softly. As the words 'He'll give her everything that she needs' floated in the air, I fondled Darren's balls. I felt them churning. Miss Lust told me he was making semen for me. It always excites me when I feel balls making semen for me. At that moment, a feeling from Miss Love came over me. I realized I loved and needed Darren. I had to have him to complete myself as a woman. I lusted for his semen inside me more than anything else in the world.

"I led Darren onto the bed with me. It was a firm mattress, the kind I do my best work on. He was anxious to become a man and I was ready to help him. I put two feather pillows under my head and tucked one under my bottom. My pussy was elevated to Carol's eye level. She watched us and began crying openly. Miss Iniquity reveled in the mental torture my cunt was visiting on Carol. I next spread my legs widely and held my pussy fully opened with both hands. Miss Shameless assured me she was the most beautiful thing Darren had ever seen. Miss Lust pulsed inside her, craving Darren.

"By then I'd had my upper thighs tattooed to look like the wings of a giant Monarch butterfly. My pussy formed the body of the butterfly, and when I spread my legs open, the effect was priceless. Every boy who saw my butterfly and scented my pussy wanted to put his cock inside me. It was a terrific advertising promotion.

"Darren stared at my pussy. He salivated to come into me. Miss Lust took him by his hand and brought his cock over my cunt. Carol was shocked and mortified by my shameless display, but I was determined to give no thought to her sensibilities. All I cared about was pleasing Darren and letting him know I wanted him.

"Just as the words, 'He'll even leave his best friend' floated in the air, I said, 'I'm ready, Darren.' My pelvis lifted my pussy. She reached upward and outward for him. She yearned for him. Miss Lust urged my cunt toward Darren as she urged his cock toward my cunt. I opened my arms to hold him and beckoned him to come inside me.

"I said, 'I'm ready for you, Darren. I want you. Come inside me and make love to me.' I was so anxious to fuck Carol's Darren, I tingled in anticipation. He was about to become my Darren. My skin flushed and became hot from my rushing blood like it did that time in the movie theater before I fucked the twins. Thousands of tiny fingers tickled the surface of my skin. My skin was alive with lust for Darren. Little tiny sweat beads prickled my forehead. I anticipated how wonderful I was going to feel when his cock slipped inside me. I salivated. I couldn't wait to fuck him. I was already thinking of sucking the last drop of semen from Darren's cock after we finished fucking. I was in a world of my own. Miss Determination blocked all thoughts of Carol and everyone else in the room. I was totally focused on fucking Darren. He focused on fucking me, and his friends focused on watching us. Miss Love told me I could have Darren all for myself and that he wanted to escape Carol's clutches and fall in love with me. He wanted to forget the insane world of Goody-Two-Shoes Carol and surrender all his love to me.

"'Oh man, fuck her, Darren,' one of the boys urged.

"'Oh God, she's beautiful. You just have to fuck her,' seconded the other boy.

"Carol stared at my pussy like she'd seen her worst horror movie and cried out, 'Don't do it with her, Darren. Please don't do it. Don't fuck her, Darren. She's just a slut. Don't do this to me. Please wait for me. Save yourself for me, Darren. It will be special if you wait. Pleeeease, Darren, don't. If you love me at all, Darren, don't do this. I'm begging you, please don't.' Carol then cried deeply from her stomach. She brought a handkerchief to her eyes in the vain hope that staunching her tears would somehow relieve her aching heart. Her world was being destroyed before her eyes.

"I took Darren's cock in my hand and rubbed it gently, lovingly, around the outside of my pussy. His shaft was rock-hard and straining to plunge into me. I could tell he was feeling the same wonder I felt. We both had that glorious, anticipatory sensation just before penetration. My heartbeat quickened, and I felt by the strong pulsing in Darren's cock that his heart was racing also. Then Bette's words lifted us to another world as her voice repeated the song's refrain and strengthened. 'When a man loves a woman.'

"I pulled Darren's cock head ever so slightly into my pussy, letting it feel the inside of my inner lips. He could feel I was hot, slippery wet, and anxious to fuck him. Then I gently guided his cock all the way, deeply into my pussy. He was oh so hard! He had a splendid cock. It went way in to my very depths, and then Darren let out a groan of happy escape from Carol's puritanical idiocy. I never felt a man so immersed in happiness like Darren was at that moment. I French kissed him and held him tightly while he fucked me in front of Carol.

"I softly whispered to Darren, 'You're home, baby. You're with me now. We are one. You're safe with me, Darren, and I love you.' That seemed to solidify his complete surrender to me and me to him. Carol choked back a scream. We drove her crazy.

"After Darren's initial power thrusts, the two of us settled into steady, rhythmic, slow, sensuous fucking. It was the kind of fucking where every part of my pussy felt the smooth gliding strokes of Darren's cock. He was a very good, giving lover. He appreciated the love only a woman can give a man. He moved his shaft around and rubbed his penis against all my walls as he plumbed my depths. I fell in love with that boy.

"At that moment, the first song on the CD player ended. I followed it by a violin orchestra playing 'Here Comes the Bride.' Darren immersed himself in me when the violins began playing. He hugged me tightly, squeezing me close to him as if he'd never let go of me. I loved his passion. He French kissed me, squeezed my tits, and then put one hand under my ass and pulled my pussy up into his groin, ever so tightly against him. We were engulfed in rapture sex. We were in our own private world, right there in front of Carol and his two friends, as if we were married and it was our honeymoon night. No one else mattered to us then. Darren loved me and I loved him.

"Darren did his utmost to please me. He was so hard and tender with his loving penis. It was a wonderful fucking experience. I've never felt happier for myself or the man I was with than I was that afternoon. I was a woman satisfied.

"I put my hands behind my head and lifted my head on the pillows. I looked at Carol and smiled in happiness and satisfaction. It was a smile that proclaimed to her that I was completely content with who I was and what I was doing. I was in heaven. I smiled at Carol for the longest time. Miss Happiness felt the need to share my joy with her, even though she loathed everything about me. I then rubbed the back of Darren's neck and brushed my hand over his cheek.

"Finally I said, 'Darren didn't want to stop, Carol.'

"Carol sobbed the whole time. That titillated me. I had my long, sweet orgasm as the violins played their melody at the completion of the wedding ceremony, when the bride and groom leave the chapel. As the violins, trumpets, and piano burst out their proclamation of the union of man and woman, Darren and I both burst into orgasms. We had our union! It helped me continue a long, gushing orgasm knowing Carol watched in deep distress. But I couldn't feel sorry for her. After all, to achieve a great relationship with a man, often a woman has to first break his old relationship. That's just what fairness in love is all about. Miss Iniquity mocked everything Carol represented. She had no concern for Carol's feelings.

"When Darren shot his prodigious wad of cum, he pushed hard into me. He heaved against me like a bull that wanted to drive me through the bottom of the mattress. He kept shooting and shooting. I thought he'd go on shooting cum into me forever. His stream was so strong and continuous I felt like he had a fire hose that streamed endless cum. I loved every second of his prolonged release. I rubbed his back and praised him. I French kissed him again, long and passionately.

"When I felt his cock starting to soften, I pulled my pussy hard against him and gave his cock a long Kegel squeeze while I reached under his testicles and pushed upward into his taint. That's the soft spot between the anus and the penis. I calculated correctly. There was a vestige of semen holding there. After I pushed up on Darren's taint, I gently squeezed his balls. My pelvis gyrated against his shaft and I thrust my pussy hard against him.

"My efforts were rewarded. A final gush of thick, creamy cum pulsed out of Darren's cock. He sighed from exhaustion and total satisfaction. I continued French kissing him as I wrapped my arms around him and stroked the back of his neck. It was a glorious moment, what Darren and I did that day. Miss Love kissed him sincerely. Real feelings can't be withheld. I always keep my customers satisfied long after they come. It's important to keep long-term relationships.

"I praised Darren's performance and whispered to him, 'That was beautiful, Darren. You can fuck me whenever you want. I loved having your wonderful cock inside me. I'll never be able to get enough of you. Please call whenever you want me again. I'm here for you. I love you, Darren, and I will always love you, and I truly do want you.'

"I believe in telling my lovers that I love them. It makes the experience more enduring and less clinical. Every man needs love. They're like little boys who need a mommy substitute. The expression on Darren's face was priceless. He looked awestruck and dazzled in wonderment, as if he fell into an Elysium field with a sex goddess—which, of course, he did.

"Carol bawled, snot running down her nose like some sloppy two-year-old toddler. Her words came choking between breaths. 'What did you do, Darren? What did you do? How could you? I loved you so much.' That outburst from her pissed me off. She lost him because she acted like a horse's ass, and she was trying to make the poor boy feel guilty about finding happiness. I wasn't about to let her get away with it.

"After Darren finished, he kissed me on the cheek, like a boy might kiss his mother. Then he rolled off me, completely spent. He looked up at the ceiling, ignoring Carol. I took his weary cock into my mouth and sucked its last drops of semen into my mouth while I squeezed his balls. I took everything he had into me. He groaned from exhaustion.

"At that point, I sat up and then knelt on the bed facing Carol. I cupped my hand under my pussy. I was so full of cum it felt like I was the Hoover Dam holding back Lake Mead. I captured a large pool of Darren's white semen in my hand, and then I rubbed his cum all over my tits. I put some of it in my mouth and basked my tongue in it. I loved the taste of Darren. I showed Carol the underside of my tongue with semen in my mouth. Darren's semen was in my pussy, in my mouth, and on my tits. I tried to help Carol understand her new reality. I wanted to slam her face into a wall, but I restrained myself. After all, a whore can still behave like a lady.

"'This is what Darren did, Carol. Can you see what Darren did? Look at all this wonderful cum Darren shot into me! And, Carol, he did it so very well! He's got a wonderful cock. He's magnificent. He made me feel wonderful, the way a woman wants to feel. The way a woman should feel. I hope Darren calls me again. I want him to call me. I need him in my life, Carol. I want him to fuck me often. I love him, Carol, and I love fucking him. I'm going to fuck him all summer long. Thank you so much, Carol.' I spoke sincerely.

"I noticed the two other boys staring at me with awestruck looks. I had Darren's cum smeared all over my stomach and breasts. Long, dripping cum streams, like strings from the egg whites of a dozen cracked eggs combined with droplets of white cake batter, reached down in descending tendrils of procreation from my pussy onto the bed sheets. The slow, gravity-pulling drip of the strings mesmerized Darren's two male friends and horrified Carol. I smiled at the boys while Darren's cum drip continued for what seemed like an eternity. I did nothing to wipe up, just let it flow, drip by drip.

"And I continued staring into the boys' eyes, smiling at them, inviting them. I captivated those two boys with my wanton display of lust. Their eyes moved ravenously between my eyes, my smile, my semen-covered tits, my spread legs, and the cum stream dropping from my pussy. The boys' breathing became quick and shallow. They both repeatedly licked their lips. Reluctantly, they slowly stood to take a shaken Carol home. It was obvious they had huge hard-ons pressing against their pants. They wanted me too.

"I said to them, 'If you boys would like to be with me after you take Carol home, I'll wait here for you.' I smiled my special welcoming smile. Their eyes widened at the thought of coming back. Their spirits skyrocketed and they nodded excitedly.

"'I'd love to share intimacy with you boys. The thought of you both together with me like Darren was excites me beyond words. I promise you'll enjoy it. I'll be here for you.' With that, the boys took Carol out of the room. They helped her stand and steadied her out the door. Instead of taking her home like they'd promised her, they just took her to the concierge and called a cab for her. Then they returned to my hotel suite. They were hot to fuck me. They didn't want to keep me waiting and I wanted to oblige them. After all, they'd helped me and Darren.

"I French kissed them, sucked them, and fucked them both for a very long time and completely emptied them just as I emptied Darren. They were delightful and glorious. It wouldn't be right for them to just sit there, watch me fuck while holding Carol down, and not have any fun themselves. I never had so much cum shot into me than I did that night.

"I thought about the way Darren's friend first approached Jimmy with the idea of sex and realized a lot of men are shy about asking. Ever since that night, whenever a boy or man I desired asks me if he could have sex with me or if I'd like to go with him somewhere and fuck, my response now is to immediately take him by his hand or to kiss him on his lips. That establishes an immediate bond of intimacy. I then respond by saying, 'Yes, of course you can. I hoped you'd ask,' or 'Yes, I'd like that very much. I'm so glad you asked me.'

"Then, when we're at the place where we'll be having sex, I immediately give my partner encouragement and reinforcement. I press my body to his and give him a long French kiss and rub my hand over his cock. I then undress and say my magic words. 'I'm ready.' Men go crazy when they hear their woman say she's ready. Those words summon them like it's their call to duty.

"That night with Darren, Carol, and friends was a wonderful, special night for me. I realized I could be in love with many different men at the same time and thoroughly enjoy fucking each one of them without feeling guilty or possessed by any of them. I was exhilarated by this new revelation. Men were my love, per se, and fucking was my uninhibited expression of love. I was serendipitous about that evening. It was a delightful, fantastic success. I made three new boyfriends who positively adored me. All three became my regular customers. I stayed in the room after the boys left and lay on the bed naked, staring at the ceiling and gently rubbing my clitoris. I felt the boys' cum ooze from my pussy onto the bed and relived every moment of the experience I just had. I felt complete peace and satisfaction with myself and my path in life. There was no tension within me, only wellness and tranquility. I wondered how long I'd wait until I heard from the boys again.

"As it turned out, I didn't wait long. They called the next day. They wanted me every weekend for the next month. They postponed and rearranged their schedules to meet mine whenever there was a conflict and never once groused about it. As luck would have it, they were all from wealthy families and payment was never an issue. They booked me for sailing excursions to go to Easton on the Eastern Shore with them where one of their families had a huge estate on the water, complete with servants. The boys wanted to pamper me, and did they ever!

"I sailed with them and sucked and fucked the three of them those entire weekends and went dining with them to some of the country's finest restaurants in Cambridge, Easton, Chestertown, Annapolis, and Baltimore. The boys gorged me on blue crab cakes and soft-shelled crab.

"Annapolis was and is my all-time favorite place in the entire world. When we were there, the midshipmen were out on leave wearing their white uniforms. They are without doubt the handsomest, smartest, most virile young men on the planet. I was a budding nymphomaniac seeing an endless supply of eye candy. That was the night I had my revelation dream, when I knew I had such a strong addiction to sex that I was possibly mentally ill.

"I was falling asleep that night in Darren's arms, but I kept thinking about all those midshipmen. I remembered a study I'd read that concluded the average male has a penis that is five and a half inches long and four inches in circumference when fully erect. As I dozed off to sleep, I imagined that, in addition to high academics and athletic abilities, the midshipmen each had to take a special examination of their penis sizes to ensure that the Academy's reputation for extreme masculinity remained intact.

"Every midshipman had to have at least an eight-inch penis to be admitted to the Academy. I mentally calculated that, based upon an average nine-inch penis size, there was over a half mile of cock inside the Naval Academy. As I slipped off to sleep, I fantasized I was lying in bed in a drag house, one of those homes where the middies keep their girlfriends. There was a long line of four thousand midshipmen standing outside the house. They all took their turns coming into my bedroom to fuck me.

"During that night, I dreamed that, somehow, all four thousand midshipmen penises became united into one giant-sized penis. It was the size of a main water pipe. I was trying to get my head into a good position to suck off the tip of it. My legs and arms were wrapped around it as I clung underneath it floating six feet over my bed. Just as I got my mouth to the open end of it, a huge wall of pasty cum came gushing through the pipe. I swallowed all of it that I could, but I was over-whelmed by this tidal wave of hot, tasty cum. It filled my stomach and then gushed over my face and hair. Then it spilled over my entire body, drenching my blouse and skirt.

"I was drowning in pasty, savory, erotic cum in my dream when I awoke in a puddle of sweat. I was breathing hard and my heart pounded like it was about to burst from my chest. My pussy was wet and hot, and I desperately craved sex. I felt like a female cat scratching the walls. I was possessed by this ravenous craving to shove a hot, fat, slimy, giant cock into my pussy. I wanted this imaginary cock to impale my pussy, to thrust into me, to lift me upon it like I had my cunt stretched over the top of the Washington Monument. I was nuts with lust.

"I panted with insane desires. There was this incredible intensity about it. Seeing those men in whites made a total mess of me. I shook Darren awake in the predawn. I sucked him hard. Before he was fully awake and able to understand what was happening, I began fucking him. I absolutely had to fuck at that very moment. I had this urge I couldn't control. I was in heat, crazed out of my mind for sex. Poor Darren didn't understand why I was the way I was. I'm glad he didn't ask questions. He just obliged me and performed very well.

"I fucked Darren with a wild, frenzied intensity. I couldn't waste time with foreplay. I screamed 'Yes!' dozens of times and fucked with a ferocity I never knew I had within me. I continued my wild abandon past both our orgasms until I finally collapsed onto Darren from exhaustion. I smiled from gratitude knowing Darren was there when I needed him. If I were a kitten, I would have purred. Darren just laid there with his softening penis inside me and patted me on the back, hugging me like I was a baby. He knew me by then. He understood my needs and was tender about it. He never made fun of me or mocked me. He just loved me. He understood I'd surrendered to unbridled nymphomania.

"It took me days afterward to stop thinking about fucking those men in whites. I don't trust myself to ever go back there. I'm afraid I'd throw myself on one of them right there in broad daylight. I don't believe I could help myself. I fear that erotic dream would come flooding back and I'd lose control of myself. A girl with a healthy libido shouldn't be allowed anywhere near Annapolis.

"Another weekend, the four of us went to Ocean City, and again I sucked and fucked my way through the entire weekend. One of the boys' parents had an oceanfront condo with an oversized king bed and a balcony overlooking the ocean. We, all four of us, spent hours on that bed with the balcony doors open. I loved the feel of the ocean breezes on my naked body while I made love. Darren became obsessive about licking my pussy while I sucked off the other two boys. They all took turns fucking me in the maiden position, with a pillow of course, while I sucked the other two. They became a fuck family with me. I was their constant sex partner. I remember how they all loved kissing my nipples. Eventually, the other two boys also got into licking my pussy. I was having perpetual orgasms. They couldn't get enough of me. They even gave me backrubs and rubbed my feet and massaged my legs. They wanted me in tip-top shape for fucking, and I really was!

"We spent many summer afternoons sailing on the Chesapeake Bay. I had my favorite selections on my CD player. As we sailed along, I sat in the boat's cockpit with my skirt lifted above my waist. The boys licked my pussy and fucked me as we skipped along past other boats. My music favorites, especially 'When a Man Loves a Woman' and Wagner's 'Bridal Chorus,' and Mendelssohn's 'Wedding March Recessional' played often that summer, as well as love songs from Elvis, Sinatra, and Barbara Streisand.

"I fucked and sucked my way over a thousand miles of beautiful water that summer, with seagulls hovering over our boat and gentle breezes filling our sails. We moored off islands, went ashore and camped, and I had orgies with all my boys many nights. We were like crazy wild dogs and I was their bitch in heat.

"The boys arranged a place for me on the boat's forecastle. I had a kapok-filled pillow, a soft canvas mat, and tie downs. Many times, when the boat was tacking to windward, I laid naked on my mat listening to my music playing with my legs spread wide apart. Semen from the boys' ejaculations oozed from my pussy while I lay there on the bow. That white cum flow displayed my uninhibited sexuality and made those boys crazy to fuck me more. It also felt wonderful and natural. I loved the stimulation of cool bay breezes blowing gently into my cunt and caressing my body. The sun and breezes relaxed me after some great fucking and excited me about getting fucked all over again.

"The boys were always thoughtful and protective of me. When I was resting on the bow, one of them always sat next to me, watching over me. The lookout boy, as they dubbed the forecastle station, was ever ready with a blanket to cover me in the unlikely event the water police saw us. That never happened, thank goodness. Those exhilarating windward tacks usually lasted a full hour or two. So there I was, bow maiden with legs spread wide open, as if my glorious pussy were the prized trophy for those three boys. They revered their prize. They thrilled displaying me to passing boats.

"I didn't care. I just laid there with my pussy taking in the breezes. Sometimes I'd look up, and smile and wave at their friends. None complained about guarding me. Each one of them took the opportunity to sit close to me, massage my temples, and kiss me about my eyes and face. I knew all three loved me. A woman can tell when she's loved. On the forecastle, when I wasn't fucking, the duty lookout boy fondled my tits. All three loved massaging my nipples. I got endless stimulation and I loved it. I think it was on that boat that I became open and uncaring about being an unrepentant, sex-crazed, mindless nymphomaniac.

"We experimented using the rhythm of the swells and the chop of the waves to enhance our sexual pleasure. The sloop had a large middle bedroom amidships aft of the galley with a queen-sized bed. The lift of a swell raised my pussy effortlessly into the boys' cocks, and the swell drop at their bottoms drove the cocks deeply into me. On some tacks when the waves got choppy, we took advantage by fucking while sitting upright with my legs wrapped around my boys. The wave chop acted like a natural vibrator. It was all so exhilarating. Since then I've always looked to Mother Nature to assist with lovemaking experiences.

"I was in this euphoric stupor of perpetual arousal while on that boat. It's impossible to describe how wonderful it was. I was getting continuously fucked, licked, fondled, and massaged by those three boys. I had serene thoughts. It was magical. 'We sail over endless water under endless skies. I'm fucking while my music's playing. It's all so exciting and erotic, but fucking to the soft sounds of wind and water makes me feel at one with nature, and I'm starting to like lovemaking better that way. Maybe I'm becoming a free spirit girl who likes to fuck when surrounded by nature.' I think the boys liked lovemaking better with the music off as well. That way there was no distraction. Which boy I was fucking and the trim of our boat were the only things on their mind. I was often near dizzy from my euphoria and close to exhaustion, but I loved every minute of it. I'd love to look them up someday and relive that summer with them. I was in heaven on earth, or on water, and wished that summer would never end. I was truly blessed to be discovered by those three boys.

"It's probably a professional blessing that those boys pounded my pussy as hard as they did. I felt some irritation after a few days with them, so when we were in Annapolis, I stopped in a drugstore and picked up some KY jelly. I've used it ever since. My pussy is always a smooth, slippery, velvet glove ready to envelop a penis shaft. By taking away irritation and staying lubricated, there's almost no limit to the hours I can fuck. It's gotten so that now, when I don't have a cock thrusting inside me, I feel like there's something abnormal about being without. Having a cock plugged into my pussy just feels natural and right.

"The boys were always loving and considerate, always pleasing me in every way imaginable. They also referred four other boys to me. They were true gentlemen and completely unselfish. After that summer, they went on to win their high school divisional title. My boys—the center, Darren; left guard, Brian; and left tackle, Phil—provided the offensive power that dominated the line of scrimmage.

"'Venimus, vidimus, vicimus, they announced to me after they won first place. 'We came, we saw, we conquered!' They told me my pussy contributed to their victory. It was the bonding and teamwork they'd developed over the summer. One boy was always pumping cum into me even while another boy's cum was still oozing out. I was their melting pot. They lovingly called me their cum blender. We were sworn fuck buddies forever!

"That fall I was chosen as their high school's homecoming queen. The boys told me they voted for me because I was the best fuck, the most often fucked, the most beautiful, and most beloved girl from both my high school and theirs. At that point, I officially became their trophy girl. My cunt made me famous! My picture was in the two local newspapers. I was smiling and waving to all the boys and holding several dozen red roses. I also achieved notoriety that year. My phone in the dorm rang constantly. That's when I knew with complete confidence that I was going to be a highly successful whore. My pride was unbounded.

"During that memorable summer, I learned something remarkable about Carol. She went home that night I made love with Darren and became catatonic. She didn't leave her bed, nor did she eat anything for three days. She developed an eating disorder and became anorexic. She told her friends she broke up with Darren, but never told them why. I guess she was embarrassed about her own inadequacy. I was shocked that watching me fuck the love of her life affected her that seriously, but I didn't try to figure her out.

"Miss Iniquity entered my mind in a special intimate dream that explained everything to me. She appeared to me as a gorgeous red head. I often have dreams about her. We were naked and we French kissed feverishly. We went down on each other and gave each other wonderful orgasms. When we finished, we lay side by side and she whispered to me. 'You did a wonderful thing for Darren. Be proud of yourself. Carol spent years developing her relationship with Darren. She invested her life in him and she loved him. You destroyed their relationship and their love in just one hour of glorious whoring. I love you for that. There's a beautiful, irresistible evil about you. I can't get enough of you. I am with you always. Hold me close and never let me go. We are one and the same. Whenever you have doubts about whom you are or your power, have your mind come back to me and kiss my lips. Feel the way you feel at this moment. You will be courageous enough to repeat your performance with Darren whenever you want with whomever you want. Always remember we sisters of evil are entitled to our rightful place in the world. We are just as important to humanity as the forces of righteousness. God himself loves us and blesses our role. Embrace and cherish what you did to Carol as the unstoppable progression of humanity.'

"Carol was everything good and moral and honest love, but she was like water going past us, sliding down the side of our sailboat and slipping into our past. Everything she represented drowned in the ocean of my iniquity. My pussy triumphed over her antiquated Puritanism and became exalted by those three boys. They figuratively left Carol in their water wake without a lifeboat. They never spoke her name again. My cunt purged her from their minds. Fucking me became their sole obsession that summer. That fall when I heard she was seeing psychiatrists, I broke into a laugh. I couldn't help myself. What she really needed was a good fucking, but she'd never understand that. She was such a fool. I have no idea what ever happened to her.

"When I heard about her catatonia, I realized when I fucked another girl's boyfriend, I'd likely have a devastating effect on the girl's psyche and self-esteem. I never forgot that lesson. Adult women behave no differently than Carol. They just hide their emotions a little better. The lesson I took away from my experience with Darren is, if a man wants to have me, it's important for me not to hesitate or get myself into a mental quandary about it.

"The advantage of his desire is already mine, and it's a huge advantage. I learned I just need to cut through the pretenses and fuck him. And yes, fall in love with him, and not worry about the consequences of offending his wife or girlfriend. I believe morality must, ultimately, be each person's own subjective matter. I love to liberate men who need me and have the courage to come to me, and I believe making love is life's highest moral calling.

"I learned something else during those years. Once I seduce a man and put his cock into my mouth or my pussy, he'll try his best to give me anything I ask for. The case in point was my plane geometry teacher in eleventh grade. I was flunking the course and I needed to get a good grade to become a senior. I noticed he looked at me a lot during classes, and I suspected he knew about my extracurricular life. After class I went up to him at his desk, put my hand on his arm, and just rubbed slightly. I asked him if there was anything I could do to improve my grade. I was almost seventeen by then and I had more experience in the bedroom than most women twice my age.

"Sure enough, my instincts about him were spot-on. I was soon going to his home while his wife and kids were away and fucking him and performing fellatio on him right in his wife's bed, right in front of the pictures of him with his wife and kids. That teacher loved to perform cunnilingus on me, and I learned a lot from him about how to relax and be receptive to his tongue. He was good at it. I already knew it was important to keep my pussy fresh, clean, and properly scented. I continued experimenting with perfumes and oils until I had the perfect fragrance and tasty lubrications coming from my pussy. It's those little extra touches I do that drive men wild and place me above ordinary whores.

"I was determined from early on to become one of the most successful whores in the world. Being with that teacher, working with him on scheduling our rendezvous, that's when I realized that most married men desperately need to be liberated from their marital obligations, at least for occasional periods of time. They just yearn to get relief from all the stresses and responsibilities a wife puts on them. I think it's because men are just larger versions of little toddler boys who depend upon and love their mommies.

"Once Mommy is out of the picture and the boy is an adult, he still has that deep need for Mommy's unconditional love. His marriage gets dull. His love for his wife is unrequited, so what does he do? He returns to Mommy, only Mommy is no longer there for him. He's supposed to be a man. He is a man, but psychologically speaking, he is still a toddler. He must have that unconditional love. So here is an adult man in desperate need of Mommy's unconditional love. He desperately wants to return to Mommy's womb.

"The only way to get back there is to crawl into her pussy, but he can't do that. He's outside and grown now. His head won't go back in there. It doesn't fit! So he does the next best thing. Actually, he does something even better. He sticks his dick in a pussy! All men's brains are in their dicks anyway, so this is what comes natural to them. Understanding this male drive helped me with my geometry teacher. He needed unconditional love. He needed my pussy. That teacher pushed his kids and his wife away, made up all kinds of lame excuses to get away from them to free up his time to be with me. He got to the point where he was willing to risk wife, kids, and career just to have his pecker and tongue inside my cunt. He also helped me discover something else many married men have.

"He had a secret contempt for his wife. It was obvious when he dressed me up in her dresses and had me lie on her side of the bed. Then he'd pull her dress up above my pussy, and he'd bunch up her bed pillow under my ass. He loved it when we fucked like that. I felt his deep penetration in that position and the pussy fluids from my orgasms squirted out of me and dribbled onto her sleeping pillow along with his semen. I don't know whether she ever noticed or if her pillow stains and smells became an issue for them, but I didn't care. I thoroughly enjoyed myself, and I learned that fucking with a pillow under my ass is positively glorious. It helps me wrap my legs around a man and pull him tightly into me and rock his body over my clitoris while we fuck. I learned a lot from that teacher.

"He also liked to sit me on their kitchen table. He positioned me on a gorgeous decorative pillow she'd made. It was a hand embroidered one she made with frilly white lace and beautiful, intricately stitched pink roses on its cover. Embroidery was his wife's favorite hobby. He placed the pillow under my tush and sat me on the table at the place she took her meals. Then he spread out my legs and stood where her chair would be. He knelt down and licked me softly, titillating my clitoris until I released an orgasm right on that pretty rose flowered pillow. Then we fucked.

"There I was my legs widespread and my pussy where her plate was when she ate her meals. My fluid squirts and his cum soaked into her lovely pillow. I actually felt remorse for what we did when I looked at those pink roses with my orgasm fluids and his cum stains on them. I could tell she worked hard to sew those intricate rose petals on that pillow. Miss Iniquity told me that if I wanted to become a world-class top whore I had to lose those sentimental caring impulses.

"Maybe he wanted to spite her by fucking me on her artwork. He never said. He always held me close and tenderly after we fucked and told me how much he loved me and how beautiful I was. I suppose his vision of an appropriate place mat for his wife's meals was my cunt squirting orgasms on her beautiful artwork. I don't know what was happening between them, and I didn't want to know, but I loved fucking him.

"I could only imagine what was going through his mind when he saw his wife getting into bed and putting her head on her pillow, or when she slipped into some of the dresses we lifted over my head while he fucked me, or when he saw her sitting at her place at their kitchen table. Thoughts of me fucking him had to race through his mind because of the association of our sex acts with those places in their house. The memory of my cunt was everywhere he looked. I'm sure my cunt was perpetually on his mind. He often told me how he adored my cunt, how he loved to lick her, how he couldn't wait to get his cock into her, how juicy my cunt was compared to his wife's dry hole, and how he woke up in hot sweats after dreaming about me. He was obsessed for sure. My cunt was his mommy substitute and refuge from his wife and kids.

"I knew my cunt positively dominated their marriage. You have no idea what a thrill it gave me as a young girl having carnal relations with an older man, having controlling sexual power over my geometry teacher. I was on cloud 9. He became so obsessed with me that he left his wife and kids for entire days and weekends, just to be off somewhere with me. He didn't even bother making excuses to them anymore. He just told them he needed to leave.

"When we were in class, he'd sneak quick looks up my short skirts at my open legs. The first time it happened, I teased him into looking up my skirt by sitting with my ankle over my opposite knee. He was standing with his back to the class writing a geometry theorem on the white board. Midway through the theorem he turned, facing the class to explain where he was in the proof. That's when his eyes riveted on my pussy with her widespread butterfly tattoo. She leaped out at him. I didn't wear panties.

"He stopped talking midsentence and sat down at his desk. He just sat there for a long moment saying nothing. He brought his fingertips up to his temples and began slowly massaging them. Then he said 'That's where I want to stop for today, class. Quietly read the rest of the theorem in your textbooks and the next three pages for the rest of the class period. We'll pick up where I left off tomorrow.' The rest of the class didn't understand why he stopped mid-proof. They just began reading. Meanwhile teacher continued sitting there. He was paralyzed by thoughts of my cunt like a small animal immobilized by a scorpion's sting while the insect's poison seeped into its nervous system and brain. I watched, as a scorpion would as its poison took effect, while his thoughts of licking and fucking my cunt shut down his reasoning processes. I watched his lust for my body course through his blood.

"I didn't study my theorem. I studied him. He had very strong arms and huge hands. I could tell he wanted me so badly he actually salivated. He'd lost his ability to think. When the bell rang ending the class period he said 'Miss Maloney, would you please stay for a moment?' Two periods later, school let out. He picked me up in his car three blocks from our class building and took me to a motel. Once inside our room, he told me he loved me. Then he kissed every inch of my face, tore off my clothes and forcefully thrust his cock into me. He became like a wild animal consumed with desires to mate. I loved having him like this. We French kissed passionately and our hands touched each other everywhere. He was a wild torrent of unleashed raging heat. I responded in kind. I met his thrusts with violent thrusts of my own. He squeezed my ass hard with both hands. I loved it! He was a total animal. We fucked until I drained every drop of cum from him and he lay by my side, his chest heaving from exhaustion.

"He was beautiful. He had a steel jaw and wavy, dark hair and dark eyes. As he lay there, I ran my fingers through his hair and kissed his closed eyelids. He kept telling me how wonderful I was. I lay on my side and softly ran my hand over his wiry chest. I played my fingers on each of his nipples for a while until they were very hard. I could tell he loved to be touched. His wife must not have touched him much. My hand naturally found its way to his testicles. As I kneaded his balls with my hand, I kissed him again on his closed eyelids. Then I asked him 'Do your nipples and your balls make an isosceles triangle?' When he responded yes, I asked 'Did I earn a passing grade for this extra instruction period?' He assured me I was his best student and I'd get a fabulous grade.

"Then I held him tightly in my arms like he was my little child. He repeated how deeply he loved me. He told me he knew he shouldn't be involved with a student, but he loved me so much he couldn't give me up. I told him everything was all right and reassured him that I loved him too. I told him everything about our relationship was wholesome, natural, and beautiful. I promised I'd never tell on him. I told him he could trust me and that he was always safe with me. In the back of my mind, I heard Miss Shameless tell me she was thrilled with my brazen behavior. Miss Iniquity held me in her tight embrace, kissed me, and whispered, 'I idolize your iniquitous whoring and congratulate you on your recent conquest. You are my mirror image now. When I see you, I see myself and I love what I see. I love everything about you. You've done everything I would do. This man's married life and career are completely beholden to your money requests. His heart and soul worship at the altar of your cunt. When you hold his balls in your hands and his cock in your cunt, realize you have the power to crush his life if he displeases you. Also realize that a few words from you to his wife would devastate her and shatter her world. Know that you own their lives and you may do with them as you please. Way to go, girl!'

"I felt deliciously wicked inside. I succeeded in my goal of attracting and seducing my teacher, then wrapping him in dependency on me for sex. He was like a fly captured in the web of a spider. But I was a loving spider. I wrapped him tightly with my delicate, loving threads of endless sexual favors. I loved him. I understood then how strongly men were attracted to my beaver shot, how quickly their dreams of sex with me will displace their trains of ordinary thought, and the incredible risks many men will take to be with me. I'm convinced my butterfly tattoo amplifies the effect of my beaver shot. It sends an unmistakable signal to a male that I want him to come fuck me.

"I received an A in that class. I had the most fun ever in school, earning my A that way. I got all the test answers from my teacher the week before, and when I still screwed up a question, he wrote 'I believe you meant this' and wrote a big A on the paper. Smarter kids than me got B's and C's. That teacher later paid me serious money for the privilege of fucking me all through my senior year, long after I'd earned my A. I even got extras like perfumes, exotic panties, silk stockings, camisoles, and sweaters.

"A lot of whores thinking back on a relationship like I had with that teacher would conclude he was an asshole, but I never felt that way about him. He was lonely inside and he needed me. Our love affair was a life changing experience for me. Most kids feel their graduation marks the beginning of an adult life. My adult life began when I seduced my teacher. I graduated from boys to men. I discovered that the intensity and depth of a man's feelings greatly overpowered anything I ever knew before. He knew how to command my body. He melted me and I could never get enough of him. It was so easy to surrender to him; I wanted to do everything he asked of me. Pleasing him was so important to me. I was a whore just beginning my career and I wanted every second he spent with me to be special for him. I still have flashbacks about our romance and the wonderment of my seduction of that teacher. It was all so beautiful. He was beautiful and I was beautiful. He had such big strong arms and hands. He liked to seat me on his lap and hold me in his strong manly arms. Then he'd touch me all over and kiss me. He fondled my tits and kissed me for the longest times before we made love. I loved his hands on me and how he liked to play with my boobs and kiss my face. He'd reach his big hands down into my panties, spread my legs and work his fingers around and inside my pussy. I loved that too, absolutely loved every second of it.

"I was no longer a silly student girl but a woman being held in a man's arms. I knew what I was doing had to be hurtful to his wife and kids but I didn't care. Our pleasure was more important to us than morality or second guessing. What we had together was so delicious, oh so beautiful. We would hug and kiss and play together like the first man and woman who ever met on Earth.

"I remember it all so well. I already had my woman's body but he was able to bring out this inner rapture that I held bound up within my feelings. He took my feelings from a girl's to a woman's. When his fingers made my pussy begin to moisten and swell, I would hold his head in my hands and kiss him all over his face. I would kiss his eyes, lips and forehead while I ran my own fingers through his beautiful hair and massaged his magnificent head. Then, when I was ready I would put my mouth against his ear and titillate it with my tongue. I remember how I used to giggle when I told him that my butterfly was ready to flutter. That was his signal to take me. He'd hold my ass with those huge hands of his, slip his cock into me and we'd go into a kind of fuck frenzy. In just a minute's time we'd both be gushing orgasms all over everything, over his wife's pillows, her artwork and her dresses. We were free from any thoughts of consequences. We just drank in our pleasures. Then, we'd get our strength back and settle down and fuck slowly and sweetly for hours.

"We blocked the rest of the world out of our minds. We shut out his wife and kids, the school, everything. I still get a burning desire in my breast to be held in his arms again, just like the way we were then. It was my first time with a real man and I was proving to myself that I was a beautiful desirable whore that could have real men falling in love with me. Here I am years later and I still find myself falling asleep nights imagining I have his manly arms tightly wrapped around me and his big hands holding my breasts. I was completely, madly in love with him. I was lost in that love, absolutely consumed by it. I lived that entire year on cloud 9.

"My seduction shattered his inhibitions about being with a student and it dispelled any hang ups I had over becoming a career whore. Our passions transcended societal norms and took us to some higher magical place. We didn't care what anyone thought or suspected. Nothing mattered to us except our feelings for each other. We fell into this bottomless abyss of obsession with each other and our love. I tremble inside with happiness for him and myself whenever I think back upon that lovely wonderful year. I learned to never get judgmental about a man's human needs or why he is like he is. All men need someone to love them. I learned to provide that service for a price and put my whole heart into it. I get intimate and personal with all my men and I learn all I can about them. They are real people and real lovers. I crave their closeness and the warmth of those relationships. I've sought out married men to be my lovers ever since. They are always grateful for the relationship, they pay very well, and they are extremely discreet."

"How many men have you had, Marty, and how many were ready to leave their wives for you?" David licked his lips while staring at Marty's pussy. He then leaned forward and once again kissed her upper thighs close to her butterfly tattoo. He behaved like a priest at an altar ritual, paying homage to the cunt nestled between the wings of the tattoo. His kisses were gentle love pecks of worship and deference, as if he was awestruck by the powers of the goddess before him. He appeared to be praising Marty's cunt and blessing her thighs for their seductive accomplishments.

"Oh, if you count the times I was at boarding school and college, and all the tricks I did with Jimmy's help, I'd guess I've had around three hundred different men in my lifetime thus far. And quite a few of them, like the twins, the football players, and Jimmy and that teacher, I've fucked many, many times. Why, I'll bet I've fucked those twins, the football players, and Jimmy easily a hundred times each. I know it sounds like a lot, but I was a very active young girl and it was easy for me to fuck four or five different guys in one night during my dormitory years. The twins, Jimmy, and the football players each had many days when they fucked me several times a day. It's not like I wanted to take time off from fucking. I didn't. I got to where I just lived to fuck. I couldn't get enough sex. I was making great money and I loved fucking. I've become addicted to fucking, and now I almost go out of my mind if I'm not fucking. It's what I live for. I can't help it.

"I often tell myself I'll stop my nymphomania, but it's very hard to control an addiction, David. And believe it or not, the relationships I've formed are very solid. A lot of my lovers stay in touch with me and they care about me. Take Donny for instance. I still get a Christmas card each year from Donny, my first lover. He is so sweet. He always includes his phone number. I know I could go back to him any time I wanted, even though he's married now."

"Do you find it hard to translate your sex drive into sales when there's a wife in the picture?"

"The wife usually isn't much of a problem. When I have a really great salesman, it takes me a while to get him to the point where he's willing to throw away all he's built up over the years. Occasionally those affairs get messy because the wife often has a lot invested in him and she doesn't want to give it all up. The wives will call the salesman's firm, the owner, the branch manager, whoever she feels close to and cry her eyes out to someone. The wife looks for a sympathetic ear to try to get someone on her side, to try to get someone to help her stop me, to keep me away from him, but that never works. The thing about a really great salesman is he has an ego. He feels he deserves the best. When the wife reacts by trying to enlist others to save her husband, that behavior by a panic-stricken wife only makes the man want me even more.

"When a wife tells a great salesman he can't have me, or he must choose between me and her, that's a fatal error for her because great salesmen feel they should have anything they want. That's when I know the wife is playing out of her league. That's when I get brazen. I tell him he has to prove himself even more to me because I don't want to have to deal with the distractions of a wife and kids. If he wants to keep seeing me, I demand more sales from him.

"I let him know in a subtle way that I want him to take me on a trip to someplace far away from his wife, and that I'll fuck him all weekend long. But to afford my time away from the office, he has to give me double his sales from the last month. A great salesman loves a challenge like that and a reward for performing. At least ten salesmen have told me they'd leave their wives and families for me if I'd only agree to marry them, but I never agree to that. That would end my sales career. A great salesman can get very possessive, so I'm always careful to waltz away from marriage. Right now there're four men who are telling me they'd throw away their wives and families to have a life with me."

"That's really impressive, Marty. You really know how to gain their loyalty. I like that about you, always have. But do you ever feel any remorse for the destruction of their family?"

"No. That's never my problem. That's always the wife's problem. She had to know the nature of the man she married. If she didn't know, then she was just stupid. Stupid people just fall behind in this world. They get weeded out. If I weren't fucking her husband, then someone else would be fucking him. No, that's her problem, not mine. Now, when it comes to the children, I figure the guy already conceived them and he's always going to be obligated to pay for them, so he's already done his part. The woman raises the kids anyway, so what he does with his life after he conceives them is his decision. If he'd rather be off fucking Marty than being at home pitching baseballs with his son or watching his little girl doing a piano recital, well, that's the man's decision. I never question that decision. I always honor it, either way.

"I have no feelings for the little girl who's missing her dad at her recital because he'd rather be off somewhere fucking me, and I don't feel like I've lost anything if he decides to ditch our plans to be with that little girl. I know he'll come back to me when he's ready. What angers me is when a wife tries to jerk me around and interfere with my work."

Just as Marty began explaining to David how she dispatched an irate wife, a beautiful Monarch butterfly flew into the barn and attached itself to the door frame above the hay bales where Marty lay with her legs widespread for David. The butterfly seemed to listen for a while. Then it closed its wings and rested for the night. Marty and David continued talking while the butterfly dreamed of its migration to Mexico.

"So what got you interested in having orgies, Marty?"

"That was Rita's doing. She's a girl I met shortly after I came to Plaintown. She was looking for a partner girl to do a short nudie movie. Anyway, I answered her ad for a partner, and I've known her ever since. We went on to doing sports teams together, but I've pretty much separated from her. She started doing really kinky stuff for big money.

"She fell in with this group of real weird guys who had her sucking anthropoids, you know, monkeys. They'd tie up the monkey—they even had an orangutan once—tie up its arms and legs so it couldn't move and then have Rita suck it off. The monkeys went crazy wild for it. These guys got a kick out of watching it. They thought it was hilarious to watch a monkey having an orgasm. Then they fucked Rita afterward. She told me they also got this pony. They pretended Rita was Catherine the Great of Russia. They put her on this huge bed and had this pony rigged up on pulleys and they lowered it over her and had her suck it off. Somehow this one time they made sure they got all the piss out of it and they had Rita stroke it really hard, and then they tried to get its cock into her pussy. It didn't work. The pony wouldn't cooperate. I can't believe Rita let them try that kind of stuff. I don't know if they'll try it again. That's a whole other story I won't hear until I see her again.

"Rita's a really sweet girl, but she needs money badly. She'll do practically anything for money. She's pretty, but not beautiful like me, so she has to do the kinky stuff to make enough to get by. I, on the other hand, have a well-established high-end, sales-based clientele and I can be selective. I don't do cretins or guys who are perverts. I also avoid smelly men who don't bathe properly. Well, I have made a few exceptions to that. When nymphomania overwhelms me, I will take on some rough guys sometimes, but usually not. After all, I am a woman with extremely high ethical and moral standards. I have my reputation to consider."

"Marty, forgive me if this question makes you feel uncomfortable, and you don't have to answer it if you choose not to. I'll understand. I'm just really curious if you've ever made love with a black man, or if you avoid interracial sex?"

"Oh, David, don't be silly. I told you I wouldn't hold anything back. I love making love with black men. I also enjoy sex with women. I don't have any hang-ups when it comes to sex. In fact, I still book myself with Rita for her orgy parties when I have a free weekend or evening and our schedules mesh."

"Can you tell me what it's like, having sex with black men?"

"Sure, David. Actually, having sex with black men is my most stimulating sex. They're so loving and sensitive. They appreciate a woman much better than white men do. I love to have orgies with them. Let me explain what it's like, and how they make me feel like a total woman."

"Yes, I find this whole area fascinating."

"Well, first you need to visualize the setting. I like to have at least five black men fucking me during a single orgy, but I prefer to have seven or eight men. That way I can totally release all my passions for them. First I welcome them to my body by French kissing all of them, putting my tongue deeply into their mouths and using my tongue to play suggestively with theirs. When I can feel they are ready to fully enjoy me, I like to start the fucking by sitting on the first man with my back to his face while he's lying down. I suck up his cock to get it hard, and then I guide it into my pussy. Now I'm lying near the edge of the bed or a table when I do this. Next I like to have a second man stand at the edge of the bed. I spread my legs wide and hold my pussy open for him and I insert a second cock into my pussy above the first cock. Now, I'm fucking two cocks with my pussy. Are you following this?"

"Yes, of course. Go on."

"Well, here's where the black men are so wonderful and loving. I next have a man kneel down on the bed with his knees planted under my shoulders. Then two other men kneel on the bed with their cocks next to my head. The man who has my shoulders upon his knees massages my shoulders and the back of my neck. He's very loving and gentle and unselfish. His fingers pull up on my neck muscles, stretching them. This is incredibly relaxing. He also softly rubs my temples and caresses my forehead. This helps me immensely because it honors and glorifies the act of giving blow jobs and fucking simultaneously. The whole experience transforms me into a modern-day temple goddess, put here on earth to glorify nature and human feelings by fucking and sucking my black lovers for hours on end. I totally love this indescribable, otherworldly feeling the orgies give me. While my masseuse works to keep my shoulders, neck, and head relaxed, I begin sucking the cocks of the two men who are kneeling beside me. These two also squeeze and massage my tits and suck my nipples and finger them between their thumbs and forefingers. As you can imagine, I'm getting stimulation that is out-of-this-world glorious and wonderful. But the sexual act and the positioning of bodies is actually the smallest part of it."

"What else happens?"

"Well, besides all the men taking turns in the different positions, and each of them licking my cunt until it throbs ready to burst into a volcanic orgasm, I do what I like to think of as a transformation of the nature of the orgy relationship."

"What do you do?"

"It's not complicated, David. I talk to them like men like to be talked to and I tell them the truth. I tell them how I feel."

"Go on, please."

"Well, for starters, I constantly tell them they're beautiful because they *are* beautiful. I tell them how honored I am to know that they want to fuck me, and how wonderful they make me feel when they are fucking me because that's truly how I feel. It's beautiful. It's the most wonderful thing any white girl could ever feel. I believe that. I tell them to keep fucking me and to never stop fucking me. I tell them I want all of them, everything they have to give, and to not hold anything back. I tell them to squeeze my ass and my tits. I tell them I want their tongues in my pussy and licking my clit. I let them know I want to take all of the semen they have into my pussy and into my mouth. I want their cum gushing out of my cunt and drooling out of my lips. I want them to rub their cum all over my chest and tits. I tell them how much I love having their cocks in my mouth and how delicious it tastes to have their balls in my mouth. I let them hear me talking to their penises' heads as if they were real people, which to me they are.

"I tell their penises how much I love kissing and sucking their beautiful heads and titillating their circumcision line with my flickering and caressing tongue because I know that is so erotic and sensuous for their adorable penis heads. It makes their cocks swell ever harder. I tell them I love it when their penises shoot cum into my mouth because I truly do love it. I tell them I love squeezing their balls and sucking all the remaining cum out of their cocks after their first shot of cum because I do love doing that so much. I tell them how much I love swallowing every last drop of their semen and how wonderful it tastes because it's the truth. I tell them that I'm taking their life essence away from their wives and girlfriends, that what they have to give is mine now and no other woman's. I tell them that because I feel it's true and believe it's true. I believe I'm having the most unforgettable experience I've ever had when I'm in the throes of an orgy, and I tell them that. I tell them that they please me beyond anything I've ever known. I tell them that because it's true.

"All the while I'm fucking and sucking these beautiful men, my mind and all my bodily movements are silently saying to them that I truly love them, all of them, and I can be completely relaxed, uninhibited, and erotic through the whole orgy because I do honestly love them. As I'm thinking about my love for them and their gorgeous cocks, I'm all the while being caressed and massaged about my shoulders, neck, and face, so I'm feeling like I'm loved more than any goddess ever was loved. But then I do something to forever impress upon them how special they really are."

"What's that, Marty?" David was astounded at her insatiable lust for the penis.

"I tell them that whenever they feel lonely, whenever they feel their woman doesn't appreciate them, whenever they want to be loved like no other woman can love them, to call me. I tell them I'll make myself available for them just as soon as I possibly can and to wait for my call. I tell them that I understand that it's hard for them to love their woman after they've been with me and they shouldn't expect their woman to adore them the way I do because other women just aren't capable of feeling the same lust for their beautiful bodies that I feel. And I believe that's true, so I tell them."

"But aren't you afraid you'll cause them to leave their wives or girlfriends when you tell them that?"

"No, why should I? The color of a man's skin doesn't require that I concern myself about his home life. If he wants to leave his wife or girlfriend so he can be available to me, to fuck me more often, that is his free will choice."

"But what about the families of these men ending up with broken homes, children growing up without a man in the house?" David seemed to have sudden empathy for the human condition, something Marty hadn't observed before.

"I couldn't care less, David. If a black man would rather have his hands on my lily-white tits than on his wife's tits, if he'd rather squeeze my beautiful, tight, white ass with his massive hands than holding his wife in them, if he'd rather have his mouth French kissed by mine than by his wife's, if he'd rather have his beautiful black cock in my mouth or in my pussy than in his wife's, that's his business. How his wife deals with it doesn't concern me."

"But what you're doing may cause a child to grow up without a father."

"Oh, David, don't be naive. I've already been the catalyst that broke up several black marriages. I don't lose sleep over it. Actually, I feel a certain evil, joyous thrill in being the home wrecker. You already know that about me."

"And you have no feelings for the fatherless child?"

"No, I don't. Everybody in this life has to play the cards they're dealt, David. Let me make something very clear to you. I am a woman who has no morals, David. I have no sense of moral duty to others, none. You knew that when you hired me for marketing. I told you the truth about myself. You told me you wanted a whore to go out and bring in sales. You set me up to make a lot of money, and I brought in a lot of sales by fucking my ass off.

"You can't now expect me to have a sense of morality or feelings of guilt, David. I lost morality and feelings for those I hurt back in boarding school. I choose to live my life as an amoral whore, and I love my life. The only love I feel is for the passions and lusts of the physical sort, the love I feel for whichever man or cock I'm fucking or sucking at the moment. I am in this life for my own pleasure and the money only. I love to fuck. I love sucking cocks and swallowing cum. I love orgies. I love destroying other women's families.

"I believe the whole concept of family is just a farce from the get-go anyway. If some little girl gets hurt in the process of me taking her father away, that's just that, a little girl's tough luck. The kid will just have to deal with the fact that her daddy would rather fuck me than be with her. I simply don't care one wit about the kid."

"Marty, you are both beautiful and amazing. What I like most about you is you're clearheaded about who you are. How are you planning to give up these nymphomania cravings when you marry Bob, or are you planning on continuing to have affairs and orgies after you're married to him?"

"Bob's very special, a very special man. He needs to be in love with a woman, and love happened for Bob and me. He's the only man I've ever felt I could love and care for the rest of my life, so I have some real mixed feelings about that issue. I don't ever want to hurt him, and once we're married, I will never do anything to hurt him.

"I'm hopeful that after we are married and he gets to know me, gets to understand me and my feelings, and once I'm sure he has no inhibitions and he can love me totally for who I am when I'm expressing my feelings, and once he understands my deep need to have this glorious thrill, this peak intensity of nirvana I feel when bonding with other men through the orgy experience, then I hope and pray that he'll want to join with me in that experience. He already understands that I really love to make love with him, and by joining me as I release all my passions and exhilarations through orgies, I have faith that he'll see the joy of it and he'll learn to love me all the more."

"And what about some of the other lovers you have?"

"Well, I've given that a lot of thought. I can't live without Carl in my life. He's so good to my clitoris, little Gloria would never forgive me if she couldn't have Carl. He's developed wonderful techniques with his tongue and Gloria is thrilled out of her mind with the way his tongue caresses her. He gets his head down very low on my pussy, and then he uses the underside of his tongue to slowly massage little Gloria. It's sensational. It's better than having a slippery, velvet glove just slowly, lovingly coaxing her to enjoy herself and take all the time she wants. Carl is extremely patient.

"Most men approach oral sex like their mouths are the human replica of a mechanical vibrator and they hammer little Gloria with rapid tongue movements, like there's some kind of urgency to get the job finished. Not Carl. He's so much the opposite. He loves to have the underside of his tongue caressing Gloria because he loves me. It's an expression of complete love, totally unselfish love. When Gloria erupts into orgasm while the underside of Carl's tongue is embracing her, I completely lose my mind and enter a euphoric state. I'm so enraptured by the sensation Carl is giving Gloria that I want to pull his entire head up into my cunt and keep him there inside me forever. The sex is that good. It's a feeling that comes over my whole body. It's not a feeling from this earth, or like anything else in the world. It's a spiritual feeling, a heavenly feeling, and it lifts me up into the universe and I become part of eternity. I can't get enough of that feeling.

"Most men just want to climb onto a woman and shoot their rocks off. There are only a few good men who really know how to love a woman up so she feels like she's part of eternity. I guess it's kind of like the Marine Corps. There are really only a few good men in this woman's world. A woman knows the difference between getting fucked and getting loved when she experiences it. Thankfully, I've been able to work with Bob on his oral sex techniques as well as his penis techniques. Now Bob is every bit as good as Carl when it comes to oral sex with Gloria. Now I get that feeling with both Carl and Bob. That's why I want them both."

"I don't understand, Marty. If Bob's oral sex is every bit as good as Carl's, why do you need Carl after you've married Bob?"

"Oh, David, this is the crucial difference between a man and a woman, especially a woman like me. A man can have sex and he's good for a week or at least a few days without sex before he feels he needs it again. A woman can have sex every day, even several times a day, and she still wants more sex. Ever since boarding school, I've gotten progressively more and more accustomed to having sex as an integral part of my life.

"I've embraced my condition of nymphomania rather than trying to fight it. Whenever I try to fight it, I know in my deepest heart that I can never stop my craving for more sex. So, David, looking at it from my perspective, I have this deep human need to have Gloria licked and to have a man fucking me almost every moment I'm alive. Sex is my reason for living. If I have two men who know how to give Gloria great oral sex and then fuck me so I orgasm twice with each man, then I can possibly have four orgasms in one day. That makes me feel wonderful and complete as a woman. If I had more men who could kiss Gloria the way Carl does, I'm sure I'd include them as well. I'd make love every minute of every day if I had the stamina to do it. I believe every woman on earth should have at least two lovers who know how to perform oral sex with them just as Carl does with me."

"So two men are better than one? You look at your lovers, your men, as commodities, like two ounces of gold are better than one, am I right?"

"Well, yes, but the tongue and the techniques of cunnilingus are only the first part of the lovemaking I need from a man.

The penis is so very special, such a wonderful gift to a woman. That's where Carl and Bob separate themselves from all my other lovers. That's why, after marriage to Bob, I need to find a way to keep fucking Carl no matter what. Carl is such a wonderful, unselfish lover. He's twenty years older than Bob, and Bob could learn more patience to become as good as Carl.

"In time, I have confidence that Bob will be a perfect lover, even better than Carl, possibly, but Carl really gets into rhythm with me and his techniques are what set him apart. It's like, after our oral sex, Carl slowly runs his huge, hard penis along my outer lips until I start to throb and gush inside all over again. I just go out of my mind crazy when he first penetrates me, when that huge shaft starts slipping into me.

"I just can't give Carl up. Whenever I think of him and his hard, monster-sized penis, I get so moist my panties dampen. I can't wait to gyrate with my pelvis while his huge penis is inside me. I orgasm so easily with Carl. He can stay hard for me while I just keep coming like my orgasm will never end. I could never give him up. The man adores me, loves me no matter what I do, no matter that I have other lovers. Carl lives to give me pleasures and make me happy. Every woman should have a man like Carl in her life, even if that man isn't her husband.

"There are a few other men I can't give up either. I'm their only relief from their miserable home lives, and they love me very much. It takes years to develop healthy male relationships like the ones I have, and those relationships are a special part of me. They are who I am. My lovers will all understand my situation, and I'm sure they'll all work with me, work around my married life schedule. I'll just have to manage my logistics and make sure everyone is discreet about their times with me. In a funny way, I have to believe that by having extramarital liaisons, I'll be that much more sensuous with Bob. No man wants a deadpan wife who doesn't enjoy being fucked in her own bedroom."

"Tell me this, Marty. Have you ever considered renouncing your life as a prostitute and pleading to the cross for forgiveness, lest your soul be condemned to damnation? I mean, is there any chance that you could change your ways?"

"Ha! No, David, never! There's no chance of that. Long ago when I was in the movie theater with the twins, I heard a voice from my sister soul mate, Miss Promiscuity. She told me to be unafraid of sin and wrongdoing. Our other sisters, Misses Shameless, Wantonness, and Iniquity helped me discover that the path of godlessness and evil was right for me. I swore an oath to my sisters to love them as they love me and to follow the path I chose. I praise and give thanks to them, not to God. I could never forsake them or the ways they have taught me. That would be to betray my very soul. Evil and debauchery have been wonderful to me, David. I love the good life it brings me and I enjoy the powers it gives me over others. I don't concern myself with dreams of an afterlife. I believe that is the realm of simpleminded fools. No, David, I am in my soul a whore in love with whoring. I will never change."

"Marty, that's beautiful. Thank you for helping me to understand you better."

"Was there a second thing you said you wanted to cover, David?" Marty recalled that he had two things to ask of her before she earned her necklace.

"Well, yes, there is. Please hear my proposal to you. You see, Marty, I've looked at you from afar as an ugly, older man who wishes that just once in my lonely life I could know what it's like to make love to you." Marty's eyebrows went up hearing that. Before she could speak, David continued. "Wait, let me finish. You see, I run the company kind of like a feudal kingdom, and I try to do my best to look out for people because I care about them.

"Well, in the olden days of feudal kingdoms, the lord of the fiefdom had the right to be the first lover of the women in the kingdom who were about to marry. So, I'd like you to honor me, just this once, and let me make love to you, right here in the barn. I promise you that, if you'll do this one little thing for me, the diamond necklace will be yours, a 20 percent pay raise will be yours, and Bob will never hear a word about it. It'll be our secret, and I promise no one else will ever know. Please, just do me this one honor as a loyal subject who is adored by her lord. Just humor me this one time."

Marty thought for a moment. She pitied David some. He was short, ugly, and smelled repulsive. She could just imagine his frustrations with never having had a beautiful woman.

"Making love to me would really mean that much to you, after all I've told you about myself, after knowing what a calculating, immoral whore I am?" she asked with a bemused pity in her voice.

"Yes. It would mean the world to me for the rest of my life. Just one time is all I ask. Please grant me this one simple request."

Marty thought some more. She'd promised Bob she'd marry him. She really should say no to David, especially since he and Bob were so close, but she rationalized that she'd soon be back with Bob in the company by David's good graces. Refusing a man who just gave her a diamond necklace was foolish. She'd been with numerous other men before and performed all sorts of sex acts for far less compensation.

I promise myself this will be the last time I open my legs for any man besides Bob, at least until after he and I are married and he consents to my participation in orgies. I'll soon get my income back, and Bob will never have to know this took place. And I'll look and feel so triumphant and glorious at my orgy parties wearing those diamonds! The diamonds will raise the bar for every man who wants to be with me, even for Bob. Men will beg on their knees to fuck me! Rita will want me at least twice a week! Yum!

"Okay, David, let's have some fun." Marty giggled with her winsome wide-mouthed smile. She was so enthralled with the thought of wearing the diamond necklace, she was now anxious for David's penetration. She thought to herself that she'd probably never be able to stop being a whore, but at least with Bob as her husband she could be a whore who was in love with a man for all the right reasons, as a true life partner.

David arranged a second heavy blanket over the hay bales. He asked her to assume the doggie position because he didn't want his bad breath to offend her. He'd planned this moment perfectly. As Marty bent over, he summoned Muscle Boy to come around from the side of the barn to take his place. Muscle Boy was bisexual. He was glad to accommodate the wishes of David, his master, and happy to act as David's substitute for the chore of fucking a woman.

Marty was anxious for David to enter and was pleasantly surprised by the hardness and sheer size of the cock that probed her outer lips. Soon Muscle Boy found her vagina and quickly penetrated her. He thrust his huge cock into her as if he were a stallion upon a mare. It was beyond wildly satisfying for Marty on many levels. There she was, fucking David, or so she thought, getting paid a bonus to rejoin the firm, and getting a diamond necklace and a floppy-eared rabbit. Could it be, she wondered, that she would become David's female bitch whore as well as Bob's wife? Could it possibly be that David had such a splendid cock that would service her occasionally right in his office, perhaps when Bob was out of town, or better yet, while Bob was in his office, making sales calls on the floor below.

Muscle Boy gripped his hands upon Marty's shoulders and pulled her tight against his cock. She twisted her neck around and recognized to whom the giant cock belonged. She saw she wasn't fucking David. He was standing aside and slightly behind Muscle Boy, taking in the scene.

He was obviously pleased to see her getting ravaged by the brute with the beastly cock. Muscle Boy grasped her hair and lifted her head with his pull. Her back arched upward and her pelvis canted slightly skyward. Now Muscle Boy's penetration was complete. The rock-hard, throbbing cock shoved deeper into her than any cock had ever gone before. The feeling was intense, electrifying. She loved it and wanted more. She couldn't think about why David switched Muscle Boy for himself to do the fucking. It made no sense based upon David's previous claim that he wanted her. But now her logical mind shut down. She'd think about that later. Right now, her libido was in the on position. She was having the greatest fuck of her life and she didn't want to stop.

Marty closed her eyes. She knew she was having fabulous sex. She breathed deeply while Muscle Boy grunted and strained behind her, giving her every measure of his splendid, throbbing cock. His exertions brought to her memory her first experience with orgies through her meeting with Rita Hernandez. Her thoughts drifted to an earlier time and place. She was lying on her sun porch that day, perusing the paper, when she noticed an ad from a modeling agency. Specifically, it sought white girls with dark hair. Ordinarily she'd just toss the paper away, but she thought, *Why not?*

At least she could confirm whether or not she had "the look." Rita wanted her right away, that very night, to join her in making a short clip for a porn movie. They'd be fucking some black studs for about twenty minutes, and they'd get paid five hundred dollars each. She felt like experimenting, went along with Rita to the porn shoot, positively loved the whole experience, and never looked back. Her face was never shown in the video clip, so she was free to live her dual life. Rita booked her for orgy parties and soon they were in demand from sports teams visiting Plaintown.

While in the throes of an orgy, Marty proclaimed she was the liberating goddess of oppressed souls to her black male partners. Her exhortations served to skyrocket her into great demand. She beseeched her lovers, smiling and giggling the whole while, making light of their hang-ups about white people.

"I am here to release you from the evil, shameful destruction heaped upon you by my white forefathers. I am your pathway to freedom from the resentments and bitterness you hold against the white race. I am here to show you a better way, a better place in your hearts, a place where all of us know love, understanding, and acceptance.

"Cast aside your gods of the past. Forget the teachings of those who tell you that one tribe is better than the other, those who tell you to harm others who are outside of their own belief system. Cast them out, for they are evildoers who seek to sew strife among us, who seek to destroy love. Those who exhort you to war upon others do not make war themselves. No, they just hide behind you beautiful men and urge you to give them your power by making you do their bidding.

"Shun them. Their teachings are dung piles of nonsense. Cast them aside. They have no power over you. There is no glory in death. There is only death in death. Is a dead bird glorious? Does it fly to heaven? Of course not! There is only glory in life. Those with evil minds fear you will open your eyes to the beauty of life. They are not God. They do not speak for God. They are cowards."

Her opening lines always took them aback. They couldn't tell if she were serious or if she were a nutty broad jesting with them. That's when she'd begin to wiggle her hips and ass in front of them. They knew they were in for a great time when she got suggestive.

"My pussy is your new goddess. She is here to show you the way and share her love with you. Come and worship my beautiful pussy. Lay your troubles upon the altar of her throbbing clitoris. Venerate her glory with the praise of your semen streaming into her Holy of Holies. Feel the rapture of your heart beating close to mine as we press against each other in our union of love. My pussy comes to you and with you as the voice of all white women who want you to join with them in lovemaking. Together we rise above the shames of our forefathers."

As Muscle's strokes became more rapid, Marty's imagination drifted to another place and time. She dreamed she was once again the centerpiece of a wonderful orgy. She was hostess to eight male partners, all of them young, strong, black men from a visiting basketball team. They had beautiful bodies and handsome faces, and all of them were eager to get their penises inside her, to give their sexuality completely to her, holding nothing back. Yes, they had to be blacks in her dreams and fantasies. Her experience was that black men were so much stronger and had far greater endurance than whites. Their penises were longer and they swelled up so marvelously to such a wonderful hardness.

She imagined two of them were sucking her nipples and squeezing her breasts while rubbing her sides softly with their free hands. The eroticism of their titillations was making her moist and eager to receive the others. She was being held up by another partner who had his hands propped under her ass, squeezing her behind like he was holding up a basketball as he kept her positioned two feet above the floor. She was stroking the scrotums of the two of them who were standing beside her, sucking their penises alternatively in her mouth.

Two others spread her legs and held them apart, rubbing her inner thighs and massaging her feet. She was relaxed, anxiously anticipating their penetrations. Another orgy partner began licking her vagina. His tongue flicked over her clitoris, arousing her to an even greater height of eagerness. They were all experienced lovers, and she was anxious to fuck. She wanted all of them so badly she couldn't contain herself any longer.

The first one to enter was a beautiful man of about twenty years of age. As she received him in the maiden position, she could feel the hot blood of his penis coursing through it, making it pulsate and swell to an incredible hardness. His strokes were slow, methodical, gentle, and beautiful. She loved this man and canted her pelvis upward, rhythmically moving her hips to receive all of him into her wet, throbbing pussy. Her mind and hands worked in harmony with her hips as she concentrated on the penises in her hands. She imagined she was performing on stage, holding the penises, flicking her tongue over their eager heads, coaxing them ever higher to their hardest erectness.

Her fingertips massaged their scrotums, beckoning their sacs to swell with semen with the promise and anticipation that their shafts would soon be inside her and their hot payloads would be discharged into her. She dreamed she was hearing the Puccini Opera, *La Boheme*, as she suckled her partners' penises. Her head and lips moved rhythmically to the music, reaching an explosive eroticism as the opera moved from the "Alcindoro" to the climactic "Sergente dei doganeiri."

As the full opera chorus burst into their forte finale, her passions and her lovers' capitulation to her reached their simultaneous climax. She squeezed down with a gentle, encouraging force on her first partner's sac. He responded beautifully, swelling to the music, the opening of his vascular tube like that of a flower stem in the throes of piercing through its leaf sheaf to first reveal itself to sunlight. She felt his throbbing head in her mouth as the semen rushed up the shaft. It shot up in a bubbling fountain of white life's procreative essence atop its proud, strong, yearning black column.

She was so proud of him. She licked his penis head and curled his semen into her mouth, savored it and then swallowed it. She continued to suck the head as her hand pulled upward upon the glorious shaft. More sperm erupted, which she greeted with her partially opened lips. She swallowed his second offering and kissed his throbbing penis head with a grateful reverence for his power.

As the music continued to resonate in her mind, she turned to the second penis and performed her glorious, loving fellatio upon it as she had the first. As she sucked, her second lover's penis hardened noticeably. Her mouth and the music had coaxed his hot blood into his organ stem with such pressure its veins stood out along the glistening shaft as if they were straining to contain an explosion. When he shot, she felt his force hard inside her mouth as the penis strained and pulsed, releasing its powerful stream. Her mouth filled to overflowing and semen ran down her cheek and chin. She gathered it up with her hands and rubbed it on her breasts and chest.

She looked up into the faces of her two swains. Their eyes were full of awe and lusting for more of her. Her hands went to their chests and she pressed her palms hard against their hearts. She could feel their strong heartbeats; they were both excited and eager to have more of her. She spread her legs wide apart and positioned two penises into her pussy, one from a lover lying beneath her and one from a lover entering her as she presented to him in the maiden position.

She imagined for a fleeting, erotic moment that she was Tosca, from Puccini's opera, willing to kill Scarpia in order to escape and run away with her lover Caveradossi. She remembered the beautiful aria from the scene and dreamed of being with her true love. Her imagination returned to her lovers in her orgy. No one would ever take them from her. They looked into her eyes and swore to her that her eyes were more beautiful, her hair was more lustrous than even Tusca's, and they wanted her forever.

She took each lover by his arm and pulled them close to her face. She began kissing them full on the mouth. She gave them searching, inviting, lustful, sensuous French kisses, running her tongue deep into their mouths, rubbing her tongue over theirs, her first lover, then her other. Enraptured by their releases and entranced by the music, she held their sacs in her hands, looked into the eyes of both of them, and declared herself to them, "You are beautiful lovers and I will love you both forever. We will make love often."

These two men were splendid specimens of masculinity. She wanted to feel them inside her as well as having had them in her mouth. She squeezed their testicles and bit down lightly on their penises. They responded beautifully, both returning to their fullest hardness. Only black men could exhibit such marvelous stamina, she thought. That's why she loved fucking them so much. One of them lay on the floor below her. One lover had just spent himself, his semen still oozing from her onto the bed, and her newest partner now inserted his penis into the bottom of her vagina. Now there were again two penises inside her and she was thrusting her pelvis as she moved her hips to help them stroke her vaginal cavity. The upper penis was gliding smoothly over her throbbing clitoris, causing it to swell and sending a flood of endorphins into her brain.

She was rapidly reaching her wild, uninhibited, shameless, lust-craven, frenzy of orgy, an insanely driven quest for harder, more rapid penis thrusts into her vagina than ever before, pushing her over the edge of sensuality, beyond her earlier euphoric state. Her heart pulsed and her breathing quickened as her exertions increased. Her maiden-positioned lover shot a stream of hot semen over her clitoris. She came to orgasm in response to the hot flood. More white cum and hot juices from her pussy trickled onto the bed.

Another lover took his place and began gently thrusting into her pussy. Her clitoris continued throbbing in its swollen state, her orgasm offering her juices onto the newest cock that titillated her clitoris. Tongues and penises entered her pussy and made their rounds like visiting bees entering and caressing the opened petals of a fragrant rose, each trafficking in pollen dusts from its predecessor, each stimulating fresh releases of fluid squirts and erotic pheromone scents. Her thoughts drifted away to the subliminal world of euphoria and Elysium meadows, and her conscious thoughts departed to a place she could not retrieve them. She was getting the attention she needed to quench her souls and the sex she craved to slake her carnal lusts. For Marty, fucking was ecstasy.

She began fondling the scrotums of the two beautiful men who had been sucking her nipples, all the while meeting thrusts of penises with thrusts of her hips. Her actions were automatic by that point. Her mind was in the stupefied world of never-ending sex, and all she could still comprehend was that she had to have more of all of it. A ravenous need beckoned her every action and took complete control of her. More cocks, more tongues, more touches, more penetrations, more semen, more kisses, and more slaps and squeezes became her demanding quest.

She took turns putting first one of their penises in her mouth and sucking it and then the other. Both of them were very hard. She could tell they were eager to be inside her vagina. Then her maiden-positioned lover, the one who was gliding his shaft along her clitoris, fired off his first ejaculation. The heat of his semen against her clitoris caused her to burst into a new and deeper orgasm. She moaned with the joy of this otherworldly sensation and called out to all of them to fuck her more and harder. They all complied, each taking turns in their positions. She imagined herself as a female snake in a mating ball of male snakes with all of them showering her and rubbing her with their semen. Her lovers were rubbing their semen over her breasts and stomach and pinching her nipples as she writhed in ecstasy and squealed for more.

Then she imagined herself on her knees, a position she always craved taking during all her orgies, with a penis penetrated deeply into her anus while she received another of her gorgeous black lovers as he drove his shaft deeply into her vagina. She was feeling the erotic sensation of the throbbing member in her rectum as that lover pulsed stronger and stronger until he expelled his semen into her. After each of them took their turns inside her, they were still able to continue releasing semen after their initial spurts into her vagina or her ass. She had that effect on men. Her release of endorphins caused her to radiate an uninhibited state of nirvana. The men responded to her eroticism with releases from their reservoirs of testosterone and seminal fluids from the deepest wells of their prostates that they never before knew they had.

She imagined she was copulating on a stage. She and her beautiful, muscular black lovers were being serenaded by a full six-sectioned, hundred-piece orchestra playing the music from the mass of Saint Cecilia. She imagined hearing herself whispering to her lovers, coaxing them, urging them to drive their thrusts with feverish intensity as she burst her floodgates of passion, simultaneously releasing a massive streaming orgasm as the orchestra reached its crescendo climax of the clashing cymbals. "Yes. Yes, my sweet lovers. Yes. Fuck me. Fuck me. Fuck me more. I want you to give me more. Give me all of you. Come some more. Please give me more. I love you so much. Keep fucking me. I know you can, baby."

The music strengthened as she further exhorted her lovers. "Forget your wife, baby. I love you the most, and I want all of you. I'm the woman who loves you, baby. I'm the woman you want. I'm your woman, my love. Our love is all that matters. Nothing else, no one else.

"Cast away all your cares, all your responsibilities and commitments, and worship my glorious pussy. Venerate her.

Surrender your life to her. Keep fucking me, my lovers. Give yourselves to me completely. Don't hold anything back. There is no tomorrow, only now. Give me all of you. Now kiss me, baby. Kiss my mouth. Put your tongue in my mouth. Kiss my tits, my darlings. Bite my nipples, sweethearts. Squeeze them. Hurt me a little. That's it. Now kiss my pussy, each one of you. Put your tongues deep into my pussy and then lick my clitoris. Run your tongues up and down over her, then from side to side. Suck the tip of her. Feel how she pulses with the joy of your tongue touching her. Kiss her with love in your hearts. She wants you so much. Let her know you adore her.

"That's it, my darlings. Now put your tongues at the base of her and vibrate your tongues against her. Make her come some more, my love. Caress her with your tongues. She loves you so much. Oh, baby, that's it. Show me that you all love me, just me. You all love my pussy, my darlings. My pussy wants all of your tongues inside her. Make my pussy happy, my darlings. Feel her coming onto your beautiful faces. Oh, my loves, that's it. She's coming again. OOOHHH! I love all of you so much.

"Now fuck me some more. Don't stop, darlings. Revel in the joyous shelter of my loins. In my pussy you are in heaven, and in her you will know the pleasures of a thousand kings. Be her whoremaster. Let her be a slave to you, and fear not the voices of the wicked moralizers. Cast them from your mind and feel no inhibitions. You are safe in nature's warm, loving bosom. Release all your semen into her and be proud of your manly powers. Push deeply into her, reach her depths and spend your beautiful seed into her. You are a god and my pussy is your protector. My pussy loves you so much."

She took each penis in turn into her mouth and continued drawing out all vestiges of semen, taste testing all of their sperm before she swallowed.

As she sucked each of them dry, she wished with all the strength of her thought, as if she were intensely concentrated in prayer, that each of them would remember her forever and that they would come together to fuck her often, and that each of them knew she truly loved them. She quietly prayed that she would always be the most sought choice of women guests for visiting sports teams whenever Rita booked an orgy party.

Muscle Man finally neared his climax. Her orgy dreams would have to be put on hold for a while. She realized that David had gotten her to think about who she really was. She was an unrepentant, unabashed, and unashamed nymphomaniac whore, and she loved her sexuality. She knew now that she would never stop loving the act of fornication with other men in an orgy setting. The endorphin release, the nirvana of the experience, the collapse of her and her group of lovers into an exhausted pile of bonded humanity joined by unquenchable desires, her kissing them on their mouths, the smells of their sweat, and her final loving caresses of each of their expended members would be impossible for her to give up. She knew that now.

No marriage license could ever lock her nymphomania in a closet, and a wedding ring would never collar her passions. She would lie to Bob, swear to be monogamous, marry him, and bring him around to understanding her needs later. When she wanted other men, her cravings nearly drove her insane with lust. She knew she'd have to have them. Her urges would be slaked.

Her duty to David was coming to an end. Muscle Man fired off his shot. Her duty to him was over, thank God. She made a mental note to go to confession as soon as possible. She felt she'd betrayed Bob's trust, both in her imagination and by fucking Muscle Man, but she intended to keep that necklace, and she intended to remain true to her innermost self.

"Now, there's just one last thing, Marty. I'd like you to sit here looking out the barn door. Let me put the necklace on you. Then I'll bring your rabbit to you." David fastened the necklace around her neck and kissed her warmly on her cheek with a lingering kiss. "This is a small token of my esteem for you, Marty. I am so proud of you, words fail me. We'll have to do this more often."

Marty was on cloud nine. *David is eccentric all right, but how many girls wouldn't fuck an ugly old man or his fantasy substitute for a diamond necklace and a floppy-eared rabbit? I'll play along. It's quirky, but it's fun too. Maybe I'll soon be fucking Bob, all my other lovers, and Muscle Man too, while David watches. Maybe I'll be called on to do private fuck sessions with Muscle Man and David on David's day bench, just like mother did with Marvin. We'll fuck our afternoons away in our "private strategy meetings" while Bob works hard on his sales on the floor right below us. That's a wildly intoxicating, kinky thought. I can't believe this. I feel myself getting wet again just contemplating the wickedness of it all.*

Miss Iniquity will be so pleased with me. My cunt will soon rule the entire UGGA complex. I'll have Barbara fired. Bob and I will stand next to her desk and kiss while she cleans out her drawers and packs to leave. That will crush her heart. Oh, Miss Iniquity, I do so much wish I could find you real in the flesh right now. I so badly want you to be close to me as a real live person. I want to celebrate with you right now. At nights, after I fuck Muscle Man all afternoon, I want you to come home with me and my new husband. We'll both fuck him all night long. We'll be wildly sensuous with him. I'll imagine I'm fucking Muscle Man and starring in an orgy while we fuck my husband. We'll make him appreciate the wildcat whore that lives within me. He'll love me so much more once he understands me, and he'll fall asleep at night with his penis cradled in my pussy. When he goes out of town, I'll fuck Carl and my other lovers. I'll have Rita schedule me for orgies again. I'll never be long without a hot, throbbing cock inside me. You'll come with me to my orgies, Miss Iniquity. We'll embrace and kiss while I fuck all my lovers. We'll toast each other with champagne and congratulate our insatiable lust. I'll show you I'm your truest, most faithful disciple.

I wonder if Muscle Man likes oral sex. Oh, please, Miss Iniquity, tell me he'll love licking my cunt as much as I'm going to love sucking his monster cock. I can't wait to have his powerful semen shot explode in my mouth. I want to kiss his cum-covered dick head. The two of us will do sex acts for David's pleasure. I'm going to love my new job assignment. David said we'd have to do this more often. I can't wait. I'm the luckiest girl in the world. Maybe I'll soon replace mother's private duty services. I'll be a much better hostess to those old men she fucks. I'll ease her out of the picture and fuck them myself. Those old boys will experience pleasures they never dreamed existed.

Marty heard what sounded like pigs scraping at the big sliding side door to the barn. *They must be hungry.* "What's the grunting and squealing all about?" Marty asked playfully. She was feeling more and more at ease in the barn.

"Oh, those are my pigs," said David. "One's named Gutah, another's named Pileo, and the third one's name is Scraps. I've only had them a couple months, and I'm not used to feeding them on schedule. I guess they think I'm a little behind schedule today. They can just wait a while until I get your bunny. Ignore them."

While she sat looking outward into the sun-drenched barnyard waiting for her bunny, Marty was overcome by euphoria. *Many men know my reputation and think of me as a whore and nothing more, but David knows I'm a valuable corporate asset. He recognizes I'm a uniquely talented and proud woman. I'm finally getting the recognition and status I've always craved and deserved. Of all the men I ever knew, only David has the insights into my personality that can unlock my feelings of pride and specialness. He just confirmed to me that I am special and unblemished by conventional morality. He doesn't pass judgment on me. Instead he respects and admires my unique, unashamed mindset and encourages me to use my talents to earn as much as possible.*

Marty's ego soared. She put her thumb between her lips and softly kissed it, thankful to whatever eternal being there was that she had the blessing to have such sensuous mouth and tongue and the skill to use them to such advantage, to tease semen from prostates and to revel in her wantonness. She was grateful that her tongue had rolled and basked so often in the ejaculations of so many lovers. And her legs, her beautiful legs! How appreciative she was sitting there with her hands upon her knees. These lovely, sculptured legs were a true gift to her. *How often have these gorgeous legs cradled men and boys and guided them, held them tightly while their cocks stroked my pussy? I'm so blessed to have legs that men crave to cradle them. I must remember not to tell Bob all the details about this afternoon. After I have my bunny, I'll go home and make a place for it in my yard. Then I'll bask naked in my sun room. I'll oil myself and relax. Then I'll call Bob later and tell him the good news. We'll be together again. I'll try to behave like a dutiful wife to him, at least for a while.*

"Now, close your eyes and don't turn around while I get your bunny," David spoke as he opened the door to a little tool room in a corner of the barn. Marty waited for her bunny. He walked up behind her.

Suddenly, David put an ether-soaked handkerchief over Marty's nose and mouth. She struggled briefly while he held her arms. Her thoughts were of a woman crazed. What was he doing? Where was the bunny? She was gasping for a breath, but the air was so cool and she was suddenly overcome with dizziness, like when an anesthesiologist gives you something. Marty fell unconscious. David had timed his attack perfectly, just after Marty exhaled. She deeply breathed the ether. After a brief while, she stopped struggling and succumbed.

When Marty awoke, she was sitting on a hay bale naked. Her hands were chained behind her, her ankles were chained together, and her mouth was covered with duct tape. Her mind was groggy. She shook her head as if to dispel this surreal happenstance. She thought this must be some kind of joke, but she didn't like it. David was way out of line doing this. She squirmed and groaned to free herself, but the struggles she put forth were of no use. She looked up. There was David, standing about three feet from her, out of kicking range. She shook her head up and down and gyrated back and forth as if to demand that he free her at once. David just stared at her. He was like a man transfixed. After a little while, she stopped her struggles and just looked at him, as if requesting an explanation.

She glanced off to the side. Both her diamond and her pearl necklace were hanging from a nail on the side of the barn.

David finally spoke.

"Marty, I need you to know that I have the utmost respect for you. You are not an ordinary woman. Most women are trivial creatures. They are selfish, vain, incredibly boring, pathetic beings who go through life focused on trivialities and obsessed with their petty jealousies. They are insufferable company for most men who have ambitions and purpose in life. They do not know their purpose for being alive. They obsess over who among their circle of nitwits lunches with whom, who attended whose parties, and who said what to whom. They are maddeningly boring, despicable, narrow-minded beings that men are made to suffer.

"You are different, Marty. You identified your purpose in life early on. You understood a woman's only purpose was to please a man, and you made the most of it. You are like your mother that way. You both figured out that you could go far in life and make considerable fortunes by shamelessly plying your best asset. You both mastered the techniques of using feminine guile to get men to do your bidding. You, more even than your despicable mother, learned how to conquer men with your cunt. For that genius in you, I salute you, Marty. My purpose was to harness your genius for the good of the firm. I'm sure you can appreciate that.

"But, Marty, here are some things you should know. I know you have a tiny scar on your right little finger. You had a little nub of flesh there when you were a child, didn't you?"

Marty was silent. David had a knife, which he now held up to her nose, threatening her if she refused to answer. "Well, didn't you have it removed?" She nodded. Suddenly she was afraid.

"You see, Marty, I saw the nub when you were a little girl. You were over at Dad's house in Rondel Hills, bouncing a ball with me. Remember?" Marty shook her head. "Well, that's okay. I remember. That's all that matters. I knew someone else who had that same nub in the same place, on his right little finger, and he had his nub surgically removed too. Do you know who that was, Marty?" Again, Marty shook her head. "It was my dad, Marty. I remember seeing his nub when I was a boy. Then I was sent to summer camp. When I came home, the nub was gone.

"So you see, Marty, you and I have the same father. You didn't know that, did you? You are not Joseph Maloney's daughter. You are Marvin Sustack's daughter. You and I are half-brother and sister." David paused for a while to let Marty absorb that. "It's okay, Marty. I don't hold anything against you because you are beautiful and I am ugly. Our mothers were just different people, and they were the ones who determined what we looked like, not Dad. Dad was handsome. You are beautiful. Your mother is beautiful. My mother was ugly and I am ugly. Nature just worked it out that way for us."

David smiled as he stared at Marty before he continued.

"But we do have a serious problem, Marty. Because we're brother and sister, we're not supposed to fuck together, but we did, vicariously. We broke a Jewish mitzvah. And you broke another mitzvah, Marty, when you fucked Muscle. You broke the mitzvah that one who is betrothed is forbidden to fuck anyone other than the betrothed one, and you shouldn't even fuck your betrothed until after you are married by a rabbi. I see you're shaking your head to everything I'm saying. Is that because you're not a Jew? These rules don't apply to you?"

Marty nodded.

"Well, ordinarily that would make a difference for you, and since your mother is a gentile, that really makes you a gentile, so Jewish law shouldn't apply to you, but this is not that ordinary, Marty. You see, Dad treated your mother as his wife in the office. She wasn't an ordinary shiksa. Your mother was more of an office-wife shiksa, and by being Dad's office wife, that makes you the daughter of a woman who wanted to be a Jew.

But Dad wouldn't marry her and let her use marriage to convert and join the tribe. It's complicated, Marty. I don't expect you to understand everything I'm saying here, but Dad wanted Susan to be his wife and, but for Eloweiss, my mother, I believe he would have married Susan.

"You see, I know Dad loved Susan and you more than he ever loved Eloweiss and me. Dad pushed Mother and me aside to be with Susan and you whenever he could, but you probably don't remember that, do you? You two are beautiful and we are ugly. There's just that simple truth. Dad loved Susan, your mother, so much that he has me tied up with her through his will until she dies. So you see, Marty, I think of Susan as Dad's wife and that makes you a Jewess in my eyes. Now, that brings me to why we're here now, and why I have you chained up.

"According to our faith, when someone comes into contact with a corpse, we have to have a Red Heifer sacrifice. That's a heifer with not a single hair on it that is not red. Sometimes people used to cheat a little. If a heifer had some white hair, they'd just pull it out, figuring the rabbis wouldn't notice. Well in our case, Marty, I figure that, while you are not a corpse, your soul is dead. You are a hopeless, base whore, forever committed to your whoring, which makes your soul a corpse. I know that for sure because you just fucked me for diamonds and betrayed your husband-to-be. I think of Bob like he's a son to me, and I didn't like seeing him betrayed."

Marty now looked at David and rolled her eyes as if to say she thought he'd lost his mind. *David is one sick asshole. First he gets his jollies off by learning about my personal feelings, and then he watches Muscle fuck me. Now he says everything I did for the company was immoral. What's he going to do next, spank me? I've never felt this alone and abandoned since Mother sent me off to boarding school to get rid of me. I wish Bob would come along and put a stop to this craziness. I wonder where he is on a nice weekend like this. I wish I hadn't told him to stay away.*

Men! They surprise you when you don't want to be surprised, but when you need them to surprise you, they are just off somewhere doing something else. Damn it! This is too frustrating. It isn't fun anymore. I can't think straight. Just wait until David takes this tape off my mouth. I'm going to give him a piece of my mind! After all I've done for UGGA and for him to treat me this way! He got company loyalty from me, bottom-up loyalty. I fucked my ass off for this company. Where's the loyalty from top down? Nobody should ever treat their best employee this way. Why am I being treated this way? When do I get my necklaces? Where's the floppy-eared rabbit?

Shut those fucking pigs up, please! They're making way too much noise. I wish he'd hurry up and feed them so they will shut up! Where did he go? David, I can't see you. You can't just leave me sitting here like this. I can't think with those pigs grunting like crazy, and I can't speak. David! Come back here. What kind of company are you running, you crazy bastard? You made a promise! You're not going to break your promise, are you?

David, you're frightening me! Stop this! What are you doing? Where are you?

CONTINUED

With

WHEN THE BUTTERFLIES COME

For information, contact:
rosemarylightfootnessbitner@aol.com